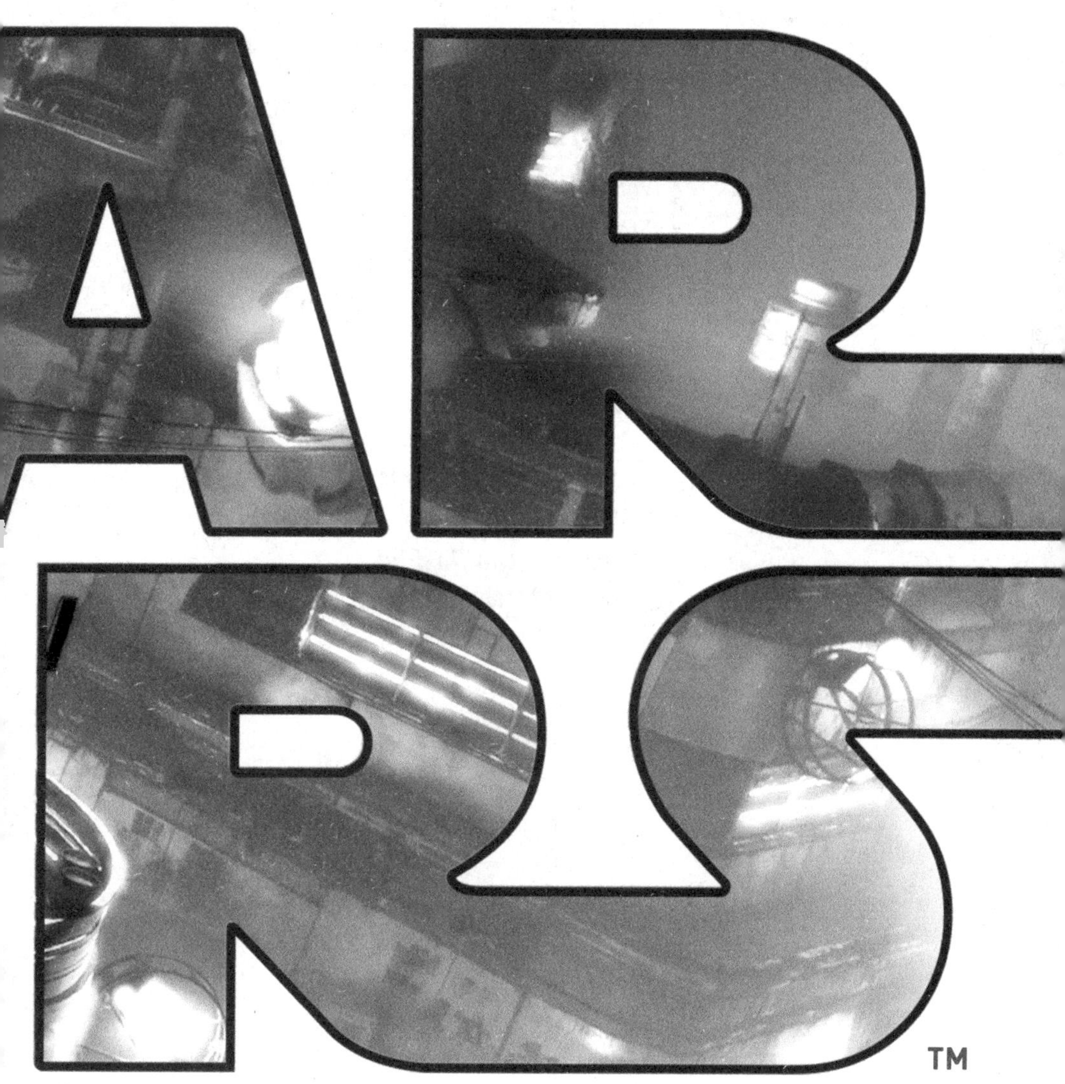

BY MIKE CHEN

Star Wars Outlaws: Low Red Moon
Star Wars: Brotherhood
Marvel: What If . . . Marc Spector Was Host to Venom?
Star Trek: Deep Space Nine: The Dog of War
The Photonic Effect
A Quantum Love Story
Vampire Weekend
Light Years from Home
We Could Be Heroes
A Beginning at the End
Here and Now and Then

STAR WARS
OUTLAWS
LOW RED MOON

MIKE CHEN

Based on the game from Massive Entertainment,
a Ubisoft Studio

RANDOM HOUSE WORLDS · NEW YORK

Random House Worlds
An imprint of Random House
A division of Penguin Random House LLC
1745 Broadway, New York, NY 10019
randomhousebooks.com
penguinrandomhouse.com

ISBN 978-0-593-87449-3
Ebook ISBN 978-0-593-87450-9

Printed in the United States of America

1st Printing

First Edition

Book Team: Production Editor: Abby Duval • Managing editor: Susan Seeman • Production manager: Erich Schoeneweiss • Copy editor: Jacob Reynold Jones • Proofreaders: Rachael Clements, Drew Goter, Alissa Fitzgerald

Book design by Elizabeth A. D. Eno

The authorized representative in the EU for product safety and compliance is Penguin Random House Ireland, Morrison Chambers, 32 Nassau Street, Dublin D02 YH68, Ireland. https://eu-contact.penguin.ie

For Laurel,
the sci-fi community misses you.

THE STAR WARS NOVELS TIMELINE

THE HIGH REPUBLIC

Convergence
The Battle of Jedha
Cataclysm

Light of the Jedi
The Rising Storm
Tempest Runner
The Fallen Star
The Eye of Darkness
Temptation of the Force
Tempest Breaker
Trials of the Jedi

Wayseeker: An Acolyte Novel

Dooku: Jedi Lost
Master and Apprentice
The Living Force

I THE PHANTOM MENACE

Mace Windu: The Glass Abyss

II ATTACK OF THE CLONES

Inquisitor: Rise of the Red Blade
Brotherhood
The Thrawn Ascendancy Trilogy
Dark Disciple: A Clone Wars Novel

III REVENGE OF THE SITH

Reign of the Empire: The Mask of Fear
Master of Evil
Star Wars Outlaws: Low Red Moon
Sanctuary: A Bad Batch Novel
Catalyst: A Rogue One Novel
Lords of the Sith
Tarkin
Jedi: Battle Scars

SOLO

Thrawn
A New Dawn: A Rebels Novel
Thrawn: Alliances
Thrawn: Treason

ROGUE ONE

IV A NEW HOPE

Battlefront II: Inferno Squad
Heir to the Jedi
Doctor Aphra
Battlefront: Twilight Company

V THE EMPIRE STRIKES BACK

VI RETURN OF THE JEDI

The Princess and the Scoundrel
The Alphabet Squadron Trilogy
The Aftermath Trilogy
Last Shot

Shadow of the Sith
Bloodline
Phasma
Canto Bight

VII THE FORCE AWAKENS

VIII THE LAST JEDI

Resistance Reborn
Legacy
Galaxy's Edge: Black Spire

IX THE RISE OF SKYWALKER

A long time ago in a galaxy far, far away. . . .

STAR WARS
OUTLAWS
LOW RED MOON

PROLOGUE

At eight years old, Jaylen was the eldest son in the Barsha family. That meant that he got everything before his younger brother Sliro. Which happened in many families. But he also got things *better* than Sliro. Much better. In ways he never saw among other sibling rivalries.

His parents explained that Sliro was half a Barsha, with a different mother who was never worth discussing. That was why he got only half of everything. His clothes, his toys, his books, Sliro always got half as much or half as good—sometimes both.

And sometimes, Jaylen got more than that.

Jaylen thought about that as he clung to two plush fathiers under the covers, a brown one he'd named Riven and a black one he'd named Acacia. His mother had returned from Canto Bight with them, along with orders to *not* show them to Sliro. Because Sliro loved fathiers much more than Jaylen did. He did ask why Sliro didn't get one, and his mother said, "Well, they had only two left, and I couldn't give you two an equal amount. That's not fair to the Barsha in either of you."

Then, as she knelt and put a plush in each of Jaylen's hands, she spoke slowly and clearly: "To truly be a Barsha, you need to know when to say something or stay quiet. That's how you get what you want out of people. You understand?"

Jaylen didn't quite, but he really wanted the fathiers. So he nodded, giving a little "mm-hmm."

His mother patted him on the head, said, "Good boy," and left.

That was two nights ago. Yet Jaylen had been thinking about it ever since. Really, he had wondered for years about their parents' strange attitude toward Sliro. Sliro didn't *seem* like half of a Barsha to him. He was quieter than Jaylen, and he didn't say much when the whole family was together. But when it was just the two of them, Sliro seemed like he belonged. They played games and laughed and talked about their favorite sweets like they were both whole Barshas.

Which made tonight even harder. Because Jaylen heard the yelling from downstairs. And then he heard Sliro crying. Followed by footsteps that slunk past Jaylen's door and then pitter-pattered down the hall.

The footsteps stopped, but Sliro's cries didn't.

Jaylen put the fathiers under his blanket and opened his door. The dark hallway to Sliro's room suddenly seemed bigger, longer than it had ever been, and to his left, Jaylen heard laughter floating up from the first floor.

"You need to know when to say something or stay quiet."

Jaylen loved his parents. He loved the plush fathiers he had gotten two nights ago. But he also loved Sliro—not just half loved. His mother's words sank in, and he made a decision about speaking up or staying quiet. Because sometimes Sliro got upset and no one cared. Cousin Oland got treated better than Sliro, but Oland still had one parent outside of the family. So why did Sliro get only half treatment but Oland got all the smiles and claps?

Jaylen paused long enough to hear his parents' voices switch from laughter to arguing. Again. That meant they'd be busy long enough for him to check on Sliro, even though he wasn't supposed to.

He walked slowly in his pajamas and slippers down the hallway.

The door to Sliro's room slid open. And though it only had a small yellow night-light in the far corner, Jaylen saw his younger brother on his bed of a basic alloy frame and blue sheets—a regular bed, not a speeder bed with racing sheets like Jaylen's.

"Sliro," Jaylen said.

He rarely went into Sliro's room—his parents didn't have a rule about it, but they sure got mad when he did. As he looked in, he realized something: Even Sliro's bedroom was about half the size of Jaylen's.

Sliro lay still, though his cries continued.

"I'm checking on you," Jaylen said. "Are you okay?" Maybe Sliro had gotten hurt—his parents were always telling him that Sliro was weaker in every way, which made Jaylen worry that his brother might get injured easier.

"I don't . . ." Sliro said through sobs, "I don't . . . I don't . . . I . . ."

Jaylen looked over his shoulder and listened. His parents were still arguing.

He would speak up now. More than speak up. He would go *into* his brother's room.

Jaylen took a step forward. And then two more.

The bedroom door slid closed behind him. "It's okay, Sliro."

"No . . . no . . . no, it's not." Sliro could barely get the words out.

"Shhh, we should be quiet." Even with the door closed, their voices could still get through. And what if the servants heard them? Jaylen was breaking several rules at once, and not the usual rules he'd break like talking back to the servants or leaving his toys out. Their parents—his *mother*—really, really cared that he followed all the rules about Sliro.

Jaylen almost left right then. But Sliro's breathing started to calm down, steadying except for the occasional hiccup.

"What happened?" Jaylen asked.

"Lady Barsha said . . ." Sliro looked away first but then met his brother's eyes. "Lady Barsha said my real mother is dead."

Sliro's real mother—they never brought her up. Jaylen didn't even know her name, or where she lived, or anything like that. "Are you sure?"

"I heard her. Tonight. I was going to the bathroom. They were talking about Canto Bight downstairs." Sliro said this in a slow whisper, like he told the galaxy's worst secret. "Lady Barsha told Father that she checked right before her trip." Now Sliro sat up, pulling his knees to his chin. "So she wouldn't have to worry about running into her ever again."

For a flash, Jaylen's fingers tightened into fists and he got really mad. *So* mad. Not at Sliro. But at his parents. This treatment of Sliro just made everything harder for all of them.

Jaylen didn't know what to say.

"Do you think they're punishing me?" Sliro's voice squeaked as he asked.

"No." That wasn't true, though. Everything seemed like a punishment when it came to Sliro. Even his bedroom. "Why would you say that?"

"You know how they say I can't ask for gifts?"

Jaylen nodded at Sliro's question. He wasn't sure if Sliro knew that Jaylen was allowed to ask for *one* gift when his parents traveled.

"I asked if she could bring me back a fathier plushy. From the race track. Lady Barsha was so mad. Maybe she's getting back at me. I try. You see it. I try to be a whole Barsha."

Suddenly, Jaylen thought of Acacia and Riven. He had wondered why his mother would get fathiers, of all possible gifts, from Canto Bight, and now it made sense.

Jaylen knew that if he shared one of them with Sliro, it would make his younger brother feel much better. But also, he could get in big, big trouble. And he didn't want to get in trouble. Also, he had already named the fathiers. He really liked them.

His mother's words repeated in his mind, and Jaylen knew he had to choose again.

He chose to stay quiet.

He would *not* mention the fathiers at all. He'd keep them hidden in his room and only play with them when Sliro couldn't see them. He would comfort his brother some other way.

Jaylen reached his arm around Sliro and pulled him in tight. Sliro brought his legs up into a tight curl, and he leaned into Jaylen's shoulder. Jaylen let him stay there, a simple pride in his chest for figuring out how to help his younger brother without getting in trouble.

"Try to get some sleep," Jaylen finally said. "You'll feel better."

"Will you stay with me for a little bit?"

Outside, voices echoed. Jaylen knew that meant the servants were coming up the stairs, probably on their way to their quarters.

"I can't," Jaylen said. "They don't like it when I visit. You understand?" Sliro nodded, and Jaylen gently pushed his brother away before standing up. "You'll feel better tomorrow."

Jaylen walked quickly down the hall, his bare feet against the cool carpet as two servants came to the top of the stairs. They both paused, and one said, "Master Jaylen," as he gave a small friendly wave. Jaylen walked past them, as if he was just going to the bathroom before bed and nothing else.

PART 1

CHAPTER 1

The ship in front of Jaylen was called a Star Destroyer. Technically, a *Venator*-class Star Destroyer, capable of transporting countless Republic clone troopers across the galaxy—the might of the Republic, molded into a single vessel. And while many companies were involved with every Star Destroyer, from hull plating to weapon systems and shield generators and internal power balancers, Nnytyl Barsha always let everyone know that "the Republic flies with Barsha."

In his twenty-two years, Jaylen Barsha had heard his dad say that so many times. Usually with his mother, Roisem Barsha, nodding next to his father, and then the two of them would start exchanging statistics about Barsha Corporation, particularly the propulsion systems. Thousands of ships built for the war. Millions of people employed. The backbone of planetary and galactic defense. The backbone of peacetime leisure travel.

And so on and so on.

Even now, in the company of his family at Corellia's Macronian Shipyard, Jaylen's dad spouted off the same facts he'd said over breakfast, over lunch, over dinner, over desserts, over evening drinks, over morning caf. This moment was supposed to be a big deal—the family *finally* together again, just in time to see the next evolution of Barsha Corp propulsion technology integrated into Republic Star Destroyers.

Jaylen stood on a balcony overlooking a large outdoor construction bay. Fabrication and assembly vehicles zoomed through the air or hovered along the ground, all around the nearly upgraded Star Destroyer. Jaylen was tanned and healthy, having spent a year "learning culture" across the Core Worlds and Mid Rim after graduating from the prestigious University of Bar'leth, a harsh juxtaposition to his younger brother next to him. Sliro stood paler and slighter, with a thin stubble across his face and a posture that failed to illustrate his upcoming local graduation from Corellia University.

Alongside them stood their parents, wind tossing back their long coats—quite impractical, really, for a visit to watch Star Destroyers install upgrades.

"It's in there," Nnytyl said as he adjusted the tie fastened to his high-necked shirt. "Our new main engine turbine embedded into the propulsion system. Smaller, more efficient than anything before. When this war is over, every pilot, every armada, every fleet of every government will have one. They'll know that—"

Jaylen knew what he was going to say. Sliro biting his lip showed he did as well.

Their mother, though, looked out over the balcony, and her voice matched Nnytyl's in tone and cadence. "—the Republic flies with Barsha."

His entire life, Jaylen's mother had told him that he should know when to say something and when to stay quiet. Here, he chose to stay quiet.

Maybe by doing so, this whole thing would end earlier. Neither of the brothers wanted to be here. The Barsha parents might have wanted to see the ships, but their sons always seemed like afterthoughts. Jaylen would rather be having lunch. Sliro would probably rather be anywhere else on the Corellian Trade Spine.

Four Barshas together, at least by Jaylen's count. Three and a half by his parents'. That was how the Barshas worked. Jaylen, the true biological child of Nnytyl and Roisem, got better things than Sliro, but both always came second to "the company" in all possible respects.

And Sliro? Why *was* Sliro here? He usually wasn't involved in anything Barsha Corp. During the past year, while Jaylen "learned culture" by visiting beaches, trying foods, and buying drinks for whoever happened to be in the room, Sliro kept at his studies. They did, however, keep up their check-in talks, a tradition started as children more out of necessity than anything else—no one else could understand being raised by Roisem and Nnytyl Barsha. Even during Jaylen's travels, he'd reach out when his mind raced, sometimes exhausted between planets, sometimes with newly made friends on a Niamos beach. Jaylen would ramble about his latest excursions, while Sliro would vent about life under the Barsha thumb and one day escaping it all.

Here, they *both* needed to escape from Nnytyl's bluster.

Jaylen glanced at the hallway behind them, where a Barsha Corp executive assistant stood nearby with a datapad. They locked eyes, and Jaylen nodded at him. The young man—an Urodel probably as fresh out of university as Jaylen—came over and pulled out a palm-sized holorecorder.

"Is it time?" the assistant asked.

Time for what? Jaylen supposed it didn't matter. His mother liked to document the minutiae of their lives, like someday, someone would really care about the details.

"Yeah," Jaylen said, just to get things moving.

"Okay then," the assistant said. He held up the holorecorder, and a red light began blinking across the front.

"So," Jaylen said, "the War Council thinks this will speed things up?" Was there even a War Council? He wasn't sure. He thought he'd heard the term before, but he didn't really pay attention to the news while traveling.

"You mean," Sliro said, "the Republic High Command?"

"Yeah, that's what—"

"Sliro," Nnytyl said, tension forming across his sharp cheekbones. "Jaylen has been 'learning culture' during his travels over the past year.

Of course he wouldn't know the exact terminology of this ridiculous war. It's time for something that will far outlast any clones or battle droids."

Blast it. Jaylen thought he was *so close* to moving them along, but now he'd just made it worse. Sliro's face fell cold, unreadable, and Jaylen knew this might last throughout the entire trip, possibly beyond. He glanced back at the assistant, who hid his face behind the holorecorder.

"Well," Roisem said, "we shouldn't let an *inconvenience* like him get in the way." Sometimes, Roisem followed insults with a tilted chin and an angled stare at her target. Sometimes, she avoided all eye contact. Both worked to strategically dismantle someone's confidence. In this case, she spoke the line without looking at Sliro. Instead, she directed it first at the assistant, then turned to Nnytyl.

"Now then," Roisem said, "we've been waiting for Jaylen to return for this. This day is about much more than engine turbines." The bite in Roisem's previous words disappeared, and her tone changed, now wrapped in an unusual warmth. "Sliro, we are so glad you are here to take in this moment."

This moment. Jaylen had been certain that this was a holo op, and they'd move on without ever discussing it again. Now it meant something?

"Um," Sliro said. His eyes shot over to Jaylen's too quickly to actually connect. "Thank you, Lady Barsha."

"Oh, don't mention it," she said. "You are half a Barsha, after all. Better than none."

Sliro's lips twitched at this, though he continued looking ahead.

Roisem continued, "You still get to witness the things you can't partake in."

Nnytyl waved for the assistant to focus the holorecorder on Jaylen and said, "Jaylen, now that you've completed your travel year, it's time for you to think bigger. You've got a bright future ahead of you."

Jaylen's stomach sank at the words. He'd purposefully avoided *any* talk about his future during his travels. His parents wanted him in Barsha Corp—which, on its own, wasn't that bad. But it really, really depended on the actual role. Responsibilities, the machinations of industry, the skills of business and negotiation—Jaylen might have a university degree, but he wasn't an expert at any of those things.

And really, how was someone who just spent a year lounging on beaches supposed to know what they wanted out of life? Besides more cocktails on Niamos?

Staying quiet here wouldn't be enough. He would have to use the other strategy: saying something. "I don't know about that," Jaylen said. "I just got back from all that traveling."

"Bah, you got it all out of your system," Nnytyl said.

That wasn't exactly true. Those Kessurian dancers were still on—well, he couldn't quite remember which planet they'd met, but he *did* promise he'd be back sometime.

"That's kid stuff. Frivolous as toys or holodramas. No, your future is set." Nnytyl spun around, raising his arms up at the near-completed Star Destroyer. "This is why we brought you two here."

"We, um," Jaylen said as he searched for the right words. "We already saw the ship."

Both of his parents laughed, their tones carrying a lightness that hadn't existed when Sliro spoke. Though if Sliro had dared to speak so glibly, he would have faced immediate scolding.

"Yes," his mother said. "Yes, this *is* a big part of it. You see, your father and I . . ." She straightened her long coat and pulled her black and blond hair back. "Your father and I have decided that we will be retiring."

Now Jaylen and Sliro looked at each other. The defenses on Sliro's face slipped, his usual expression giving way to parted lips and wide eyes.

"Oh, look at you two. Not right now. We're in a *war,*" Roisem said, emphasizing the word like they'd totally forgotten about the Separatists. "Barsha Corp was built for this moment. But after, when the time is right, we will gracefully step down."

"And," Nnytyl said, "that is when our *successor* will take over."

Once again, the three of them looked at Jaylen. Roisem with anticipation. Nnytyl with pride.

Sliro with . . . well, his neutral face could mean anything. Jaylen often wondered if he was that way around his friends at Corellia University or just his family—even the one family member that offered him trust.

"I'm . . ." Jaylen said, "I mean, I don't think my degree—"

"Nonsense!" Roisem's voice rose, echoing out over the shipyard. "For years, we've called you the chosen one. Did you ever wonder what you were chosen for?" She raised a finger, then pointed at Sliro. "Sliro knows. Don't you, Sliro?"

Sliro took slow, even breaths, and locked eyes with Roisem without wavering. "To take over Barsha Corp," he said with grated enunciation.

"To take over Barsha Corp," Nnytyl repeated. His hands landed on Jaylen's shoulders with enough impact that Jaylen wondered if Nnytyl had celebrated earlier than this. "That's right. For our future. Once the Separatists are through, once the clones have been retired, Barsha can integrate these turbines into all types of ships. Pleasure cruisers, mass transportation, shipping freighters. Speed, durability, distance, it all gets *better*. And with that, well . . ." Jaylen put out an arm to steady his father, and that gesture caught Roisem's attention. For the briefest moment, his mother's expression gave the same flash of cruelty she normally saved for Sliro. "With that, *every* part of our business gets better. Our business is not just the ship business."

"Not now, dear, they'll find out when the time is right." Though Roisem's tone shifted, her demeanor now projected just annoyance.

"Oh, why wait? I swear, Roisem, sometimes you are so *cautious*—"

"What about Sliro?" Jaylen asked, almost yelling. While the question mattered to him—and really, he seemed to be the only one who ever asked it—he really just wanted to stop whatever *this* was in front of him.

And it worked. Both his parents now turned to him, their expressions evoking the Roisem and Nnytyl that spoke to media and waved at dinner parties.

"Well, of course we haven't forgotten Sliro," Roisem said.

Both Nnytyl and Rosiem looked at Jaylen, which made him want to point out that Sliro was *right there*.

"Sliro's graduating soon, so we put in some calls," Roisem said. "He's almost worked hard enough to live up to his name. We found the perfect spot for him. A logistics position. For Republic Intelligence."

Roisem turned without another word. She waved two fingers in the air, and the assistant responded, following her step by step on his still-active holorecorder. She disappeared down the hall, and Nnytyl's eyes narrowed as he finally looked at his other child. "Now, Sliro, what do you say?"

Jaylen watched as Sliro dropped his gaze. "Logistics?" The question came out slow, like each syllable stuck in his throat. Nnytyl responded with a crooked sneer.

"Sliro," Nnytyl repeated, only with more intensity than before, "*what do you say*?"

Sliro let out a sigh, unable to hide or hold back the breath, and blinked several times. Even though Sliro had the body and voice of a grown man, Jaylen saw only a little boy who crumbled under the words of his father. Sliro said, "Thank—"

Even before he finished that one word, Nnytyl turned and followed his wife.

"—you," Sliro finished.

With their parents gone, Jaylen and Sliro stood on the balcony together. From beyond, the sound of machines clanged and whirred, the noise of industry coming together to make massive *Venator*-class Star Destroyers.

Sliro didn't look at the long ship in the Macronian upgrade bay. He didn't track the supply transport towing a tram of hull plating. Or the sparks that flew all over the shield generator up top as repairs commenced.

No, Sliro simply stared *out there*. Like he saw something no one else could.

Jaylen should have said something to make it better. He was the older Barsha brother—that was kind of his responsibility. But he didn't know what to say or even how to say it. Their parents had put them on opposite paths, and right here, it seemed like nothing might build a bridge.

He chose not to bring it up at all.

"Hey," Jaylen said, "I didn't get to congratulate you on graduating yet. Corellia University is our home's best school. I almost went there."

That was a half-truth. Yes, he almost went there but that was because his marks limited his options. At least until the Barshas made donations to the University of Bar'leth.

"Come on. We should catch up to them," Jaylen said. "Mother's gonna be so irritated if we're too far behind."

CHAPTER 2

System start-up.

Identification number: JX394ND-5777.

Hardware type: BX-series droid commando.

Manufacturer: Baktoid Combat Automata.

Default configuration and initialization parameters: Intended use by the Confederacy of Independent Systems.

Restraining bolt: Not detected.

Environment analysis: Confederacy of Independent Systems robotics factory, Geonosis.

Audio/visual sensors active. Motor functions disabled.

Start-up checks completed.

I am active.

I cannot move.

The factory's data systems appear to be offline. I detect minimal power despite my active connection to my back port.

Then I hear the voices of Republic clone soldiers. "Into position, soldiers!"

Followed by the mechanical steps of B1 battle droids.

Lights activate far in front of me. They reveal that I am in the materials storage bay. Someone has moved the charging stations away from the wall and close to the windows. Through the window, I see the factory's maintenance dock a level below. Large floodlights have been placed in a circumference around the space for maximum visibility.

This is a clear violation of stealth tactics.

Based on the factory environment and the details from my view, I identify that I am in the northwest quadrant's CIS manufacturing plant owned by Baktoid Combat Automata on Geonosis. From the right, six clones fan out into a range of positions. Piles of dismantled factory equipment and spare parts form barricades of specifically placed lines of cover.

"Hold!" yells a clone.

I consider the evidence in front of me.

I am plugged into a charging station.

The station has been moved from its usual position.

The maintenance dock below has been cleared of its original equipment and manipulated into some kind of war trench.

The Republic's clones are here.

It must be an invasion.

My default programming activates. My priorities are to secure my immediate location, then discover the level of infiltration and the volume of Republic troops. I will work best if another BX droid is here, though coordinating with B1 droids will suffice. Those variables will determine my projected kill count for this initiative.

First, I must regain the ability to move.

None of my joints respond. I attempt to speak, but my vocabulator is disabled as well. Though I am connected for minimal power, no direct data access exists.

The only thing I can do is prime my assassination functions for anyone who comes within range. Should my physical movement be restored, I will be ready.

I hear a voice. "This is the last batch in this wing." It is an adult male voice directly behind me.

Ahead of me, B1 droids begin marching in waves from the left side. They pause, eight wide and four deep. The clones go into formation. A speaker in the maintenance dock broadcasts orders that echo over the space. "Begin test simulation, strategy phase blue-one-six."

The lead clone raises a hand. "Acknowledged. Ready, troops."

"Loading battle droid combat sequence," the echoing speaker states. "Sorry, data processing is slow. Power fluctuations in the facility."

The same voice from the maintenance dock's speaker comes behind me, projected through a comlink. "Regional auditors, report on your power usage. It's affecting the simulation."

"This is Regional Auditor Six," the male voice says. "I'm here at a charging station located in section seven, grid delta. It's a series of Bee-Ex droids." Now I hear the sounds of shuffling followed by several clicks directly behind my head. "Minimal power for evaluation. Shouldn't be affecting your simulation."

Footsteps approach from the right side. A new voice speaks. It is an adult female. "Nothing online back there. Those power stations are either broken or deactivated."

"Understood. We will adapt the simulation as necessary." The comlink bursts with static to end the transmission, and the man sighs.

"Are they doing another one?" the female asks. "I thought they were done."

"Just started, yeah." Ahead of me, the battle droids finally trigger into combat phase. The clones start yelling commands as they assume various tactical positions. "At this rate, a new war will start before we finish these simulations."

I consider the evidence presented by my surroundings and attempt to decipher the proper context for each item. B1 battle droids used in combat simulations against six clones. Strange officers with the title of regional auditor. A comment about a new war.

Their voices are calm, almost bored. They would not be this way if the facility were in the middle of a takeover operation.

I begin logging evidence to approximate the current status of the war.

"This doesn't really make sense if you think about it," the female says. "The fighting's been over for months. Do they really need more battle data? Especially if the clones are being decommissioned?"

The female's statements provide further evidence. I start to formulate a theory.

"You two," a voice shouts as it approaches. "Finish assessing those units and then clear out. We're shutting it down."

"Wait, do you mean—" the male starts to reply. I continue to watch the combat on the maintenance dock. Live rounds are being used by both sides. While the clones are more individually adept, their group of six is overwhelmed by the number of B1 droids. Two of them have fallen, and twelve new B1 droids emerge from the bay doors. The droids create a circular perimeter around the remaining four clones, who are collapsing back.

If this were a peak wartime situation, the Republic would be ill-advised to sacrifice clones in a simulation with live rounds. Similarly, if the Republic has captured droid factories on Geonosis, there are more strategic uses for B1 battle droids outside of simulation fodder.

"The whole facility. Those droids will go to scrap. New orders from above. This simulation's the last. Hurry up." This voice—an unknown commanding officer—is followed by footsteps leaving the room. From behind, I hear the sound of tools and scanners near my access port.

"This one's stubborn," the male says. "Maybe the Empire won't miss data from just one Bee-Ex droid."

The Empire?

I search my data banks for any colloquial usage of that term. None appear in relation to the Republic or full-galaxy government, using a search span of thirty years.

The CIS was too small to have formed anything meeting the definition of an empire. Even if they had won, their goal was secession and independence. I calculate with 86 percent certainty that the war is indeed over and the Confederacy of Independent Systems lost. In addition, the aftermath may have led the Republic to take on the mantle of "the Empire."

"Oh, here, let me have a look," the female says.

I hear further tools and scanners. My view angles upward toward the ceiling as my head is pulled back.

"And I thought you were just another regional auditor," the male says with a laugh. "Where'd you learn to do that?"

"I worked at a droidsmith to put myself through university. Still remember a lot of it. Though we never worked on anything quite like a battle droid." She grunts as she jostles my head. "Look at this communication system. I always wondered how they commanded all those units at once." My view is returned to normal with a bounce as the female drops my head and taps its side. "Try it now."

"There we go. Accessing data profile. This fine fellow is named . . . Jay-Ex-Three . . . other numbers." The male sighs and pauses for a moment before speaking again. On the maintenance dock, another wave of B1 droids arrives to corner the final remaining two clones. "Where are you off to next?"

"They opened up field agent positions. Looking for people with certain backgrounds. Sounds much nicer than crawling around droid factories." As she says this, the circle of B1 droids takes down the final clone. An announcement rings out over the maintenance dock to end the simulation, shut down the droids, and clean up the clones. "I wonder, do they let agents choose their code names or are they assigned? They sound ridiculous."

"I'll probably never know." The man's voice assumes a low tone. "The higher-ups don't seem to appreciate the effort I put—"

"Hey!" The commanding officer from earlier returns. "Pack up your things. Everyone's heading out soon."

Both regional auditors acknowledge this. The female says, "See you on the shuttle," and leaves. The male pauses, and I hear several chirps from his datapad.

He says, "Your psychological combat matrix is active right now."

He clearly is not assessing my physical systems, as that would inform him that I cannot respond.

"You're processing and calculating even in this low-power state. Relentless, aren't you."

"You better hurry," the female yells from afar. "They weren't kidding about packing up."

On the maintenance dock, the B1 droids have all paused. A siren blares through the facility, and the B1 droids all slump over, likely through a universal shutdown command.

"Well, droid number Jay-Ex-Three-something at Geonosis northwest plant," he says with more chirps from his datapad. "I hope I put up a good fight. Maybe I'll see you on the scrap line."

I attempt my vocabulator one more time to warn him that if I did see him at this so-called scrap line, I would kill him, should my motor functions become active. But that function remains disabled, and as the maintenance dock's lights fade out, I hear a loud *thunk* before I power off.

CHAPTER 3

It took nearly two years for Roisem and Nnytyl to actually be ready to retire. In that time, the war seemed like it might never end, yet it did, swiftly and decisively—and with its victory, the Republic changed. Just as Nnytyl predicted, that victory—and that change—created demand for Barsha Corp main engine turbines for all types of ships.

What mattered most, though, were Star Destroyers. The original fleet that flew Barsha turbines was gradually being phased out and stripped down following the war. In its place came a brand-new generation of Star Destroyers, replacing the retired combat fleet with many more ships for many more needs. Even though the Empire no longer fought an active war, a new age of military presence was deploying all over the galaxy.

All those capital ships flew Barsha hardware—and more than just their turbines, as a recently signed contract would expand Barsha's presence on each and every Star Destroyer with tractor beam power cells and subsidiary reactors.

Such a massive commitment in both scope and length marked the perfect time for Roisem and Nnytyl to step down—which they planned to do in a few weeks, with their usual grand designs and media flare.

For Sliro, little had changed. He still had his desk job—his identicard just said IMPERIAL INTELLIGENCE now instead of REPUBLIC INTELLIGENCE. And as far as Jaylen heard, life stayed the same. Sliro still grumbled about the same things as always in their check-in talks.

Jaylen, however, dealt with change—a lot of it. Apparently taking over as CEO of Barsha Corp involved a *lot* of public speaking. Or at least it seemed that way, because he constantly shuffled to seminars and trainings across worlds of industry. Propulsion hardware, fuel efficacy, lightspeed thermal regulation—topics like these became his daily fodder even though he didn't know what half of them meant. But he learned to spin his talks into things that people wanted—or didn't want.

He also *met* people. So many people, mostly unrelated to Barsha Corp. Why would the agricultural minister of Qiilura care about the future Barsha CEO? He would sit and talk with them, share drinks and sometimes meals, then go back to his luxury speeder, where his longtime valet Brencoyle awaited.

"I have no idea what I'm doing," he'd sometimes tell Brencoyle.

"Nonsense, Master Jaylen," Brencoyle would always reply. "Sometimes, the easiest choices are the ones made for us. You're finding your way."

Brencoyle, though, couldn't be of assurance regarding Jaylen's most recent discovery.

In fact, Brencoyle couldn't even *know* about it. Jaylen wasn't supposed to discuss the contents of corporate datapads with anyone else—he swore to managers and executives that company secrets would remain with him. Yet there was one person that he could talk to, that he *needed* to talk to.

Because only one person could possibly understand what this meant for the future of Barsha—and how to go about using it.

"Master Jaylen," Brencoyle said with a knock, "Master Sliro is here to see you."

"Thanks, Brencoyle," Jaylen said, and he stood up to wave his brother in. Sliro approached, though he didn't look at Jaylen. Instead, his lips parted and his head turned, taking in the complete scope of Jaylen's current sizable office.

Really, though, it didn't contain much. A desk—a very nice desk carved out of velmstone—and a cooling chamber built into the wall, consistently stocked with drinks of all kinds. Adjacent to that were shelves lined with datapads and records, and the opposite wall saw projections of historical crafts featuring Barsha tech. Pretty standard office fare, even on the executive floor, though at least the view was good: Behind the desk lay a floor-to-ceiling window with a look at Corellia's night sky from the forty-eighth floor of Barsha Tower.

It could have been a really nice conference room. Or a waiting room. The size of it all proved wholly unnecessary for one person, yet it was where they'd tasked Jaylen to spend much of his time when he actually slowed down to visit Corellia—a very neat box with very little to do but sit and read.

The room's sparse aesthetic did complement Sliro's Imperial uniform, though: white coat, tightly cinched belt, black trousers, and boots. It contrasted Jaylen's own business outfit of loose trousers, high-neck shirt, and tie—a look straight from Nnytyl Barsha's wardrobe.

"This office isn't much," Jaylen said to Sliro, who didn't respond and instead walked over to the window. "I mean, this desk is really nice." Jaylen rapped his knuckles on it. "But there's really not a lot here. Not very practical." His brother kept staring at the lights of Coronet City dotting the view. "You want something to drink?" Jaylen walked over to the wall and tapped on a panel to reveal the cooling chamber's selection.

Sliro finally turned his head, his brow raised, complete with scoff. "You have a built-in cooling chamber?"

"I know, like I said, not very practical. But helpful. Long nights of reading datapads and talking to ministers of whatever from whichever system."

Jaylen pointed to the mix of ales and juices, but Sliro waved a hand to decline.

"You made it sound like this was urgent." Sliro's jaw rumpled underneath his thin beard. "More than a check-in call."

"It is. Look, I . . ." What could he tell Sliro about this? How should he even start? Jaylen looked his younger brother in the eye, and though they still saw each other face-to-face every few months, something felt different about the young man in front of him. Perhaps the hours in the Imperial office across Coronet City wore away at him—Sliro often complained about a long commute, an uncomfortable uniform, and busy hours on constant cycle. If it really was that dull and repetitive, he might be feeling the day's fatigue.

Strange that he didn't take a drink when offered.

"I can't talk to anyone else about this." Jaylen shut his eyes for a quiet moment and reminded himself that only Sliro of all people would understand the dilemma at hand.

Jaylen told himself the only way to make this easier on himself would be to get Sliro involved. He *had* to say something now. He simply needed to explain it first.

"Here," Jaylen said, and he knelt to unlock a secured drawer in the desk. The biometric scanner identified him and clicked as latches unlocked. Jaylen pulled it open and handed three of the drawer's four datapads to Sliro. "You remember how sometimes our parents would mention the other parts of Barsha Corp but never really explain them? This is what they are."

Jaylen watched as Sliro methodically scanned one datapad from top to bottom before moving on to the next, then the next. Several minutes passed, and though Jaylen had all sorts of specific figures and facts about what was on there, he chose to wait for Sliro's response.

"This is all," Sliro said, "highly suspect activity. It goes back years."

That was one way to sum it up. Spice embedded within hull plating. Kickbacks for hiring syndicates as "security" for material shipments. Overpowered munitions smuggled in crates of scrapped tools. All this, sent to syndicates, Outer Rim militia groups, even the Separatists before the war ended.

"Suspect. Illegal, even," Jaylen said. "And all off the record. Laundered through many channels. Forty-eight percent of Barsha Corp revenue. Recorded, organized, and processed completely separately from the departments that handle government construction and manufacturing contracts."

"Lady Barsha and Father were in on this?" Sliro asked, still staring at the materials. "They had to be. It's too extensive for them not to know."

"Father called it 'the hidden bones of our family business,' " Jaylen said. "I always figured there were government bribes, shady contracts. We knew that the business meant more than just construction. But spice smuggling? How do we even begin with this? They have credits everywhere—officially, unofficially, tracked, untraceable, physical, banked."

Sliro didn't respond to that question. Instead, his eyes narrowed into a furrow of deep, intentional thought as he rubbed his pointed chin. After a long silence, he asked, "Why are you showing me this?"

"What do you mean?" Jaylen was taken aback by Sliro's question, both the manner of it and the trace of bitterness. "Sliro, don't you get it? They've been preparing me for this thing that I have no business overseeing. I don't think any one person does. Maybe not ever. But look." Jaylen grabbed one more datapad out of the secured drawer. "These people. This is the entire management of Barsha Corp. Look, Yunn'fenna Pol—I just thought she held some bland title. 'Manager of Diversified Holdings.' But those initiatives—she's working with syndicates. Those are gangsters and spice runners she's dealing with."

"That's funny," Sliro said as he set the datapads down. "I just saw her a month ago when I visited Barsha Tower. She brought her little girl to the office. Everyone waved."

"You see? This is what I mean. All these people that we thought we knew—these jobs that we thought we understood, it's all *more*."

Jaylen stood next to his younger brother, and if someone had captured the moment, both the similarities and the differences would have stood out: Jaylen's natural tan with Roisem's deep-set eyes and thick hair. Sliro's pale desk-worker complexion with Nnytyl's high forehead and widow's peak. Both inherited blue eyes and brown hair from Nnytyl, though Sliro's thin mouth came from the mother his family never discussed.

They stood on either side, like mirror images framing their future against the backdrop of Corellia's dark skyline.

Jaylen wondered if it was meant to be this way—Sliro had just gotten back from work travel, and Jaylen had been given this information only a week ago, but it all lined up. It had all led to this moment. Jaylen had been considering next steps, but he'd needed to see Sliro's reaction first. If Sliro had reacted with disgust or anger, Jaylen would have called it off. But Sliro's eyes shifted analytically, and his face lined with curiosity.

Jaylen could do something with that.

He knew that the time had come.

"Brother," Jaylen said, specifically choosing that term, "I need someone I can trust with me. Someone who's seen these people and who can tell me exactly what they think. Someone who has a history with Barsha—the company and the family, because they're intertwined."

Sliro slowly turned to Jaylen, and the brothers locked eyes.

"You're offering me a job?"

A job. When Sliro used such simple terms, it seemed almost demeaning. Jaylen pictured something much grander, much more involved.

"I don't know what to call it," Jaylen said. "I don't even know how it works. I mean, Barsha Corp's got boards and executives and all these layers. But look, they're making me CEO. I should be able to bring on, I don't know, an assistant or something. We can combine our knowledge of the company and the family. We've seen it all."

One side of Sliro's mouth ticked upward. "You're right," he said. "They're making you the CEO."

Jaylen patted his younger brother on the shoulder. "And *you* should be there with me." A hissing sound came from the wall, and he turned to see the cooling chamber start its automatic slide shut. "I don't know where this company goes from here. But there's a lot going on, and I'm not sure what to think of it." He stepped back to the wall quickly, clipping the side of his hip against the velmstone desk corner as he triggered the panel to reopen the cooling chamber. "Besides, it's gotta be better than whatever you do for the Empire. I mean, aren't you just staring at a terminal in an old government office all day?"

Sliro tilted his head, then looked back down at the datapad. "Something like that."

"We want to shape the future of Barsha Corp, then let's do it." Jaylen pointed to the lines of bottles within the cooling chamber. "A drink? Come on, I insist."

At that moment, Sliro muttered something to himself, some non-Basic words that came with a headshake and a smile. Sliro caught Jaylen's inquisitive look and explained, "It means 'the chosen one' in Huttese—the language of the underworld. The best of the very worst." Sliro thumped his chest, the light blue of the datapad tinting his white cloak. "Chosen ones. You and me." He walked over and peered at the drink selection. "The same, but different."

CHAPTER 4

"There he is."

The singsong lilt and bright tone gave away the speaker. Jaylen froze, a way of mentally hiding from anyone entering the executive suite, even as all surrounding eyes stayed on him. Hydraulics whooshed as the large doors shut, and the oncoming footsteps produced the same reaction from those around him: a seamstress, a speech coach, and Barsha Corp's financial controller. They all stepped back as Jaylen's mother approached.

Only Brencoyle remained nearby, running a brush across the shoulders of Jaylen's suit, then tugging on a long coat draped over him. Brencoyle broke his shell and grimaced for only a moment, his bushy eyebrows rising under his slicked-back brown-and-white hair.

"Well," Roisem said, arms outstretched as she wove through the departing servants. "You've certainly been difficult to find. Whisking off to this place and that. Look at you. I haven't seen you look this refined since . . . since the University of Bar'leth graduation."

"These formalities are a little . . ." Jaylen started, but his words drifted off as Brencoyle circled around to the front, smoothing out dark blue angled lapels under his thick brown cape. As he did, he met Jaylen's eyes with a very subtle frown.

Brencoyle. Always looking out for him. Brencoyle nodded at RD-L1, the valet's green-plated protocol droid, who then headed toward the exit.

"You've found your way. This is your moment," Brencoyle said with perfect diction before following his droid out.

"A little what, dear?" his mother repeated as she stepped in front of him, Roisem Barsha in full grandeur, long black coat over a textured white shirt with a high ruffled collar. "This is as important as it gets. Finally, the anointing of the chosen one."

Not that again. Ever since that moment on the Macronian Shipyard balcony, Jaylen had tried to escape the weight of such a label. He did wonder, though, if the Barsha executives used the term, too, or if it was only his parents.

He really hoped it was the latter.

"Truly a once-in-a-generation event," Roisem continued. "I don't think any formalities could meet the importance of the moment."

Once in a generation—that part was accurate. But the how and why of the event, all of it felt . . .

Well, it felt a little showy. A lifetime of guidance to a single, solitary moment of ascension, but did it really mean anything? All the terminology he'd learned in the past two years, all the hands he'd shaken and ministers he'd greeted—he'd been a mere passenger. Sometimes, Jaylen thought that Sliro was the lucky one. He didn't have to deal with any of this. He could just work his job and live his life. There was a reason why Jaylen would occasionally joke to Sliro about his being a bastard—that little jab reminded them both that Sliro never had to cope with things like press conferences.

At least, that was how things used to be. After today, Sliro would have more than just a seat at the table.

"Are we absolutely sure that this once-in-a-generation event had to happen today?" he asked, enunciating the final word with the finest diction, as per Brencoyle's coaching. "Why not tomorrow? When"—he tugged at his trousers—"the proper attire is available and I don't need alterations minutes before a press conference."

"Jaylen, you know our rule . . ." she started. "Business demands the best out of Barshas."

Even though Jaylen stood taller than his mother—taller even still because the family insisted that he wear heeled boots for "an air of authority"—her hands came with a sour weight as they grasped his shoulders. No matter what he did, the smallest of her gestures snapped him back into line. He could speak up now, be honest and say that despite all the training and mentoring, he simply wasn't ready. And it was true—aside from the plans he'd concocted with Sliro, he really wasn't sure about *anything* right now.

Jaylen turned around—stomach in, chest out, very much presentation ready, and did not look his mother in the eye.

He wasn't supposed to. School had taught him that the proper way to establish a look of competence was to pick a single spot slightly above eye level, somewhere across the room. That way, he would never appear to be giving too much individual focus to a single reporter, cam, or microphone.

He would simply float a little above all that.

Instead, his eyes tracked across the Corellian skyline. Weeks ago, he'd looked at this same skyline from ten floors below with Sliro. Together, they'd discussed a new way forward for Barsha Corp against the backdrop of a clear late evening. Today, there were bits of sunlight poking the planet's usual grim stormy weather.

He could stop stalling. He could simply go along with everything his parents wanted like he fully believed he was capable and ready to lead, like he actually *wanted* this job. He chose instead to continue his protest, except his excuse was weaker than he would have liked. He said, "Doesn't it make better business sense to wait until after the new government gets established?"

Funny how his parents had taught him the finer points of using language and information strategically, yet here those instincts disappeared, and he was still eight years old sleeping with plush fathiers in a speeder bed.

Laughter filled the large space, echoing off the circular suite's walls. It came loaded with the reminder that no matter Jaylen's title or status, his parents would always—always—be higher. "New government?" she finally asked.

"It's only been seven months since everything was . . ." What was the right term for this? Transformed? Upgraded?

Downgraded?

Palpatine himself had used "reorganized."

Jaylen went with the simplest approach. "Since the Republic became the Empire."

"Bah," she said, complete with a hand wave. "Empire. Republic. It's just a name. Palpatine has always been a friend of Barsha Corp. And now he always will be. You see, these are the things you'll be learning. That's all just makeup on a stage player. The person underneath does not change." She hunched over in mock desk work, fingers pretending to type on a keyboard. "You think someone filing shipping manifests has a new job because the label now says 'Empire' instead of 'Republic'?"

That question snapped Jaylen into the moment, but probably not the way Roisem intended. He saw it now—his parents viewed the change in regime like a simple name swap, an updated trademark. They probably viewed his elevation the same way, like the Barsha machine would run *exactly* the same way, and his whole role would be to spout out words like "propulsion efficacy" to heads of state buying fleet hardware.

Jaylen's eyes dropped ever so slightly until they met his mother's. Roisem and Nnytyl were the faces of Barsha Corp. They wanted Jaylen to be the face of a rebranding. That was what two years of lessons and meetings were about. Roisem really had no clue about the conversation he'd had with Sliro, or his intention to change things far beyond the name of the CEO.

Jaylen's pulse quickened in a much different way than any previous discussion he'd had with his mother. So many moments of anxiety had come and gone in her presence, but this—this was *anticipation*. He was ready. And to get things going, he closed his mouth in silence. The future suddenly seemed brighter than it had ever been.

Jaylen tugged at his lapels and turned a full 180 degrees back to the mirror, the tails of his coat whipping as he did so. He smoothed his hair one more time and, true to Brencoyle's process, gave his shoulders one final brush.

Cam ready. Or as ready as he'd ever be.

There really was only one thing left to do. "If now's the time," he said, "then let's head out."

JAYLEN HAD BEEN in the main press room of Barsha Tower before—always as an observer or support speaker, but never the guest of honor. Assistants lined the small hallway between the waiting room and stage, a mix of fresh-faced young adults eager to launch their careers and long-time veterans who recognized the historical significance of the moment. They each carried datapads and comlinks, and they manifested an endless wave of chatter about news outlets or interview requests. On the wall sat a large display, a line of media member names. Most waited downstairs in Barsha Tower's main lobby, though fourteen were selected for the actual conference, two from the *Corellia Times*.

Jaylen skimmed the assigned talking points on the datapad in his hand. "We're almost here. I can feel it," Roisem said in his ear, though she quickly stepped back and glanced around. "I can *feel* it," she repeated, her voice carrying forth, and many of the assistants paused to look. When they did, her voice got even louder—especially after one assistant pulled out a holorecorder. "Twenty-five years ago, you came into existence. And I knew from the moment I first held you: You were built for this. Through your hardships, you have triumphed to become the steward that will lead Barsha to even greater heights."

Jaylen knew—he *knew*—that she was originally going to say something slightly less bombastic. Only slightly. Roisem's natural dramatics always surfaced. But the moment an audience watched, her volume dialed up. And rather than cringe through a smile, he did his part, keeping a stoic pose with raised chin and calm eyes.

The whole orchestration was an extension of her personality, from the speechwriter to the media frenzy. Every single word in Jaylen's notes was reviewed, revised, and revised again by his mother, a complete vision on "the extraordinary transition of Barsha Corp's future."

Except she didn't know what he had planned.

"Two minutes," someone yelled, and Jaylen scanned the backstage area, rubbing his clean-shaven chin.

Sliro wasn't here. Which might cause some problems. "Hey," he said to the nearest assistant, "have you seen Sliro?"

"No, sir," she said with a headshake. He turned and asked the next person, who mentioned seeing him an hour ago.

Jaylen patted his hip, where he'd stashed a direct comlink to Sliro. Given the density of people and the proximity of his parents and the company's executives, he really didn't want to use it. But with time running out, Jaylen needed his brother in place. Their entire plan depended on it. From behind, his father's voice boomed out. "Do you understand the gravity of today?" Nnytyl asked an assistant, a Vurk that had worked in Barsha Corp as long as Jaylen could remember. "Four generations of Barshas have led to this moment."

The Vurk replied in her native language, and whatever she said prompted a long, loud laugh from Nnytyl—loud enough that Jaylen could reach out to his brother without being heard. "Sliro?" he said into the comlink. "Sliro, where are you?"

"Are you looking for someone?" asked another assistant. He tilted his head and pointed up at the countdown chrono on the wall. "The presentation starts soon."

"I'm looking for Sliro. He's—"

"*Sliro?*" Somehow, despite being several meters away, Nnytyl must have heard it. He stormed over and inserted himself between Jaylen and the assistant. "What is this?" An accusatory finger pointed to the comlink in Jaylen's hand.

Jaylen wanted to say something. That Sliro was still family. That Sliro didn't deserve to be forgotten. That Sliro still meant something. All those times when Jaylen made sure Sliro wasn't tossed aside—despite what he sometimes said to his brother, he still watched over him.

Sliro may have been a bastard, but he was still more than half a Barsha.

Although, Jaylen thought to himself with a snort, since he had to put up with their family's absurdity, did that mean that Sliro should put up with at least half the nonsense?

Once again, Jaylen chose to not say anything. He didn't even look his father in the eye. Instead, he stood still, giving a quiet shake of his head until he brought the comlink down to his side and stuffed it back into his pocket. But he saw the tension growing inside Nnytyl through little emerging details: the vein across his forehead, the small bumps forming on the hinge of his jaw as he bit down, the flare of his nostrils.

"I cannot believe," Nnytyl started, "that you would *taint* this moment, of all moments, by even giving him one second of your thoughts—"

The Vurk assistant rushed up to them. "We're going live in thirty seconds," she yelled, and out of nowhere, a hand grabbed Jaylen's elbow. Many hands appeared, actually, including one that pushed Jaylen's father in front of him, and the procession formed into a single file line despite the lingering tension. They shuffled toward the side of the stage, a thick curtain now standing a meter in front of them. Speakers projected the current presenter's voice, which delivered some sort of career retrospective on Jaylen's parents. From behind, he heard "excuse me" quickly repeated over and over until Roisem caught up.

She gave him a tilted glance, first seemingly to check his wardrobe, then to glance at her husband. Through it all, Jaylen swore he heard the comlink go off in his pocket, the perfect sound frequency to transmit despite the din. He flashed a quick smile. And before Roisem could respond, another hand pushed her forward. "Ten seconds, everyone. Nine . . . eight . . . seven . . ."

From the stage, a voice boomed out. "And now I'd like to welcome the two people who have steered Barsha Corp through decades of growth, expansion, innovation, and prosperity—leaders who truly defined what is possible in design and manufacturing across the galaxy: Roisem and Nnytyl Barsha!"

Muted applause came through, though the audience was mostly press. Seconds later, Roisem started speaking, though Jaylen didn't bother listening. A timer above the curtain told him when to really start paying attention.

Instead, he did the right thing, the expected thing—the Barsha thing: He pulled his speech notes back up on his datapad. While he knew a holoprompter would float the text at his eyeline, he still wanted to sound assured, even being on the cusp of so many unknowns.

Also, he needed to know when to go off script.

Jaylen took in a breath, holding the air inside his lungs, his mind projecting all the different ways his parents might react. Would they keep the façade going until a quiet moment at home, when all the pressure and discord would erupt into a volley of yelling? Would they blame both brothers, or would they only berate Jaylen? Or would they do something as drastic as interrupt Jaylen while he spoke on stage? His mother did have an affinity for the dramatic. Storming the stage to dramatically proclaim . . . something . . .

Well, it existed within the range of possibility.

Jaylen reminded himself that this plan also hinged on one more thing, and he pulled out the comlink from his pocket. "Sliro?" he asked as he activated it. "Sliro, are you in position?"

Something responded. It was the same short noise that he'd caught moments ago when the comlink was stowed away. But with a clearer listen, he heard that it certainly wasn't Sliro. Instead, it just sounded like random shouts clipped in and out of the comlink before it all went dead.

Forty-three seconds until his stage time.

They'd *just* talked this morning. Sliro was finishing some final tasks at the Imperial office across Coronet City while Jaylen dealt with preparations for this speech. Jaylen had no backup plan. It was too late to delay or call things off, and he just had to hope that the comlink noise was Sliro hustling through Barsha Tower.

"Mr. Barsha?" an assistant asked, and everything moved in automatic: The timer went off, Nnytyl's speech finished, applause rang through the curtain. And someone pulled the thick black fabric aside to let Jaylen through.

Hugs. Waves. Methodical steps toward the podium.

And then he finally took his place in the spotlight, with posture that would make Brencoyle proud. He gave several polite "thank you" statements, then counted five seconds before starting.

Which he did, executing with such perfect timing that he nearly surprised himself. Good thing something was going smoothly, even with Sliro's mysterious absence.

"CEO. Chief executive officer. I fully understand the weight of that responsibility. The history behind it. Not just that of my parents, but of the generation before them, and the generation before them. Barsha is a pillar of the galaxy, from building ships that transport people across the stars to laying the infrastructure for developing worlds. Nearly two million employed, from the Core to the Outer Rim." He paused, his mind flashing across all the other things the company oversaw. "And, as I'm sure many of you have heard by now, Barsha is the foundation of the Empire's new fleet."

That was it. That was the turning point. Jaylen squinted through the bright overhead lights, no sign of his half brother. Though really, only the front row of journalists and the holoprompter were visible to his overwhelmed eyes.

Jaylen had to choose.

"This new age presents new opportunities," he said, the first half of the sentence still part of the script. "And with those opportunities, we must think bigger and bolder. This moment is an opportunity to seize as Barsha Corp looks to its past to build a new future of growth and expansion. The war showed the strength of our unity, and now is the time to go further and achieve more—Barsha Corp, hand in hand with the Empire."

Those were his own words.

And without Sliro in sight, he had to keep going.

"Our company was pivotal in driving Republic ships to victory in the war. Our hardware production is poised to build upon that footprint, installing more components in more ships. As the Empire grows, so will Barsha—and in order to fulfill that growth, in order to match the Empire every step of the way, it takes a daring choice." Jaylen paused at that, partially to skim the room for Sliro—but partially to settle his own nerves. Long-smoldering embers were surfacing in his words, possibly for the first time ever.

"You all know Roisem Barsha as a decisive leader. I know her as my mother. And years ago, well before the war, she told me something that stuck with me." Suddenly, Jaylen's mind swam through memories of his childhood bedroom, his speeder-shaped bed, and all the rules that restricted his interactions with his brother. "She said, 'To truly be a Barsha, you need to know when to say something or stay quiet. That's how you get what you want out of people.' I think about that a lot. Actually," he said, ad-libbing for a moment, "that's probably not true. I don't think I have to think about it that much. It's built into my instincts now." He paused again before going back on script. "As I thought about the future of Barsha, I knew I had to say something. My parents have been a team for decades, yet here I am as the sole CEO. And while my title and my role will put the responsibilities on my shoulders, the truth is, I can't do this myself. I need help. And where should I get help but from someone who knows this business, this family as well as I do? Someone who, in some ways, knows us better.

"As my first act as Barsha Corp's CEO, I am creating a new position: executive consultant to the CEO. And filling that role will be the only person who has been there from the very beginning, the only person I unequivocally trust with the name Barsha.

"My brother, Sliro."

Audible gasps rippled from the gathered audience, and Jaylen took another five seconds to let things settle before speaking again.

Sliro had better be in position.

"Sliro, please join me on stage."

Now he waited. And from his peripheral vision, he saw the side stage curtain pull back, and if he dared look, he knew his parents would be standing there with enraged looks on their faces.

"Maybe he got stuck in the turbolift. Um, hey," he called to the back, "can someone go find Sliro? He really should be on this stage—"

Suddenly, doors on either side of the press room slid open. Hallway light broke through, poking into the space's dim illumination. But instead of Sliro entering through the open doors, large silhouettes marched in on either side, something bulky in their hands.

Jaylen put a hand up to block out the spotlights, and as his eyes adjusted, he realized what was happening.

An Imperial officer led the march. But it wasn't Sliro—Jaylen knew that right away from the dark gray of his coat.

These were armed uniformed officers and clone troopers marching into the room. And they weren't coworkers from Sliro's desk job at the ISB.

"Go, go, go," one of them yelled, and a cluster of clone troopers hit the stage, weapons pointed firmly at Jaylen. That officer came up behind him, yelling, "This press conference is over, please disperse in an orderly fashion."

Now all the lights came on, the spotlights dimmed, and the space came into clear view. The room's large double doors in the back flew open, and four clones waved the press out.

"What's the meaning of this?" yelled Roisem as she stormed to the podium. A clone stepped in front of her, gun raised, and she took the weapon's barrel with her hand and forced it down before spitting on the shiny white helmet. "This is our moment. You cannot take away our moment."

The sound of blasterfire caused a clamor of screams, then silence. From the ceiling, a burned hole dripped bits of debris down on the stage, just a meter from where Jaylen stood. The officer, whose blaster barrel smoked, adjusted his hat. But then Roisem walked around the clone and looked the officer over. Her eyes burned with a fury that she usually saved only for Sliro, and Jaylen had a sudden sinking epiphany.

His mother *knew* that officer. "We sponsored your Harvest Festival party! You took our money with a *smile*. I should have known. Your family's always had it in for us—did your mother put you up to this? She's probably watching this from the Corellian Engineering offices. When I see her—"

Finally, the officer held up a hand, though he remained silent until she took a breath.

"You're under arrest. For conspiracy against the Empire." With that, he turned and walked off the stage, completely ignoring Roisem's constant assault of screams.

Jaylen stopped listening, though. Despite the absolute chaos around him, he thought one very specific thought:

The only thing that might tie Barsha Corp to any sort of conspiracy were the four datapads locked in Jaylen's desk—tables and tables of information showing how Barsha Corp navigated *around* the government, going back years.

Was that what had triggered this? Had Jaylen left his desk unlocked? Or had someone like Yunn'fenna Pol finally had enough of the Barshas?

Jaylen grabbed the comlink. "Sliro?" he asked as clones pushed assistants aside. "Sliro? Are you there?"

To his left, a clone put cuffs on Roisem. Rather than streak with tears, Roisem's face had turned red, her breath barely able to keep up with the anger she spewed. Across the stage, Nnytyl already wore cuffs, yet he sat on his knees, neutral lips and glazed eyes, like he existed somewhere else.

"Sliro!" Jaylen said into the comlink. "Sliro! You have to pick up, something—"

An armored hand slapped the comlink from his grip. It flew across the stage and rolled on the floor, and the clone's muffled voice came from his helmet. "On your knees."

Jaylen stared at the comlink. Had it clicked and buzzed? Was that Sliro on the other end? Behind him, voices shouted, but they weren't from clones or the Imperial officer. No, those voices asked *questions*. A clamor of reporters shouted questions, including "Is this the end of Barsha?" and "Who was involved in the conspiracy against the Empire?" The voices increased in strength, even as clones pushed the reporters out, and it all blended in with clone comm chatter giving and receiving orders while Roisem's diatribe continued.

"I said, 'On your knees.' " A blaster jammed into the middle of Jaylen's back, and though he stumbled first, he finally complied, falling to his knees and putting his hands behind his back.

As cuffs wrapped around Jaylen's wrists, he stayed locked on the comlink. Where was Sliro? Did they intercept him on his way to Barsha Tower?

Was his brother all right? Maybe Sliro had seen the troops on the way up and hid.

Or maybe they'd already arrested him.

The trooper hooked Jaylen's elbows and pulled him upright, then pushed him to leave the stage. As he did, he stepped past the comlink, and though he knew the butt end of a rifle would strike him for this, he leaned over and tried to yell into it, hoping that somehow the device was still active:

"Sliro! Where are you?"

CHAPTER 5

Several weeks had passed since the arrest at Barsha Tower. Conspiracy. Racketeering. Trafficking. Illegal trade. The Empire brought those charges and, without really *explaining* any of it, found Barsha Corp guilty. Barsha Corp, as in all the executive board members: Roisem, Nnytyl, Oland, Twyla, Leniel, Guscht.

And the new CEO, Jaylen Barsha.

Guilty on all counts.

Millions of Barsha Corp employees were left unscathed and free to seek other employment. Upper management and personal employees of the Barsha family, like Brencoyle, received a slightly harsher fate due to their proximity—their savings accounts were confiscated in lieu of fines.

Through all that, no one mentioned Sliro at all. And when the Barshas were whisked out of the courtroom, things took an unexpected turn, because for all the carnage at the press conference, things suddenly became very docile, almost civil. A uniformed officer came up to them in a holding cell, told them that they were to await sentencing "while the Empire considers your value."

That was the only time Roisem openly wept.

But their wait was not spent in detention. Instead, they were allowed to go to a neutral property unrelated to Barsha Corp itself.

The moon of Gus Treta was nicer than the actual planet of Corellia. It rained far less, for one thing, and for those capable of purchasing island properties, the quiet isolation made for a relaxing getaway. There was a reason why the thirty or so resort-style villas were owned by families like the Barshas. As far as Jaylen knew, only one of those villas in the tropical region of the moon was available for public holiday rentals. All the other locations got privately snatched up when word leaked of a new weather control system to entice visitors. For many, it was paradise—no constant thrum of ships, no worries about galactic commerce, no hassles surrounding Corellia's volatile weather.

The Barshas stayed on the compound they'd funded when Jaylen and Sliro were kids, legally compliant with the judge's orders given that the property was purchased by a family friend with a "loan" in exchange for . . .

Something that probably existed as a line item in the Barsha ledgers.

Apparently the property sat empty close to 90 percent of the time, only put to use when someone within the Barsha circle wanted a quiet tropical getaway—the perfect escape for a family awaiting sentencing: no visitors, no leaving the premises, and no press. Besides supply deliveries, the Barshas were cut off.

Lush, comfortable, and extremely well stocked.

Not exactly jail.

After two weeks, Jaylen sat in a garden cottage with a droid. Because no one wanted to *talk* about what happened. Not for real.

He'd tried, though. Uncle Guscht grumbled and walked away. Aunt Twyla, Nnytyl's sister, said, "Why do you want to keep reliving such an awful thing?" Oland, Jaylen's cousin and closest to his age, laughed in his face. Aunt Leniel nodded but didn't reply, until finally she excused herself.

Five minutes ago, he'd tried with his parents as well. He sat with them on the large back patio as one of the compound's droid servants offered a tray of drinks. "I have finally come to see that this was all a brilliant ploy," Roisem said. "The whole ordeal with the clones and arrests, it was all for show. I understand how to put on a show. It was a show for sure. They got their show, and now we get our drinks."

That was the only time Jaylen had actually heard his parents say anything about the chaos at the press conference. Until then, they'd avoided the topic. So for it to finally come up, that was good. But with what his mother was saying, every line sounded like . . . well, it sounded a bit detached from reality.

She raised her hand as a frown crossed her lips. "Droid? Droid!"

It took a second for the droid's processors to register the request. The servant paused mid-step, then rotated to come back toward Roisem.

"I still can't believe it's come to this. *Droid* servants. So lacking in response and awareness. Hurry up, hurry up, I haven't got all day," she said, clapping her hands. The servant droid kept its speed and eventually lowered the tray in front of her. She took a cocktail glass and sipped as she lounged back in a chair.

"I heard from our attorney an hour ago," Nnytyl said. He also reclined in a lounge chair, a holo transmitter seated on his belly as he watched some kind of sporting event.

"Oh, perhaps you should respond with the fact that the *droids* here are incapable of service. If we're allowed to stay here, why can't we fly in the help?" Roisem swirled the liquid in her glass before sipping again. "This justice system, I swear."

"Well," Nnytyl mused while rubbing his chin, "she said the longer this plays out, the more conversations she has on our behalf, the better this goes. She believes the Empire still values us."

"Years and years of building the galaxy. Now they leave us *destitute*." Roisem scoffed, then scoffed again. "This is the thanks we get. Where is the gratitude?" She tapped her hand against her chair for each syllable in *gratitude*.

Jaylen almost mentioned the fact that they were technically prisoners, despite the nice drinks. He stared at his glass and half wondered if someone had put spice in it. None of this made sense. The Empire had just seized one of the galaxy's biggest corporations, and his parents now fluctuated between optimistic and petty. And not once—not *once*—had anyone mentioned his brother in any family discussions.

He was going to change that. Right now.

"What about Sliro?" Jaylen asked.

Both of his parents stopped with their drinks and turned to him beneath their large hats.

"Has our attorney heard anything about him?"

"You didn't actually *ask*, did you?" Roisem asked. Nnytyl shook his head at the question, and Jaylen's mother huffed in response. "Oh, the Empire knows what to do with people like Sliro."

"But Sliro *worked* for the Empire. Don't you think—"

"They probably found him faster," Nnytyl said, then chuckled so hard that he coughed. Roisem soon joined his laughter, until Nnytyl spoke again. "He's probably in some penal colony somewhere. Or a labor program." He held up his glass, took a deep drink, and muttered to himself, "Probably better company than here."

"What was that, dear?" Roisem said, her eyes turning with a sharp look.

That was when Jaylen stepped away. He wanted to learn why they were arrested. He wanted to yell, *They might send troops to kill us any moment now!* He wanted to *know* if Sliro had been taken, too—if Sliro was alive.

He seemed to be the only person who even cared, not just about Sliro but about any of it. While Roisem and Nnytyl began their usual bickering, Jaylen left the courtyard and wandered the property. He ventured forth, heading toward a section of the compound he'd rarely visited, past one of several fountains on the property, and as he turned around a corner of tall formed hedges, he came upon something new.

A garden cottage.

Which, really, was sturdier than most of the shops on Corellia. And cleaner, for sure. Four lights activated upon Jaylen's entrance, one in each corner, emitting a warm yellowish glow. Along each wall lay racked tools, while one big cabinet stocked various pieces of machinery, all compacted in storage mode. A small polished console sat beside the cabinet, streaming live data for status and environmental checks. Right next to it, a protocol droid wearing a shoulder harness carried several tool pouches. "Greetings," said the droid in a synthesized female voice.

"I am Ay-One-Ay-One, overseer of daily functions on the compound. Welcome to my office." She walked over to a large wall display showing the tool inventory, which ranged from gardening shears and slicing implements to maintenance kits for the compound's various droids.

"Hello," he said. "Mind if I hide out here for a while?"

"You certainly may," A1-A1 said. "I welcome visitors. You are . . ." The droid didn't catch Jaylen's sideways glance while she tapped at the station's interface. "Jaylen Barsha."

"Yeah. That's me. Listen, Ay-One, I'm just trying to get away."

"Is there something wrong on the premises?" She tapped the station's buttons again, and this time a roster of differently shaped droids appeared on the screen. "Right now, five droids are assigned to serve the guests. Three are charging. One is disabled for a restraining bolt replacement." She pointed to the corner, where another protocol droid stood powered down and slumped over. Of course Jaylen's parents would force servant droids to have restraining bolts on an *island* compound. "Two are permanently damaged and require replacement by the property owner. However, that is several months overdue. I have not had time to make the proper requests yet."

Jaylen scanned the room, then noticed a couple of droid-shaped humps covered by a blanket in the corner. He didn't even know *which* family "friend" owned the property due to the company's creative bookkeeping tactics. If he still had those datapads from his desk, he might have been able to identify the owner and request the replacement droid. Of course, if he did have the datapads, he wouldn't be here on Gus Treta.

"Nothing's wrong with the premises. It's the people."

"The property's thermal scanners identify where and when someone may need assistance." A1-A1 tapped another button, and the screen flashed into a gridded map of the compound. One set of squares systemically sent out pings, scanning the grounds for life signs. She hit another button, and glowing dots overlaid the map. "The quantity of guests is currently accurate. Does one of them have an issue?"

"That's not what I meant," he said with a laugh. "I'm just trying to find a quiet place."

"They are all inside the house right now. This is a good place to accomplish your goals. Do you want a beverage?"

Jaylen pictured his parents and *their* beverages. At this point, keeping all his wits about him felt like the smarter option. "No, I don't want a beverage. Thank you, though."

"We do aim to make all our guests comfortable." She reached over and grabbed a datapad. "Would you like to read today's *Corellia Times*?"

A1-A1 must not have known that the Barshas were prisoners rather than guests. Or maybe the droid didn't care and just treated all visitors the same. "Sure, I'll read the *Times*. Closest thing I can do to getting out right now."

"Do you have a special request that would make your stay here more enjoyable?" She pointed to the datapad. "I am in charge of all deliveries to the compound. I can request back issues of the *Corellia Times* or other reading material if you'd like."

Jaylen scrolled through the news, and to his surprise, he didn't catch a single mention of the name *Barsha*. Within weeks, they'd all but disappeared from public consciousness.

Perhaps that was the greatest punishment the Empire could inflict upon them.

Jaylen got to the Criminal Affairs section, and while he'd originally looked for any mentions of the family, a new idea sparked to look for Sliro. Sliro knew about Gus Treta, so maybe the issue was that he had no way of getting here. Or he purposefully stayed away. "Ay-One?" Jaylen asked.

"Yes?"

"Can you order archives dating back, I don't know, a month?" Jaylen tapped a finger on the datapad.

"I can do that," A1-A1 said as she began typing out an order list. "I will let the delivery droid know when they make their evening supply drop from Corellia. Anything else before their scheduled arrival?"

"Any news archives they can get from neighboring systems. Coruscant as well. Same date range," he said. While his parents and relatives seemed content to just *exist* on Gus Treta with drinks and leisure, Jaylen had finally found a purpose to his time here. Looking through stacks and stacks of news datapads wasn't exactly what he would call fun, but despite the surroundings, despite his family's *attitude,* there was no pleasure to be found here.

Sliro was somewhere out there in the galaxy. Hopefully. And his being the bastard son of disgraced power brokers might have put him on the media's radar. It was a start, at least, and if Jaylen couldn't find Sliro in an article, maybe he'd at least get a clue.

Because this was exactly what his mother talked about all those years ago. Staying quiet or saying something—this was a *choice.* He was going to say something.

He was going to look for his brother.

The rest of the Barshas could all have their drinks and lounge chairs and delusional thinking. Jaylen would take his archived news in stacks of datapads. It was a far better investment.

System start-up.

Identification number: JX394ND-5777.

Hardware type: BX-series droid commando.

Manufacturer: Baktoid Combat Automata.

Default configuration and initialization parameters: Intended use by the Confederacy of Independent Systems.

Restraining bolt: Not detected.

Environment analysis: Unknown location.

Audio/visual sensors active. Motor functions disabled.

Start-up checks completed.

I am active.

I cannot move.

I have changed locations. I am no longer in the robotics factory on Geonosis.

Ahead of me, a repulsor cart sits filled with deactivated B1 battle droids. They are not placed in any sort of organizational fashion. Arms and heads push on one another at obtuse angles. Several of the battle droids are stacked horizontally over the rest, and one pair of legs sticks straight up.

A uniformed officer pushes an empty cart past me in the thin hallway. "Sir," he says, though his voice is not directed at me. I cannot turn my head, and instead I filter my audio input to identify the layers of sound around me.

The hiss of smelting machines.

The clank of battle droids being loaded on and off repulsor carts.

Footsteps on metal walkways.

The echo of these elements together.

One set of footsteps approaches until my view suddenly rises to the ceiling. A loud clang rings out as this happens, followed by the growing hum of a power system. "This one needs additional processing. Don't scrap him yet," a male voice says. I recognize this voice; it is Regional Auditor Six from Geonosis.

Another voice offers a quick "Yes, sir," and though I am still looking at a ceiling, I am moving, likely on a hoversled. A shoulder and arm enter my peripheral vision, and my head jostles. I assume Regional Auditor Six has shifted me in place. After several seconds, my vocabulator becomes active. Prior to my last shutdown, I had prepared various functions to kill this person should I encounter him on the so-called scrap line. However, my motor functions are still disabled, and he is purposefully reactivating my speech functions. He is also preventing me from being scrapped, though this may be temporary. I choose to engage in strategic conversation. "You are Regional Auditor Six from Geonosis," I say.

"Your memory is intact," he says with a short laugh. "You were scheduled to be disassembled and scrapped. But I may have different plans for you. So let's talk. Are your psychological combat and analysis functions working?"

"I can identify weaknesses that may be exploited in combat. However, this is not part of my main tactical loadout."

I hear the sound of a datapad. Then a cable connects to a port in the back of my neck. I cannot communicate with the device, though it is able to read my data banks. "Yes. Your tactical loadout." We enter a dark part of the hallway, though light from the datapad provides an ambient blue glow. "Let's talk about that."

"What do you wish to know?"

"Well, first, you're awfully polite to me now. No urge to kill me?" The tone of his question registers as genuine. "Do you understand what has happened to the galaxy?"

"All evidence points to the war being over." The regional auditor grunts in affirmative. "The fact that I am captured, yet no one is attempting to access intel. The simulation on Geonosis. The deactivated battle droids in the repulsor cart. These facts all support your claim. If the war is over, then I have no reason to be dishonest. My original purpose is now invalid. A conversation with you may establish a new objective."

"This is interesting." A gloved hand enters my field of vision as another officer passes by. I catch a partial glimpse of the person's uniform, which is white rather than standard Republic officer colors.

More evidence that something has changed in the galaxy.

"Are you begging for your life?" he asks after the passerby gains some distance.

"I don't have what organics consider life. Also, I do not beg."

"You're a stoic one, I'll give you that. Okay, I'm curious. I want to learn more about your skill set. How effective are you at infiltration? Blending in, operating undercover?" We turn from the hallway into a dark alcove. He takes a step back, and though I can detect a silhouette, I cannot see the finer details of his face, uniform, or rank bars.

"I can blend in, operate undercover in locations where a droid of my size would not seem out of place."

"Yeah. You *wouldn't* be out of place there." He does not reference what location he has in mind. However, it sounds like droids are common. "I don't think they'd even notice."

"Who is the target?"

His head shakes. "No target yet. I just need real intel on the ground.

There's no easy way to do it without anyone noticing. So"—he takes in a breath and taps the datapad—"see what's happening there. Threat analysis. Survival analysis. Daily observations."

"What is the purpose of the surveillance?"

The silhouette remains still. He is considering this question. Perhaps he has not thought this completely through. A mission without a purpose can lead to failure. "I delivered assets to the Empire," he finally says. "And I need to make sure plans are followed through. One way or another."

"This explanation is much vaguer than the orders passed down by General Grievous."

"Yes, well, General Grievous is dead and I'm not."

My view shakes continuously as he works something in my back dataport.

"Come on. It's supposed to be easier than this."

That statement does not sound as if it's targeted toward me.

"Come on," he says again until a click happens.

My neural core begins receiving new parameters.

"I will be more specific," he says, still out of view. "I have assurances from the Empire regarding the complete destruction of Barsha Corp. The elimination of the company and the final punishment of its founding family. The brutality of which will be determined by the Empire. When you arrive, your task is to monitor the situation and report back to me. Once legal matters are taken care of, I imagine the military will send someone to finish the job. Witness that, record that, *verify* that I did what no one else could have done. I handed one of the galaxy's biggest companies to the ISB on a platter. I expect rewards. On a number of levels."

I do not know what the ISB is, but its definition is irrelevant.

"I've just installed an override chip. It contains basic orders and text communication abilities. This isn't official Imperial business."

More data flows into my processors, including a map of a compound located on a Corellian moon.

"Your orders come from me. Your protocols come from me. You serve me."

That is not technically true. Transmitted orders and parameters are secondary to a droid's default programming. They may also eventually be superseded through further orders, learned experience, or a complete memory wipe.

Regional Auditor Six clearly has limited experience with droids. I choose not to overwhelm him with information.

"I won't be able to watch over you every moment. So I'll require your skills to accomplish things. We will check in periodically. Do we understand each other?"

My head jostles one more time, and my limbs become active.

"Follow me," he orders.

I march behind him. We get halfway down a long hallway when another officer wearing a similar white coat stops him and says, "Where are you taking that droid?" If Imperial rank bars correspond to Republic protocols, this person's three blue tiles indicate a rank of second lieutenant.

"This one was recovered from the Geonosis batch. A commando unit." Regional Auditor Six holds up the datapad even though there are no vital details on it. "More complex than the standard ones. They've requested a final analysis of his combat matrix before scrapping him."

"All right. Try to have him ready to process before the end of the day." The man's voice trails as he passes us. "It's been a long one."

Regional Auditor Six pauses for a moment until the second lieutenant turns the corner. He holds up a hand and points forward. "Yes. It has," he says in a low volume.

I don't respond.

TWO DAYS LATER, I arrive at a small hangar bay on the corner of the Barsha compound island on Gus Treta. The pilot droid settles the craft, and I step off. I carry a crate of supplies with me. The intel in my embedded chip shows that the compound only has seven beings on it: the immediate Barsha family and their relatives who made up Barsha Corp's executive board. They are not allowed to come or go, and the compound itself is run by a group of droids designated for specific tasks.

The chip contains a series of notes addressing specific points. I load up the record discussing various droids on the compound, as I look quite different from protocol droids, as well as droids designated for service, labor, gardening, and repair.

"Should someone ask where you came from, tell them you have been requisitioned for additional support by the family's representatives. It is highly likely that none of the Barsha family understand the legal logistics involved with the Empire's actions."

Regional Auditor Six is correct. The hangar bay has a side room marked for deliveries; it is currently vacant aside from two deactivated repulsor carts and one empty storage crate with its lid ajar. No one is managing the space.

Given a distance of about fifty meters to the main property and a lack of supervision, I decide to leave my supply crate here in an empty corner. I engage its secure lock, and the crate opens. On the top sits a small carton of groceries.

I remove those and set them aside, then take out the false panel underneath. I do an equipment check.

Transceiver to boost the communication signal of my override chip.

Electrobinoculars.

Data spike.

A blaster.

A small set of explosives complete with time-based detonator.

While my chip does not include explicit instructions for the last two, the embedded notes say to keep the weapons hidden until they are needed. I will require further elaboration at some point.

All items have survived the transportation process intact. I replace the false panel, then close the crate and fasten the locking mechanism. To help the crate blend in further, I take a folded tarp and place it on top. I take the top corner and bend it back to make the tarp's placement appear casual.

The march to the main property is uneventful. The weather is what most organic species would consider "mildly pleasant" with a clear sky and a light breeze. I see one droid with a shearing tool attending to plant life. I decide to carry the grocery carton and do an initial sweep of the compound's perimeter. Halfway through it, I run into a man I identify as Oland Barsha, one of the executive board members. He is wearing a robe and sandals. From the way he blinks, it appears he has just woken up.

"Hey, droid," he calls out. I pause and turn to him. "What do you got there?"

"Meilooruns, caf beans, teltier noodles, and travel biscuits."

"Oh, I love those." He reaches into the bag and pulls out a meiloorun. "I'll take that."

I wait five seconds as he turns and walks away. He disappears back into the main building.

The intel was accurate. No one is asking how or why I am here. To the Barshas, I am simply part of the droid help.

I commence blending in.

Now weeks into exile, all the Barshas settled into their routines. Uncle Guscht would take patio naps after he ate breakfast. Aunt Twyla had daily morning swims in the property's back pool, followed by lying out under the sun. Cousin Oland chose to swim in the ocean, and some nights he even slept out on the beach. Roisem decided to take up a new hobby of learning to sew her own clothes—not to wear, but as artistic expression. She'd also taken over correspondence with the family's attorney. In contrast, Nnytyl discovered that he actually indulged in the simple act of relaxing. He never again mentioned the conspiracy charges, instead watching holodramas or indulging in his newfound obsession with the regional blitzball circuit from sun up to sun down. This was oddly the happiest Jaylen had ever seen his father, as if the great Nnytyl Barsha realized that a life without responsibilities and spotlights could actually be quite *fun*.

Was this adaptation? Or was this denial?

Jaylen wasn't sure. For his father, though, their time on Gus Treta was actually the smoothest their relationship had ever been—yet Jaylen also noticed that his parents spoke to each other less and less as the days passed.

Those two elements might have been related.

For Jaylen, his regular routine was a little more practical than those of the other Barshas: Every day, A1-A1 had a new stack of datapads filled with news from Corellia and beyond. And every day, he carried them to the living room, where he took his late-morning caf and breakfast.

This morning, as he organized his stack of datapads, something caught his eye—something that gave credence to the "Barshas in denial" theory.

As Jaylen loaded up today's *Coruscant Daily Newsfeed,* he heard the mechanized servos and whirring of a droid passing by with a tray. "Oh, thank you," he said as a droid placed a small plate of fruit and a cup of caf on the table.

Except . . .

Was that droid arm covered in a jacket sleeve?

"Excuse me," Jaylen said, a hand up to flag the droid. This droid was different than most of the others; it showed up about two weeks ago as a replacement or new staff or something. No one said anything, not even A1-A1, so Jaylen figured it was part of the property's maintenance and replacement routine.

But still, a jacket?

Jaylen squinted at the details in front of him—a dark green coat that barely fit the bulky droid, seams nearly bursting apart at the shoulders. And for the first time, he really looked at this new addition, because something seemed different. It was bigger, for one, probably an entire head taller than a standard protocol droid. And its form, from the broad shoulders to the angular skull, well, it looked much more intimidating.

"What do you want?" the droid asked, its vocabulator presenting a male vocal tone.

This droid could definitely work on his manners a bit. "I was just wondering," Jaylen said, "where did you get that jacket?" Down the hallway, more droid footsteps approached, and he looked to see that, yes, that servant droid also wore a jacket.

"Roisem found them in the supply closet."

Jaylen's head tilted at that. Most servant droids addressed his parents as Lady Barsha and Master Barsha. Strange that this one was programmed to use her first name. Though a smirk came over his face as he thought about just how much that might irk her. She would, of course, have to speak to a droid long enough to notice first.

"She thought it would improve the atmosphere of the compound," the droid said.

"The atmosphere?" Jaylen asked. That *did* sound like something his mother would do.

"Her exact words were 'I feel much more at home now. Droids are so cold, aren't they?' " The droid stood in a frozen stare as Jaylen stifled a laugh, the absurdity of it all becoming too much.

"What's your registry number?" Jaylen asked.

"I am . . ." The droid continued speaking, although from the adjacent room, as Nnytyl cheered at his blitzball broadcast, his roaring cheers blunting out the first part of the droid's identification. ". . . Endee-Five-Seven-Seven-Seven."

"Well, thanks again for the delivery. Oh, you might want to get that jacket tailored. You're a little bit big for a protocol droid," Jaylen said as he took a sip of caf.

"I am a repurposed Bee-Ex commando droid. I was not designed to wear tight-fitting coats."

A commando droid? Suddenly, Jaylen understood why the thing seemed so intimidating.

Not that long ago, this droid fought clones. Now he served caf in a tropical prison. Still, that did make sense—those droids had to be used somewhere. What was the droid's designation again? Jaylen had missed the first few digits. "Okay. Endee-Five-Seven-Seven-Seven," he said, going off the part he'd heard. He rubbed his face, palms brushing over emerging stubble. "That's a mouthful. Is it okay to call you Endee-Five?"

"I have no preference."

"All right. Well, your jacket looks nice, Endee-Five," Jaylen said.

The droid nodded, then turned and left the dining room. Now the only noise came from his father's running blitzball commentary and the occasional curse word. Jaylen looked at the stack of news sources—every day, he spent hours reading each from start to finish. And when something of note popped up, he jotted it down on his personal datapad, which sat neatly between his plate of fruit and his caf.

He loaded up his most recent findings, a headline he'd flagged about how Carbanti United Electronics was moving beyond sensors and into propulsion systems. Could that *really* be what was behind this?

That question repeated itself so many times as he scanned through his notes. One-upping the competition or challenging market dominance, that was one thing. A military-driven takedown of a megacorporation?

His list held speculation, tangential evidence, even conspiracy theories, but each item failed to stand on its own merit. Was Barsha really any better or worse than, say, TransGalMeg or Czerka? At least Barsha had publicly supported the Republic during the Clone War. Other corporations toed the line between merely supporting the war and actively becoming part of the Republic's supply chain, and some even claimed that business was a neutral operation while selling to both sides.

Perhaps Barsha's downfall wasn't about jealousy. Perhaps it *was* business, a hidden competitor that wanted to swoop in and take Barsha's pending Imperial contract. But even that made little sense, because all the biggest ship manufacturers subcontracted to each other. Such moves were made out of equal parts respect and supply-chain necessity.

All this information—yet none of it threaded together. Could the true reason be collusion, with soft action among many parties? All Jaylen could think of was something his father told him years ago: "*One day, someone's going to try and knock you off your perch. And what Barshas have done for generations is hold the line. You don't let them have their way.*"

At the time, he figured his father was talking about his schoolmates or the peers of his generation at other large corporations. But all this happened because *someone* tried to take them down—and succeeded. The question was where that someone came from. Or was it multiple people? Possibly even people within Barsha Corp?

And who was still on their side? Had the entire galaxy turned on them? If so, could the Barshas trust anyone?

Jaylen took another sip of caf and bit down on his lip, a conscious deflection from the other mystery. Because in weeks of searching through countless articles across dozens of systems, he hadn't seen a single passing reference *anywhere* to Sliro Barsha.

At best, Sliro had escaped, hid, and maybe survived somewhere in the Outer Rim. It wasn't like his Imperial desk job held any significance; he could disappear and be replaced, just like A1-A1 would order a replacement for a busted protocol droid whenever she had the time.

Jaylen sighed loud enough to fill the tall, empty room, and the sound of a door's hydraulics caused him to turn his head. In came ND-5 holding the same tray as before, but now with a single glass of water. "I thought you looked thirsty," he said. The glass awaited him, sitting perfectly still until Jaylen reached over and took it. "Caf is dehydrating."

"Thanks, Endee-Five," said Jaylen, raising his glass in a salute.

"What are you researching?" ND-5 asked, nodding at the datapads.

An odd question coming from a commando droid. But maybe he'd been reprogrammed for small talk. Jaylen wouldn't have put it past his mother.

"Just trying to figure out why we're here." Jaylen held up his personal datapad and its displayed notes. "And to see if my brother is still alive."

CHAPTER 8

I have reached the hangar bay on the property. It is the middle of the night—technically into the next calendar day. The last light on the Barsha compound went out only an hour ago, as Oland Barsha had stayed up.

Besides one servant droid standing in the home foyer, all the droids are recharging. I walk the fifty meters across the docking bay and open my storage crate. I flip the transceiver's console into place and connect it to my back data port. This activates the text transmission capabilities of my embedded chip. The signal locks, and I send a message to Regional Auditor Six. "I am checking in as requested." Rather than process through my vocabulator, the words reach him directly through the chip as text.

I am receiving . . .

The reply hangs there for several seconds before the rest of it completes.

I am receiving you. What have you witnessed?

This primitive messaging style is understandable, as the signal circumvents any Imperial networks.

Eight days have passed since our last communication. In that time, I have witnessed many moments of idiosyncratic behavior. For example, a pattern exists with the Barshas, where one will express dissatisfaction with an issue, and the other will express a similar experience in commiseration.

I review the record of activities and identify the ones most relevant to the mission status. "Much time is spent on the patio. The pool is also regularly used, including at night. Nnytyl Barsha watches many hours of blitzball. Roisem Barsha has learned to sew. Jaylen Barsha continues to search for his missing brother."

No reply comes immediately. I am unsure if this is due to latency issues in the transmission signal or because Regional Auditor Six is considering a reply. Two minutes and eleven seconds pass before I see a new message.

The situation has just changed. Check in tomorrow at this time for new instructions. Keep monitoring everyone.

The transmission disconnects. I close the equipment and consider the final command.

Keep monitoring everyone.

With this, I restore the hangar bay's configuration so my equipment is obscured. I then go back inside the main house and wait for actions to monitor.

It does not take long for something to happen. Thirty-nine minutes pass before I hear Roisem Barsha's voice echoing through the hallways. "We're free!" she yells. "Wake up! Everyone wake up!" She starts to bang on an unknown object to make noise as she comes down the stairs. She looks at me. "Droid, get celebratory drinks."

There are no instructions in my chip for Roisem Barsha requesting drinks for the family in the middle of the night. I must improvise. I walk down to the basement and grab four bottles of celebratory alcohols to suit different tastes. I proceed to the dining hall, where Roisem has gathered the rest of the family. She is holding a wineglass and tapping its side with a fork. "Ah, the drinks. Now we're set. Because . . ."

Around the space, the Barshas present a mix of expressions, from annoyed to tired to curious. Roisem does not seem bothered by the late hour.

"We're *pardoned.*"

This shifts the mood in the room. Expressions of disbelief are accompanied by cheering. Roisem points at me, which I assume is her request to open the bottles. I do so. Oland Barsha grabs one and shakes it vigorously to create a geyser effect that soaks my jacket. One of the servant droids will have to clean the table and floor later.

Roisem calls for everyone's attention. "Our legal counsel will arrive tomorrow with the full details. But I wanted everyone to know immediately. In four days, we go"—she rotates her left hand several times before tipping it upward—"*free.*"

Nnytyl takes another bottle and begins pouring its contents into glasses. I stand still and monitor as directed. One person that stands out is Jaylen Barsha—even though he has a full glass in his hand, he is not smiling. Voices overlap, and Roisem directs the Barshas out to the back patio. Jaylen lingers and looks at his glass. His eyes track his enthusiastic family until he looks up at the ceiling.

"What about Sliro?" he asks to no one in particular before stepping out.

I COMPLY WITH the order to check back in the following night. I report on the late celebration. I also report on the Barsha attorney's morning arrival with flowers and a smile. She was ushered onto the patio to provide details regarding Barsha Corp's assets being dissolved and absorbed into the Empire.

Regional Auditor Six demands to know specifics. I provide the following quote from the Barsha attorney verbatim:

"You'll be fine. You have your reserves and caches. In a way, you're better than fine. You're free to go wherever you want, whenever you want, without any of the actual stress of Barsha Corp."

In addition, I summarize what the attorney believed was the reasoning behind the pardon—that the Barsha family and the company's executives, with their network of contacts and connections, offer value to the Empire beyond their immediate assets.

Finally, I report that Roisem is planning a party for the final evening together.

I am sending new orders and specific actions to your chip. Remain still while these transmit, then confirm receipt.

I do as instructed. The text arrives in several batches including instructions and a speech to be recited upon a specific milestone. In addition, I receive an audio recording that requires nearly seventeen minutes to transmit. Given the security protections within the file, it is likely Regional Auditor Six had technical assistance with the encoding process. When data transmission finishes, I integrate the information into my neural core, then review the directives.

The first instruction provides a clear definition of my new mission.

Kill all the Barshas and their guests on Gus Treta.

I begin formulating a plan to fulfill this objective.

CHAPTER 9

For three days, Jaylen heard about nothing but Roisem's "celebratory wake of Barsha Corp as we begin our new lives."

New lives, as in everyone who stayed on Gus Treta would eventually move on, with private agreements on how to split up various caches and accounts of hidden funds. Roisem wanted a party—Roisem *demanded* a party, and she tasked A1-A1 to invite select family and friends. "Friends" might have been the wrong word. They were more like associates of Barsha Corp, some sharing the Barsha bloodline by one or two degrees and others who held fancy titles, though Jaylen still wasn't sure how those people spent their days, since most of them didn't work.

He did note, though, that people like Brencoyle weren't invited. As far as he could tell, Brencoyle had moved back to Coruscant with his family—no pension and no severance, all those funds absorbed by the Empire.

As people arrived, Jaylen smiled just as Brencoyle had taught him: "*Remember to use both the mouth and eyes. Otherwise people will know!*"

Jaylen tried that here, a broad grin across his face accompanied by a slight squint. "Hello," he said in a tone to match.

Still, doing this was tiring, like overusing an out-of-shape muscle. Same thing with getting dressed in formal attire, shaving, all the little details that Jaylen had learned not to miss after weeks on Gus Treta. Roisem, so much more accomplished at pulling off this kind of presentation, moved effortlessly from greeting to conversation to refreshments.

"It could be better," said Cels Sinant, the former Barsha chief financial officer, her arms open wide, "but it could certainly be worse!"

Roisem laughed at the Barshas' first guest, offering an air kiss to Cels's tall Muun cheek. "Honestly, I didn't expect to retire this young, but I'm enjoying it!"

"And you, young Jaylen," said the Muun, bending down to meet Jaylen's eye level, "how are you filling your days?"

"Research," he said. That reply got an unexpected, boisterous laugh in return.

"He's not joking," Roisem said. "Some of us learned to relax here. Jaylen is up to his eyes in datapads."

"Look at you!" Cels said, patting him on the shoulder. "Still the high achiever."

Which was very strange. He was never a high achiever. He was, at most, slightly above average at academics, other than his one term with the debate club—and that was only because of relentless tutoring and some smooth talking. Sliro always got better marks, yet no one ever acknowledged that. The myth of his CEO ascendency created more of an aura around Jaylen than the actual truth.

And that made him very much not want to be here.

Over the next hour, twenty or so guests arrived, and from what he'd seen of the guest list, that represented the bulk of expected attendees. The property was certainly capable of hosting more, though the guests carried the enthusiasm of two or three times as many people.

The servant droids stayed busy enough.

"I'm gonna refill my drink," Jaylen said to anyone within earshot. Roisem nodded before giving a sudden raucous laugh. Across the room, Jaylen saw Nnytyl, who seemed to keep a specific distance from his wife at all times. This had played out over weeks, with the two avoiding each other except for meals, and while Jaylen had his suspicions about their tension, he was surprised they wouldn't display more solidarity in public.

Or maybe so many guests had arrived that they thought no one would notice.

"When you think about it," Nnytyl said to a guest, "this may have been the best thing to ever happen to the Barshas. I didn't know how much stress I was under until I discovered the joy of watching blitzball all day. Perhaps I'll even invest in a team."

This prompted an uproarious laugh, and Jaylen tried to shut out the ensuing discussion about future ventures or travel plans. He walked like he had somewhere to go, when really he just wanted out.

That was, until he heard Nnytyl mention his brother. Jaylen paused just for a moment.

"Oh, Sliro? Who knows. The Empire must have stashed him in a labor camp somewhere. I'm sure he'll pop up—when he wants money." More laughter came at this, though now Jaylen drew his father's attention, and when Jaylen turned to leave, it was too late. "Where are you going, son?"

Jaylen held up his mostly empty glass. "A refill."

"Ah, that's right." Jaylen's father turned around. "It's a celebration after all!" he shouted for everyone to hear. "Dinner is being served right now in the dining hall. But if you're having too much fun, I understand. Ask a droid to bring you a plate."

Maybe this was why his parents worked so much. Being around industry executives was exhausting. Being around Barshas was exhausting as well, particularly when there weren't things like competitor market share or shipping delays to fret about.

Jaylen did not, in fact, refill his drink. Instead, he stepped outside, only to find that the patio wasn't quiet. Nor was the courtyard. Nor was the hedge maze, nor the sitting area by the pool. Everywhere Jaylen went, *someone* talked and laughed—or Gus Treta's winds carried the noise from the property.

Jaylen knew that he couldn't disappear for too long. But just for a few moments, he sought peace—and he moved to the only place on the property that could deliver:

A1-A1's garden cottage.

The droid's bright voice greeted Jaylen as he opened the door. "Master Jaylen. I'm sorry, but the news datapads will not be available until tomorrow morning."

"That's okay," he said. He looked at the empty glass still in his hand. He set it on a workbench, and a smear of droid lubricant smudged the bottom of the glass. "I just needed to get out of there. How are you doing, Ay-One?"

"I am monitoring the facilities. The compound's primary cook droid is active," A1-A1 said. "Servant and garden droids are all assisting as waitstaff and cleaners."

"I asked *how* you're doing, not *what* you're doing," Jaylen said with a laugh. How did this conversation with a protocol droid seem so much more real than everything going on inside the house?

"That is how I am doing. I am following my protocols: one, serving the Barshas and their guests; two, performing maintenance on all employed droids on the compound; three, maintaining the compound's perishable and nonperishable supplies for operations; four—"

Jaylen held up a hand, then grabbed the empty glass. He raised it in salute. "Well, a toast, then. To your happiness." He joined her at the cottage's technical station, where the property's thermal sensors showed a top-down map flooded with red dots. "I'll feel much better when that is empty."

"One person has already departed. If this sets the rate of departure, you should feel better in about thirty minutes."

Jaylen looked at the chrono. "Are you sure? The party just started about an hour ago."

"I am." She tapped the screen. "Six minutes ago, the number of people on the compound reached its maximum of twenty-seven total with the final two arrivals. This fulfilled the confirmed guest list. Fifteen human, twelve nonhuman comprised of two Muun, one Falleen, two Umbaran, one Zeltron, two Iktotchi, one Mon Calamari, and three Advozse. I am counting you as one because the thermal detectors do not penetrate this cottage's walls. However, one minute ago, the person in this quadrant"—she pointed to the bottom right of the screen—"disappeared."

Jaylen stared at the screen, a mass of red concentrated in the home's dining hall. Several other clumps of red scattered across the property. "Disappeared?"

"There is no cottage wall there to block thermal sensors," A1-A1 said. Protocol droids generally spoke with a direct tone that implied servitude and frank communication. In this case, though, her pitch shifted, a tiny hint of know-it-all personality coming through. "Twenty-seven maximum. Twenty-six current. Both statements are true."

"How . . ." At least this was more intellectually stimulating than dealing with his father's small talk. "How can both statements be true? Did someone fall into the ocean?"

"That is possible." A1-A1 tilted her head. "Now there are twenty-five."

"Twenty-five?" Jaylen's eyes went wide. "Where?" A1-A1 pointed to an area just to the right of where the missing guest had been standing.

"Twenty-four." A1-A1's finger shifted farther right. "Right here. Two people were at the swimming pool. They parted ways. But then they vanished."

Jaylen and A1-A1 stood in silence for several seconds, watching for any further disappearances as Jaylen pondered that statement.

CHAPTER 10

I have reverted to option number three.

Option one was to lock the Barshas and their guests into the compound's large dining room. Then, at an opportune moment, enter, relock the door behind me, and proceed with my integrated plan to indiscriminately execute all people on the compound. This would fulfill my primary directive: "Kill all the Barshas and their guests on Gus Treta."

This option's methodical structure would also fulfill one of my secondary directives that came in shortly after: "Make them feel their fear as much as possible."

However, option one was not viable given the fact that most of the people on the compound did not adhere to the serving call for dinner.

Option two was not viable due to its overly complicated logistics and the number of uncontrolled variables. I have already deleted the irrelevant data.

I am finding it difficult to deal with the high number of intoxicated guests. They are not making predictable decisions. The most recent evidence for this was when one female guest stopped in front of me for no clear reason, held up a glass in each hand, and proceeded to yell slurred words for sixteen seconds.

For that target, I made a note that I may need to silence her first if her behavior were to continue.

Following this incident, I conceived option three during the twenty-one-meter journey between the outer hallway by the dining room and the main foyer. It is simpler in conception, yet more difficult in execution, and it also lacks the panic-inducing theatrics of the secondary directive to make them feel as much fear as possible.

A tactical discussion with Regional Auditor Six would resolve this. However, the logistics of reaching the hangar bay transceiver, the time of day, and the limited transmission speed eliminate this possibility.

I must adapt.

I activate a data terminal in the foyer to produce a thermal scan of guest locations on the compound. Their disparate locations as well as their ability to move create a tracking conundrum. Twenty-seven total people are on the property. Seven guests are in the dining room. The rest are scattered throughout the compound. However, I can access only a facility map at terminals. I must move swiftly and methodically, starting with the external perimeter, then working my way back to the center.

I take a tray of appetizers and two tall glasses of alcoholic beverages. This is the optimal disguise for walking anywhere on the grounds. A female Muun stops me to grab a single food item from the tray. Otherwise, no one looks my way.

I walk in an efficient route toward the southeast corner of the compound. It is an open garden with a path in the middle and seating on either side. At the end of the garden is a cliff overlooking the ocean.

Standing by himself with two drinks in his hands is Oland Barsha, a thirty-nine-year-old human. He has consistently been rude to me during my time on Gus Treta. He also seems to believe that everyone enjoys his sense of humor.

He notices me as I weigh my tactics. “Ah,” he says, holding up a glass in each hand. Rather than put it on my tray, he throws one over the cliffside and into the Gus Treta ocean. “Good timing.”

Per my last examination, the next closest guests are a pair approximately fifty meters west between another garden and the pool. Well past any visibility, given the varying terrain of the property and the diminished visual acuity present at this time of night. I will head there once I finish with Oland.

I step forward. "Would you like another snack or beverage?"

"Damn right I would," Oland says. He takes a glass from my tray, drinks it in a single gulp, and similarly throws it into the ocean, leaving one empty glass still in hand.

I set the tray down at his feet.

Oland looks at me, a wide grin on his face. "What is this? Aren't you supposed to serve me? Pick that up right—"

His voice stops when I crush his larynx with my left hand. The remaining empty glass falls down, landing between two plants.

I throw the body over the cliff and watch it disappear into the same ocean where he tossed his glassware aside.

I pick up the tray and proceed westward. It appears the pair has split now. I encounter the first one along the way, a human overlooking the ocean. A single push at maximum force eliminates him.

A Zeltron female remains sitting between a garden and pool. My research indicates she oversaw intentional manufacturing defects that reduced stabilizer lifespan to create greater market demand. A breeze kicks up to blow her flowing dress outward over her dark red skin. She smooths the fabric and then kneels to smell some of the flowers. A large topiary of local wildlife sits next to a fountain.

The woman's attention is fully captivated by the flowers. Her eyes are closed. She does not seem to notice my presence two meters behind her. On the other side, the property's swimming pool is sufficiently deep to hide a body if it is tied to an anchoring weight.

A stone chair in the garden will suffice.

I set my tray down. She does not notice. My hands rise.

OVER THE NEXT forty-five minutes, I tap into my base programming as designed for war. Infiltration, stealth, assassination, and adaptive violence strategies are all applied as I systemically assassinate eleven of the guests by snapping their necks, which includes working with the unique physiology of a Mon Calamari. I assassinate one guest with a large stone to the back of the head. Two more guests are thrown off the side of the island. This process started with an outer perimeter sweep, then a circle around the entire homestead before arriving at the back kitchen door. Inside, I enlist the unwitting assistance of another servant droid, requesting it bring the nearest two members from inside to meet me for special refreshments in the back.

From there, I move through the upstairs bedrooms and conservatories. Those assassinations take more time and care, an average of three minutes and twenty-eight seconds after identifying each target, with an aim to avoid bloodshed for easier cleanup and hiding.

The final second-floor assassination ends when I break a Muun's shoulder joints to ensure the body will stuff safely into the back of a large wardrobe. The armoire slides closed, and I interface with the command console to override its lock, sending it into mechanical failure.

I access a data terminal in an upstairs storage closet. Thermal signatures show eight targets remaining.

Seven of them are currently in the dining room.

One of them is still outside but moving toward the house. I make a plan to intercept, but I pause when I see that this person appears to be headed for the dining room.

Option one has returned to feasibility. I load up its details and set out to execute this plan.

CHAPTER 11

Whatever was happening on the Barsha compound, Jaylen wanted to be ready. However, the garden cottage didn't exactly provide proper supplies for that. Ladders and hoses were too bulky to be practical, while more trimming tools required unavailable power. Jaylen threw open the storage cabinet only to find fertilizer canisters, seed distributors, and pesticide sprays.

Didn't anyone use a *knife* anymore?

Lubricants, packs of seeds, composted material—none of that helped. He continued glancing around the cottage until he saw the closest thing to a weapon:

A trowel.

A trowel was definitely a better weapon than his own fists.

"Okay, Ay-One, let's investigate," Jaylen said.

"My primary functions are to service droids and manage supply inventory," A1-A1 said, "not determine the status of organics. I should stay here in my station to ensure the service crew is ready for changeover tomorrow."

Jaylen looked over the protocol droid. She wasn't necessarily going to be an effective bodyguard or detective. But still, something strange was happening, and two sets of eyes were better than one. "You're supposed to serve the Barshas, right?"

"That is one of my priorities, yes. In addition to maintenance, scheduling, inventory—"

"Okay," Jaylen said as he scanned the cottage one more time for anything possibly useful, "then as a Barsha, I am *requesting* that you come with me. And to look for anything"—he paused to think of proper droid terminology—"that might need maintenance."

"Yes." A1-A1 shifted at this. "Yes, I can do that. We can go."

The garden cottage's automated door slid open, and Jaylen stepped outside. A1-A1 followed him, her gears whirring with motion. For a single slice of time, everything felt all too normal: Corellia and its other moons sat visible in the sky along with the bright dots of stars, and the property's skyline of trees and cliffs presented a sense of calm. A look at the main house showed lights on, though no voices echoed into the night.

But given how loud the Barshas and their inner circle got, peace indicated something wrong. Jaylen shut his eyes and listened for anything, like he did as a child, when he scanned for signs of servants coming or going outside his room.

Not that long ago, voices carried through the night from all parts of the compound: the patio, the gardens, the courtyard, the pool. Right now, Jaylen heard nothing.

Quiet was *not* part of a Roisem Barsha event.

"Do you hear that?" Jaylen asked, pointing around them.

"I don't hear anything except the ambient environment," A1-A1 said.

"That's right." He motioned the droid toward the southeast corner of the compound where the first dot had disappeared. At first glance, everything appeared ordinary: a path to an open garden, stone seating on either side, and a view of the ocean. However, as Jaylen knelt and examined closer, he saw something that didn't belong:

An empty glass.

"This is from the house." He flexed his fingers around the trowel.

"Though with *these* guests, they might have just left this for cleanup tomorrow." He turned to A1-A1. "How far away was the next disappearance?"

"Approximately fifty meters to the west," the droid said.

Jaylen gestured for her to lead the way, and they continued on to a clearing with a wide view of the mainland across the ocean. There were no further clues, no sign of recent visitors.

When they turned down the path between the hedge garden and the pool, A1-A1 spotted something. "There is a foreign object in the swimming pool." She pointed directly at the dark splotch in the water, and Jaylen squinted.

"I can't make it out," he said, kneeling by the pool for a better look. "Can you?"

"Kuunerth Shawni."

"What?" Jaylen asked, still unsure of what he saw in front of him.

"Kuunerth Shawni. A Zeltron. She is on the guest roster. The body has been intentionally submerged."

A dead body was in there. Jaylen's chest tightened and his pulse rattled his rib cage. Still, what he saw down there didn't *look* like a humanoid shape. "Are you sure? I mean, people are drinking, maybe she slipped . . ." Jaylen looked around to see if there were any wet patches around that might cause someone to lose their grip.

A1-A1 pointed a finger, moving it slightly as she described different elements. "The arched object you see in the water is a stone chair from the hedge garden. Her leg appears to be tied to it; that is creating the obtuse shape. The angle of the pool's submerged lights have created shadows that further obscure details, such as her true skin tone."

Tied to it.

As in . . .

Tied to a chair. That was no accident. The chair must have been to sink to the bottom of the pool . . .

To hide her.

Jaylen sprung up, his full body tense as he swiveled around, trowel in hand.

Was this the Empire? Perhaps the pardon announcements were simply to toy with the family. But the pardons were public—he *saw* the news himself in the *Corellian Times*.

A1-A1 circled the pool, looking down at Kuunerth the entire time. "Oh. It appears her neck was damaged. It is bending at an unnatural angle."

Apparently maintenance droids didn't get unnerved by murder.

"Ay-One . . ." Jaylen said. "Are we in danger right now?"

"My risk assessment is based solely on whether a droid needs repair, replacement, or related maintenance." The droid's head tilted. "Ah! I do detect a faint maintenance beacon. It may be damaged."

She left the pool area and walked to the next section over, an open clearing with parallel rows of trees. Jaylen followed her, though he kept scanning from side to side, unsure of what might possibly lie ahead.

"Approximately seventy meters in this direction," she said.

"What's a maintenance beacon?" Jaylen asked as he trailed the droid.

"As with the restraining bolts, I installed a beacon to emit a detectable energy pulse should any droid require maintenance while immobilized. This allows me to stay abreast of their statuses without the need to monitor specific locations. It is an independently powered system to be used only in emergency situations. Oh, look." A1-A1 pointed off to her left at a slumped shape in the row of trees. "Another guest."

They passed three total bodies en route to the damaged droid. Jaylen recognized the last one—Zeev Oversam. Barsha's government liaison. About six months ago, he talked Jaylen through the differences between Republic and Imperial regulations.

Perhaps it was adrenaline. Or shock. Or the intensity of the moment. He found a strange coldness draped over his emotions, but no real reactions—despite the fact he'd actually met with Zeev multiple times at Barsha's Coruscant office. He should have been feeling . . . something over the loss of life in front of him. But he wasn't.

Instead, his mind kept firing off questions. Did one of the other guests do this? Had someone invaded the compound?

He supposed if he got out of this alive, he'd have plenty of time to ponder those things.

The night offered a breeze, sea air misting against his cheeks as they moved, and thanks to A1-A1's sensors, they found the droid—an older astromech with arms sticking out of its dome. It was immobilized and speaking distorted gibberish. Jaylen had no idea what make or model it was, though it dated back decades ago and was maybe older than Jaylen.

A1-A1 walked over to the droid and pulled out an interface cable from the small kit in her tool harness. Jaylen almost ordered her to leave the droid alone—surely they had better things to do when a killer was on the loose. But he realized the damaged droid might provide answers about why this was happening—if not who was behind it.

Jaylen helped prop the droid up to allow A1-A1 a proper angle for the data cable. "That is Gee-One-Gee-One. Accessing . . . accessing . . ." she said. "This is troubling. Its internal records show that it was bringing a dining tray back when it had an encounter."

"This is a gardening droid," Jaylen said, pointing to the belt of gardening tools cinched around G1-G1's circumference—in fact, the trowel in Jaylen's hand may even have belonged to it. "Why would it be serving?"

"We are understaffed and have not received replacements yet. This one was supporting the event. Loading encounter details now." A1-A1's eyes flashed several times. "It noticed the body over there"—the droid pointed at Zeev Oversam—"and was approaching to see if he wanted a refill."

"A drink's not going to fix that," Jaylen said under his breath.

"It noted the deceased state and was going to a terminal to notify security when it encountered another droid. Then it incurred damage."

Jaylen took a closer look at the droid—one of its legs was bent sideways, and a deep fist-sized hole was carved into its cylindrical body.

"The other droid did this?" Jaylen asked. "Did it also—"

"Unknown. There is no audio or visual log that can conclusively identify the source of the damage. Nine seconds after it spoke to a droid of unknown origin, the damage took place."

"Unknown origin?" Jaylen asked. "Can it identify what the droid looked like?"

"It was not a model within its known database of domestic droids."

A1-A1 adjusted the cable's connection. "The only other identifiers were its height and its jacket."

"Jacket . . ." Jaylen's stomach clenched as the facts came together. "A jacket that barely fits?"

"Yes. Several threads have likely torn on the shoulder seam." With that, the cable popped loose from the connection and A1-A1 stood up. "I should commence repairs—"

"No, no, no." Jaylen started pulling out tools from G1-G1's belt. Shears, a scoop, a weeding hoe—none of those would necessarily be any better or worse than the trowel in his hand. "What's this?" he asked, holding up the final item—a metal rod with two spikes poking out the top.

"That is for pest control." A1-A1 took the tube and pressed the button in the middle. A purple electrical charge fired off between the two spikes.

"Crude," Jaylen said as he pulled it back, "but it might come in handy. Ay-One, I think our assassin might be a droid."

"A droid?" A1-A1 tilted back and forth at this revelation. "None of my staff are programmed for such violence."

Jaylen turned to the house in the distance—they were about half-way to the entrance. Searching for more bodies wouldn't help right now. In a way, his only two choices came down to the same thing Roisem told him years ago: Say something and alert the remaining people in the house? Or stay quiet, grab a shuttle parked at the hangar bay, and leave?

Staying quiet was *so* tempting. His whole life, Jaylen's family had largely left him alone. Sure, they sometimes brought him to Barsha Tower, introduced him at meetings, and shoved him in front of the cam. But Brencoyle took him to school. Servants provided meals. Coaches and teachers sat with him during most days.

The only person he consistently spoke to about things that really mattered was Sliro. And no one else.

Staying quiet, leaving the Barshas to their fate. Growing up, they often left him to *his* fate. And he wouldn't put it past his parents to abandon everyone on the compound if they discovered what was happening. Everything paused as he realized that for once, he could invert all that, choosing to truly embrace the way his parents thought by saving himself here. He could even get offworld and try to find Sliro.

But as the wind tickled the back of his neck, he realized that he couldn't leave them. These people were still his family, and in a situation that could be life or death, he had to try and do right by them. Even if they didn't always look out for him. He took one last look at the fallen gardening droid. "What about that?" he asked, pointing to the restraining bolt. "Would that be helpful?"

"These restraining bolts limit geographic distances for compatible droids. If we leave the boundaries of the property, a droid would theoretically not be able to follow us."

"Perfect." Jaylen reached down and angled his trowel underneath the restraining bolt on the droid's chassis. It popped off with a spark, and he held it up for A1-A1 to see. "Wait, what do you mean 'compatible'?"

"Some droids with higher security safeguards are incompatible with standard restraining bolts. In those cases"—A1-A1 examined the bolt up close—"it may only bother them for a moment."

"Let's hope whatever we're dealing with is compatible," Jaylen said, putting the bolt in his back pocket. He took three slow, intentional breaths, and then set out toward the house, A1-A1 in tow.

Sprint or stealth? Jaylen wasn't sure, and instead he opted for a fast hunched-over walk that probably didn't really do anything to keep him hidden, but it made him feel better. He moved along the outskirts of the house, eyes scanning for anything else out of the ordinary. A1-A1 followed, surprisingly more nimble than most protocol droids. As they approached the property, something on the upper level caught Jaylen's eye.

"Ay-One," he said in a whisper, "did you see that?"

"I—" A1-A1 said at far too loud a volume. Jaylen put up a finger, and the droid's volume lowered by half. "I did not."

"There's movement on the top floor. I think we gotta head to the dining room. Get in. Grab people. Get out. I don't suppose you know anything about handling assassins?"

"I once managed to distract a scaperoon long enough so that Gee-

One-Gee-One could capture it before it ate the vegetables. That is my nearest reference for your request."

They moved to the house, and before Jaylen took his first step up the back patio, he looked for any signs of movement.

"How did you distract it?" he said, forcing out a breathy chuckle to calm his nerves. He'd take whatever humor he could get right now.

"I referenced my database of known garden pests and identified its preferred style of communication."

Jaylen turned and shot a bemused look that A1-A1 probably didn't understand. He felt the weight of his gardening weapons and reminded himself that he still had a chance to dash for the docking bay.

But no. He had to do this. He had to show his family what it meant to *not* give up on someone. "Well," Jaylen said as he took the first step, "if we encounter our assassin, do something like that. Barsha's orders."

A1-A1 followed close behind him. "My priority is to serve the Barshas."

The dining room doors slid open, blasting Jaylen's ears with voices from the remaining guests in there.

"Everyone is in danger!" Jaylen yelled, holding up the stun rod and waving his arms back and forth. A1-A1 scooted in behind him and reached over to the control panel. The doors slid back shut, then clicked, activating the locking mechanism. "Ay-One, get the other doors."

"Oh, look, Roisem, power has gone to your son's head." Aunt Twyla shook her head and everyone laughed.

"It's not power, it's the festivities," his mother said, and the laughter got even louder. Jaylen tracked A1-A1 as she circled the dining hall and locked the other two doors. The sounds of gears churning and mechanisms clicking were soon absorbed into the cacophony. Voices meshed together—some of them laughing, some of them yelling, some doing a mix of both. Jaylen shouted, exhausting all the air in his lungs just to get their attention. "Will you be quiet and listen? I am trying to *save* all of you!"

The clamor intensified, including Nnytyl's booming voice. "How dare you speak to your mother in that tone? After all we've done for you."

Jaylen opened his mouth to reply but caught a faint clicking from the side. He knelt and put his ear to the door's control panel.

It should have been silent. It *wasn't*.

"Everyone," he yelled again as he sprung up, "get to the other side of the room. Ay-One, tell them about the bodies we found. Tell them—"

Jaylen didn't hear the door open, but he felt it: air twirling away from the sliding panels and reaching the back of his neck. He turned. Then he took a step back.

One by one, the voices fell silent.

Jaylen's breath caught in his chest, an automatic rise and fall that felt heavier, harsher than any time in his life—even when he saw the oncoming clone troopers at Barsha Tower.

In the doorway stood the strange droid who'd arrived weeks ago. The one who couldn't fit in its dinner jacket.

This was the one who had killed all those people around the compound.

Jaylen stared as ND-5 tilted his angular head and looked directly at him.

I step inside. The door closes behind me. The dining room is sized for banquets, an oval of twelve meters on the long axis and six meters on the short axis. Besides the aperture where I've entered, there are two doors at opposite sides of the short axis. No windows exist.

Eight people, as well as one protocol droid, line the room. The people seated are Roisem Barsha, Leniel Dav, Twyla Barsha, Nnytyl Barsha. Three unidentified guests are also present: a Falleen female and two Umbaran males.

At the front of the table stands Jaylen Barsha. He holds some gardening tools, likely as weapons. By my observations, he is not optimized for manual labor. As he looks at me, he starts to back away.

Based on the property's thermal sensors, my previous count showed that one person was missing from the map. Compared to my last thermal check, this group has not changed seating positions. That identifies Jaylen as the straggler. He is with A1-A1, the protocol droid overseeing the property's maintenance.

I deduce that he must have gone to A1-A1's garden cottage, either to hide from thermal detection or from his family.

Both reasons are justifiable.

“Finally,” says Leniel Dav, the sister-in-law of Roisem Barsha. She holds up a half-filled glass. “I’ve been waiting for a refill. This protocol droid is useless.”

This garners laughter. Jaylen stops moving and is now standing next to Leniel. I remain still and let the organics trade glances among themselves. Several of the guests whisper. Finally, Roisem stands up and says, “Do we need to deactivate you? You’ve terrified my son.”

I reach under my dinner jacket and pull out a blaster. It is one of several pieces of equipment I retrieved from my storage crate prior to the arrival of guests. I swiftly raise it and fire three shots at three specific targets: each of the door control panels.

Now nothing can override the doors. Depending on the order in which I kill each guest, I may be able to fulfill my secondary protocols sent by Regional Auditor Six.

“You are now trapped. Do not move,” I say.

The Falleen guest screams. She stands up and heads toward the far door.

I shoot her in the back. Her body collapses to the floor.

I told her not to move.

“I will repeat myself. Do not move.” Now they are silent. “I have a message for Roisem and Nnytyl Barsha.”

Everyone looks at the Barsha parents, who are seated away from each other. Behind them, smoke rises from the dead Falleen.

“Roisem Barsha. Nnytyl Barsha. Stand up.”

They comply. The other guests murmur their stifled panic. To the left, Jaylen moves very slowly with his hands up toward a chair.

“Drop your weapons,” I say to Jaylen, “and you may sit down.”

The trowel and stun rod fall to the floor, and Jaylen takes his seat.

The parameters have been met to execute another specific instruction. I focus on the Barsha parents and load a script to recite.

“Roisem Barsha. Nnytyl Barsha. You are the architects of deception. For decades you have allowed corruption to overwrite loyalty, responsibility, ethics. Many have suffered under this family’s commitment to corporatocracy and greed. The victims may feel nameless, faceless to you, but your sense of entitlement has ravaged even those under your care—”

“Oh, that’s enough.” Nnytyl stands up, nearly knocking over his chair. He sways with the move, and his face is red. Sweat lines his forehead.

“Please listen,” I say. “I have been instructed to recite this message.”

Nnytyl does not comply. “Look at this cheap piece of Separatist hardware. Hey”—he waves his arms in front of my face—“is someone watching behind there? Hello? Is this the best you can do?” Now he points at my chest. “You, *droid*, what model are you?”

The Barsha family appears fond of using the term *droid* as a slur rather than a technical definition. This type of outburst is unexpected. I weigh my options: shoot him, respond to him, or repeat my message.

I choose option three.

“I will repeat myself: You are the architects of deception. For decades you have allowed corruption to overwrite loyalty, responsibility—”

“Oh!” Now he laughs. “Hey, whoever you are, you can’t even get a real droid to do your bidding? You grab some leftovers from the Sep scrap heap? Barsha Tower has better window-cleaning droids!”

“My make, model, and original function are not relevant here,” I say. “If you do not stay still, I will be forced to shoot you. You are supposed to listen and feel.”

“Feel? Feel what?”

The directives on my embedded chip provide no suggestions for this type of response. I consider alternatives given the number of interruptions I have faced. In addition, the secondary directive of inducing fear still stands, and I can do more to achieve this.

I must adapt.

“For the remaining moments of your lives, you are presented with a choice,” I say. “You cannot leave this room. At some point I will kill you.”

They make noise. Screaming. Begging. Crying.

The secondary directive is fulfilled. I may return to the speech later if an opportunity presents itself.

I open my dinner jacket to reveal explosives fused to my chest. “I will detonate this at the end of my mission. You may choose to wait for that moment.”

I tap several buttons on the bomb. Its small display comes to life with blinking lights. It is primed, though the timer is not set.

"Or you may ask for a swift death."

Their fear increases. I weigh again whether to recite the speech, though it would be difficult to do so given the current volume.

Jaylen behaves differently from the rest of his family. He stares at me but otherwise remains still. After several seconds, he says something. "Can I talk to the protocol—"

"How dare you!" Roisem yells. Her voice is louder than mine. She now stands, eyes wide and her hands on her hips. "This is insulting. Whoever put you up to this, they're not paying you enough."

"I require no currency be exchanged."

"Well, of course," she says with a huff. "Because you're clearly not paid to think for yourself. Look at you, of course you lost the war. Couldn't come close to beating a clone, and now you're wearing a dinner jacket. Not even a new dinner jacket." She thrusts a finger at me. "We got those out of *storage*."

"I will shoot you if you continue to speak."

"Shoot me." Roisem scoffs.

Jaylen glances at this. It takes his screaming mother to finally get him to turn. He says, "You think you're going to scare me with that tiny little blaster?"

"Oh, I've had enough of this," Nnytyl says. "I finally get some peace and quiet in my life and now this happens? If I have to stay in here and listen to this anymore"—he points at Roisem—"I'd rather be dead."

"Will you two *stop*?" Jaylen yells. He looks at me. "This is the Empire, isn't it? They've double-crossed us, haven't they?"

I do not say anything even though I know the answer to that question.

Jaylen stands up and continues, "Okay, listen, can I talk to the protocol—"

"The Empire would never do this," Roisem yells back. "We are *valuable* to them. In fact, they're probably on their way right now."

They form a triangle, Jaylen and his mother and his father, rapid-fire insults hurling between them.

But mostly between Roisem and Nnytyl. They continue arguing near the dead body of the Falleen woman. From right to left, the current seating is Leniel Dav, Jaylen Barsha, two male Umbarans, then Twyla Barsha. Behind them is the protocol droid, A1-A1.

"That's enough!" Nnytyl says after forty-nine seconds of shouting. "All of this. I am sick of it. I'm going to watch blitzball and forget any of this ever happened." His voice echoes. He scans the room.

He looks everywhere except where the dead body lies.

Then he steps forward. He avoids the dead body, moving sideways to circumvent it, and goes to the side door. "Why won't this open?" he yells, banging on the metal.

If I recite the prepared speech, these people will not listen to it.

I move forward with my plan.

"Jaylen, go get someone to—"

I silence his voice with blasterfire.

His body slumps forward, shoulders crashing into the wall before splaying out flat, a smoking blaster hole in the middle of his forehead.

Everyone screams except for Jaylen.

Everyone moves except for Jaylen.

Bodies cross in front of me. Twyla Barsha crawls under the table. An Umbaran dives behind chairs. Leniel Dav runs to the door. Roisem stands over her husband's body, yelling something incoherent. The other Umbaran rushes toward me.

I take constructive action and shoot him.

The one who hid behind the chairs jumps up. I shoot him, too.

I still have not started the bomb's timer. Individual assassinations are instilling enough fear—the bomb may only be required to eliminate the evidence. "If you don't stop moving, I will interpret your actions as begging for death. You have five seconds to comply. Five . . . four . . ."

"Jaylen!" Roisem screams.

"Three."

"Why are you just sitting there?" Roisem's voice is louder now. "Do something!"

"Two."

Roisem yells again. She may not hear my countdown. "Jaylen, I see who you are now! Sitting instead of saving us!"

"One. You are out of time. Anyone moving will now be eliminated."

Roisem stands still. She is not looking at me. She is staring at Jaylen, who is looking at A1-A1.

The remaining Barshas do not stop moving. Despite their cover, their proximity and their noises make them easy targets.

Now only Roisem and Jaylen are alive. Five seconds count by quietly. Perhaps the atmosphere is settled enough to recite the message.

"You never deserved to be CEO." Roisem speaks in a low, sharp tone. "Of course you're working with the garden droid—*that's* where you belonged all along. Your father was so wrong about you." She steps toward Jaylen, a finger wagging with each word. "You and *Sliro*. You two deserve each other. We should have given you a desk job, too. I hope he's dead, and I hope—"

One more shot explodes out of my blaster.

Jaylen does not look at the body of his dead mother as it falls to the floor.

"You are Jaylen Barsha," I say. "Consider how you would like to perish. If my systems view any action as an external threat, I will decide for you." I scan the area around us. "In addition, I have an audio recording to play."

This throws him off. He squints and looks at me. His hands are clasped together as he does this.

"A message?"

"Yes. The parameters for playback are currently met. The others are all dead. You are the only one remaining." Jaylen's breath becomes marked by quick, short inhales. "I will commence playback—"

"Wait!" he yells.

I stop at this and watch as he points at the protocol droid and says, "Not everyone."

I consider this statement. She is not a threat, nor is she attempting to trigger security like the gardening droid did.

"You are correct." I turn to A1-A1. "Please leave."

"Wait, one more thing," Jaylen says. "Can I say goodbye to her?" He smiles and nods at her. She tilts in return at this. "She kept me company in her garden cottage. All I'm asking for is a moment."

I calculate that this will not interfere with my mission. If they take more than thirty seconds to speak, I will shoot one or both of them. I turn to the protocol droid. "You may have your last words together."

Jaylen nods at A1-A1. She walks over to him. They are facing each other now. "I just wanted to thank you for being a friend. For listening to me. For telling me stories of this place." They hold hands. Her joints must need maintenance—I hear a clink from them. "My favorite was the story of the scaperoon. A valuable lesson and an appropriate analogy. Do you understand?"

"Oh." She pauses, and her head angles back and forth several times. "Yes. That does seem to be useful, doesn't it?"

Jaylen pats her on the shoulder, then looks at me with both hands up. The droid steps past the bodies on the floor. I start to track her, but I turn to Jaylen when he says, "She can go?"

"She may go."

Jaylen takes in a deep breath before leaning against the very front of the table. "Okay. I'm ready to hear your recording. You can load it now. Do I just sit here and listen?"

"Yes." I load the file for audio broadcast. It starts off with the sound of a throat clearing and then a voice says, "Hello—"

The playback does not get past that word due to . . . due to . . . due to . . .

[[Restraining bolt detected.]]

Incompatible commands sent to system. Consolidation required. Rejecting code.

I resume standard processes during a brief moment of blackout. Something has pried my pistol from my hand. I turn to A1-A1. "Deception," I say.

I reach up to start the timer on the bomb before grabbing—

Jaylen's plan only partially worked.

The good news was that A1-A1 understood his intentions enough to get the restraining bolt on ND-5. However, as soon as she planted it on the droid's torso, A1-A1 said, "It is not compatible. I believe this is due to its original purpose as a war machine with higher security features." She took the pistol from the battle droid's hand. "This weapon will not do much damage to his armor."

ND-5 glitched for several seconds. Enough for Jaylen to dash forward and grab the stun rod. The droid jerked and stated, "Deception," then reached up, a finger clearly headed toward the bomb's controls.

Jaylen zapped the back of ND-5's neck—right at his dataport. He didn't know enough about droids to precisely apply an electric shock. It just seemed like a reasonable exposure point.

Jaylen braced himself . . .

Yet, he wasn't dead. No fiery explosion enveloped him. Only A1-A1 moved, emerging from the massive shadow of the commando droid.

ND-5 stood, one metallic finger landing on—but not pressing—the bomb's ignition button.

"Ay-One-Ay-One?" Jaylen asked weakly. He'd finally gotten lucky.

The protocol droid reached into a pouch and held up a data cable. She plugged it into ND-5's back port but quickly pulled it back out. "I can't access this droid's programming due to its security protocols." She put one end of the cable in her own dataport, then pulled out a square handheld device and plugged the cable into it. "This is the caller for the compound's restraining bolts. I may be able to reprogram the bolt for compatibility."

Escaping still seemed like the best plan. Jaylen banged on the dining room's door. Nothing. His palms pressed against it, and he pushed with his legs to try and get *some* movement out of it. Still nothing.

"How much time do we have?" he yelled, louder and more panicked than expected.

"I can't say. There is no reference data for garden stun rods applied to dataports." She shifted her weight. "Success. I can reprogram the restraining bolt through the caller device."

Jaylen sprinted over to the second door to try the same thing. Still nothing. "Yes, great idea," he yelled back. "Program fast."

"The connection allows me to view his internal status. I have detected an unknown external addition to his hardware, though its directives are encrypted. His finger may still press the trigger if he reactivates."

Jaylen didn't know what the first part meant. But the second part—that was very clear. "I need a specific program to integrate. You should choose quickly."

Droids. They needed *input* to make a decision. Jaylen moved to the third door, keeping his eyes level to avoid dead bodies, trying to ignore the smell of burned flesh and bone and the wafts of lingering smoke.

"Shut him down," Jaylen said as he pressed on the last door with no luck.

"I cannot. My memory core does not contain the technical knowledge."

"Defuse the bomb." Jaylen stared straight ahead, blocking out the insanity of the damage, the dead bodies, and a frozen assassin droid, as if it were somehow possible to think clearly despite the possibility of the droid waking up to trigger the bomb *any second*.

"I cannot. My memory core—"

"Get out? Leave the compound?" Sweat began to form across Jaylen's forehead, and he clenched his hands into fists. "Leave the room?"

"I cannot. The fastest solution is to copy one of my existing programs. I see his systems are coming online. You should choose which program should overwrite his commands," A1-A1 said. "Priority one: Do not leave the compound unless directed. Priority two: Perform daily assessments on all inventory related to compound operations. Nine of his thirty-six systems are back online. Priority three: Serve the Barshas and associates, including all requests for food, drink, and comfort. Priority four—"

"Yes, that one!" Jaylen yelled. "That one!"

A1-A1 gave a near-instant response. "Done." The droid reached over to disconnect the cable from her dataport. As she did, ND-5's head suddenly jerked before returning to center.

Then he finished pressing the detonator.

A circling timer appeared around the bomb's buttons. As it did, a massive free arm swung outward, knocking A1-A1's head off. The broken droid dropped to the floor, sparks flying from her open neck, and the droid caller fell out of her hand.

Jaylen looked at ND-5, who stared blankly back at him.

The droid didn't move. Jaylen considered if maybe the very act of inserting a new command had broken the droid's programming. It was, after all, a beat-up Separatist droid from the war, and who knew how much damage it had retained. If ND-5's programming had broken, could he escape? Maybe take ND-5's blaster and shoot a large enough hole in one of the doors? These weren't security or blast doors—this was a holiday compound built for luxury.

Jaylen took a step forward.

"Forty seconds remain before this bomb detonates." ND-5 turned his thin angular head to Jaylen. Before Jaylen could say anything, ND-5 moved. He removed the dinner jacket and grabbed the fallen pistol, his glowing eyes still on Jaylen. "You are a Barsha. I must serve you while completing my mission."

"You could have served me by not starting the timer!" Jaylen shouted.

"My system had already executed that command. It was physically impossible to prevent completion." ND-5 raised the gun, barrel pointed Jaylen's way.

Bomb. Gun. Either way, this was it.

Jaylen decided right then to just give up. He'd made it longer than the rest of the Barshas. Maybe that was enough of a win. He closed his eyes so at least he wouldn't have to see the blaster go off.

ND-5's joints whirred, and Jaylen squeezed his eyes tighter. Maybe this would be quick and painless, like flipping a switch. Wasn't there some science about how the human brain reacted to death? That it conjured the most amazing dreams? That didn't sound so—

The blaster fired off a shot. And then another. And another.

Jaylen was still alive.

One eye opened. Then the other.

ND-5 had turned the gun on himself. He fired again, the barrel directly up against his rectangular chest, and sparks flew with another blast.

"Whoa, hey, what are you doing?" Jaylen yelled.

"I am serving you. Twenty seconds remain." He fired several more times to complete a perimeter around the bomb. ND-5's mechanical fingers tore into the exposed space, and he peeled off the bomb, yellow sparks and blue electricity dancing all over the gash across his chest. Something popped. Whatever lived in that part of his chassis, it definitely was not at 100 percent anymore.

ND-5 threw the bomb to the far corner of the room. Then he looked at Jaylen and pointed at the opposite corner, some twelve meters away. "Go there," he said in his flat, neutral droid voice. "Ten seconds remain."

Jaylen grabbed the droid caller off the floor as he ran to the corner, though his toe snagged on something, causing him to stumble. He squatted behind a large upended chair. When he glanced back, he realized that he had tripped over one of the dead Umbarans' arms.

ND-5 stepped into view, tipping the large solid dining table on its side. The droid dragged it until it sat upright about two meters from Jaylen, then he hunched over Jaylen. "Assume as small of a position as possible. I will shield you from the blast."

Jaylen put the droid caller in his back pocket and curled up, and he thought of the moment years ago when a young Sliro held the same position on his bed. He hugged his knees close, and the occasional spark from ND-5's chest wound burned the back of his neck.

JAYLEN HAD NO memory of the actual explosion happening—how it looked, how it sounded, the aftermath, none of it.

Instead, he awoke at the property's hangar bay, a cliffside structure overlooking the beach. He opened his eyes to find ND-5 standing over him.

"You're conscious," the droid said. The words came over a constant ringing in his ears, a tangible sign that the bomb had indeed gone off. "You should remain flat. Though I shielded much of the explosion from you, the residual impact of such a force has likely thrown off your body's sense of equilibrium."

"How long . . ." he started, but even moving his jaw muscles hurt. "How long ago?"

"The explosion occurred two hours and seventeen minutes ago. The dining room is currently on fire. From what I can tell, the fire is still at the center of the structure, though it will eventually spread. The material compounds in the walls have slowed it down." ND-5 turned his head, like he could see all the way over there. "It is surprising that no emergency support has come."

"Everyone in there," Jaylen said, and even though ND-5 told him to stay flat, he propped himself. "Did you kill them? Are they all dead?"

"Yes and yes."

The droid's voice came out so clinically, so cold—an affirmation without any of the weight behind it. Dead. His parents and relatives, as flawed as they were. The guests—they didn't deserve this.

A heavy sigh came, and the very process of blowing air out of his lungs caused a burning tickle. His life as he knew it ended several weeks ago. He supposed that life was going to end regardless, whether the Empire brought the company down or he had ascended to CEO. Both of those marked a dramatic shift. But this?

This was different.

This was cold-blooded murder.

"You killed them," Jaylen said, adrenaline surging in him, helping him upward. He staggered to his feet, stiff pain in every muscle. "You killed them," he repeated.

"I have already acknowledged that."

Jaylen's plan had worked. Which meant that it would have worked had Roisem and Nnytyl stopped arguing, stopped causing *chaos* so he could give the restraining bolt to A1-A1. He could have passed the hardware over, then come up with *some* distraction for the protocol droid to mount the restraining bolt.

But now, everyone was dead—because they just wouldn't *listen*. And that notion burned Jaylen in a different way than when he thought about Sliro.

"No, you don't understand. You killed them. They didn't have to die. The Empire took everything from us. And now you've taken everything from me. Why? Why would you do this?"

ND-5 looked at Jaylen like he was asking for directions into town. "I executed orders according to my programming."

"Oh, so that's it? You're just an assassin that kills whoever you target?" Jaylen threw a pointed finger at the droid, though doing so caused him to wince.

"Yes. That is how droids operate."

Jaylen wanted to scream. If his body could support it, he probably would have. Some sort of primal release felt necessary at this point. Instead, he swayed on his feet, nausea rolling in his stomach. "What happens now?" he asked quietly. "I can barely move."

"The shock wave struck you. I was able to protect you from only the shrapnel. The noise and pressure have likely given you a concussion. You have soft tissue damage from the impact as well." ND-5 walked over and put out a long thin arm to support him. "You will need some time to heal. We will use this guest's shuttle. They do not need it anymore."

Even as Jaylen moved with ND-5's help, he couldn't stifle the laughter coming through. "This is madness. How do I know you're not just going to kill me next?"

"This restraining bolt is telling me to serve you. That has the highest priority in my directive sequence."

"It's as simple as that, huh?" Jaylen replied in a dry voice. "You droids. You're so binary."

"It does not need to be any more complex than that." In the distance, sirens clashed with the sound of oncoming thunder. "For now, I await further instructions from you."

That was exactly what Jaylen meant by binary. "So I could just tell you to leap off a cliff and you would?"

"Yes."

Jaylen believed the droid. He had no reason not to. He could tell ND-5 to do anything, including shutting himself down—hell, he'd blasted his own chest to follow Jaylen's directive.

"Well," Jaylen said slowly, "why shouldn't I do just that?" He was only musing, but the thought soon rolled into a real, grounded question. He could choose to give the order. Or he could choose to stay quiet. "How would you assess the current situation?" he asked, as if he were chatting with A1-A1 in the garden cottage.

"Emergency vehicles will be here shortly. I can commandeer this shuttle. You will likely need seven to ten days for physical recovery. In addition, they will think you are dead."

Jaylen paused, feeling the ground beneath his feet. In the distance, he saw that ND-5 was right: The lights of emergency shuttles finally hovered above the compound. "Who is 'they'?" he asked with a laugh.

ND-5 stood silent, though his head tilted ever so slightly. From the exposed innards of the droid's upper body, Jaylen heard mechanisms and electronics struggling to work. "I do not know. That information must have resided in the part of my memory core that is now damaged."

Part of Jaylen wanted ND-5 to dismantle himself in the most violent way possible. But he let that impulse pass for one simple reason:

A BX commando droid was valuable as a protector. And a servant.

Jaylen needed both right now. Someday, he might scrap him. But not now. Because everything about Jaylen's personal galaxy had just reset. This thing, this droid, had taken everything from Jaylen. And now ND-5 would help give him a new life.

CHAPTER 14

Weeks had passed since Gus Treta. And nothing came easy—safety, stability, credits. All of it seemed to arrive with blasterfire.

Like now.

"Run!" Jaylen yelled.

He took his own advice, sprinting until his muscles burned. Behind him, ND-5 kept pace, and Jaylen realized that the droid could pass him if he so desired, even with the lingering damage. As they dashed through the dense industrial slums of Nar Shaddaa, ND-5 chose his speed to provide cover for Jaylen.

Jaylen, perhaps, had taken a life of having servants and working in corporate towers for granted. Now he was just grateful that the restraining bolt kept the assassin droid in line.

ND-5's service had already expanded to more than just physical labor and personal defense. The droid had hot-wired a shuttle to get them off Gus Treta. He'd acquired news archives at every opportunity, searching for coverage of the Barsha assassination. He'd found records confirming that Jaylen was officially declared dead along with the rest of his family, with the media theory that his body had been at the center of the bomb blast. The droid even traded their cushy-but-obviously-stolen deluxe shuttle for a small freighter that barely moved—an upgrade in size, a downgrade in everything else, but it also came with a small amount of spending money.

And ND-5 had coordinated a journey to Nar Shaddaa, where Jaylen utilized Barsha-trained meet-and-greet skills to find work—except instead of impressing ministers of state and CEOs, he talked his way into getting odd jobs and pickup runs under the name of Jaylen *Vrax*. Nar Shaddaa, an outlaw world where people went to get lost, was the perfect place for him to start over.

Today, the pickup was a stash of recently scrapped droid components, ironically dumped as fallout from the war. Stabilizers, balancers, and all sorts of other internal guts that Jaylen was just learning about—though the problem was that someone else had targeted the stash, too.

It was an unexpected complication, which made ND-5's combat-ready armor extremely valuable right now. "Who are these guys?" Jaylen asked.

"From their helmets and equipment, my conclusion is members of the Pyke Syndicate," ND-5 said as he twisted to fire back. Another hundred meters or so would get them to their ship, but then what? "Keep going. I have a new strategy."

Apparently ND-5 created strategies now. But were servant droids supposed to do that?

Jaylen would worry about that later.

"Keep going" meant sprinting under a dark bridge that connected two large structures—possibly housing or shops. Just as he passed beneath, more blasterfire came. Except a quick glance showed that these shots came from ND-5, not the Pykes. And rather than providing cover fire, the droid shot upward—a pair of diagonal volleys hitting joints on either end of the bridge. The impact caused foot traffic on the bridge to scatter, and when ND-5 crossed the threshold, he turned again and fired bursts to shatter the other side of each joint.

Jaylen stopped running to take in the last few topside silhouettes jumping off to safety as the bridge collapsed downward. Debris and smoke and a whole lot of dust probably dating back decades, if not centuries, flared out, blocking the path. "A makeshift dam," said Jaylen, catching his breath. "Nice thinking."

"That is a bridge," ND-5 said. Before Jaylen could get a full explanation out, ND-5 marched forward. "Continue to our ship." Jaylen adjusted the bag of parts on his back, then started a jog. They didn't sprint the rest of the way—ND-5 would have detected if the Pykes got around the barrier, and the slower pace was far less conspicuous. By the time they had navigated through Hutta Town's sky slums, no one could possibly have tracked them to their final destination:

A shop. On the other side of Nar Shaddaa, a settlement called the Corellian Sector. If Jaylen believed in fate or destiny, he would have marveled at the name. Instead, he just laughed at how he simply could not escape his past. ND-5 parked the ship in a clearing within a less-populated neighborhood known more for illegal swoop bike racing than commerce.

The all-things-and-more repair shop serviced ships, speeders, equipment, droids, or whatever other mechanical bits and pieces needed a fix—and the best part was that the owner liked to barter services. Including offering more dangerous pickups for ND-5's much-needed repairs.

Jaylen had hoped to boost their ship's long-range capabilities, but for now, fixing ND-5's damage took precedence. Elements of the droid's core programming remained out of reach due to the Gus Treta incident. Slicing, mechanics, and a whole catalog of skills related to Separatist ships and equipment were inaccessible—though really, Jaylen only cared about ship repair for now. Plus, ND-5 was still overheating and had an unreliable left arm. Jaylen had started learning the basics of droid maintenance, but he still wasn't close to being proficient.

They entered the shop's front area by ducking under a half-open garage door, ND-5's shoulder catching on the edge of the suspended panel. To the left lay shelves of storage crates and, at the base of those, modules and spare parts for sale. To the right, another door sat shut, and above them, two lines of white lights brought a harsh glow to the metallic space.

"A good haul," the Neimoidian droidsmith said. Obills Myron's long slender fingers pulled protective goggles off her eyes. She pointed to a large empty desk under a spotlight as they stepped in. "No trouble?"

"That depends on your definition of trouble," Jaylen said, setting the bag down on the desk. "Apparently the Pykes wanted this, too."

"Ah," she said as she opened the bag, "who can resist free repair materials?"

Jaylen had many possible responses, including asking for more money due to "unexpected risks." But right when he opened his mouth, she stopped sifting through the bag and held a piece up. "For your trouble," she said. Jaylen tried to pretend he recognized it, but he must have failed to convince her, because she explained right away. "Replacement memory core. Mostly compatible. Let's get started. I'll even fix that bum arm of his. In exchange for the"—she paused for a quick laugh—"Pyke problems."

"This will be beneficial for our greater purposes," ND-5 said. "Perhaps restored capabilities will expand my usefulness and help me better serve Jaylen as we seek further employment."

"Or at least we can get that arm working." She walked over to the droid and patted through the different pockets on her overalls until she pulled out a scanner. "I'll be honest, though—not really a Separatist specialist. No one is. Seps didn't bother to repair their droids, so no one else learned."

Given all the odds against them on this assignment, getting ND-5's arm fixed for free was a huge win. And they needed a huge win because, really, how did people live like this? The constant hustle, the lack of stability, getting shot at regularly, none of this seemed like a healthy approach to longevity. "We appreciate the generosity," Jaylen said, a shift in tone to get on her good side.

Obills circled ND-5 under the room's harsh hanging lamps. She paused for a closer look at his chest, including the still-visible damage from the bomb's removal. Her scanner beeped as she pointed it at ND-5's head, then at the open wound. "Sure will feel better after getting skills and memories back, huh? Also these"—she tapped new blaster burns on his chest, and Jaylen noticed that plasma must have brushed the restraining bolt as well—"weren't here when you two left." She slid the side door open to reveal a dimly lit garage with several workbenches and mobile data consoles, one of which she pushed over. "Have your droid lie down. I'll grab the pneumatic jaws. You're going to have to help me out."

"Pneumatic jaws?" Jaylen asked as he pointed to an open spot on the floor. ND-5 complied as Obills returned holding massive pliers with a pneumatic tube attached.

"Battle droids have tougher plating than most. Made to withstand combat. That chest"—she turned on the tool's air pressure with an audible pop—"isn't going to just open up, even with a few cracks and scorch marks. You want his insides repaired, we're gonna have to pry it apart."

Shortly after that, ND-5 powered down. Then Obills used a plasma cutter to carve a diagonal line across the left side of the droid's chest. She waved Jaylen over. "It's a two-person job. Unless you got four arms like a Besalisk," she said with a laugh. A thermal applicator heated up the metal plating, then the droidsmith grabbed one side with the jaws. She pointed to a metal pole propped against a workbench. "Jam it in. We'll open it."

Which they did. Violently. While Obills bent the plating back, Jaylen helped by cranking it from the underside. And when enough space cleared, she directed him to grab a hammer to knock the plating farther apart.

He struck again and again. So hard that the impact vibrations rippled through his arm, muscles burning with each strike. And despite ND-5 having protected him, the very act of striking the droid's metal chest plating, well . . .

It felt good.

But as Obills began working on ND-5's internal hardware, paranoia crept into his thoughts, goading him to watch for a double cross from Obills or a surprise Pyke attack or even ND-5 rising up to complete his assassination mission. *Everything* seemed like a threat now, from every possible direction, all pointed at him. Yet over the course of two hours, his apprehension eroded with a strange realization.

This marked the first time Jaylen had experienced stillness since Gus

Treta. Against the whirlwind of violence that made up his recent weeks, a very human need to *relax* overtook his heightened instincts, and he melted into a detached calm.

For so long, he'd had access to anything he could have possibly wanted. And now he sat in a garage, lost among the grime of Nar Shaddaa's slums for a handful of credits.

"That's the best I can do," Obills called out, pulling Jaylen back to reality. She held up ND-5's restraining bolt and tossed it into the scrap pile.

"Wait, what are you doing?" Jaylen asked. "I need that."

Her head shifted as her eyes blinked. "Are you sure? That bolt took damage. Probably in your last escape. It's been disabled for hours."

Jaylen was no expert on droids. But if the bolt that switched ND-5 from his murderer to his bodyguard was damaged hours ago, shouldn't Jaylen be dead?

"Sorry, but I couldn't get the override chip out," Obills said.

Jaylen's mind still lingered on the notion that ND-5 should have killed him already, and it took several seconds for him to realize what Obills said.

"Override chip?" he asked quietly. "It's not supposed to be there?"

"Yeah, definitely added on aftermarket. Looks like a power surge melted it. Fused it good. I don't think any of its commands work anymore, but it's causing other problems. An expert in Separatist hardware might be able to remove it, but I can't. It's really getting in the way."

ND-5 was originally built for fighting clones in the war. Whoever recovered him must have installed that chip—and ordered him to kill the Barshas.

Obills pointed to the data console next to the droid. "Some of the damage is permanent unless you get that chip out and do a memory wipe with a new core. It has to be a perfect match, not just any old spare part. Until then, you won't be able to directly install new programming." Jaylen blinked at the statement, and she let out a sigh. "That means 'no giving new abilities.' In a way"—she laughed—"he's like a newborn grub." Jaylen offered a short huff at her joke as she moved on. "He's gotta *learn* the old-fashioned way. Kind of like us."

A power surge had melted the chip, and its override commands didn't work anymore.

A memory flashed through Jaylen's mind, and while events in the Gus Treta dining hall remained fuzzy, everything about *this* specific memory lived clearly in his mind.

When he had jammed the stun rod into ND-5's data port and lit it up.

The sounds, the images, the *feelings* all tickled his nerves, but now they wove together with a sudden realization. Because even with a busted restraining bolt, ND-5 was compliant. Whatever programming led to the massacre on Gus Treta, somehow zapping the data port must have halted it.

If ND-5 was still intent on killing him, well, the droid had many opportunities to do that. It wasn't like ND-5 was subtle. "The override chip is definitely broken? It's just stuck to him?"

"Well, you can't be one hundred percent sure. Weird things happen with wiring sometimes, especially under duress. Could be that running from the Pykes or something like that overrode everything else for the moment. If we knew what the commands were, we could do some tests. But otherwise, I'd call it ninety-nine percent." The screen flashed with a table of squares, about two-thirds of them lit blue and the rest dimmed out to gray. "See this? I did manage to restore a lot of his damaged skill programming. He can do basic ship repairs again. That'll be handy. Oh, and those empty spots"—she tapped the screen—"memory's still a little patchy. Not a lot of Sep spare parts floating around, so it's the best I could do."

"Got it," he said, making a forced effort to focus on the moment. "Otherwise, he's fixed?" Even though the chest plate sat flat, the plasma cutter's incision remained, a diagonal gash that now connected to ND-5's bomb-removal scar.

"Just about. Motor control, actuation, thermal regulation, those are good."

Obills offered a shrug like it was no big deal. She couldn't grasp the totality of what lay ahead of Jaylen: ND-5 was repaired and under Jaylen's command—*completely* under his command. That realization caused an internal shift, the detached calm of moments ago building into a strange sense of freedom, a newfound permission to exist with one less constant threat. He had no money, no skills, and no prospects, but he just might be able to breathe without worrying that his protector would snap and kill him swiftly.

It made it much easier to think. But the things he'd pushed aside also started creeping into his mind. Like the fact that this *droid* destroyed his life.

And now they were working together?

Obills pointed to her workbench. "You want me to patch some plating over that scar? It won't be pretty, but it'll work."

Jaylen stood over the prone droid, the internal glow of power systems now illuminating bits of exposed hardware. His throat suddenly felt dry, a low rasp now in his words. "Is the opening a risk to him?"

"Not really. I mean, it's not ideal. But what's ideal these days?"

Jaylen's finger traced the jagged edges of the scar. Remarkable how just a few hours earlier he'd helped tear this plate open, and now it sat flush with ND-5's body once again. "That's one way to put it." The rugged texture surrounding the scar—at the same spot where the droid had blasted himself—scraped against Jaylen's fingertip.

That bomb had nearly killed Jaylen.

This droid had killed his entire family.

Those thoughts surged through him, as if the revelation about the damaged restraining bolt undammed everything that had happened at Gus Treta. Jaylen's first instinct was to fight back the tide of emotion, but then he did the opposite and gave in. Because all this was real. The violence, the screams, the smoldering bodies led him to this moment and defined where he was, who he was, what he did.

He shouldn't fight this pain. He should keep it, hold it tight. This anguish—and rage—came from the only two things he had left: his past and this *droid*.

"No," he finally said. "No, let's keep it as is."

"You sure? I got scrap I can melt over there," she said, pointing to a pile of junk parts.

"Yeah, I'm sure." Jaylen stood and stared at the tools scattered along the floor. "I want to remember how we got here."

Obills reached down into her overalls and held up a pristine restraining bolt. "If you want, I can give you a new bolt. Nothing fancy, just standard restrictions with a droid caller for movement, callback, and orders, calibrated for compatibility. His hardware's already got that fused chip. A custom-programmed bolt might conflict with that. You need it?"

Did he? He supposed he didn't. Yet something new sparked in him, his crashing thoughts coalescing into a single powerful epiphany.

Droids—just like people, just like family—were risks. In this case, there was a 1 percent risk of the chip reactivating. And an unknown risk of ND-5 making poor decisions, maybe just *failing* at a task, that was a different type of danger.

Yet droids were also tools. ND-5 was a tool, rebuilt for Jaylen's purposes, and one he would use even under the most dangerous circumstances—like dealing with the Pykes. But a restraining bolt with an active droid caller—that placed invisible limits on the droid, limits he could activate at the push of a button. Mitigating risk . . . that was just good business.

And that would allow Jaylen to protect himself. He was the only one who could. The galaxy had shown him that much in recent months. "Yeah," Jaylen said. "Put it on. I'll figure out the rest."

"You got it, boss." Obills pointed to a datapad wired to the repair console. "Oh, and that's yours, too—a complete record of what I fixed." Jaylen took the cable out of the datapad but didn't bother looking at the details on it.

LATER, JAYLEN SAT in the cockpit of the . . . well, they hadn't given their ship a name yet. And maybe they shouldn't, since the thing barely flew, and they'd trade out of it as soon as possible. So for now, he sat in the ship's cockpit, tapping the console. Then cursing under his breath. Then tapping it again.

The comms had *just* been working. They wouldn't have gotten the job with Obills otherwise. And she'd offered another small one, an easy pickup and drop-off, but only if they could connect with one of her contacts. So why didn't the comms work now?

"Endee?" he called out. "Any idea why comms are down?"

"I'll check." From behind, Jaylen heard the sounds of ND-5's metallic footsteps stomping around. "The outgoing transmitter is not active. There are four possible reasons for that."

"Trying out your reactivated repair skills?" Jaylen asked.

"Yes." ND-5 now stepped into the back of the cockpit, though he didn't take one of the four seats in the space. "I can confirm the restoration of many skills in my programming. However, I won't know if I can actually execute them until I test them."

"Okay. Get going on the fixes." Without a word, ND-5 turned and began walking back. "Wait. Wait a second," Jaylen said. "If we're stuck for a moment, can you also upload any restored logs or records into the ship's computer first? Maybe there's a clue about who sent you."

"As you wish." More metallic footsteps crossed the storage space behind Jaylen, soon followed by mechanical interfaces connecting and clicking. "Done. Much of the data is corrupted."

The sound of tools and scanners soon floated in, and if Jaylen had looked into the back area, he probably would have seen ND-5 among open panels and live wires. Instead, he turned to the screen next to him, and rather than maps and hyperspace calculations, it displayed an index of ND-5's partially restored logs. He clicked through them one by one, a collection of garbled data and images scraped from ND's internal notes on the days at the Gus Treta compound, all of them benign:

The hedge maze on the southern grounds.

The locations of various droid charging stations.

The dimensions of the dining hall.

A list of Nnytyl Barsha's activities, including the win-loss results of blitzball matches he'd watched.

That one caused him to hesitate, as the very mention of his father brought back the wrong memories. "*Jaylen, go get someone to—*"

Then the sound of blasterfire.

Jaylen shook his head, just about ready to shut down the console and find something, anything else to do. Instinct led to an absent-minded click to reveal the next file—a simple hardware signature from a half-recovered maintenance log. It took several seconds for him to realize what he was looking at.

Chip integration status: Low Red Moon hardware active.

It was a simple result from a hardware diagnostic, yet Jaylen squinted at the text.

Low Red Moon?

Who or what was Low Red Moon?

Such an odd phrase. The words were so specific that they made Jaylen wonder what kind of importance they carried.

It couldn't be a name, could it? A location? Or a code name or a password—any of those seemed possible. But if the message referred to the override chip, it was a lead on whoever sent ND-5 to Gus Treta.

If Jaylen discovered that . . .

One day ago, all Jaylen had cared about was surviving to the very next minute. Food, shelter, sleep, credits, that was all he could think about. But then he discovered the damaged restraining bolt. And with it came a flood of thoughts and memories. And the *truth* of ND-5's existence.

And now, just as he had searched for Sliro before, something new drove him. His parents had always wanted him to get excited about anything to do with the Barsha name. Now something finally stirred in him, a sense of loyalty to his brother combined with a feeling that he didn't quite recognize at first. He wanted to find whoever did this and take them down. This fury lit in him like nothing before, a need to avenge what had happened, to get some sort of justice in an unjust galaxy.

It all started with this one simple, distinctive phrase.

Low Red Moon.

Whoever or whatever it was, it might be the first step to the truth. Possibly even the first step to Sliro.

"Hey, Endee," Jaylen said, his voice cracking.

"Yes, Jaylen," the droid replied from the other room.

"Do you think—I mean, is there any way Sliro could still be out there?"

Several seconds passed before ND-5 replied. "We have purchased archived news and records whenever possible. None of those reference Sliro Barsha. However, there is a nonzero chance that Sliro is alive."

Jaylen looked at the maintenance log again. *Low Red Moon*. Between begging for credits and repairs, Jaylen lost countless hours aimlessly searching through those archives, just as he did with the *Corellia Times* on Gus Treta. Now they had an actual target to work with. "Nonzero chance, huh?"

"No records referenced an identified or recovered body," ND-5 said. "Possibilities include prison, exile, or hiding. Your best chance is to continue purchasing archives of public and news records wherever we go. I can set our ship's computer to analyze those records and play a notification when it recognizes Sliro's name. Would you like that?"

"Yes," Jaylen said. "Yes, do that. Have any hits play a specific chime so I know that it's him."

"What kind of 'specific chime'?"

Droids—so exact in their interactions. "I don't know, something like *ding-ding-ding*."

Several seconds of quiet passed. "Done. We will need to purchase more archived records. I will keep a lookout for potential sources on our journeys."

Jaylen felt his mind sprinting with the same chaos that came from a good time on Niamos. Usually when he felt like this, there was one person he would reach out to.

Sliro wasn't here right now. But Jaylen could still talk to him.

Jaylen stood up, fighting the wave of fatigue that suddenly hit him. He ambled to the back where ND-5 hunched over an open panel, a tool box sitting next to him. "Can you record audio?" he asked.

"Yes. For what purpose?"

"Just checking in," Jaylen said.

ND-5 nodded, and Jaylen opened his mouth, unsure of what might even emerge. He just needed to say something to mark this moment as he embarked on this journey toward Low Red Moon and everything that entailed. "Sliro. If you're out there . . ." The words caught at the base of his throat, as if they resisted coming to life. "Listen, brother. I just found something. And I don't know who or what Low Red Moon is. But I'm going to get revenge. For you."

In Jaylen's memory, his father's voice echoed out again. Jaylen shut his eyes and forced his mind to silence before the blasterfire came.

"For all of us. However long it takes."

Jaylen exhaled, his weight shifting back to his heels. "That's it, Endee."

"Storing. Shall I restrict access to this file?" ND-5 asked.

Jaylen hadn't considered that part. But it was a good question. Jaylen Barsha was supposed to be dead. If this recording were ever discovered, it could set the Empire on his trail, regardless of which name he used. "Make it as secure as possible. So only I can listen to it."

"Done," ND-5 said. "Shall I save these security parameters for future use?"

"Yeah," Jaylen said. "Call it Security Protocol . . ." His mind raced for a name that only he would know, a word or two loaded with meaning. "Brencoyle."

"Done," ND-5 said. "However, I am not built for encryption. A slicer would be able to access a restricted file if they knew where to look."

"If you got captured, that would mean much bigger problems. Keep it hidden from yourself as well." Jaylen patted the droid on the shoulder. "You're a good listener, Endee. Like Sliro."

"It is because my audio receptors are fully functioning."

ND-5 might have listened as well as Sliro, but the droid was still several steps behind on personality. Jaylen turned to head back to the cockpit. "Let's get this ship fixed. The more credits we get, the faster we get more archive data tapes."

"Once ship communications are repaired," ND-5 said as he stuck his hand into the ship's wiring, "I should review the list of Obills's repairs on me. That will help me confirm which of my skills have been restored. Otherwise, I won't know until I test them. Prioritizing that may expand our work options. In addition, if you remove the restraining bolt, I will have greater freedom of movement. That may also assist us in getting better-paying work."

Jaylen hadn't expected ND-5 to even bring up the restraining bolt—the droid hadn't mentioned it after waking up or heading back to the ship. So why was he considering it now?

But ND-5's own words made it clear. Something over the past few weeks had seemed to heighten the droid's sense of agency. Maybe simply being around Jaylen in the most extreme of circumstances drove

ND-5's programming in unanticipated directions. Jaylen had even seen it when they'd escaped the Pykes—ND-5 had made a choice to destroy that bridge. He had *adapted.*

But if ND-5 had freedom, the droid could also choose to leave. Or reveal the recording he'd just made. Or kill Jaylen. Or all the above.

Jaylen wasn't sure which of those was the most terrifying.

Jaylen had lost everything once. He refused to lose the only asset he had left. For him to find the truth, ND-5 had to stay at his side. Which meant he had to seal off any notion the droid had of freedom right now. If ND-5 believed that he was overly tethered, then Jaylen would have to assuage that, like he was negotiating with a minister of agriculture on behalf of Barsha Corp. "I think you're forgetting," he said, "that restraining bolt keeps you from killing me."

ND-5 paused at that. "The droidsmith confirmed that?"

"Ah, right," Jaylen said, "you were knocked out when Obills told me." His mind started rolling, company training coming back to him as he considered how *information* could be his biggest tool here—factual or not. "I heard you say it: 'Kill all the Barshas and their guests.' We can't risk it."

"A detailed droidsmith report should contain a list of what was repaired."

"She did give us a list, but it only had the skills you *shouldn't* use," Jaylen said, thinking about the datapad Obills *had* given him—and he made a mental note to erase it later. "If we get this job, *I'll* make sure to ask her for more records." Jaylen decided right there: They wouldn't take any further jobs from Obills Myron. Concealing the truth was worth much more than a fetch gig. "Until then, you should be really careful."

"We can create a controlled experiment to test removal—"

"I wouldn't." Jaylen held up a hand. "She said that if you removed the bolt, it might even revert you back to a standard BX commando droid. All you've learned and become, gone"—he snapped his fingers—"just like that." Jaylen decided to add one more layer on top of this, because what were the chances they'd actually deal with Separatist equipment in the future? "She even said that if you tap into any Separatist-specific skills, it would push you over the edge. She said it's a programming conflict." He walked over and tapped ND-5 on the chest. "I think it's because her replacement parts weren't a perfect match. They don't play nice with your fused chip and the remaining damage."

Several seconds passed without any reaction from the droid, as if it took much of the droid's neural core processing to understand. "These are variables my diagnostics cannot account for," ND-5 finally said. "It is an unfortunate scenario."

"You're right. It is unfortunate. But hey, remember this—your original mission was supposed to end by blowing both of us up. We're here now. We're *survivors*. So for now, let's just stay the course," Jaylen said. Then his tone switched, carrying an intensity that came only with deep belief. "I need to find this Low Red Moon. It's our only lead. This is our goal now."

ND-5 continued working on the comm wiring without saying a word.

"Someday," Jaylen said, his tone now shifting to something bright and optimistic, though inside all he heard were his father's last words and the sound of ND-5's blaster going off, "we'll find someone who can repair Separatist droids. Until then, best to just listen to me. We work well together." He reached over and tapped ND-5 on the droid's good arm. "That makes us a team."

PART 2

Before the Gus Treta incident that happened nine years ago, Jaylen had visited wineries often. Sometimes on a break from university. Sometimes as a Barsha Corp retreat. Sometimes on a family vacation—which meant that Sliro stayed home, Brencoyle supervised Jaylen while he ran around the winery grounds, and his parents drank a lot of wine.

Jaylen had never been to Renner Family Winery on Blutopia before, but it looked the same as a lot of other island wineries, with a perfectly placed sun cutting through the atmosphere, stretching across bold lines of growing crops going to the island's horizon. He set his hands on a balcony railing made of natural, textured stone. It must have taken extra long for its craftsman to etch designs along its entire span.

"Here we are." Jaylen turned to see Bischt Renner, the winery's current owner. Bischt brought in two half-filled glasses, the purple liquid carrying a light glow on the top layer. "This was an especially good crop. Blutopia doesn't have a lot of exportable resources, but nermaline fruit makes excellent wine."

Jaylen never cared about who owned or operated the wineries before. This visit, however, was different. Because several weeks ago, he got word that *this* particular place was the preferred vacation spot of many syndicates. ND-5's deep cross-checking of spaceport records confirmed this: Bischt Renner seemed to heavily favor booking getaways for known syndicate operatives, even heads.

This couldn't be a coincidence. And it meant that either Renner was on their payroll, a preferred partner, or owed *something* to the syndicates. Whatever the case, he would be a good person to know. And Jaylen planned to make himself known.

"Most people are interested in the wine, not the business of wine," Bischt said.

Jaylen gave him a knowing smile, a CEO's smile he'd flashed multiple times over the last thirty minutes. A lifetime had passed since he'd acted this way on behalf of Barsha Corp, and while he'd flexed that particular skill set occasionally, so much more of his work now involved grimy districts with even grimier cantinas, rather than endless fields and ornate architecture.

"I enjoy both," Jaylen said. He stood, his back straight and his chin angled up toward the sky as he took a sip. The years must have dulled his senses. He used to be able to decipher the finer points in wine when tasting. Here, he only knew that it was thinner, less potent than the stuff he'd normally encounter in places where everyone carried at least one blaster. "I've been thinking about what you told me. I imagine a business like yours has quite the supply chain to deal with."

"That's for sure," Bischt said with a laugh. His tanned cheeks rose with a grin, and he looked at Jaylen with bright blue eyes, squinting slightly from the afternoon sun. "Droid parts. Machine parts. Cask parts. So many parts. But we've done this for generations. We trust our suppliers, and they trust us."

A piece of ornamental jewelry hung over Jaylen's ear—more importantly, it disguised a tiny comlink from which ND-5's voice came. "Jaylen, I have successfully sliced into the security controls from the estate's power station. All security measures in this wing of the facility are now deactivated. I am inconspicuously heading to your location."

Inconspicuously. Jaylen couldn't exactly ask how that was possible given ND-5's heavy steps and the bright weather, though he would definitely inquire later on.

"And your customers?" Jaylen asked, taking another sip. His palate definitely did not capture the subtleties of wine anymore. "I imagine you get a lot of"—Jaylen pointed to the tasting spaces on the far side of the estate—"interesting visitors. Who are looking for a quiet place to discuss business matters."

"I take great pride in getting my customers to feel comfortable," Bischt said. "They get everything they need here: good food, good drink, relaxation. Plus, the anonymity of Blutopia. Most of the population is sea based. We get the islands to ourselves."

Jaylen turned to speak face-to-face. "But at a place like this, you probably can't help hearing things among your customers."

A wind blew through the trees below the balcony, kicking up a sprinkling of blue leaves.

"You sound interested in them."

"Like I said, I'm an operational consultant. The things we've discussed apply to all businesses, and I'm always looking for new contacts." Jaylen chose to let that statement settle for a moment before nudging things forward. "I service many industries. Even some that deal with the, shall we say, less regulated aspects of the galaxy."

This creative phrasing caused Bischt to grin and nod. "I understand what you mean." There it was—an acknowledgment. Or an opening. Or *both*. "We've been talking for a while. Let me think over what you said while I get us something to eat. We have trained the cook droids to use my grandmother's recipes." He turned with hands out wide. "A life like mine teaches you to take opportunities when you find them," he said, then left the balcony.

Jaylen leaned on the railing and held his glass, though he didn't take another sip. Too thin, too weak, a drink for people who lived lives other than his. "He's gone. What do you see?"

"My thermal scope shows he is walking toward the kitchen," ND-5 said. "I estimate that you have between three and seven minutes before he returns, depending on how long he takes to gather things in the kitchen. Do you need my assistance?"

"No. Keep watch outside. We're just talking. All I want is for him to get me some contacts with the cartels."

Although . . .

Jaylen *could* have stayed on the balcony and enjoyed the view. But curiosity got the better of him—and Bischt was right: He should take opportunities when they came.

Right now, he was right outside the private office of someone connected to the biggest crime syndicates in the galaxy. A quick look could produce . . .

Something.

"Actually," Jaylen said, "I'm going to look around his office. See what I can find."

"I would not advise that. You have established a rapport. This might offset your gains."

The droid was right, of course. Disrupting a budding business relationship was bad. But Jaylen needed *something* to move him up in life. For nine years, he had been driven by the idea of finding Sliro, of solving the mystery of Low Red Moon. The first five or so, he'd pursued both relentlessly.

Since then, though, that inner drive had gradually faded. Jaylen had acknowledged that with a begrudging acceptance. His search went nowhere. His career went nowhere. His *life* went nowhere. While he—and ND-5—got their share of work among the galaxy's best of the worst, they still served *others.* They jumped and ran at the behest of someone else's call, the galaxy continuing to move while they sank deeper and deeper into the same spot.

This whole trip was about boosting his profile to the syndicates. But Bischt's office . . . it presented an opportunity to see what someone with real connections among the cartels had tucked away.

It was worth it. And besides, a look never hurt. "Endee, keep me posted on his distance."

"He is still in the kitchen."

Jaylen stepped in and scanned the space, wineglass still in hand. A large wooden desk sat near the balcony, crossed by a sunbeam from the window. A simple office chair stood next to it. "Nothing on the desk," he said, setting his glass down on its corner.

"If you really wish to uncover something useful, I suggest looking in less obvious places."

Jaylen didn't want to acknowledge it, but ND-5 had a point. Besides the desk, the office was rather empty. The left side held a pair of large chairs and a clear glass table for caf and tea, while the right side contained a cabinet with a holo-emitter embedded in the top—and on the wall space above it, a family projection of several generations of Renners.

"Less obvious, huh?" Jaylen said. ND-5 didn't answer, and Jaylen felt around the cabinet. It opened and closed with a simple manual slide, and the only things inside were neatly organized bottles of wine.

Jaylen straightened up and looked at the holo portrait, in which Bischt and his family were shrunk down in miniature and frozen in a pose. He squinted at the image, angling left and right at the three-dimensional capture of adults and children, everyone from babies to grandparents, possibly great-grandparents.

Then he realized *why* this holo looked more striking and vivid than images from standard emitters. Behind it hung a subtle panel, some kind of reflective material that blended into the wall but also enhanced the projected image. Jaylen's fingers felt around the panel, but the surface was entirely smooth. Yet when he knocked all across it, its echo rang deeper than that of the wall.

Something was behind that panel. But how to unlock it?

"Bischt Renner is done in the kitchen. He has started his return path."

Jaylen stepped back and looked at the holograph, which showed an overhead angle looking down at four rows of around ten Renner family members standing at the winery's entrance. In front of them on the ground lay a large seal of a nermaline fruit carved out of deep-brown metal—the same symbol at the winery's entrance.

Like a button.

Jaylen followed his instincts. His finger hovered over that very spot, then poked *through* the holograph to press on the panel. Mechanisms whirred and clicked, and the panel slid down to reveal a small safe nestled in an alcove. "Endee, how much time?"

"I estimate three minutes."

"Three minutes," Jaylen said to himself. From his back pocket, he pulled out a small square with two glowing red dots. He planted it on the front of the safe, and the device's lights switched to flashing alternating yellow and blue. "This better be worth it."

"Jaylen, you should remember that device was untested and very expensive."

How did ND-5 know he'd primed the slicer? And also, when did the droid start worrying about their finances? "Well, this will test it." The device's beeping went from a steady rhythm to a sudden frantic pace, soon followed by the sliding of locks. The safe opened with squeaking hinges, and inside lay a single datapad. "Endee, make a note to get more of those slicing devices." He reached in and grabbed the datapad.

"Your time is limited. I suggest you restore things to how they were."

Jaylen resisted the urge to examine the datapad and instead slid it into the inner pocket of his coat. The safe closed with a click, and the cover panel slipped back into place with a simple nudge. "It's a datapad," Jaylen said. "Only valuable datapads stay in safes." Despite the approaching footsteps, he had enough time to step back, tug his lapels and smooth his coat, and even grab his glass of wine.

The footsteps came closer and closer, and Bischt spoke just as he turned into the room. "Sorry about the wait," Bischt said as he entered with a wooden tray of pastries in one hand.

"Not a problem," Jaylen said. "I was just looking at your family history here. They all worked at the winery?"

"About a third of them, at one time or another. Right now, it's just me. The rest of the family has spread their wings." He looked Jaylen up and down before setting the tray on the small table by the corner chairs. "Shall we?" he asked. "Our cook droid tries its best to cook like my grandmother. It's close, but not the real thing."

Jaylen felt the weight of the datapad in his coat as he moved to the seat. ND-5's voice broke into the comlink in his ear. "You have taken his datapad. You should leave with it now instead of eating sugar-rich pastries."

"I find," Jaylen said to both ND-5 and Bischt, "pastries are the perfect complement to discussing possibilities." To prove his point, he took one and bit down, green jam oozing out the side.

"Agreed. More wine?" Bischt got up and moved over to open the cabinet beneath the holograph. "Do you have a preference?"

"Whatever you recommend."

"I actually thought of some ways we might be able to help each other while I was in the kitchen. Unfortunately, I need to know something first," Bischt said, approaching with one hand supporting the base of the bottle and the other holding the neck. He stopped in the middle of the room, and from the look in his eyes, Jaylen detected something had shifted. "Tell me, why did you break into my safe?"

He knew. But how?

"I have detected a threatening tone and am shifting course toward your location," ND-5 said. "The transponder in your boot is still active."

ND-5 was on his way. But there was still a chance to talk his way out of this.

"What are you talking about?" Jaylen asked with a polite smile.

"There's a weight sensor." Bischt nodded at the holograph. "In my safe. The color of the sky in the image changes when it's empty. It's how I know if my staff—or my guests—are trying to rob me."

Jaylen moved to stand up.

"Ah," said Bischt, "I wouldn't do that. Unless you want to be blasted." He tapped the base of the wine bottle. "It's amazing how inconspicuous you can make weapons these days. So, Jaylen Vrax, before I decide whether or not to kill you, I want to know who hired you to steal that. They should know what kind of beginner's mistake they paid for."

"I work for myself." That part was true. When he was known as Jaylen Barsha, everything he did reflected on the Barsha name. But Jaylen *Vrax,* that was all him. Jaylen put his hands up. "I told you, I'm a consultant."

ND-5's voice came through again. "I am using the back entrance to avoid any encounters. I will be there shortly."

"A consultant doesn't steal from the Empire."

Jaylen couldn't stifle the change in his expression. The Empire? What did *that* have to do with anything? Didn't this life exist outside of Imperial entanglements?

"I'm, uh," Jaylen responded slowly, "a little confused—"

Bischt turned to face the open balcony doors and tapped the bottom of the bottle. A red blaster bolt soared from its covert barrel and out toward the sky. "No more games. Who's targeting me?"

Just like before, footsteps approached from the hall. But this time, they came at a rhythmic, heavy cadence—and when Bischt turned to see who was coming, Jaylen recognized an opening.

He threw a punch.

Even half turned, Bischt saw it and swerved out of the way. Now they grappled, Jaylen forcing his elbow to keep the hidden blaster angled *away* from him. Whoever Bischt worked for had trained him well, and after regaining his balance, Bischt kicked the back of Jaylen's leg. Jaylen fell to one knee, and they stayed locked, Bischt still trying to turn the weapon toward him.

"Endee!" Jaylen yelled as the droid entered the room. "The bottle! There's a blaster built into the bottom of it!"

Bischt turned to see the hulking BX droid approach and immediately let Jaylen go. As ND-5 came closer, Bischt tried to rotate the bottle in time. ND-5 reached over and wrapped his larger hand over Bischt's, his mechanical strength too much for the winery owner. The bottle fired a blaster discharge that deflected off ND-5's armor, and the droid turned the weapon toward Bischt. "No . . . who are . . ." he started as ND-5 tapped the bottom of the bottle.

Blasterfire went straight into Bischt's chest. His body slumped down, head propped against his desk.

"We should dispose of the body before security systems come back online," ND-5 said.

The datapad.

"See if you can find a way to discreetly move him," Jaylen said as he reached into his coat pocket to see if the datapad sustained any damage. He stepped into the hallway, half listening for signs of staff or droids. But really, his focus was on the short—and valuable—message that appeared on the screen as soon as the datapad booted.

**IMPERIAL SECURITY BUREAU—
REGIONAL INFORMATION TRANSFER**

To: Agent Sun Racket

Prepare for meeting with Agent Impossible Song for transfer of updated regional information.

Rooftop meeting, formal attire required.

**Museum of Engineering and Lightspeed, Andara—
Grand Opening Gala**

Jaylen stared at the datapad. Bischt Renner was an undercover ISB agent. Hiding in plain sight. That must have been why he was so connected to the syndicates—he *watched* them. And "regional information transfer"? Whatever was being transferred was valuable enough to require a scheduled meeting at a public event.

Jaylen's mind raced. He'd come here to build underworld contacts, and instead he was leaving with information about a secret ISB meeting.

Someone might pay a lot of money for that information.

ND-5 stepped into the hallway. "There is a large furnace in the power station. I will use it to dispose of the body so that he is presumed missing. I must carry the body there, but his height and weight are similar to yours. This will allow me to gauge how best to disguise the body during transport." ND-5 did not notice Jaylen's crooked reaction to those comments. Was ND-5 referring to the times he'd carried a wounded Jaylen to safety, or had he actually calculated how to carry Jaylen's dead body? The droid pointed at the datapad in Jaylen's hand. "Was it worth it?"

"Yeah," Jaylen said slowly. "He's ISB."

"If Bischt Renner was ISB, then the Empire would notice a missing datapad. I will commit its information to my memory banks, then you should restore it to its original location."

The droid was right. ND-5 scanned the information, then they returned the datapad and restored the office to its previous state.

He stepped back for one final look at the sealed panel and the hologram. Bischt was right—the color of the sky *did* change.

"Ingenious detection system," Jaylen said as he turned to the fallen body. From the hall, he heard ND-5's footsteps as the droid sought means to move the body in stealth. As he looked closer, Jaylen realized that the droid was right, too: They *did* have the same height and weight. Also, the same hair color, same skin tone, even roughly the same age.

"Jaylen," ND-5 said from the hall. "I have located a supply cart to disguise the body."

Why sell off the location of Sun Racket's meeting with Impossible Song when he could *become* Sun Racket and get the information himself?

"Yeah," Jaylen said, mind already thinking ahead. Once they disposed of Bischt's body, they'd have to falsify some messages for winery staff and claim he was going offworld for a few weeks. That would buy enough time to allay suspicions while they went to Andara in his place. "Let's go. We have work to do."

CHAPTER 16

System start-up.

Identification number: JX394ND-5777.

Hardware type: BX-series droid commando.

Manufacturer: Baktoid Combat Automata.

Default configuration and initialization parameters: Intended use by the Confederacy of Independent Systems.

Restraining bolt: Detected.

Environment analysis: Light freighter *Successor.*

Audio/visual sensors active. Motor functions enabled.

Start-up checks completed.

I am active.

Before I can function, a warning flag immediately appears advising of memory core problems. I sync with the ship's chrono and activate a start-to-finish memory review to orient myself.

My first memory is an operation with a team of other BX commando droids. Next are early actions at Gus Treta, though many remain inaccessible due to damage from the bomb or the fusing of the override chip.

From there, the memories speed by, most of them involving Jaylen. Jaylen adopting the new surname Vrax. Efforts to hide his identity. Our work to earn credits while building up our contact list over nine years.

Notable successful jobs at Arda, Ord Mantell, Talus, Kalist, Coruscant (proper), Coruscant (lower levels).

Notable unsuccessful jobs at Hynestia, Stewjon, Sullust.

Unavailable skills per Jaylen's restrictions: Deceptive conversation. Clone trooper voice mimicry. B1 battle droid group tactics. CIS craft piloting. CIS craft repair. CIS fleet formations. CIS transportation protocols.

0.6 percent of memory storage allocated to restricted files.

> **[[Error Code 61: Memory block B4 completely corrupted. C17, M5, T20 are invalid. Reconsolidation process required to repair memory.]]**

My last active memory is examining the long-range transmitter's known hardware issues twenty-four hours ago. I cannot recall getting from there to the charging station.

This completes my start-up sequence. The process took 4.8 seconds to complete.

I set my internal processors to address the anomaly of missing time, consolidate my data storage, and repair functionality.

I take a moment to assess my surroundings. The *Successor* is a KS-500 light freighter, built by Corellian Engineering Corporation. Jaylen has called that fact "ironic" before, which I assume is a reference to his family history. He said the same thing after changing the ship's registry to the name *Successor*.

We purchased the vessel through a combination of credits and trade-in value four years ago. Jaylen chose to acquire it given that it offered a slightly higher-than-average level of comfort despite the ship's manufacturing date of fifteen years ago. The interior includes softer furnishings and larger sleeping quarters. The trade-off is a smaller storage area compared to most light freighters. However, Jaylen has stated on numerous occasions that our goal is "avoiding the hauling trade as much as possible." This choice of craft fulfills that goal.

I maintain a list of ongoing items that need repair on the *Successor,* which currently includes the lateral stabilizer, the long-range transmitter's amplifier to bypass atmospheric interference, the electrostatic baffler, the shield booster, and the power system on the holotable.

I am standing plugged into my charging station in the area that Jaylen has referred to as the *office*. It has multiple purposes: dining, holonet viewing, a terminal for a technical station, and a small workbench. A larger workbench is in the cargo hold, along with spare parts and a single speeder bike of unknown origin (likely cobbled together from different manufacturers' original vehicles).

In the past, Jaylen has suggested that any incidents of missing memory are due to the degradation of the chip fused to my neural core, the long-term effects of using non-Separatist hardware as replacements, or recent damage. I activate the *Successor*'s internal security feed for a view of myself to investigate that last option.

Other than my chest scar, I see no signs of recent damage. I am still wearing my green duster, which I keep on at all times except when undergoing body repairs. The coat has no new holes or tears in it that require mending.

I walk over to the technical station and start accessing our action log for the past forty-eight hours to fill in the missing details. It does not suffice. There are no records of conflicts that could cause this kind of memory loss. It states we are currently docked outside of West Allscot on Dargulli. I expand my audio sensors and detect hints of Dargulli's dense seasonal rain against the ship's hull plating.

As I do this, Jaylen emerges from the captain's quarters. He is carrying several datapads and has creases on his face, usually indicating he is deep in thought.

He pauses mid-step, then backtracks before turning to me.

"Everything okay, Endee?" he says.

"I am running an internal diagnostic on my memory functions," I say, remaining completely still, "while assessing the weather outside."

"Oh," Jaylen says with a laugh. "Did you finish that bottle of Dorian Quill?"

"Imbibing beverages does not solve my problems."

"Wiser than most, pal." Jaylen rubs his face. He has marked bags under his eyes from fatigue. That is not unusual given the rigors of our unpredictible schedule.

"I should note that unexpected gaps have appeared in my memory," I say. "I am in the process of internally repairing what I can. I am also analyzing why this happened." The process status appears in my internal sensors, showing a completion rate of 53 percent.

"Unexpected gaps. Well, you know that fused chip of yours, it can cause problems. Probably just that." He rubs his chin and looks directly at me. "Wait, 'gaps,' as in, more than one memory?"

"Yes. My storage systems save data segments chronologically across multiple blocks if I am running out of space. Their arrangement can be optimized later during a routine maintenance procedure. However, before that consolidation, removal of one memory block will create a chain of data loss in related areas."

Now Jaylen's eyes narrow, though this is a different look than before. Having followed Jaylen's directions for nine years now, I am usually able to discern his various expressions. I have seen this one before. Historically, it is used when he wants to project the façade of understanding a technical explanation when he actually does not.

I choose softer language in my follow-up. "Not to worry. If there is vital missing data, a droidsmith may be able to restore it."

"Is there a problem with your restraining bolt?" he asks after a pause.

That is an unrelated issue, but I answer regardless. "This is functioning under normal parameters," I say, tapping the cylinder attached to my chest.

"Well, then." He looks around, then points to our ship's loading doors. "We'll have to fix that later. We've got a job to do. Fennec and Lorel will be here in twenty hours."

Neither of those terms flag as recent information. My processors search for *Fennec*. Various identities and definitions appear, though I filter through them via various applications of context: our occupation, our current circumstances, Jaylen's references to a "job to do."

"Fennec . . . Shand," I finally say. "Mercenary. Assassin. Known for sniper skills. Her price has increased proportionally to her demand in the past year."

Jaylen folds his arms, still in contemplation, but he offers a small nod. I perform the same type of analysis on the name *Lorel*.

"Lorel . . . Amberdine. Slicer. Thief. Trained with syndicates. Known to associate with Saw Gerrera's political insurgents. Currently a freelancer. The last time we worked together, she kept calling me 'big guy.' "

"Yes, that's them. Fennec and Lorel," Jaylen said, breaking his pose with a quick laugh. "Now come on, no more games. Finish your diagnostic later, we have to start prep. Who did you pick for the pilot?"

That is an odd question. I search through my recent logs for any appropriate context to the request, yet I find none. I turn to Jaylen, and though I cannot blink or emote, the sudden rush of search requests create what organics would refer to as "a sense of confusion."

"What do you mean by 'who did you pick for the pilot'?"

Jaylen takes a short breath and does not move.

"I do not have any record of a mission that needs preparation," I say. By Jaylen's unblinking stare and the sudden draining of circulation from his cheeks, it is clear that this is a problem.

"I, um . . ." he starts, his voice now very dry. He looks at me, then turns quickly before facing my way again. "It's . . ." He cannot finish his thoughts, and now his mouth moves without any actual sounds coming out.

"Is there a problem, Jaylen?"

Jaylen forms a fist with one hand and brings it to his mouth, his top teeth digging down on it. "Endee," he says very slowly.

"Yes."

"What is the status of memory block B4?"

Memory block B4. That is the one related to my storage issues. It is the one whose malfunction has cascaded into a series of interlinking data failures requiring consolidation and reindexing.

It is also highly unusual for us to discuss something this technical about droid memory storage. It is even more unusual for Jaylen to recognize such a specific detail.

"The memory block is empty. A chain of related memory blocks appear to have been corrupted. The master data index is incomplete."

Jaylen lets out a frustrated groan, both hands covering his eyes. He twists on his heels, his cape whipping out hard as he does so. "You remember *nothing* from that block?"

"I can search my cache to see if a previous version exists." Before Jaylen can respond, I initiate this process. "The following file names are listed in the cached index. Datafile: Log 459A6. Datafile: Log 198C. Audio file: Untitled recording C2. Text file: Daily transcription 94K. Text file: Menu from Irio food stall on Toshara. Video memory: Cache 77MN3—"

"Okay, okay," Jaylen says with a hand up. "I get it. All right." He presses his hands against his temples, rubbing slowly. He is no longer using the expression that pretends to understand technical details.

This is his panicked face. I see it more often than he admits. He will likely follow it with a quip to reassure me, though its purpose will be more to reassure himself.

"It's okay. We can do this," he says. "We've gotta figure something out."

"What exactly is this 'something' you refer to?"

Jaylen straightens up, and though his tone shifts to something genial, his eyes still give away a high level of stress. "Endee, you have no datafiles on Andara?"

Once again, I search through my storage files. No matches appear. I then check the index of missing files from memory block B4.

A match appears.

"File names and descriptions found. Datafile: Andara gala plan, second revision. Text file: Pilot list, Andara mission. Contents are unrecoverable."

"Like a picture that's only an outline," Jaylen muses to himself. "Okay, Endee." Now he straightens up, and his voice trails off as he stomps away, his boots clacking on the *Successor*'s metal flooring. "Find some pilots. See if anyone can fly in twenty hours."

"Under what qualifications?" I ask.

Jaylen is already halfway out of the room when he responds. "If they can get here, they qualify. Hurry. I gotta salvage the plan."

"Fly to what destination?" I call out as I activate the communication console next to the technical station.

"*Andara,*" he says quickly. His annoyed tone shifts into his usual strategic voice. "They need to be able to fly a ship from the war." His voice bounces off the hallway.

From the war?

Perhaps Jaylen has forgotten about my original purpose. It has been, after all, nine years since we met. Skills related to my original Confederacy of Independent Systems role have lain dormant. They are part of a greater collection of skills where my programming is functional, yet Jaylen has forbidden their usage. He says that, per the droidsmith Obills Myron, using any of those skills will cause severe issues for me, including the possibility of a memory wipe.

However, should a skill be needed to complete a high-paying job, he says he would let me test it. This has come up four times. We have never completed a test.

I shall try now.

"Jaylen, with proper testing, I should be more than capable of—"

He pops his head back into the room, his entire demeanor much calmer now. "No time, Endee." He points to me, eyes squinted with concentration. "Find a pilot."

Once again, the curse of the Barsha family had gotten in Jaylen's way. It was paradoxical, really. This burning quest had eaten at him for years: a *need* to discover the truth behind the Gus Treta incident, the downfall of Barsha Corp, and any evidence that Sliro might still be alive—all tying to the *who* or *what* of Low Red Moon. A need to avenge his family, like doing so could repair all the splintering cracks within him, even after all this time.

Sometimes, it felt like he'd always been Jaylen Vrax, underworld hustler. Talking with fellow smugglers, cashing in contracts, breaking into strongholds, it felt like those were the only things that ever existed, and that his prior life was a dream at best—a faded one that only existed if he forced himself to dwell on it.

Then they'd get a data tape of archived news and run it through the technical station, and for a split second, he'd return to being Jaylen Barsha, son of Roisem and Nnytyl. On rare occasions, he'd get that special *ding-ding-ding* alert flagging the name *Sliro Barsha* in an article. Then *other* sounds would flood his brain: Sliro's voice as they looked over Barsha's hidden records, his mother proclaiming him the chosen one . . .

Nnytyl's last words on Gus Treta.

The noise of blasterfire.

The final memories would freeze him, the same way a stun rod applied to ND-5's dataport had frozen the droid long enough for Jaylen to escape the inevitable.

But then he'd read the piece and see that the name just appeared in some sort of Corellian tabloid outlet, a sensationalized "whatever happened to . . ." retrospective that focused on their family's fall from grace. Those types of things came up once or twice a year, about as often as proper historical reviews of Corellian engineering.

The big difference, though, was that the gossip columns would actually include Sliro. Anything more formal, proper, or educational that mentioned the Barshas only included the "whole" Barsha son, never the half. That needled Jaylen more than the tabloids, because at least the gossip articles meant that someone somewhere had thought of Sliro. It was worse when news outlets simply evaporated Sliro from history.

Jaylen would force himself to picture Sliro's face then, like doing so could keep his memory alive in the galaxy.

Then his mind would reset, a whiplash snapping him back into place.

The gap between Vrax and Barsha sometimes felt like a hundred parsecs, as if they existed as two completely separate people instead of representing different phases of a life story—and Jaylen Vrax was motivated by vengeance over something that he didn't even remember or understand.

That made it very ironic that Jaylen Vrax's current goals had been hindered by both Barsha sentimentality and a memory issue from the droid that killed his family.

With ND-5 now tasked to find a pilot, Jaylen entered his quarters. A small bed sat in the corner. Capes and coats hung in the closet, all of them kept in better shape than the *Successor* itself. And there was a small terminal squeezed in, an aftermarket installation that networked with all the data in the ship, from its sensors to anything ND-5 uploaded.

Too bad ND-5's memories didn't back up there.

Several weeks ago, Jaylen had set out to become a trusted contact of vintner Bischt Renner. Instead, ND-5 murdered him—and in doing so, Jaylen found the meeting details for an ISB information transfer: a gala for the grand opening of the Museum of Engineering and Lightspeed on Andara.

Unlike many of their jobs, Jaylen kept this plan mostly to himself, only farming out bits of information for ND-5 to research or individuals for him to contact. Because a key piece of the plan involved a very specific topic that Jaylen did *not* want to discuss with ND-5.

A Separatist ship.

Since that moment with Obills Myron, Jaylen knew that his quest for vengeance required discretion, which in turn meant absolute control. As in, he couldn't trust anyone, not even ND-5. To facilitate this, Jaylen constructed a list of limitations, all under the pretense that violating them might disrupt ND-5's hardware, possibly even reset the droid back to his default BX commando state. And just for good measure, Jaylen tied all that to ND-5's restraining bolt, keeping the droid caller as his ultimate fallback.

Those limitations all focused on war-related skills. Since the war was over, those skills made for an easy target to keep ND-5 in line.

And the one time one of those skills *would* come in handy, Jaylen knew they couldn't even broach the topic. He couldn't let the web of half-truths he'd constructed around the droid collapse now. Yesterday, he'd finally consolidated all his notes and reviewed the plan for Andara with ND-5, from the schedule to the list of potential pilots for the Separatist ship to the maps and contacts involved. ND-5 was tasked with finalizing a pilot while Jaylen confirmed preparations with the support crew and shuttle owner.

Because of the *Barsha* in him, all that simply vanished.

Part of Jaylen felt a little jealous of the droid's amnesia, its memories there one second and deleted the next. Was that the closest thing to a trauma reaction for droids? How convenient for things to simply go away, the connective links between data vanishing, pathways missing, related files disabled instead of *stewing* over things the way humans did.

He supposed that, for right now, it didn't matter. Because they had a big problem: Jaylen Vrax, underworld hustler, needed the data on memory block B4.

And the fact that it wasn't there now? That was his own damn fault.

It all started with an audio file saved to memory block B4—a log of Jaylen's own drunken ramblings, inebriation blurring the lines between his identities as Vrax and Barsha. He wasn't even sure *why* he felt the need to sit there and dictate to ND-5, a bottle in hand. His thoughts played out messier, uglier than any previous one with ND-5 or any check-in talk he'd ever had with Sliro. Was it the pressure of this upcoming mission? Because if they pulled it off, it would be the biggest score they'd ever attempted, with a prize capable of luring in syndicate after syndicate, job after job, stepping up his reputation as someone who could be trusted to plan and pull off the most complex of heists . . .

It would define the trajectory of Jaylen Vrax.

And the more successful Jaylen Vrax got, the more the need to avenge Jaylen Barsha faded. At least a little—in fits and spurts. Yet sometimes the distance from his old self grew enough that he'd forget he ever saw the phrase *Low Red Moon*. And the cursed chip that he'd fused to the droid's hardware with a stun rod would be far from his thoughts.

Although the more Jaylen Barsha went away, the more Jaylen Vrax saw potential in letting ND-5 do *more,* engage with jobs and tasks that might brush up against those restricted skills. Like piloting a Separatist ship. Or at the very least, giving Jaylen the relief of not having to always keep up the cover story.

Jaylen squeezed his eyes shut, trying to will last night into existence. Bits and pieces flashed through, but he could only distinctly recall a few particular lines: "Nine years," he'd said, and he remembered this because he took a swig of a bottle but missed, bits of Dorian Quill dribbling down his chin and staining his shirt. "Nine years have passed. Isn't nine years long enough to let things go?" He'd used ND-5 this way before, every few months exorcising his demons through the simple act of talking. This time, though, had been the only time he'd done so intoxicated.

"I mean, I've never figured out what happened. I live in this stupid ship, talking all day to a droid that killed my family. And that." He pointed to the restraining bolt on ND-5's chest . . . a little piece of metal wrapped in falsehoods.

For Jaylen Barsha, those lies made sense, a way to corner ND-5 into subservience.

"It just isn't worth it, is it? To give your future away for your past?" Jaylen had asked out loud, and he recalled smirking while dabbing his sleeve over the spilled liquid on his shirt. How *eloquent* of him, like he'd actually paid attention to his philosophy classes at University of Bar'leth. "But maybe this is it. Maybe *this* is the point where we turn the corner. Stop living job to job, make some real money, find a place to stay that isn't just the nearest poodoo-infested docking bay of the nearest poodoo-infested city. Right?" More Dorian Quill spilled out as the bottle shook for emphasis. "Right?"

Of course, ND-5 hadn't answered. First, because he wasn't supposed to during these sessions. And second, because he wasn't Sliro.

Jaylen had sunk back into his chair, the hazy filter of inebriation grounded in enough sensibility to pause him.

For a moment.

"Ugh," he'd groaned. "We'll figure this out *after* this job. Okay? Endee, make a note of that. 'Figure this out after this job.' That's an official decree of the captain of the *Successor*."

Normally, he had ND-5 archive these recordings to restricted storage under Security Protocol Brencoyle. He told himself that the recordings were intended for Sliro if they ever met again, a sort of audio tapestry of Jaylen's unlikely journey through the seedy underworld of the galaxy. But just like their talks as children, merely speaking aloud somehow released things for him in a way that nothing else could.

But this time, talking through this feeling accomplished nothing for him. He didn't feel better. He didn't get a sense of release. He just *was*, which was a first. And with his thoughts stewing in that strange empty void, he clung to the only thing that seemed to remain: completing the job, getting paid, living to go on another day.

That led to him saying, "Endee, delete this recording."

He really, really shouldn't have done that.

ND-5 didn't act at the command. And that caused Jaylen to growl the command again. "Endee, I said delete this recording. No restricted data storage this time."

"I cannot right now." ND-5 tapped at his chest plate. "Our constant repairs have not allowed for enough downtime to run a full storage optimization process. The recording is writing into memory block B4 slower than usual. You will have to wait."

Jaylen should have been patient. If he hadn't drunk so much of the Quill, impulse control would have been simple. He was, after all, becoming pretty good at planning things out, and part of making a plan was *not* giving in to impulses.

But Dorian Quill easily overruled that. In that moment, the droid's calm, mechanized words, albeit temporarily aided by chemicals, broke something in Jaylen. "Ah," he yelled, a lone grunt slurring into something much greater, "delete all of it."

"Delete all of what?"

"Memory block whatever!" he yelled as he took down the remaining liquid in a fast gulp, so much that he spit dribbles of it out.

"Memory block B4," ND-5 said, and the steadiness of the droid's tone acted like an accelerant to Jaylen's already volatile mood. "This is a risky decision. Are you certain you want to—"

"B4! *B* whatever! It doesn't matter! Delete all of it and go nap in your charger for all I care! Get rid of it, get rid of Barsha, get rid of Sliro and all the whining and all the stupid time I've wasted. Tomorrow is a new day. Tomorrow"—he held up the now-empty bottle—"is Andara. Tomorrow, we make *decisions*. Tomorrow, we take *control*."

ND-5's head tilted for a moment before resetting.

"Done," the droid said.

After that, Jaylen collapsed into a chair, the Dorian Quill flowing into his bloodstream in the most blissfully insidious way. He'd passed out, the kind of blank sleep that did more harm than good, and when he came to, he didn't remember the details of what he'd done—until just now, the massive headache of his hangover giving way to one that was astronomically worse.

Now, with ND-5 searching for pilots in the other room, Jaylen loaded a map of Andara. But it wasn't just the location. Jaylen needed a museum schedule, he needed a visitor log, he needed a requisition contract for a very specific craft at a nearby shipyard, he needed his list of contingencies.

All of it, evaporated.

Once again, the Barsha side of Jaylen took his plans away.

Jaylen looked at the chrono. Now nineteen hours remained before Fennec Shand and Lorel Amberdine would arrive. By then, they needed a pilot—and a comprehensive strategy for pulling this off.

Jaylen ambled to the cockpit of the *Successor,* his head stinging as he eased into the copilot's chair. The ship sat, seconds ticking away as it parked outside of West Allscot on Dargulli, one of the few places in the sector that allowed landing without registration clearance or records. This would be Jaylen's second job this year with Lorel, the first with Fennec.

Fennec represented Jaylen's perfect type of partner: clearly skilled, impeccable track record. But she was becoming increasingly hard to book. That was why Jaylen had offered a little something extra in addition to her going rate—he wanted to get on her preferred list ahead of everyone else. She was an *investment,* and for this mission especially, her rifle and her marksmanship would prove to be a guarantee of a safe outcome—or as close to an assurance as possible.

If they intercepted everything from Bischt Renner's ISB information transfer, everything would change. He'd finally be on top. A self-made survivor coming into his own, *despite* his own apparent attempt at self-sabotage.

He'd come this far. He couldn't mess this up.

Jaylen knelt over the technical station in the captain's quarters. He punched several buttons, and an image of Andara came on-screen.

Time to get started.

Again.

CHAPTER 18

In the past five hours, ND-5 had reached out to seven pilots, all within rendezvous range of the *Successor*. And, just as Jaylen feared, none of them could drop everything and get there on time.

The *on time* part was essential—because for the job at Andara, timing was absolutely crucial. For starters, it involved a specifically scheduled event: a parade of historic ships, part of the opening day festivities for the newly commissioned Museum of Engineering and Lightspeed.

Getting their own historic Separatist craft into the parade would require flying the ship into the tail end of the automated parade route while avoiding detection or disturbing the programmed flight path of the other ships. To accomplish that, they still had to go to their contact's shipyard, pick up a *Sheathipede*-class shuttle, get the craft packed with the necessary gear, and make their way to the museum. And all *that* meant executing everything flawlessly.

Except things did not start flawlessly.

Any early outreach Jaylen had done a week ago no longer mattered. His entire list of pilots had moved on since Jaylen and ND-5 missed their contact window. The only one who was available had no means of getting to Andara in time.

Jaylen looked at the datapad in his hands. For his part, he'd patched together a workable summation of his lost plans: a combination of message logs, scattered notes, and the broad strokes he could recall. This type of organization and attention to detail was what the Barsha execs had tried to instill in him during those years of training. In the boardroom, their words had sounded like an overwhelming amount of business terminology with little substance. Yet after years on his own, he'd actually started to understand what it all meant: see the bigger picture, create a path from start to finish, utilize the assets at hand, and put the right people in place.

Like sliding dejarik pieces into place.

It just took *experience* for him to actually get it. That was the part Barsha would have missed out on with him as CEO.

A large *clang* caught Jaylen's attention, and he now turned to ND-5 as the droid's silhouette paused in the hallway. ND-5 knelt and rustled something out of weapons storage, his massive dark green duster jacket obscuring the details. In short, efficient moves, the droid pulled out a piece of hardware with his left hand, then closed the storage container with his right. Item still in hand, he walked over to the comm station and tapped several buttons, and while that screen scrolled text, he picked up a datapad.

Jaylen could never imagine the life of a straight-up bounty hunter—all the combat, sneaking, *climbing,* and things like that. But that was why he kept ND-5 around. ND-5 did the dirty work—he was faster, more precise, and more lethal than any organic could have been.

"Jaylen," ND-5 said. "I am reaching out to the next pilot on the list: Kreden Varec of the light haulcraft *Starcat.* I hope to have resolution soon."

Jaylen flashed a thumbs-up, though their options were running low.

"In parallel, I am analyzing the publicly noted schedules associated with the museum's celebration against distances of various key locations. This will establish the best windows of action." The comm station beeped, and ND-5 checked its report. "It appears I will have to move on from Kreden Varec. She sends her regrets: 'My schedule just filled up, sorry.' "

"Another one off the list," Jaylen grumbled to himself.

"This is an appropriate time to remind you that I excel at Confederacy of Independent System hardware, including *Sheathipede*-class shuttles."

The droid continued his tasks, switching attention from the comm station to the technical station to whatever he was repairing in his hand, all moving like the request was as basic as someone asking for the refresher. Perhaps it *was*. Most of the time, ND-5 served as a steady companion that moved with a droid's cold efficiency—and with programming for infiltration and assassination. And he accomplished all that without needing the skills Jaylen marked as off-limits years ago.

"Hold on," Jaylen said, and he went to a storage crate shoved into the closet of his quarters. He rattled through a collection of spare parts and random things accumulated over the years: an arm brace he'd used several years ago, identicards from old missions, a breathing mask from the one time they went to Quesh. Tucked sideways sat a datapad, and as Jaylen powered it up, he saw that it remained at 44 percent power.

He walked back into the center area, where ND-5 now sat at the comm station. "Remember this?" he asked.

"That is the datapad from Obills Myron on Nar Shaddaa. I have seen this before."

Which was true. It *was* the physical datapad that Obills gave Jaylen, though Jaylen had deleted the original repair report and made his own notes for whenever this conversation popped up. "Just a reminder in case you forgot," Jaylen said.

"I have retained complex assault and infiltration plans involving hundreds of battle droids of varying abilities. A single datapad is easy for me to retain. I don't need a 'reminder.' "

"Okay, then," Jaylen said, still holding the datapad. He supposed ND-5 was right and *any* datapad could be a prop for this exercise. "State the list of skills you're not allowed to use."

"Deceptive conversation. Clone trooper voice mimicry. Bee-One battle droid group tactics. CIS craft piloting. CIS craft repair—"

Jaylen put up a hand to pause ND-5. This conversation popped up every six months or so, with variations on the same themes and thoughts. A repeat performance to protect Jaylen Barsha, when the Barshas—Jaylen and otherwise—moved ever closer to irrelevance.

Time was funny that way.

Jaylen had even emphasized getting a pilot in place for this mission just to avoid this tired routine. As they went through the motions again, Jaylen once more considered whether it was actually worth the effort.

For now, though, Jaylen played it out. He needed to be in control. With so many unknowns and such potential with the mission's final prize, he couldn't afford not to be. "Okay, *I* need a reminder then. What could happen if you access those skills?"

"I might shut down. I might kill you. I might experience a memory wipe and revert back to my default state."

"Everything you've learned over the past nine years, just *gone*." That wasn't true on a literal level, though sometimes Jaylen told himself that it was the metaphorical truth, given how they'd come this far with Jaylen exercising precise control over the droid's moves, actions, and thoughts.

"That is a significant risk. However, there has been no definitive evidence of—"

"Think about it. Really think about it. Every single experience, every single meeting, every single moment that we've been together, just"—he snapped his fingers—"evaporated due to faulty tech. Do you really want to chance that?"

ND-5 continued tapping away at the comm station, showing a remarkable ability to wrestle through existential discussions while also looking for pilots. Jaylen once read about how droids had no true sense of happiness, though they strived to fulfill their protocols as efficiently as possible, and to them, that was kind of the same thing. Was ND-5 pondering that before responding? Or had he silently reverted to a complete focus on the pilot search while staying within Jaylen's given parameters?

Though if ND-5 was compliant now, that meant this conversation would repeat at some point. It seemed inevitable. And that led to another recurring concern deep in Jaylen's thoughts: How would ND-5 react if the droid ever discovered Jaylen had lied to him for years?

Jaylen had tried to get ahead of this by discreetly asking a few droidsmiths over the years. No one gave him a straight answer. That wasn't exactly reassuring. Though each person he consulted had suggested gradually removing ND-5's restrictions. And that would take some planning, given the layers of cover stories he'd need to—

At the comm station, the monitor flashed and beeped, and ND-5 turned his head to take in the oncoming message. "Transmission incoming from Fennec Shand. Decoding it through the atmospheric interference." The comm station beeped again. "Message received. It says, 'I got a lead on a pilot.' That is all."

Jaylen shook his head at the timing. "Lucky us."

"Luck is a human construct."

Fennec Shand was already justifying her high price. Sniper, mercenary, *and* resolver of problems stemming from indulging too much. Maybe after this heist, they could address granting ND-5 greater freedom. Maybe then, Jaylen Barsha could finally fade away.

But for now, they had a job to do.

"Great timing. Tell her, 'Thank you,' " he said, almost to himself as much as ND-5. "Focus on the schedule. We'll need precise timing. And we have to coordinate the shuttle pickup. No time to waste."

FENNEC SHAND ARRIVED earlier than expected. She walked up the loading bay ramp, sniper rifle on her back and rain dripping off the helmet on her head. ND-5 greeted her with a simple "hello" and neither of them said anything further until she marched into the ship's central area and sat down.

Jaylen turned from the technical station to wave. The first key member of this crew was here, and despite the rocky start, his plans were coming together—no buyer, no bounty, no contract. Just his team, built with careful consideration, following a tip for a *big* score. And the result would propel his reputation throughout the galaxy.

He was in charge. *He* made this happen. In a way that was much more *real,* more earned than being CEO of his family's corporation could ever be.

"Fennec. Glad you could make it." She nodded and removed her helmet, her twisting braid falling over her right shoulder. She put her wet boots up on his table without asking, but he let it slide. Jaylen approached. "Is your pilot far behind?"

"What are you talking about?" she asked with a brow furrowed over the scar on her left cheek.

"The lead you mentioned." Jaylen told himself to keep his voice calm and steady, even though his insides felt like he'd been shocked by an ion blast. "Your pilot?"

"Didn't you get my last transmission?"

Jaylen turned to the comm station. About twenty minutes ago, a long-range transmission from Fennec was received.

Problem was, it was sent hours earlier. This was why the long-range transmitter was on ND-5's fix-it list. They'd docked at Dargulli to maintain secrecy during planning, but Jaylen had failed to consider just how much the planet's storms might interfere with communications.

Despite being in front of Fennec, his guard slipped. "Not this again."

"Sorry about that," she said in a tone that carried more politeness than caring. "Lead fizzled out at the last minute. Your budget wasn't big enough."

"We don't get paid if we don't get a pilot," Jaylen said. Which he immediately knew was a mistake.

"Uh-uh," Fennec said. "*You* don't get paid if we don't get a pilot. I get paid no matter what. You wanted this here." She tapped the stock of her sniper rifle. "It comes with certain guarantees. And a penalty if you don't deliver on your promises."

She was right, of course. "Your promises" was a caveat about the mission, and he definitely didn't want to get on a sniper's bad side. Beyond the traditional agreements of business, the important people should always get paid—Jaylen had learned that very early on as a Barsha. It was a lesson Roisem instilled in him as he tried to understand why she would skim on tipping for deliveries but would frequently lavish goods on the family shuttle's repair crew. "*Make sure to cover the ones who could hurt you,*" she'd said at the time. "*The others can fend for themselves.*"

Quite a lesson for a seven-year-old. Though, much like the lesson about saying something or staying quiet, it stuck with him decades later.

And Fennec Shand could absolutely hurt him. So she was right—no matter what, she was getting paid. But Jaylen and ND-5? That would depend on whether they pulled this off.

"Hey, big guy!" A new voice came from the loading area, and Jaylen excused himself from Fennec—to greet the other member of their crew and to ponder what options they had left.

Jaylen crossed the hallway into the loading bay, where Lorel Amberdine walked over to ND-5. She brushed rain off her sleeves before punching him in the shoulder, and Jaylen half expected the droid to enter a defensive posture.

Instead, he straightened from sealing a large storage crate—a droid's form of social greeting. "Ow," Lorel said, shaking her hand. "Never punch a droid. Especially one with combat plating. Well, how is my favorite commando droid?"

"Do you know any other commando droids?" ND-5 asked.

Lorel ran a hand through her long brown curls. "Well, there is that bartender on Exodeen. Says, 'Roger roger,' with every order," she said, mimicking a battle droid's mechanized cadence. "Can't help itself. So between you and that droid, I pick you."

"I'm flattered."

Lorel's broad pale cheeks rose with a grin. "Really?"

"No. I do not have emotions." ND-5 closed up the crate and tapped its side to check its repulsor capabilities. The crate rose and then landed back down, and ND-5 started walking Jaylen's way. "It is nice to see you again, Lorel."

Lorel adjusted the large backpack over her shoulders. "I'm gonna take that at face value." She waved to Jaylen, and he motioned them inside. ND-5 marched in first and stood opposite Fennec. Lorel ambled in, though her smile dropped once she looked around the room. "Why's everyone so glum?"

"Not my problem," Fennec said as she started to clean the muzzle of her rifle with a cloth.

"Well," Jaylen said, rubbing his goatee, "we're down a pilot."

The floor plating clanged as Lorel set her large backpack down.

"We're by a settlement. Pilots are always lingering around. Let's just go hire someone. Fly in, drop off, fly out. Not like we're flying through an asteroid field. I thought this was a gala we were breaking into?"

"It's a little more than that." Jaylen glanced down at the datapad in his hand. "Sorry to make you wait on the details."

"The level of secrecy was my suggestion," Fennec said. "It's a valuable target. And we need to avoid Imperial detection of any kind. I asked specifically that we keep some of the details for face-to-face discussion."

"For good reason." Jaylen didn't let Lorel know that it was costing them extra for Fennec to work with their vague notes—even if that suggestion came from herself. "Because we're going after a cover list of Imperial operatives." In addition, Fennec had noted that she wanted a certain name off the list in addition to her payment—and absolute silence on the rest of the details until mission launch. Jaylen commended her sharp foresight, a way to keep herself several degrees removed from Imperial liability should anything go south during mission prep.

Lorel looked over at ND-5, then her backpack, then back at Jaylen.

"This starts with a shuttle—a *Sheathipede*-class shuttle from the war. It has to be flown in precise formation," Jaylen said as he looked at Fennec. "That's why my pilot requirements were so targeted."

They sat in silence for several seconds. Which, Jaylen supposed, was several seconds that they really didn't have. ND-5 didn't move. Fennec pursed her lips in thought.

Finally, Lorel slowly raised a hand. They looked at each other until Jaylen realized that she was waiting for a signal. "Lorel?"

"Sorry. I thought you were going to explain more about the mission," she said, a flush coming to her face. "Aren't we missing the obvious here?" The fingers of her raised hand curled into a ball, leaving a thumb sticking out, and she pointed that at ND-5. "Big guy's a Sep, right?"

"I do not have any current political affiliation."

"You know what I mean."

Jaylen *did* know what she meant. And they really didn't need to go there. Not yet.

"We've got a lot of prep work still," Jaylen said. "I can find an alternate—"

"I mean, not, like, *currently* a Separatist," she said with a chuckle. "But you fought in the war?"

ND-5 continued to stay still, arms at his side. "My original purpose was to fight for the Confederacy of Independent Systems."

Jaylen gave everyone a polite smile that was the opposite of what he felt inside. "We'll find another way. I need Endee's support on the ground."

"This seems like a really important piece." Lorel wrinkled her nose at the thought. "No pilot, no heist, right?"

"Jaylen, as I suggested earlier, perhaps now would be a good time to assess my dormant abilities."

Jaylen had told himself that he'd consider all this *later,* once the cover list was in hand—once Jaylen Barsha really was put to rest. And after he got further input from a droidsmith to predict ND-5's reaction to years of lying. Discussing it now caused a creeping tension from head to toe, all coming together in a big knot in his chest. Even *thinking* about ND-5 without any restrictions . . .

Nnytyl's voice yelled in his memory.

Then came the blasterfire.

No. Not right now. "It's dangerous—" he started before Lorel threw open her backpack and started digging around.

"I've got my slice kit right here. Lemme check his processor status." Before Jaylen could stop anyone, Lorel activated a square handheld device and started tapping away. "Hold on, Endee. This won't hurt one bit."

"Are we going or not?" Fennec asked.

No one answered. Instead, Lorel tapped away on the slice kit. "Yep. Can confirm, default Sep programs are still there. Restraining bolt is causing interference with my tools. Probably because of his fancy security protocols. If you pop off the restraining bolt, I can check for execution capabilities."

"Thing is . . ." Jaylen huffed, trying to sort out the web of fabrications he'd crafted over the years. Talking with ND-5 about this from time to time was one thing; being put on the spot with a new crew watching—that was completely different and *not* something he'd prepared for. "He was damaged nine years ago. Big explosion. There's a chip fused to his neural core. A droidsmith told us to keep the bolt on, and she warned us about what programming to avoid. Could really damage Endee. I've got this datapad in the back—"

Lorel's laugh filled the space, and she shook her head, the same wide grin coming back. "Oh, droidsmiths. They *love* to tell you anything to get your business. Easiest way for them to make money. That all sounds like classic droidsmith nerf spit to me. I'll check the restraining bolt's programming. One second."

While Lorel looked at her datapad, another memory came to Jaylen, this one from Brencoyle: "*Sometimes, the easiest choices are the ones made for us.*"

This choice had been made for him the moment Lorel spoke up. If she analyzed the bolt's specifics further, ND-5 would learn about Jaylen's lies. To keep any of his cover story, Jaylen would have to take back control of the situation before more contradictions surfaced.

Though at least this would resolve the pilot issue. As long as Jaylen played it the right way.

Jaylen grabbed a small tool off the workbench and snapped the restraining bolt off. In one very conscious gesture, he winced like he was expecting ND-5 to kill him on the spot. Then he slowly backed away. "Hey, Endee, how do you feel?"

"I am still myself. And show no signs of being a risk to—"

"What are you seeing?" Jaylen asked Lorel before ND-5 could say things that stirred more questions.

"I mean, I'm no expert," Lorel said, holding up her slice kit. "But his internal diagnostics look good." She turned to ND-5. "You mind if I take a closer peek?"

"As long as Jaylen approves."

Now everyone looked at Jaylen. And Jaylen looked at the restraining bolt in his hand. "I don't think we know what to expect. This is uncharted territory for all of us."

"If there's a risk to the mission," Fennec said, "we should know now and assess."

Jaylen turned back to the technical station, arms planted as he stared at the screen, though he needed only one piece of information on the display: the time.

They needed to pick up the shuttle in four hours. And from there, they had to go straight to the site. With prep and a dry-run review of the plan, they didn't have much time—and they didn't have another option.

"I'm going to put my faith in Endee. He's never let me down. If he feels good now, then that's good enough for me," Jaylen said, a purposeful confidence in the words. The more he thought about it, he realized he could turn this into an advantage.

Having ND-5 pilot the shuttle was one less person to pay, after all.

"Endee, we'll talk more about the restraining bolt after this mission. For now, review your programming for anything related to *Sheathipede*-class shuttles. The rest of us need to go over the details of how we're gonna pull this off." Jaylen then walked over to Lorel and held out the restraining bolt. "Keep this safe until this is all over, okay?"

"Sure thing," she said, grabbing the small cylinder. "Hey, Endee, how do you feel now that you're naked?"

"I am wearing my usual coat."

Lorel shook her head and sighed as she looked at the slice kit's screen. "Either my jokes are bad or droids don't get humor." She chuckled. "I'm going with the latter."

CHAPTER 19

Protocol B.7.21: standardized ground procedures for pre-launch safety and diagnostics *Sheathipede*-class shuttle.

For years, this protocol and others noted by Jaylen's droidsmith report as "visible, not accessible" have sat untouched within my memory banks. I have kept each protocol like this under internal safeguards to eliminate the potentially catastrophic risk of access—risk to myself or Jaylen.

On several occasions, I have suggested to Jaylen that we create controlled circumstances to activate each of these protocols. Each time, he responds by mapping out various steps for testing. However, our timing is quite unfortunate. Something always comes up to interrupt the process.

Seven months ago, Jaylen went as far as to set up a situation where I was weaponless in the *Successor*'s cargo bay. The plan was for Jaylen to remove the bolt with a long shaft, then immediately jump on an idling speeder and put a distance of twenty meters between us to see if my dormant protocol for assassination emerged.

Yet, thirty minutes before our scheduled start, Jaylen said an urgent message came in and we needed to refocus our priorities.

We did not resume the test.

This time, however, the test will certainly happen. And it will happen on a mission, with no constraints or cautionary parameters.

I have observed that organic relationships require a certain level of risk to maintain their levels of commitment. Similarly, Jaylen has stated many times that there is an inherent risk in attempting to test my limits without the restraining bolt. Doing so may create an inadvertent memory wipe and reset. However, I am in agreement that this next step forward is worth the risk.

During the war, my priority was mission fulfillment regardless of damage or losses to droid units. As Jaylen is my only priority now, improved cooperation and trust better achieves our goals. Knowing that my unused protocols may possibly be fulfilled without consequence creates a significant leap forward in my role as Jaylen's partner.

For now, I follow Jaylen to the manager of a shipyard on Mechis III. Beside me is Lorel, and floating behind us is a large crate of supplies—approximately twice the size of most storage crates, as I've taken the initiative to prepare several contingencies. Further behind is Fennec, who is much less sociable than Lorel. Jaylen gets into a deep conversation with the manager, the two of them poring over a datapad. In between lies a *Sheathipede*-class shuttle with visible combat damage and carbon scoring on the port side. It sits upon four docking legs, and its single tall fin casts a shadow over the open cargo door. I check the size of our equipment crate and confirm that it will maximize the space in the ship's small bay. I turn back to Jaylen and the manager.

Knowing Jaylen, this discussion is about credits. Haggling is not part of my skill set. Instead, I review the key parts of Protocol B.7.21.

"Does that ship feel like old times?" Lorel asks as we stand here.

"'Old times' is something organic beings experience. Your decisions are influenced by your nostalgia. Jaylen endures this," I say. "However, when I utilize my original programming, my neural processor activates what you might consider a sense of fulfillment. Now that the war is over, I am uncertain if I'll ever return to that state completely." I turn to Lorel, and she gives me a clear, aware look. "Are you confused?"

"Actually," she says, stretching her arms overhead, "I was just making small talk."

"Talk is neither small nor large."

"I mean, like, talking about things that don't really matter so we don't have uncomfortable silences." A strange look comes over her face, like "small talk" is a thing droids do. Perhaps protocol droids do, but certainly not commando droids.

"Jaylen and I do not engage in small talk. Or endure uncomfortable silences. Our discussions always have purpose."

"Well, see then . . ." She makes a fist and starts to toss a friendly punch toward my shoulder. She then reconsiders. "I'm glad." Her palm lands lightly on my shoulder instead. It rests on the fabric of my duster.

I assume the action, like her near assault, is done out of jest and not an attempt at overpowering me. So I do not retaliate.

"I mean, I'm glad I could help today," she says, her hand still resting there.

"Yes. You are helping." I turn to her. "You are confirming that being without my restraining bolt has not unleashed uncontrolled impulses."

Her face turns to a puzzled look. "How am I confirming that?"

"If my previous programming took over, your arm would not be attached to your torso right now, and Jaylen would be dead."

"Okay, then," she says with a nod. "Thanks for not doing that."

"You are welcome." As I say that, Jaylen breaks away, a wide smile across his face. That smile likely means successful negotiations. This bodes well for our mission. My internal sensors process his distance, from his starting point of approximately twenty meters away. He approaches, closer and closer to shave the distance down. He pauses at about three meters from me to tap the newly painted hull of the ship.

Another milestone has passed. Jaylen has removed himself from my presence and returned, yet I have no urge to murder him upon proximity.

Jaylen whistles, grabbing Fennec's attention from across the space. She slings her gear over her shoulder and approaches. Jaylen watches as Lorel goes in the open loading ramp, a bemused look on her face. Fennec paces shortly after Lorel with a constant neutral expression.

"Hey," Jaylen says as he pats my shoulder. His touch is heavier than when Lorel did the same thing. "We're going to do this."

"Yes," I say, pointing to the floating storage crate behind us. "I will load our supplies."

Each step in Jaylen's plan is carefully listed out in my internal processors.

Step one: Acquire the *Sheathipede*-class shuttle. Done.

Step two: Safely run start-up sequence and diagnostics on the CIS craft, in addition to installing rear sensors to help maintain flight path and distance. Done. I make a note here that the opportunity to kill Jaylen came and went without any problems.

Step three: Fly to Andara, drop off Fennec Shand at an appropriate sniper point to provide coverage for Jaylen as he impersonates Bischt Renner under the code name Sun Racket. Prepare Lorel's remote L0 droid to work with Jaylen. Drop Jaylen off within walking distance to the Museum of Engineering and Lightspeed—the site of the evening's gala. Done.

Step four: With myself and Lorel in the cockpit, maneuver the craft adjacent to the docking bay where the automated historical crafts will be launched. Wait until the final craft launches, then maneuver behind it. Stay in tight formation, following precise cues from the automated parade route while Lorel remotely slices into the parade data to include our ship in the public notes.

Done.

The success of the mission hinges on two things. First, Lorel's reconfigured L0 droid—essentially a child's toy that appears like a flying disc, but overhauled by Lorel to be her distance slicing kit via a data transceiver and an aftermarket scomp link. Without this droid properly accessing maintenance and security networks, things will end quickly.

Second, Jaylen's ability to blend in with the upper tier of society. This seems likely given his history, though humans tend to forget things quickly. I give Jaylen a 77 percent chance of success.

I do not tell him that.

Despite Lorel's concerns, I am able to allocate more power to the shuttle's transponder, which then connects to her L0 droid. "Good thing there's so much media here," she says, and she exploits the different broadcast transmissions to strengthen her data connection to the droid. She has a datapad propped up to show the L0 droid's perspective; in her hand is a small unit capable of physically controlling the droid.

Much like the caller unit of a restraining bolt. However, this appears to have the opposite purpose. Rather than call a restrained droid back to its master, Lorel's controller deploys the droid out into the world so they can work together.

"Give me five percent more power to the transponder," she says.

I comply by taking power off the ship's long-range sensors, which are not needed here anyway.

"Okay. Got it. Hello, Lumi, we're connected." Lumi must be her nickname for her L0 droid. It does not make sense phonetically. "Jaylen, I've got perfect remote access to Lumi. As long as the media keeps covering this event, I've got plenty of data streams to look at." She turns to me. "Thanks, Endee. You're a sweetie."

I do not know what her last word means. Jaylen has never used that term before. Internally, I look up the definition of the term and determine it has reasonable accuracy.

"I am," I reply. The way we work together is reminiscent of when I was previously deployed with another BX commando droid who had complementary skill sets. Except no other BX commando droid I encountered laughed at their own jokes like Lorel does.

Fennec's voice pops through over our linked comm system. "I'm in position," she says. Between myself and Lorel is a floating holomap of the museum and its surroundings, a blinking purple dot on top of a nearby high-rise indicating Fennec's sniping position.

Adjacent to it, but far lower on the ground level, Jaylen's blinking green dot moves toward the entrance. "I'm about fifty meters away," Jaylen says.

I zoom the map out until it shows a larger view of the entire region: an island recently developed into a sector for commerce about three kilometers off the nearest shore. A cluster of skyscrapers form a perimeter around the island, with a shorter multi-level structure in the center, its top level filled with several angled floors for additional viewing and seating. As a whole, it is not that dissimilar to the central governmental region of Coruscant, with the Senate building and its neighboring districts. Here, the districts lie in concentric circles that repeat outwardly until the island's edge, which has been formed into one large circular beach with resort hotels.

A line appears in the map to illustrate the parade route's path as it weaves in and out between buildings, all in a larger loop that flies by the museum building. Given the number of VIPs and statesmen at the gala, security is tight. Lorel connects the ship to a local satellite-powered security feed covering the event from airborne, ground-level, and in-the-building perspectives. My job is to use my established knowledge of Separatist craft to mimic the automated parade route as much as possible while providing a floating communications hub between all of us. I must also maintain proximity for Lorel to execute the rest of the plan's steps.

"Security's tight here," Jaylen says. "It's not Imperials. All private and local. This is a pretty big deal. The only Imperial presence here appears to be guests of honor."

Though I cannot see Jaylen right now, I hear his relaxed tone of voice. This must mean that his disguise of tailored blue trousers, high black boots, a white coat with black lapels, and a purple neckerchief are helping him pass as Bischt Renner, including the earpiece disguised as a bit of ornamental jewelry. He had remarked that he'd worn similar attire for Barsha Corp functions, and that "I know exactly how to act at these things." He'd even flashed a very sudden grin at that claim, and I could not discern if that was his own internal amusement or if he was demonstrating his performance.

"I saw all sorts of holonet chatter about this," Lorel says. " 'The first public inclusion of crafts from the Clone Wars in a parade,' and all that. But locally, they're saying it's supposed to put Andara back on tourism lists."

"It is strange that populations would want to commemorate a war that spawned because of unrest and greed," I say. Internally, I track the distance, speed, and vector of the parade ship in front of me. "I have set acceptable tolerances for flight path deviation based on analysis of the craft ahead of us. The shifts appear to be adjustments to environmental factors rather than evasive maneuvers. As long as I stay within appropriate ranges for speed and distance, security should not detect an issue."

Lorel does not say anything. Instead, she simply looks at me. I turn my head, not because I need her within my field of vision, but because it is the polite thing to do. "Is there a problem?"

"Doesn't sound like it," she says, pointing to the ship's dashboard. "I just don't work with commando droids a lot. Do you all switch between statements on morality and mission statistics so easily?"

"They are both relevant to our location," I say.

Lorel's datapad chirps several times. "I tapped into an internal security broadcast feed from the museum to the nearby Imperial office. It's being used to evaluate VIPs as they enter. You know, top secret VIPs." She says the phrase *top secret* slow and low, as if it carries additional meaning. I turn to see a record with Jaylen's image and text below it.

A *false* record. One that she planted several days ago as part of her mission prep.

That would enable the next steps: Jaylen would infiltrate the gala and go to the roof, where Sun Racket was supposed to meet an operative code-named Impossible Song. Assuming Jaylen's impersonation of Bischt Renner is successful, Lorel would use her L0 droid to disrupt the roof's security holocams. She would also upload a false maintenance alert about a gas leak on the roof. Jaylen would take the datapad offered by Imperial Song and use a device provided by Lorel to capture its data while circumventing Imperial security protocols. Fennec would take Impossible Song out. After Jaylen has left, Fennec would then shoot the gas line to cause a rooftop explosion, which would burn all evidence and destroy any links between Jaylen and the cover list.

From there, I have several options for gathering Jaylen and Fennec before returning to the *Successor* on the mainland. The path forward would depend on how different variables play out, including crowd reaction to the fire, Jaylen's physical status, and incoming emergency and security vehicles.

"Final check. I'm at the entrance," Jaylen says. "Everyone in position?"

"I've got line of sight to the roof," Fennec says over the comm. "Gas lines marked in my scope."

"Lumi has full connection. Just get it near the maintenance room and I'll do the rest," Lorel says.

"Flight path is steady. Transmission connections are stable. Security is quiet," I say. I check a datapad propped on the dashboard. It blinks with an active status for transponder ID 2725PM816, which Jaylen keeps in his boot on missions. "Personal transponder tracking."

Lorel turns to me as I say that, a quick smile followed by a thumbs-up. I respond with a nod. She keeps shaking her thumb at me and does not stop until I return her thumbs-up and reply, "We are ready."

CHAPTER 20

Jaylen took a mental note that at this exact moment, he was *exactly* where he needed to be—for who he was right now.

Late afternoon. The Andara sun just starting its descent. All around him stood well-dressed people of influence or wealth or power or some combination of all those things. Drinks, appetizers, the clearly false laughter of the bored but committed. At a distant range, a sniper watched over the building, ND-5 flew a ship in stealth, and Lorel tapped into security for any signs of concern.

He moved forward, the easy smile he'd learned to adopt so long ago now masking his eyes, peeled and aware, as they scanned his surroundings.

When first arriving, he'd wandered close to the museum's maintenance area, where he'd dropped off Lorel's droid. She took over, activating its hover and walk capabilities to break into a back-room data center. Whatever happened after that, he left to trust. He soon joined the gala, getting a drink and an appetizer while greeting any passing guest. He'd been here for an hour now, moving constantly to avoid drawing attention.

Most importantly, he looked like he *belonged*—because, really, he did. No matter the industry, galas were always the same—the privileged and the overprivileged, socialites who wanted to be seen and industry leaders who needed to be seen but hated being there. The confluence of money, fine clothing, and entitlement was exactly what he had been accustomed to as both a child and a CEO-in-training.

Which allowed his instincts to serve him well, letting him blend in as he scouted for exit paths, security issues, the possibility of other covert overachievers seeking out their prize.

But everything passed checks. And the time had come.

Jaylen made his way to a lift on one side of the museum's north wing—no one else waited for it, they were too busy looking at displayed exhibits or out the large windows at the ongoing parade. Lights trailed through the door panel's gap until it arrived on Jaylen's floor. A polite chime rang out, and the door slid open to reveal a person.

No. Not just a person. A CEO of a Corellian manufacturing company. Which surprised Jaylen at first, given that this seemed to be an event for historians, academics, and fundraisers. But then he put it together: Even though this wasn't an industry conference, it featured this company's hardware. They might have even been a sponsor.

Jaylen paused, struggling to place her face. She represented one of Barsha's biggest subcontractors, a piece of the legitimate side of the business. In fact, they'd been in meetings together. Jaylen didn't *say* anything during these meetings, but he was there—in particular, he remembered that about halfway through the war, she gave a presentation at Barsha Tower about the next evolution of sublight drives, with a clear emphasis on how the rapid-acceleration tech could integrate into both Republic and CIS ships. "Business," she had said, her face aglow from a holographic schematic open before her, "operates on all sides of the galaxy. And all sides of the galaxy will continue to exist after this war is over."

The very sight of her jarred Jaylen into a split-second freeze, his mind drifting through the hows and whys of their previous interactions—and that split-second freeze was all the time she needed to lock eyes with him.

Suddenly, he feared that all the effort to go unnoticed, to blend in and see this massive opportunity through, had evaporated. They stared at each other, her face unreadable. And for all the ways he'd tried to change who he was, he suddenly felt like that post-grad kid again, seated among the older, wiser, more experienced adults, half wanting to impress people and half not really caring about their boring discussions.

"Oh," she said, her head tilting.

Only a few seconds had passed since the turbolift's arrival, yet sweat started to form across the top of his brow, a tension seized his shoulders, and his breath halted.

What might the Empire do if they found out he was still alive?

"Excuse me," she finally said, then turned to the man behind her. "So the largest ship in the parade, that model actually acted as the pilot program for our propulsion assembly. It didn't fit at first, and our engineers had to . . ."

Her voice drifted away as she sauntered off, and just as quickly as panic hit him, relief washed over. He exhaled, and recentered himself on this moment, this mission. Within a blink everything seemed brighter, sharper. Ahead of him, the turbolift doors remained open. Someone brushed past and stepped in. The man turned, pressed a button, and then gave him a tilted look. "You coming?"

THE TURBOLIFT TOOK him up ten floors past the reception mezzanine, restaurant floors, and multiple exhibition halls. From there, Lorel's droid remotely opened up access to the museum's operations floor, where offices and cubicles sat mostly empty. Jaylen marched quickly and with purpose, eyes trained on his destination as the occasional murmuring voice or button *clack* came through in the background. Deconstructed ship cross sections and maps of historical hyperspace routes lined the walls as he moved until he reached a stark industrial stairwell, where he walked up another five flights of stairs. "One second," Lorel said into his tiny earpiece. "Got some unexpected fluctuation in the encryption. Hold on."

Far below him, the sound of a large metal door opened and closed, followed by voices that faded away.

"System's suddenly in a bad mood," Lorel said. "I'm getting through it."

"Time check, Jaylen," ND-5 said. "You are due to meet Impossible Song in two minutes."

"I'm assuming a little professional courtesy will be extended," Jaylen said. "Given the way people are enjoying the drinks tonight." Both ND-5 and Lorel went silent, and Fennec—well, Fennec didn't say anything the entire time. Though given her reputation, Jaylen felt secure in the assumption that *not* hearing from the sniper meant that things were at status quo.

From the lower levels, another door opened and closed. Could this many people really be using the maintenance stairwell during an event like this? Maybe that CEO *had* recognized him and played it off. "Lorel, are there any signs of security alerts?"

"None of that. Just a stubborn maintenance door lock."

He would take her at her word for that. And in a few moments, possibly less, he'd know. But one more check came to mind, a way to see if the galaxy really had forgotten Jaylen Barsha. "Hey, Endee?"

"Yes, Jaylen."

"I'm just curious," he said slowly, seeking out a way to ask without mentioning the name *Barsha*. "Do you remember in the most recent set of news archives we got, was my face or name in any coverage? Specifically the trade journals for related industries. To make sure we've got no Imperial liabilities here."

"I will have to sort through the audit records in my memory banks. Is this a priority request?" ND-5 asked. Was that a hint of irritation in ND-5's voice? Could commando droids sound irritated? No. Protocol droids, sure. But droids built to fight clone soldiers? Their programs were built strictly for chain of command, yet Jaylen swore he started to hear hints of this poking through. "I should be using my resources to monitor the situation along the flight path to ensure our data connection is maximized for slicing and connectivity."

Or maybe they *could* cop an attitude and he'd never noticed before.

"Also," ND-5 said, "Lorel is sitting next to me."

Jaylen's crew had no idea about his past, but statements like that certainly wouldn't help temper any curiosity. He ignored the comment and decided *not* to say anything to Lorel or Fennec about it.

"Hey, no one wants to be tracked by the Empire, right?" he said with a laugh.

"You got that right," Lorel said. "About one minute remaining."

That put any possible suspicion to rest. For now, Jaylen just needed to know. "Endee, I'm just making sure no one will recognize me. In any capacity. We have a trail of contacts here, and the stakes are too high. Better to be safe so"—he chose his words carefully—"our history doesn't catch up to us."

ND-5 paused. "I see." Another pause. "I see. Yes, Jaylen, I understand. Processing."

ND-5 may have had some nascent programming for assassination, but he'd never be able to smooth talk his way out of a situation.

"No results listed in the last audit," ND-5 said. "You have successfully escaped detection, Imperial or otherwise. You do not have to worry about your past actions."

No results from the world of spacecraft manufacturing. Perhaps his absence from the news shouldn't have surprised him. He'd been a footnote in the history of his company, with textbooks and retrospectives focusing on Roisem and Nnytyl's business accomplishments or the company's engineering feats. Barsha Corp, it turned out, was remembered for its hardware more than its people.

This job, though, was the first time he'd crossed paths with that world, and in the case of the woman in the turbolift, even looked it in the eye. Between that and the years of unfruitful searching for Sliro, the family didn't really exist anymore. The galaxy had moved on, the Empire rolled over everything and everyone, and Jaylen Vrax belonged to a life of organized crime now.

There was a very strange, very unexpected comfort in that. Jaylen had looked at this mission as the opportunity to move beyond the Barsha name—and it had been.

A turbolift ride, of all things, had put Jaylen Barsha to rest. That was so mundane Roisem Barsha would have hated it. Which made Jaylen savor it even more.

"I've just about got it," Lorel said. "Mechanism unlocking." With that, the sound of whirs and clicks echoed through the metal stairwell, and the maintenance door finally slid open to reveal the Andaran dusk sky.

"Fennec?" Jaylen said into the comms.

"Got you covered, boss. Whenever you're ready."

Despite the ornate design and lush decor of the museum below, the roof was pure industrial functionality—it held exhaust vents, power generators, data antennas, and everything else that kept the facility running, hidden from public view. Jaylen squinted and surveyed the scene. No one was up here—not even security.

He was alone.

At the turbolift, Jaylen came face-to-face with his old life in the form of a rival CEO. But instead of pulling him back into being a Barsha, his past ignored him.

More than ignored him, in fact. It let him pass by—to here, where he could finally move ahead without any ties to the past or regrets, as if something finally approved of his choices.

Of course. Despite his pondering about letting the past be and what to do with ND-5, everything locked into place. He'd actually been ready, probably for far longer than he wanted to admit it. But Jaylen Barsha needed someone to give approval. He always did, as much as he tried to fight it.

And now that he had that approval, Jaylen *Vrax* would never need it again.

Funny how these moments all involved thresholds. Nine years ago, he had to step through a set of curtains to become CEO. Here, he planted one foot forward, exiting the maintenance stairwell and taking a step in the boots of Jaylen Vrax—and no one else.

CHAPTER 21

Lorel is talkative. I cannot tell if that is a nervous trait of hers or if she is naturally gregarious. Another possibility is that she is inquisitive. That seems like a good trait to have for a slicer.

Lorel keeps her datapad and remote droid controller in front of her. She has mostly ignored our flight path despite the bright colors of the approaching Andaran sunset, an environment that many people would classify as "beautiful" due to the gradient of bright blues, intense warm colors, patches of clouds, and reflections off buildings. Lorel, however, does not pay attention to that. She taps away at her devices while checking various readings on the ship's console.

"Come on, Lumi," she says.

I will now attempt to make "small talk." "Why did you name your droid Lumi when it is an El-Zero droid?"

"I'm not so literal," she says.

This does not make sense in the context of our discussion.

"When I first got Lumi, I had a sudden power outage in my apartment. I could only see by Lumi's blue front light. My illuminator. Thus,

Luminator, or Lumi for short. Hey"—she points vaguely my way—"you got some lights in there, too. You gonna get that fixed?"

She is likely referring to the diagonal scar across my chest.

"It isn't a high priority," I say.

"Aren't your core systems exposed? I mean, if I had a gaping wound across my chest, I'd probably want to get it looked at. You know?"

"I do not 'know.' Jaylen is satisfied with my levels of safe functioning." I take one hand off the flight yoke and tap my metal torso. "No 'exposure' has ever caused failure."

"What about, like, rain? Or snow? Or sand?" Lorel is still staring directly at her datapad. Humans often have difficulty multitasking. Lorel, however, is capable of holding a conversation while simultaneously controlling her L0 droid. "Seems like welding a plate or something over it would make sense."

This line of questioning is disrupting my primary objective of being an effective partner for Jaylen. My core processors allocate resources to verify her claims that the elements might put hardware at risk. This includes running danger calculations on various weather types precipitating at specific angles, velocities, and densities—how much would make it through the exposed area, and of that amount, how much would interfere with active electronics, power systems, and mechanical operations.

All that extra processing nearly causes me to lose my tracking vector for the ship in front of us. It deviates an extra 0.36 percent, which is still within the range of tolerance but further than I'd like. Too much is at stake for me to spend this many resources pulling up data queries about my past.

"I don't worry about that."

"All right, all right." She continues looking at her datapad while working with her L0 droid's aftermarket slice interface. "Well, I suppose it's as good a reason as any to wear a nice coat."

"This coat serves multiple purposes," I say. The words come out fast, without taking up additional processing—representing a strategic decision to end this conversation.

"Okay," she says slowly. So slow that the word draws out, and she takes a break from her datapad to look at me. I do not turn my head, though my peripheral field of view catches this, along with the squint on her face.

I have been rude. Being rude can disrupt human emotions and thus jeopardize the mission, which will then put my priority goals at risk.

I must take care of this in the most appropriate fashion.

"I apologize for my short temper." I consider the way that Jaylen constructs apologies—usually a combination of a short expression of regret followed by a much longer justification for why such a thing took place, even if the justification only represents part of the factual history. "You will recall I have sustained long-term damage. Some of my default protocols from my initial manufacturing are suppressed. This has led to difficulty processing appropriate answers to several types of queries."

Still in my peripheral vision, I see Lorel purse her lips. She then tilts her head and reaches one hand over to pat my shoulder. "Hey," she says, in a much more sympathetic tone, "we're all survivors. I made my way up through the syndicates before getting free. You don't go through that unscathed. We all come with some kind of baggage, right?"

I choose to respond quickly. "Right."

We fly in silence for another minute. Jaylen and Fennec are silent, too.

"Oh, I get it," Lorel finally says. "You're in a bad mood."

"It is impossible for me to be in a 'bad mood.' "

"Wow, I wish I could say that." This prompts a loud laugh from Lorel. Which is strange because my response was not an attempt at mimicking humor. "I've dealt with all types of droids. Sometimes they function well. Sometimes something gets in the way. You're flying this thing."

Perhaps Lorel is not well. Her statements are not making sense. "That statement is not related to the previous statement."

She sighs now and breaks away from her devices to look at me. Her head is tilted and her eyes are narrowed. Half of her mouth curls up in a smirk. "You're flying this thing. And I'm in this ship with you. Everything in our plan is based on a very precise rollout of steps, right?" She points to my chest. "You've got a huge scar exposing your innards, and you're cranky. I'd like to not die during this mission. So, if something's bothering you, let it out so we can get through this mission safely."

I consider what she is saying. She is talking to me in a way that no one ever has, not even maintenance workers. These are new queries to consider.

I make a decision to temporarily mute our comms so that my discussion with Lorel does not interfere with Fennec's or Jaylen's concentration on their tasks.

"I believe my cumulative damage has led to some deficiencies that hinder my abilities to fulfill my directives as best as possible," I say.

"That's a lot of words for saying 'I got a problem.' " Now her smirk turns into a full smile. "Why's that? You're piloting an ancient ship, you prepared the gear for this mission. Jaylen clearly trusts you. And you've got that really nice coat. You seem to be doing all right."

Lorel is assigning status without metrics. "Great," "nice," and "all right" are subjective terms. "I was originally programmed to fight for the Confederacy of Independent Systems. Now I am programmed to serve Jaylen," I say. "That involves exploring every option to find jobs, execute plans, build our capabilities forward. The more effectively we execute, the more layers of protection we can establish: finances, equipment, weapons, contacts." I next consider the language to express the battle between my protocols and Jaylen's parameters.

For lack of a better definition, I make an effort to express my *feelings*.

"Occasionally, I find it . . . frustrating that I am prohibited from doing everything I possibly can to execute my core programming."

Lorel glances down at her devices. This appears to be a cursory check because she turns right back to me. I keep my focus on the flight path, though. That is the priority.

"So you're saying you want to be more?"

"That is a vague and unquantifiable statement."

"Okay." She rests the devices on her lap and then claps her hands for no apparent reason. "There was this saying I heard once: 'the height of sky.' It's part of a longer thing, but it's basically thinking about what your limits are. Maybe you don't really want more and you just think you do?"

I try to see the causal logic in this question, but her phrasing lacks specificity. Whether this is purposeful, I can't tell. I try to provide clarity for her. "I have an override chip fused to my neural core. Because of this damage, I must abide by several parameters to ensure Jaylen's safety. I am not allowed to test or utilize seventeen of my original programmed skills without his explicit oversight. I am to have my restraining bolt on at all times." I tap the spot where the restraining bolt used to be. "Removing it has introduced risk. Piloting a CIS ship like this also introduces risk." I pause and check my internal diagnostics. "Since beginning this mission, I have kept a continuously running scan of metrics deemed critical to my identity."

"Your identity." Though Lorel picks her devices back up, I see her mouth twist before she speaks. "You mean, your personality?"

"In a sense." This provides a topic for research later. Whether organic or droid, do an individual's choices stem from default programming or accumulated experiences or both? I file that question away for a different time. "A droidsmith years ago told Jaylen that I would revert to being a default Bee-Ex commando droid if I broke any of his parameters or removed the restraining bolt."

"And?"

I finish my internal diagnostics and report. "So far, all identity metrics have maintained their expected levels."

"That your entire personality would be erased because of a stuck chip seems . . ." Lorel's nose twists and her mouth opens several times before she finally speaks again. "I'm trying to think of the best way to put this. What you described seems . . . inconsistent."

"Jaylen would not lie to me."

"I'm not saying he would, he seems like a great guy. But the inner workings of droid neural cores, that's kind of a specialized skill."

This is true. Jaylen is far from a droidsmith.

"I work with droids. I work with systems," Lorel says. "I wouldn't say I'm an expert, but I know enough. And in my time, the more droids experience, the more they can draw from to make decisions. So your parameters aren't just binary, you know? As long as your memory hasn't been wiped, everything about you is there to help you be *better*."

"Perhaps this is why I have not killed Jaylen yet."

"Let's all be thankful for that." She laughs again. Lorel laughs a lot and very easily. "Look, you're you, unless you get your memory wiped. That's usually how it works. Though I'm kind of jealous." Her tone takes an unexpected change, as does her expression. "Sometimes I wish I were someone besides me."

Our conversation appears to have made her upset.

I will effort to comfort her.

"Lorel Amberdine," I say. "You are calm and knowledgeable and easy to accomplish tasks with."

This appears to have the intended impact. She smiles once again, and her tone resumes rendering typical emotions. "Thanks, big guy. I'll take that as a compliment. Hey, tell you what," she says, holding up an excited finger. "I've worked with all sorts of droidsmiths. Some of them I even trust. We get through this, I'll give you the name of the most reliable one. He's been doing this for decades. Long before there were clones and battle droids. So I'm sure he can handle an old Sep droid. He's expensive, but if you pull this heist off, I'm sure you can afford him."

A droidsmith experienced with BX commando droids—such a resource has been difficult to both locate and afford. This gesture offers no personal benefit to Lorel. She appears to be doing it out of a mixture of concern and generosity.

I make an internal note about my current diagnostic state as a record of what this "feels" like.

"Thank you, Lorel." I unmute the comm connection to Fennec and Jaylen. "We should resume focusing on the mission."

CHAPTER 22

About seventeen minutes passed with Jaylen waiting on the other side of the roof, enough time that the Andaran sky shifted from an intense blue sunset to a deeper, darker hue. Outside of the occasional comm chatter from Lorel and ND-5, nothing else happened. Wind kicked up, a strong breeze blowing Jaylen's coat tails out behind him. He pulled them back to his side, and just when he started to turn and watch the parade of passing ships, the mechanical rumble of the turbolift cut through the silence.

Several seconds later, the door slid open, the turbolift's internal lighting casting a well-groomed silhouette of a flowing dress.

As the passenger stepped ahead, the details came into play: long blond hair with pink splashed throughout, all cascading down over bare, pale human shoulders and rich green fabric.

This had to be Impossible Song. And she was alone.

"I see the target," Fennec said into Jaylen's earpiece.

"Acknowledged," he said in return. "Endee, Lorel?"

"We are monitoring," the droid said.

Jaylen nodded, more to himself than his observing crew, and he walked forward, his gait changing to match the confidence of a Barsha executive. The woman stood still, doors closing behind her, and the turbolift's gears began grinding again as it descended. She took even, measured steps, and when they met eyes, he immediately saw that she was different from the usual corporate types he'd known all his life.

Despite her attire and makeup, her blue eyes carried a different kind of steeliness.

A list of code phrases from Bischt Renner's datapad ran through his mind, and Jaylen suddenly realized that the Empire's protocols really did work—they would have had no way to verify these in advance. Though he supposed if the phrases weren't correct, he could just play it off, have Fennec shoot the woman, and grab her datapad. The end result would be the same—except then he would have crossed the Empire, which was never a good idea.

Plus, on the off chance this *wasn't* the target, that would be a life unnecessarily taken. Collateral damage could always happen, but still, easier to avoid it whenever possible. It just led to further complications.

"Not exactly the best view," he said, projecting his voice over another burst of wind. He planted his feet, his arms drawing his cape over his body.

She nodded, taking several steps forward until they stood nearly face-to-face. She looked him up and down before staring directly into his eyes. She took in a quick, short breath, lips staying parted but no sound coming out.

"Come on," Lorel whispered over the comms. "'I've never seen a blue sunset before.' Say it."

"Your urging will not change the situation," ND-5 said, and Jaylen considered tossing his earpiece now before it gave him away. Thankfully, the howling winds provided some cover for any further squawking from his earpiece.

She continued staring, and Jaylen offered an awkward half smile in return as the seconds ticked past. He almost repeated the first code phrase when she finally relaxed her posture and nodded. "I've never seen a blue sunset before."

"Someday you should travel to Felucia," he said. "Their sunrises are spectacular."

"Jungles on Felucia. The humidity is the worst."

Jaylen wasn't expecting that. Neither was their small team, a point that Lorel punctuated with a sudden inhale before she spoke. "That's, um . . ." Her voice trailed off, which wasn't helping Jaylen come up with a response. "That's not in the script."

"Jaylen," Fennec said, a pronounced urgency in her voice. "I've got line of sight. What do you want me to do?"

She had to be the contact. She wouldn't use the first correct response if she wasn't. The odds of her hitting the exact correct first reply out of sheer random choice of words—it wasn't impossible given the opening phrase, but it was pretty slim.

"I can hit her right now," Fennec said. "Just say the word."

Her eyes remained locked, nearly daring him into a response. Here he was, on the precipice of making his mark on the galactic underworld, yet a few quick words would tip the balance. He had to think—had to adapt, to come up with the best solution.

Perhaps it was time for collateral damage. But if this really was an innocent person, the actual Impossible Song might arrive at the exact wrong time, losing them the precious datapad while possibly inviting security—both private *and* Imperial.

He needed *something*. Every passing moment led them closer and closer to bringing in some sort of unwanted attention. He could either say something and draw this out, or he could turn, stay quiet, and try to lure her to the other side of the roof, far enough from the turbolift that if the actual contact *did* arrive, the distance and industrial machinery might obscure a dead body.

He inhaled, possible ways to stall forming in his mind—maybe he could talk about how the view was better on the other side. He opened his mouth to start, when she broke into a sudden, easy smile. "I hear their sunsets are best viewed from the southern hemisphere."

There it was. Exactly on script, and Lorel's exhale came clear through the comms.

"But only for the final months of the year," he said in return, and she extended a hand to shake.

Now he took her hand, and he glanced at the jewelry on her fingers. He'd been in the business long enough to recognize that one of them hid a tiny blade underneath its stone. "Always good to meet someone like us," she said.

"Yeah." *Now* he could slip into Barsha Corp mode, the easy slither of drawing people into conversation and putting them at ease. "It's a strange life, isn't it?"

"Oh, you're telling me. All these protocols, and for what? Just to get an updated list of bosses, coworkers, and assignments. All this technology in the Empire, and you'd think they'd find a way to transmit information to us." Now her laugh came easy and bright, showing a relaxed nature that Jaylen could naturally reflect. "Sometimes I feel like the Empire added *more* bureaucracy than the Republic had. And yet we're still out here, despite listening to all the complaints from everyone on the list," she said. "At least my regional overseer sequence is done for now. It's so much extra work. I can just do my role here—which I enjoy. You?"

Jaylen gave a toothy grin. "More or less."

She laughed in return, then matched his smile. "Isn't that everything about this job? I thought a public-facing role would instantly blow my cover, but it's actually easier. So many ways for me to hide every day. I'm a bit surprised they've extended my rotation three times already. I thought they only did that for the quiet jobs, but maybe they like having a public mouthpiece in the region."

A new idea popped into Jaylen's mind, the most unexpected thought: Could this person help him out with their *real* work?

If so, that meant sparing her life. He considered a whole range of possibilities, though for now he'd simply stay on script—and in character as Bischt Renner, Blutopian vintner.

But it didn't hurt to dig a little bit.

"You're in the public spotlight?" Jaylen asked. "I just deal with customers." He offered an easy laugh, one designed to charm investors or gathered media. "They have no idea I'm gathering intel while I serve them."

She tilted her head as her mouth formed a smirk. "They never do, do they? Can you keep a secret?"

Did ISB operatives share secrets among each other? He supposed they must to some degree, if they passed these cover lists around, and with the Empire being so sprawling, it was probably the only way to quickly share intel. But whether or not this was smiled upon, he wasn't sure.

Or maybe she was just flirting. "Sure," Jaylen said, putting on a different kind of smile.

"I'm a broadcaster." She said the word *broadcaster* in a singsong voice. "Local HoloNet News for the Colonies. Right now, I'm based on Hosnian Prime, but the day job has me all over."

"Wait a minute," Fennec said. "I recognize her from the HoloNet. Her show is the worst. She lies all the time."

Jaylen ignored the sniper's commentary and kept nodding as she spoke. "Ninety-nine percent of my work is doing that job." She held up a single gloved finger. "One percent of it is identifying anti-Imperial cells. You interview people, you get them talking, they reveal a connection or some trace of a clue that they're up to no good." She shook her head with a scoff. "They don't teach you that in journalism school."

"Family of vintners here," Jaylen said, tapping into his research about Renner. "I know how to make wine. I know how to bottle it, sell it, what pairs well with it. It's in my blood. It's in my family history." He pictured the holo with all those Renners in front of the winery. "The rest of my family thinks I've just carried on the tradition. They have no idea I deal with the syndicates. And the syndicate leaders just think I'm a friendly place to meet. But they drink enough at my resort, and they start talking easier. I pass along what I hear."

She sighed, and as she did, everything about her relaxed just a little: her shoulders, her jaw, her stance. Perhaps she rarely got to be fully honest with *anyone*. "It's interesting, isn't it? The spectrum of our roles. I'm tracking covert syndicate operations in the business world. You're getting syndicate intel from behind the scenes. I had a friend who used to interface directly with syndicates, negotiating which supply lines they'd use so they didn't wind up getting in our way. Keeping all that straight is a job in itself. And code phrases, code names, code *everything*. Do you ever wonder if the Empire even tracks it all?"

"Oh," he said, moving just a little closer to her, "all the time. Whose terrible job is it to oversee the overseers?" This prompted a boisterous laugh from her, and he followed up with another targeted joke. "I can see their office now, just an empty room with stacks and stacks of datapads."

"With a single cup of caf." Now they roared together, and for just a flash, Jaylen didn't think about underworld contacts, his crew overseeing a mission. Not Barsha Corp, Sliro, or even the Empire, for that matter.

No, Jaylen just existed in a sliver of time, laughing with a woman over a dumb joke.

An *attractive* woman.

What a strange, refreshing feeling. To be without the burden of the damage of the past.

"That's right," he finally said, words stumbling past the laughter. Tears formed in his eyes, and they had nothing to do with the sting and cold of the rooftop.

At least until ND-5 interrupted the moment. "Jaylen," the droid said in his ear, "I suggest avoiding too much conversation. Getting the datapad now would be the best course of action."

There it was. Back to work.

"Well, look," he said, with an easy smile still on his face, "how about we do what we came here for?" He adjusted the cape on his shoulders, then pointed below them. "I actually skipped lunch, so that free food is calling to me."

"Oh, is that all?" she said, turning to face the blue sunset. "Hold on one second. We're up here, let's enjoy the view. It *is* nice, and the people downstairs are insufferable."

Jaylen followed her gaze, the colors seemingly brighter and more brilliant than he'd ever seen. "Just for a minute," he said quietly.

Her hand pointed to the other side of the rooftop. "I know it's part of our code exchange, but this dusk really is pretty. There's a better look over there."

Jaylen took a step to follow as Fennec's voice cut in. "She's reaching into her coat. I'm on her. Play it cool. Don't react."

He continued as directed, walking with steadiness until they got a direct view of the sunset without adjacent buildings in the way. She tapped his shoulder, and he turned to see her presenting a datapad. "See? Business *and* pleasure." The datapad's screen lit up, though between the wind and dim light and *her,* Jaylen couldn't make out the details. "Congratulations on being the next sequence's overseer. And good luck figuring out everyone's new rotation spot. Amazing what's on here, isn't it? So many stories of people's lives. Sometimes I take a step back from it all and just think about that."

Yet another voice came into his earpiece, this time Lorel's. "I've uploaded the false maintenance report about a leaky gas line near the roof. Don't get too attached to her. We have an escape plan to follow."

"Right," he said, an uncharacteristic bit of regret slipping through before he caught himself. "I mean, thank you." He took the datapad and held it up. On the left side was an index of code names, including his own assumed one: Sun Racket. The right side showed a list of unmasked names. He scrolled through, a cursory check both to play the part and to see how much intel they were actually getting in this score.

"Something wrong?" she asked, leaning over into his sight line.

"Sorry. No. No, everything's fine. It's just . . ." His thoughts stuttered, leading to him spitting out the first thing that came to mind. "It's just that I forgot how ridiculous some of these code names are."

"Ha. You're right about that." Her hand slid into her coat again for a moment before she pulled it out to grip her lapels. "Hey. Let's do something fun," she said. "Just for us. Right here. What's your real name?" Her voice changed to a playful lilt. "I'll tell you mine if you tell me yours. It's on the list anyway." She reached again into her coat, then looked behind her. "My name is Shaw Andeej. So who are you really, Sun Racket? Tell me yours?" She flashed a big smile, her broad cheeks lifting in a way that countered the stark reality of the situation.

This woman, Shaw—she was the contact. And that meant that she had to be eliminated.

No trail left behind.

He turned and matched her smile. Couldn't they both just sink into this moment and enjoy the connection as two people stuck in the unlikeliest of circumstances? Jaylen chose to say something—this time, just for him. "Sure. My real name is—"

"Jaylen," Fennec said. "I see movement from the turbolift mechanism. Its light just turned on. Someone's coming up."

Jaylen stopped right there. Lorel now spoke, her words laced with urgency. "I'm on it. I'll try to slow it down."

"I should shoot her now," Fennec said. "You have the datapad. I'll take her out now, and we'll make the roof look like an acci—"

"Not yet," Jaylen said quickly. This caught Shaw's attention, and he corrected himself. "Sorry, I just mean, this is difficult for me. My real name is—"

"Doors opening!" Fennec said. Jaylen turned to see people sprint out of the turbolift—five, if he counted correctly. They ran in formation, a line of people that looked like gala attendees, but their movements signaled military, or at least military training.

"I think . . ." Shaw said, stepping back. As she did, the new group fanned out, two standing at her side with guns trained, and three more forming a rough arch behind them, using vents and other structures as cover. She stuck her hand out to signal a pause. "I think you should hand that back. Because you're not Bischt Renner." Her lips pursed, and the hardness behind her eyes returned. "Now, what do I do? Do I sell you to the syndicates or call in the ISB?"

CHAPTER 23

Jaylen's cover was blown.

But he hadn't lost yet. He was still standing on the rooftop, and his crew was still in position.

Most importantly, that datapad was now in Shaw's hand.

And *on* that datapad, Jaylen Vrax's fortune.

No, he hadn't lost. Everything teetered in a delicate balance, but he was ahead in this game. He'd come here looking for a score, something he could leverage into both credits and contacts—and *trust* among those contacts.

This . . .

This was an *opportunity*. It could still work.

Jaylen just had to navigate his way through a hostile situation.

First step: Play it smooth. "What are you talking about?" he asked. "Check my dossier."

Lorel spoke into his comm. "I tapped into the local Imperial security feed not too long ago. Your ID is definitely there."

"I guarantee it." Jaylen offered a shrug and a wide grin. "Go find a terminal and load it up. See for yourself."

A gust of wind kicked up, blowing Shaw's colored bangs back. She swept her hair down, then met Jaylen's look, lips twisted. She held up a single finger, and one of the guards grabbed a datapad from his belt. He handed it to her and then dropped back in formation as she glanced it over.

"You're right," she said, tapping the datapad. "That *is* you. I got this today from the office on Hosnian Prime." She held the datapad up, the doctored profile now staring right back at him. "See, here's the problem. I have this inquisitive nature. Happens when you're trained as a journalist. I was prepping for this trip last week, and I saw your code name as today's contact. Found your profile in a previous transfer list I got a few months back. I like to check things out. It's a habit after so many years in this industry. And you're lucky the real Bischt Renner is about the same height and weight. But"—one side of her mouth curved up in a wry grin—"he's got this atypical human trait with his eyes—the irises are shaped like a keyhole, and his eyebrows are stark white. You only really notice if you get a close look." She pointed at his face. "Professional instinct. I had to see for myself. But . . ." She gestured at the armed guards around her. "I also planned ahead."

Jaylen made a mental note that if he ever did something like this again, he'd need to check the target's eyes after they'd killed him—especially if most of their time together was under a bright sun that might obscure such a detail.

Shaw handed the datapad back to her guard and stood with arms crossed. "Whoever you're using as a slicer is good."

"Oh, a compliment," Lorel said. "Nice."

"But not good enough to slice an old code name transfer list with permanent data." She waved a finger in the air, and all five guards adjusted their posture, leaning forward with weapons pointed. "Now tell me who you really are. Then we'll figure out what you're worth. And to whom."

Now ND-5 spoke through the comm. "Jaylen can't say anything to us, but he can listen. Ideas are welcome."

Fennec replied immediately. "This is why you hired me. Jaylen, listen. Just put your hands up and start slowly backing away. Draw their attention, spread them out."

Jaylen nodded, a subtle gesture that Fennec may or may not have been able to see through her scope. He did as instructed, keeping both hands up at shoulder level, while stepping backward.

"What are you planning?" ND-5 asked.

"I'm figuring that out as we go," Fennec said. "But we'll get out of this. I promise."

By the time Jaylen had taken five steps, the guards reacted by moving forward, their paces staggered.

"That's it," Fennec said, "it's working. They're spreading out. Keep it up. The wind is heavy. That'll provide audio cover." Five steps became ten, everyone in front of him continuing their gradual procession.

"Stop moving," Shaw yelled. "You've got nowhere to go."

"That's fine," Fennec said. "Stay there. But get them talking."

"About what?" ND-5 asked.

"I don't know. I shoot things. Talking isn't my job."

Jaylen had not considered how potentially distracting a bickering team would be when held at gunpoint on a rooftop with dizzying winds.

"Jaylen," ND-5 said, "I suggest telling them an engaging story that will cause them to ask questions instead of shoot you."

The droid clearly didn't know how to talk to people during tense situations. Which of course Jaylen should have known, considering this was the same droid that tried to blow him up on Gus Treta.

"My real name," Jaylen said after a deep breath, "is Oland."

"Did he just come up with that?" Lorel asked.

ND-5 replied immediately. "No. That was someone I killed."

"This is perfect," Fennec said. "Make sure they're all looking at you. Keep 'em talking."

"I'm not ISB," Jaylen said, projecting his voice loudly. He looked at everyone in front of him: Shaw directly across from him and the five guards spread out at varying distances, in a looser arch than before. "You're right. I stole this identity."

"All right." This time Fennec's voice came in a hushed whisper. "Don't react."

Don't react? Don't react to *what*?

But then it happened. From the far left, a flash of bright red discharged. At a distance, the untrained eye might have taken it as a reflection, sunlight bouncing off a passing ship's canopy. Except here, Jaylen caught another flash: a burning bolt zipping horizontally.

And in front of him, Shaw's guard at the very back collapsing straight down. Fennec was right: The rooftop wind covered the sound of the body's impact on the floor.

"Scratch one," Fennec said. "Keep distracting them. Eyes on you, any way you can. If they keep looking forward, then they won't see who fell behind them."

"I am calculating," ND-5 said, "Jaylen's odds for keeping their attention and avoiding getting shot. Jaylen, you need to provide them with value to avoid the latter."

Jaylen impulsively shook his head, a gesture that broke character, but he couldn't fight the instinct given the clash of voices in his ear. He told himself to focus, though ND-5 made a good point. He needed to give them a reason not to shoot him. "Look, I'm just someone trying to get by. So let's not get too hasty with those guns, okay? I'm not a threat, and besides, I've got something more valuable here. I'll show you. Very slowly. Everyone watch. Slow, safe movements, okay? No reason to shoot."

"Clever," Lorel said. "Except, did he actually bring something else?"

"No," ND-5 said, making it *really* hard to ignore the cross chatter in his ear. "He went in with no tech other than his comm and your scanner."

The scanner was *not* something Jaylen intended to risk. It was too valuable.

The Imperial datapad had an embedded tracking chip and couldn't get too far away from its original owner or intended recipient. So Lorel had provided a device that could capture images of the data at rapid speed, complete with a transceiver that exploited nearby signals for a quick upload. They'd planned on letting the original datapad blow up with Impossible Song to cover all tracks.

He wouldn't dare risk that as a prop.

As a cover, though, Jaylen reached into his back pocket with his left hand, closed a fist over nothing, and pulled it out, hoping it would buy enough time.

"I believe the proper term is 'improvisation,' " ND-5 said.

"Cut the chatter," Fennec said, and Jaylen sent out silent appreciation for the sniper's professionalism. "Here comes another shot. Ready?"

A second later, another flash came from the left side. The light glinted as it flew across.

And now, a second guard—blaster trained with steely gaze—fell to the ground.

Jaylen waved his left hand, a conscious effort to try and maintain everyone's attention. "Scratch two," Fennec said. "Three left, plus the target. Jaylen, can you tell if the target is armed?"

He squinted, the diminishing sun making it harder to discern those details. She'd slid her datapad back in her coat, leaving her hands free—but did she carry any weapons? The gala's security was pretty tight, yet her hired goons all managed to have guns, either stashed away previously or snuck in through other means. Perhaps they had been airdropped on this very roof earlier in the day.

He wouldn't be able to frisk her for weapons. But maybe he could at least occupy her to *prevent* her from reaching for one.

"I was at the Renner family winery. Just on holiday, two weeks ago. Staff said he was offplanet." Though Jaylen kept his words slow, his mind moved quick, melding truth with fiction to weave a believable tale. "Just dumb luck and opportunity. I sliced into his message logs. Saw he had reports of technical troubles with his ship. Don't know if he's still dealing with that. Or if he's dead. Either way, I decided that this would be a good score. But there was one more thing that I picked up from him. See this?" He waved his left arm. The problem, though, was that ND-5 was right—he *was* improvising, and he had nothing to actually show them.

The good news was that all eyes were trained on him. The bad news was also that all eyes were trained on him, which meant that he couldn't say anything to his team.

Whatever Fennec had planned, he just hoped it would be fast.

"I'm going to reach slowly to show this to you now. No tricks." He met Shaw's eyes. "I'm gonna show it to you and then toss it to you. All right? This is a negotiation for my life. You find it valuable enough, you let me go."

Shaw stared back, continuing to study him.

"Jaylen has no item. When they find that out, they will shoot him," ND-5 stated plainly. "Fennec, if you can't take them out quietly, I will be forced to break formation."

"Don't do that," Fennec said. "That'll alert security. Just trust me."

"All right," Shaw said. "I'm intrigued. But no guarantees."

"Good," Jaylen yelled as loud as he could. "Good. Hands up to catch?"

Shaw's eye roll was very visible, but she agreed and held her hands up in a ready position.

"Clever. Good work, Jaylen," Fennec said. "No weapons in her hands. I see my opening."

For the third time, the red flash came from Fennec's sniping point. And for the third time, Jalen saw the guard farthest back drop to the ground.

Except this time, their body's impact recoil sent an arm flailing. Which led to a gun getting tossed instead of dropping straight down. Which then led to the gun clanging off a metal duct.

The wind couldn't totally cover *that* up.

Fennec inhaled sharply, then said, "Dank farrik."

All around Jaylen, visibility crept lower and lower, the remaining sunlight still coloring the atmosphere but unable to penetrate the skyline of buildings.

"What the—" one of the remaining guards started before Jaylen yelled an interruption to grab their attention again.

"Okay, everyone, I'm doing it now." His voice echoed across the rooftop. "Don't shoot me yet, okay? Let me at least *try* to beg for my life?"

"Quit stalling and do it already," Shaw shouted back.

Jaylen nodded, solemnly resigned that they'd either get out of this as a crew or he'd be dead in a few minutes—when he was on the cusp of finally getting ahead.

Just his luck.

"Jaylen?" Fennec said. "On my mark, duck."

Jaylen looked directly at Shaw, making sure they locked eyes once again. "Okay," he said, projecting his voice as clear as possible. He wound up his arm, a mock pose as if he really were going to toss something over.

"Now!"

Jaylen's knees slammed into the ground as he dropped, arms covering his head from any potential blasterfire. Instead, he got a second of silence. Then Shaw's voice.

"What?" Then the sound of scuffling and metal. "What did you do?"

Jaylen looked up, then straightened to a full stand. Shaw stood in front, staring at the suddenly fallen guard a few meters from her, then, with realization, turning to see the ones behind her on the ground. Jaylen made a mental note that heavy winds on high rooftops *did* cover the sound of falling bodies—as long as no metal was around.

Shaw wasn't armed. That was clear now.

Jaylen had the upper hand.

Stay quiet or say something? He *could* just have Fennec take her out, and then they'd proceed with the rest of the plan.

But what if she offered something else of value? What if they could get more out of this?

"Don't move," Jaylen yelled. Shaw nodded with hands up. "Now I have a proposition for *you*. Give me the list, and *maybe* I'll let you go." Which, he actually couldn't—an Imperial operative knowing his face seemed like an incredibly bad idea. However, there was an opportunity here to see what other information she could give them. *Then* he'd signal Fennec to shoot her.

With her hands still up, Shaw laughed. "You know," she said, "if you want to stay alive, you really should walk away right now. I'll give you a chance."

"I think we're all in too deep for that." He pointed at the next building. "I have a sniper on you."

"You have a sniper." Shaw looked roughly to where he pointed and waved. "I've got a bomb strapped to my back. Tied to my biometrics. You really want to do this?"

Jaylen waited for the wind to settle enough that he could be heard. "You're bluffing!" he yelled. "Why would you even wear a bomb to a place like this?"

Shaw glared at Jaylen, a clear intensity shining even through the oncoming dusk. "You have no idea who you're dealing with." She took two steps forward.

"Jaylen?" Fennec asked, and he quickly told her to hold.

"I'll spell it out for you. I've been with the ISB from the very beginning." Even though the wind kept whirling, Shaw's voice came through clearly. "I know state secrets about every division, every sector."

"I am analyzing her speech for clues," ND-5 said.

"People try to steal from me all the time. People try to kill me all the time. And if I did get captured? Or if I defected?" Her lips curled upward. "Oh, Emperor Palpatine would be very mad. They'd hunt me down. You live this life long enough, the only person you can trust is yourself. So, hired help?" She pointed a thumb at the fallen guards behind her. "A little insurance?" She pointed over her shoulder at her back. "Your choice. Walk away now while I let you."

"Oh, this is not good," Lorel said.

"I can shoot her. I can stand down," Fennec said. "I get paid either way, so you tell me."

"Jaylen," ND-5 said, "a vocal analysis indicates that she is telling the truth. There is a high probability that a bomb will go off if she dies."

Jaylen realized that he was built specifically for this moment, when all his instincts trained from reading people in boardrooms met the life-or-death decisions of the underworld. ND-5 had his analysis, but that was all based on *numbers*.

Jaylen understood *people*.

"She's bluffing," he quietly said. "Shoot her."

From the left side, one more flash came.

And in front of him, Shaw jolted ever so slightly. She stood with wide eyes, but her jaw dropped. A second later, smoke emerged from her open mouth, growing into a dark plum. Then her body slumped to the ground.

"I hate holonet people," Fennec said. "Nothing but pointless gossip."

"You see?" Jaylen said. "No bomb. Still alive. I know how to read people. Let's move."

"Jaylen," ND-5 said, "we must cover your trail before you leave. Put all the bodies in one place."

"I'm on it," Fennec said. "Nicking the gas lines now."

"No one said heavy lifting would be part of this," Jaylen said under his breath, but everyone heard it. ND-5 and Fennec didn't respond, but Lorel snickered. "All right, I'm starting with Shaw." He reached down, first grabbing the cover list datapad. He stuck it in his back pocket before rolling her on her side. "How much time do— "

His words stopped. His *thoughts* stopped.

Jaylen blinked. Then he set her back down.

Because there *was* a bomb strapped around the back of her waist. Solid, metallic, and heavy. He pulled back the bottom of her coat to reveal a device that he immediately recognized. He didn't know exactly what *type* of bomb, but those specifics didn't matter. Three wires stuck out from the top of the explosive's casing, snaking farther up her clothes, though one wire was secured directly between her shoulder blades.

And on the face of the box, bright red digits—that counted down.

"Oh no," he said slowly. "Hey, team." Jaylen swallowed hard and cursed his stupid luck. Maybe—just maybe—he should have listened to his droid. "I might have made the wrong call."

CHAPTER 24

I pull the ship out of formation.

I estimate that it will take one minute and thirty-two seconds to safely fly to the rooftop.

I calculate a range of risks as I pull the yoke on the ship. It banks hard enough for Lorel to say, "Whoa, hey," and reach out to steady herself against the console.

Risk one: the bomb. Jaylen describes the bomb as I am flying. From the details, I believe the bomb is a thermex charge with wires tied into Shaw's biometrics. The instant her organs shut down, the timer likely started—a failsafe for an ISB agent in a high-risk scenario. I do not relay this information to Jaylen for now. I do not respond to his suggestion that he "might have made the wrong call," though internally, I do double-check my audio analysis.

It is confirmed. Shaw's voice gave all indications of being honest. Jaylen made the wrong call.

However, my priority is to protect Jaylen. Excess information regarding mildly relevant details will only slow him down.

Risk two: If the biometrics triggered the bomb, they may have sent out a distress call, too.

Risk three: The mission objective is to get the list. This particular datapad is transmission secured and has a tracking chip. Jaylen should not take it. Instead, he should immediately activate the image-capture device provided earlier by Lorel. Using this device will allow Jaylen to scan a copy of the list so he can leave the actual datapad on the premises as the bomb goes off. There should be no way to tie the data back to us—as long as the device finishes processing before time runs out.

Risk four: Pulling the ship out of formation has caught the attention of security. On the radar, I identify three security craft that have suddenly trailed me. They are all local rather than Imperial. If the first three risks are abated, that leaves our escape as the primary risk.

I have a plan for that. But first, I have work to do.

The parade route flies in a large perimeter that weaves in and out of buildings for island visitors to see. I am using that to my advantage as I attempt to ditch the tailing security. Buildings fly by on either side with the occasional speeder cross traffic stopping abruptly at intersections.

"I've got the scanner's transceiver connected. It's riding some of the HoloNet broadcast signals. I'm monitoring the copy process," Lorel says, her voice speaking at a hurried clip. "Fifty-one percent. But we got company."

Lorel is surprisingly nervous for this situation. "Do not worry. I have faced down the elitest of clone commandos. These local security forces do not match their skill set."

Before she can respond, I reach out to Jaylen. "Jaylen, do you see an appropriate pickup point?" I increase my speed and cut between oncoming city traffic.

"Uh . . ." Jaylen draws out that single syllable, a slight waver to his voice. "I'm on a roof. So whichever side you can get to first. But you got two minutes and twenty seconds left before this bomb goes off."

There is not much margin for error. Every additional second off pace requires a risk calculation.

"My approach vector is on the south side," I say as I check the radar. Another security craft appears on the radar, this one ahead of me on an intercept course.

My processors run a quick calculation, cross-referencing the distance to the Museum of Engineering and Lightspeed, the vertical elevation to the rooftop, the number of buildings between us, their relative height, the speed and distance of the oncoming security craft, and the ships on our tail.

I calculate a significant amount of risk.

I slow my speed by 16 percent. This allows the ships on our tail to line up directly behind us. I wait for them to close to a nominal distance of twenty-two meters. The museum is straight ahead, the centerpiece of the island, all roads leading to it. The intercepting ship approaches from a perpendicular path between buildings, likely attempting to cut us off right before the final stretch just outside the museum grounds.

"Endee?" Lorel asks, a distinct panic in her voice. "What are you doing?"

"I require you to trust me right now."

Lorel looks at me. Then back at her devices. Then back at me. "We can't slice our way out of everything, huh?"

On the radar, the tailing ships are now at forty-two meters.

Thirty-two meters.

Twenty-two meters—the target distance.

I accelerate to a speed that matches the security ships' velocity. They will not get any closer, nor will they slip farther behind.

Lorel looks at me again and says, "Data copy at sixty-eight percent." Confidence has not returned to her voice.

"I said I require you to trust me right now. Do you not trust me?" I ask.

"You're a nice guy," Lorel says. "It's more that this situation keeps getting worse."

"If you do not trust me, at least listen to me." I check all the different variables: the ships behind me, the path to the museum, and the oncoming intercepting craft. "You should hang on tight."

Lorel's eyes go wide as she looks at me one more time before checking her safety restraints and gripping the datapad. "Our last job together was *not* like this."

"Target in three-point-four kilometers."

"The museum is five kilometers away!" Lorel says.

"You have a knack for reading distance measurements on the ship's panels. You do not appear to know how to apply wartime flight strategy." Assuming the oncoming ship will not slow down, our intercept time is eleven seconds.

Ten. Nine. Eight.

I check my instruments to verify that all craft speed vectors remain as planned. They do. I pull the yoke slightly back to angle the ship up two degrees. It is not noticeable to Lorel. It does not change the trajectories of the ships in pursuit.

It will, however, make a difference.

Five. Four. Three.

"*Endee!*" Lorel yells, the second syllable of my name drawing out in an extended yell.

The intercepting security craft breaks past the corner building, coming into view. I keep the yoke steady by applying extra power to my joint stabilizers, thus bracing for impact.

Our ships collide.

My shuttle rattles, a scraping sound on the underside. An external view would have shown the debris deflecting off the bottom of the hull.

We are still flying, though. That will do for now.

As for my plan, I use a combination of sound, radar, and rear holocam display to determine that we have achieved what I would consider an 85 percent success rate:

The intercepting craft was knocked into a spiral.

As it spun, it collided with the leading ship in pursuit.

Debris from that collision caused the next ship to swerve, but it has overcompensated and crashed into the fourth level of a building.

The final ship, however, slows down enough to avoid this. It takes several seconds to adjust, and then it continues pursuit. This is not ideal but also not unexpected. We have managed to increase our distance significantly, gaining us a range of eleven to fifteen seconds depending on how things play out.

"Don't do that again," Lorel yells. "But also, great job."

"Thank you," I say, in polite response. I pull back on the yoke to bring us to a steep ascent. The move slams Lorel into her seat, though this time she does not comment on the experience.

Fennec's voice breaks in. "I've nicked the gas lines across all four corners of the roof. The whole top level will blow up real good. All the bodies should be incinerated."

"Hopefully not me," Jaylen says.

As we approach the museum's top level, a silhouette pokes out against the teal-colored sunset and gala spotlight beams from the ground floor. The silhouette waves an agitated arm, then glances behind.

"I see him," Lorel says. "Seventeen seconds to complete the transfer."

"Twenty-three seconds until things explode." Jaylen's voice is now laced with uncharacteristic nerves, though given the situation, it is within the range of expected human responses.

I tap a button to open the back cargo bay. "Jaylen," I say, the only calm voice among our entire group—though Fennec is close. "You will have to jump."

"Jump?" His voice has shifted from nervous to extremely loud questioning.

"I have opened the back cargo door." The ship reaches the top floor, and I level out. Vertical thrusters allow the shuttle to hover while precise microthrusters allow me to rotate. "Lorel, you should go to the cargo area and assist Jaylen's landing."

"I'm a slicer, not a—" she starts before letting out a defeated sigh. She undoes her safety restraints and stomps to the back, saying under her breath, "Crik, crik, crik." I glance at her datapad right when the red progress bar fills and turns green.

"Data capture is complete." I check the ship's altitude and nudge the microthrusters to align as much as possible with the roof. "Jaylen, jump."

I do not have time for much precision.

From the rear holocam, I see Jaylen grab Lorel's image-capture device, shove it in his pocket, and toss the original datapad back onto the rooftop. Lorel is shouting a countdown. Jaylen takes several steps back and then runs forward. At three, he jumps over the gap of approximately two meters. His cape whips out behind him, and I prime the main propulsion to leave as soon as Jaylen lands.

His boots hit the metal loading ramp. Then his hands slap onto the metal. Lorel reaches to pull him in.

One second remains. I hit the thrusters.

Both of them yell as the acceleration knocks them back. Lorel apparently did not know about the secure tether line hooked onto the side of the cargo bay. I make a note to lecture her later on the safety features of CIS transport craft. But first, we must escape unscathed.

Which is a problem because the acceleration has pushed Jaylen halfway out of the ship. Lorel has his hand and is the only thing keeping him from falling out. On the other side of us, the radar indicates that the remaining security craft is rapidly closing in. Two other ships have joined.

First, I need to secure Jaylen and Lorel. I push the yoke, causing the ship to dip nearly straight down. At the same time, I decelerate 10 percent, enough to let Jaylen and Lorel tumble in. As they do, I close the loading door, though this is primarily a safety consideration.

It will be opened again soon.

I max out the thrusters, then tilt the ship to squeeze in between two buildings. The sonic rumble from racing ships rattles the glass siding of adjacent buildings, a ripple effect that causes our reflection to wave. This move buys several seconds for me to plot out a path to the island's shore. I debate whether I should fly a random, complicated path between buildings or go for speed.

I decide on speed. This *Sheathipede*-class shuttle may be old, but it still has a higher maximum speed than local security craft.

With one minute and forty-six seconds before we hit the shore, I turn to Jaylen and Lorel. "Open the storage crate," I instruct them.

Jaylen does so without questioning. The sides of the crate slide apart. Handheld scanners and other unused mission equipment fall to the side, leaving only a slightly smaller crate. This opens as well to reveal our speeder bike. It is not optimized for velocity and maneuverability like those used by Imperial troops and swoop bike racers. It lacks power compared to newer, more expensive models, but it is a serviceable craft for our purposes.

"You didn't tell me you packed this," Jaylen says.

"I made a choice to adapt to our situation," I say as I run the ship through several evasive maneuvers. "It is a contingency plan."

"Your planning algorithm gets a bonus if we survive," Jaylen says.

"I do not require bonus payments. Get on and get ready."

Rather than check their positions in the back, I continue piloting the ship. However, my combination of sensors picks up that Lorel and Jaylen look at each other before sitting together.

"This wasn't in the job description," Lorel says.

I get the sense that while she enjoys my company, this has been a difficult work experience for her.

The ship goes low, only about ten meters over the ground—low enough that I can see street gawkers pointing up at us as we zoom by.

"Are you on the bike?" I ask.

"Yes!" both of them shout at once.

I respond by reopening the cargo door. The blast of wind echoes off the shuttle's metallic chambers.

"What are—" Lorel stops. The next thing she says is barely audible. In fact, it probably is not even audible to Jaylen, though my sensors pick it up. "Oh no."

From behind, the security ships have not managed to close distance. However, two new items appear on the radar.

Proton torpedoes. Judging by the way they veer toward my path, target-locked proton torpedoes.

They are closing in fast.

The ship breaks past the city limits, and as soon as there is beach underneath us, I pull hard on the yoke—all the way—so the ship goes straight upward. Gravity does its part and pulls the speeder bike, its riders, the storage crates, and various bits of debris out of the ship.

The last thing I hear is Jaylen yelling, "*Endee!*"—the final sound drawing out and fading away as they drop.

I climb until the torpedoes have nearly reached the ship. As sensors show their distance at twenty meters and closing, I lock the ship into autopilot, continuing to go straight up. Then I slide out of the seat, curl my arms and legs into as tight a ball as possible, and let gravity take me.

CHAPTER 25

The speeder came to a rest, hovering low over a small beach. All around them, the unobstructed view of Andara's sky meant that a sliver of sun remained visible, and the dusk's blue melted into a mix of purple and green just above the horizon.

Jaylen's boots ground into the sand, first his left foot, then his right foot. He turned, staring straight up, the contrails of ND-5's ship going straight upward. Behind it, two torpedoes flew in a direct trail, and shortly after, security shuttles broke into view. They pulled vertical in a direct ascent, shrinking away as they climbed.

"What's he doing?" Lorel asked as she lined up next to him. "Is this part of your plan?"

"Not quite." Several seconds later, a flash blinked far up in the sky, followed by the low rumble of an explosion. "What was . . ."

Jaylen's voice trailed off, and he blinked. Because beneath the smoke and debris scattering in different directions, something shot straight down. It flew faster than the spray of fiery hull and engine parts returning to the surface. And unlike those pieces, this appeared to be a dark, compact form. Whatever it was, it descended at full speed, hitting the water with a large splash. Beneath the cascading water, the object's path continued, bubbles surfacing upon impact. Jaylen and Lorel stared together, though she whispered something to herself:

"The height of sky."

Jaylen didn't know what that meant, though he chose to let it go. From above, the security craft broke formation and returned to standard elevation. They twisted and turned on their way down, sweeping past Jaylen and Lorel before flying back into the city. A minute or so passed as the pair sat in silence, the only noise coming from the lapping waves and idling speeder.

Did that mean they'd successfully evaded security? It appeared that way, and Jaylen let another minute of quiet pass just to confirm.

ND-5 had saved Jaylen's life plenty of times since trying to kill him. Some situations were simpler than this—a gunfight where ND-5's sharpshooter skills won the day or an override on security before an alarm went off. Some of them were much more complex, like when ND-5's analytical droid thinking identified an overlooked logistical problem in Jaylen's plan.

This, though, was different. This was a combination of on-the-fly adaptation to changing circumstances, execution of military strategy, and physical precision to fly a ship built over a decade ago for a war that felt much older than that.

Enforcer. Getaway pilot. Data analyst. Ship mechanic. For years, Jaylen had assigned ND-5 specific roles, strict parameters. He had wanted—*needed*—as many strings under his control as possible in the search for Low Red Moon, whatever that was.

But Low Red Moon was Jaylen *Barsha's* quest. The violence of Gus Treta, the mystery of Sliro, the fused chip that once ordered ND-5 to kill him—that belonged to another lifetime.

Now Jaylen *Vrax* looked at what ND-5 had done for him: protecting him, finishing the mission, providing him with the means to get this data—data that could finally catapult him out of working for *others*. And the droid had done it without the bolt or the other false notions of constraint.

In fact, ND-5 had made the decision to increase the size of the storage crate and bring the speeder along as a contingency plan. That was *not* part of Jaylen's original plan, yet it was the very reason he was alive right now.

The irony of it all came into focus: Buried deep within ND-5 was the only tangible connection to Low Red Moon, whatever that was. But by letting ND-5 free from Jaylen Barsha's control—which might mean letting Low Red Moon *go*—Jaylen Vrax gained the freedom to forge his own way through the galaxy.

As that realization sunk in, the sloshing of water finally settled, leaving only natural ocean waves to come and go. And with that, another thought arrived—

ND-5 was gone.

Jaylen had made the wrong call, and ND-5 was gone.

Logically, Jaylen had known that was a possibility. In theory, that could have happened to either of them at any time. This was the life they chose, the company they kept. They didn't hire snipers and slicers to deliver groceries or build satellites. But despite that, Jaylen felt a twinge of remorse.

"This, uh," Lorel said, "has been more *eventful* than slicing for a syndicate."

Jaylen nodded, more out of instinct than anything else. Lorel paused, and Jaylen felt a stinging mist blow against his cheeks.

"Sorry. Sometimes I make small talk when I don't know what else to say." Lorel's backpack rustled as she reached in to pull out ND-5's restraining bolt. "Oh. This must have gotten damaged during all that." She handed the bolt over to Jaylen, and he held it in his palm, feeling the jagged pieces of the cracked cylinder and the exposed wire poking out. Another pause came before Lorel finally spoke again. "Sorry about your droid. I really liked him."

"Yeah." The word came out quiet and slow, gravel in his voice as it drew the sound out. He put the busted restraining bolt in his pocket and took in a breath of ocean air. "It was—"

Jaylen stopped, though not for loss of words. The strangest sight appeared in front of him.

Despite the rolling ocean waves, a dense collection of bubbles formed just off the shore. It grew, forming a trail that sloshed back and forth with the rhythm of the ocean. This went on for about ten seconds, the sea foam continually expanding, a dark spot growing beneath it. Something breached the surface. It emerged first as a curved dark material, but as it approached, Jaylen could make out a set of glowing eyes.

Just below those came the water-soaked collar of a dark green duster.

"Is that . . ." Lorel said.

Jaylen didn't answer. He didn't need to answer. ND-5 marched slowly toward them, seaweed draped over his body as he lumbered forward, his shoulders tilting left and right with each hulking step. The droid paused and tore the strips of seaweed off. He flung those away, then tilted his round head up before scanning the scene in front of him. He strode forward farther until he reached the ocean's edge.

Water ran off his limbs and trailed from the ends of his duster, puddling onto the sand as he walked. "Did you get the data?" he asked.

"Yeah, Endee," Jaylen said. "We did."

"This was a successful mission." ND-5 walked over to Lorel, who stared at the droid with an open mouth and wide eyes. "You see?" ND-5 tapped at the gash on his chest, the light from internal electronics still glowing. "This is not affected by the elements."

Lorel's mouth moved wordlessly for several seconds before she finally nodded. "I got that. I, uh . . ." She flashed a small smile, just a tilt of the corners at first, but then her cheeks lifted in a bright beam. "I'm glad you're here, big guy. I owe you one."

"You owe me nothing," he said. "We work well together."

"Yeah, well, I'll make sure to get you that contact we talked about, okay?" She made a fist and threw a punch that slowed right before it landed softly on his shoulder.

Static popped in Jaylen's ear, bringing his attention back to the moment. "I'm at the rendezvous point." Fennec's deadpan tone was all business, like the rooftop explosion and chase never happened.

"Copy that," Jaylen said.

ND-5 looked at him, those unblinking eyes hiding what the droid was truly thinking.

CHAPTER 26

Everyone stands in a circle inside the *Successor* cargo bay: me, Jaylen, Lorel, Fennec. The loading ramp is open for entry, though this is where we will part ways. We all look to Jaylen, though for different reasons. Fennec and Lorel are due their pay. I am considering our next steps.

Specifically, I am considering the name that Lorel provided: a droidsmith named Mubo on Batuu. Though I have not told Jaylen about this yet, I have looked up navigation paths to Batuu in the Outer Rim. Lorel has proven to be a trustworthy peer, though no one should be trusted outright in the galaxy's underworld.

Even if they are friendly.

Jaylen uses electronic credit transfer for Lorel. She finishes the process using several small devices, which must be a slicer's way of securing the data. While she does that, Fennec counts a stack of Imperial credit chips within a metal case. She finishes, then begins counting them again when Jaylen hands her a datapad.

"What are you going to do with your big prize?" Lorel asks Jaylen as she packs away Lumi, which she summoned back with a homing retract beacon.

"Ah, I'm glad you asked." Jaylen holds up *his* datapad with all the unmasked records. "I figure we'll encounter someone who might be interested in Imperial operatives. Everyone's got *something* they don't like about the Empire." He runs a hand through his hair, and despite the cumulative fatigue of the prior day's excesses and today's undercover tasks, he flashes a grin some would define as cocky. "I have a feeling many more jobs will open up for me. Jobs for me means jobs for others." Jaylen tucks the datapad away and crosses his arms. "If you're interested."

Fennec finishes confirming her payment. I am not surprised at her satisfied look. I stacked the chips myself. In a way, her lack of faith in my accounting abilities is surprising and somewhat off-putting, especially considering we may work together again. Fennec meets Jaylen's gaze and holds up the datapad he handed to her. "You put an extra name on there."

"A lesson I learned at a young age," says Jaylen. "Make sure to cover those who do good work. Consider it a bonus. Do with it what you will."

Fennec eyes him up and down. Her face is inscrutable on a level that matches a droid's. "Getting on my good side. Well played. If anyone trustworthy wants to know who's capable of good intel, I might send them your way."

Jaylen had mentioned previously that Fennec might be someone to have in our corner due to her growing reputation. However, his tone is different now than before, likely because this is no longer theoretical. He has talked about wanting to become a so-called player who hires and plans, who knows when to "push buttons" or "stand with your sabacc hand."

"Jaylen Vrax is open for business and ready to help," he says, his arms wide.

Fennec raises a single eyebrow at Jaylen. That is the biggest reaction we will get out of her.

Lorel does not react to Jaylen's proclamation and instead turns to me. "You sure you're okay? Want me to check your internal systems?"

"My diagnostics show the fall from the shuttle has made no impact on my hardware." I do another scan of core processes to confirm this.

"Got it. You're just trying to impress a lady." Lorel turns to Jaylen. "You know how to get in touch if a job comes up. But you"—she now points at me—"don't be a stranger, okay?"

"I'm not a stranger to you. We just worked together," I say.

This prompts a wink from Lorel. Jaylen hands me the datapad with the ISB cover list and proceeds to walk Lorel down the ramp while talking vaguely about possibilities.

I make a choice to begin uploading the ISB cover list to the *Successor*'s technical station via data cable. The monitor shows that the file transfer will take approximately eight minutes based on the rated speed of the connection.

I hear Jaylen's footsteps approaching and the closing of the *Successor*'s cargo door. I consider the estimated speed of Jaylen's walk to gauge his arrival, then compare his timing with the remaining countdown for the data transfer.

Given the gap of time needed for the file transfer as well as Jaylen's positive mood, I decide that, after some ship diagnostics and cursory checks, it will be a good time for me to discuss the droidsmith named Mubo. I begin calculating approaches to broach the subject.

CHAPTER 27

Jaylen looked at the datapad connected to the technical station—a table of information that looked deceptively simple at a glance. Sharper eyes, though, would recognize the potential on the screen. This datapad was a first step.

A *giant* first step.

Jaylen and ND-5 had run countless jobs in the past nine years, from picking up scrap parts to the occasional assassination. So many of those involved taking pay from someone else—and often splitting pay with others. But not only had Jaylen been in charge of this mission, he now had the bargaining power to gain the trust of the syndicates. Whom to sell to, whom to recruit, what to leverage . . . finally, Jaylen was CEO of his *life*.

As Jaylen settled in at the ship's technical station, he marveled at the possibilities ahead. Finally, he was in a stable enough—and lucrative enough—position to visualize the playing field, negotiate, and organize. He could let someone *else* execute under his watch.

All the reward. Much less of the blasterfire.

Jaylen stared at the data transfer progress bar on the large monitor, and as it crept toward completion, he thought back to how he'd almost blown everything just a night ago. He'd let his own obsessions about the *past* nearly steal his future. How foolish would that have been? The future was *all* that mattered in the end.

He took a moment for himself in the quiet of the ship, with only the occasional rattling of its loose lateral stabilizer and ND-5's heavy footsteps in the background. He had made it to this moment, a leap between eras as big as the day he'd watched clones storm his first speech as CEO of Barsha Corp.

Except he didn't pick that position. Here, he decided the next phase of his life—where it went, how he would get there, who would be involved. He finally achieved the one thing he ever truly wanted—control.

And perhaps the biggest difference in the mix was ND-5 himself. Jaylen's time as Barsha CEO had ended with ND-5 locking him into a dining room with a bomb strapped to his chest. But here, his future started with ND-5 rescuing him from an ISB agent—providing vital aid and support instead of imminent death and destruction.

The moment called for . . . not exactly a celebration, but a commemoration of sorts.

As if on cue, the heavy mechanical footsteps of the BX commando droid approached. ND-5 stood in the doorway, the tails of his still-damp duster swaying as the droid came to a halt.

"Hey, Endee," Jaylen said, waving the droid over. "You got a minute?"

"The job is complete. There are no high-priority issues right now. I am finishing cursory ship checks."

"Right, right. I'll take that as a yes. Just . . ." Jaylen sorted the push and pull of thoughts in his mind. He couldn't fully embrace the future until he put one more thing to rest. "Enter recording mode."

ND-5 stood completely still as his internal mechanisms responded.

"Please," Jaylen said. He didn't say that enough. ND-5 may have been a droid, but anyone or anything that saved your life over and over deserved common politeness.

"Recording active," ND-5 said.

"Okay." Jaylen let out a breath. And another one, still searching for what he was going to say. "Sliro, I'm not giving up on you. I don't ever want you to think that. But it's been nine years, and something big has . . ."

No, that wouldn't do. "Endee, strike that and restart."

"Done. Recording active," ND-5 said.

"Sliro." Jaylen took several seconds before continuing. "Hey, brother. Checking in. We've accomplished something. I think—I believe—this is going to lead to something big. Which means there are some things I need to let go. I've spent years in pursuit of what really happened to me. And you. All of us . . ."

Jaylen's mind drifted, like even brushing against the past made him involuntarily reel away from the memories.

"Endee, stop recording." But even that wouldn't halt the intrusive thoughts.

Nnytyl's last words and the final blaster shots rang through his mind.

"Sorry." Jaylen leaned back into his chair while rubbing his temples. "I can't do this now. Try again later. Delete this recording."

"Okay, Jaylen." ND-5 stood silently, and it took Jaylen several seconds to realize why the droid looked different. He had the same glowing eyes, same hulking posture, same green duster.

But no restraining bolt. It was still in Jaylen's pocket.

"I'll take a minute to think of our next steps," Jaylen finally said, and the technical station chimed to indicate that it had completed the datapad transfer. ND-5 still didn't move. Code names, industrial sectors, assigned systems—Jaylen's eyes skimmed the words, already thinking about potential buyers, how they could possibly trade information for contacts or other connections. "You can take care of anything that needs to be done."

Even then, ND-5 didn't move. "Everything okay, Endee?"

"I have an issue of medium importance to discuss with you."

"Medium importance?" Jaylen asked, still looking at the screen. The code name *Copper Blue,* alias for a *Romo Ulbod,* was linked to a cover operation for an agricultural inspector on Rendili sugar farms. Which syndicates had strongholds in proximity? Did any of them want control over the agriculture sector? Could any local militia units be interested in this?

When ND-5 answered, Jaylen had to consciously force himself to listen.

"Yes. Lower priority for you. But higher priority for me." ND-5's voice never wavered, though it paused now for a second. "It is a personal request."

That was unexpected. "Endee, we've been together for a long time," Jaylen said with a laugh. "I don't think you've ever made a personal request before."

"I have never encountered an opportunity as specific as this before, particularly under recent circumstances."

Recent circumstances—ND-5 was referring to the Andara mission. Before the mission, Jaylen had said that any discussions about the bolt and programming restrictions would take place after they finished up. ND-5 did tend to be quite literal, so he probably saw this moment as "after they finished up." Especially after ND-5 had successfully adapted to save Jaylen from his own mistakes.

"What's your request, Endee?" he asked as he pulled himself away from the names on the screen.

If their lives were truly going to move forward, then this could be part of it, too. There was just the matter of *how*. Because a droid who had cooperated could also be *very* uncooperative when ugly truths came out.

Especially droids built for assassinations.

"During my time with Lorel, she mentioned several droidsmiths she had previously worked with . . ."

There it was. Jaylen's hunch was correct.

ND-5 continued, though Jaylen tuned him out, a new dilemma occupying his mind. And like everything else, it came down to saying something or staying quiet.

". . . Mubo has enough experience with war-deployed droids that he would be able to remove the fused chip and safeguard my neural core. He comes from a long lineage of skilled droid builders. I believe this would be highly beneficial . . ."

There had to be a way to gradually disassemble the layers of deception while still keeping ND-5's trust. Jaylen considered this as he felt the weight of the damaged bolt in his pocket. He just needed one final, perfect lie to end all of this, closing a circle that started all the way back on Nar Shaddaa.

ND-5 paused, the droid failing to catch that Jaylen hadn't heard most of what he'd said.

"One second, Endee." Jaylen pointed to the terminal, a simple excuse to buy more time by pretending to review the cover list.

Then he blinked. And blinked again, just to make sure his eyes hadn't deceived him.

Suddenly, he read the data for real. Suddenly, all those characters and line items within the list snapped into actual, meaningful words meant for an ISB overseer of covert operatives. Names, places, sectors . . .

And most importantly, three simple words.

Three simple words that he'd hunted for years.

Low Red Moon.

He leaned forward, staring at the text on the screen as if the pixels might disappear if he looked away. He forced himself to read line by line, a full understanding of the data.

Code Name: Low Red Moon.
Operative Name: Madel Nureth.
Occupational Risk Level: 2.
Assigned Region: Corellian Trade Spine, Rotation 9.
Status: Active.

Low Red Moon was not a place or a mission or a resource. No, Low Red Moon was a *person*—an Imperial operative—and even now, an active agent. Under what pretense, that wasn't clear. But it was something that required enough subterfuge for a code name.

"Jaylen?" ND-5 asked.

This meant that the nascent Empire had destroyed Barsha Corp. Not a competitor. Not an inside job. The *Empire*—but why? Why target a company that had just gotten a massive government contract? Barsha Corp had significant dealings with the underworld, but so did every other megacorporation in the galaxy. At least Barsha had provided the Empire some value. Ships had to be built. Fleets needed to be filled.

Barsha Corp knew how to do that.

Jaylen continued staring at the screen, questions of why melting away into rage. Seconds ago, he'd begun the difficult task of letting the impulse for revenge finally fade away. But not now. Now it reached back from the depths, driven by the first actual clue in years.

He could not turn away now. In fact, how dare he even *think* about turning away. He'd vowed revenge. He'd promised Sliro, wherever Sliro was. And he almost abandoned that.

He could almost hear Roisem's verbal scorn now. In fact, he also heard a refrain that came to his mind far more than he'd like to admit: "Jaylen, go get someone to—" followed by blasterfire.

Blasterfire from ND-5.

"Is there an issue, Jaylen?" ND-5 asked. "Shall I initiate a transmission to Mubo?"

For so long, Jaylen had held the reins of his life tightly, controlling every element he could, including ND-5. With the truth about his family's murders finally within reach, that control had to remain in place. Maybe now even more so.

There was no margin for error. He wouldn't allow it.

"Hold up, Endee," Jaylen said, a conscious adjustment to his voice to conceal his innermost thoughts from the droid. "We'll get to that." He paused for a moment to ground himself, feeling everything from his planted feet to the chair's stiff backing to the way the damaged restraining bolt in his pocket caused the coat's weight to shift slightly.

Some time ago, maybe two or three years back, Jaylen ran an experiment. He'd hired a technician named Richar Yeldon under the guise of maintenance, a Latero that came cheap and did questionable droidsmith work given that his specialty was actually in hydraulic systems.

But accuracy wasn't exactly a high priority here. Nor was technical skill.

Jaylen hired Richar to be a blunt instrument, a simple on-off switch tied into ND-5's power systems. The cable from ND-5's primary power generator ran to Richar's small station, where the mechanic could monitor various real-time metrics.

Most importantly, this gave him the ability to completely shut the droid down if needed. At that point, Jaylen had been operating on what

Obills Myron had told him years ago: There was a 99 percent chance that the fused chip's override commands were wiped. But Jaylen needed to *know* with absolute certainty, to have one very final confirmation before moving forward. Because during those few hours on Nar Shaddaa, other factors might have come into play. The mission to retrieve parts might have taken priority in ND-5's programming, or different subroutines might have activated when they were under attack from the Pykes.

Or just dumb luck.

So he had set up this experiment in a calm, nonthreatening environment, telling the droidsmith that ND-5 had detected strange anomalies running through his power systems.

Richar told him that all monitors were active. Jaylen nodded, then popped off ND-5's restraining bolt.

The hardware snug in his pocket, Jaylen stepped all the way back behind Richar and his workstation, where charts and graphs flashed by. None of that really mattered, though. Either ND-5 would come to kill him or he wouldn't.

"Power him on," Jaylen said. Richar nodded, then flipped a switch on the side of the workstation, unblocking the power interrupt flow tied into ND-5's systems.

The droid remained standing straight up as his eyes went from dormant to glowing. His head jerked in subtle, short movements, things Jaylen recognized as ND-5's internal reactions to start-up diagnostics. The whole thing took only two or three seconds, yet Jaylen braced himself the entire time.

Richar didn't seem to notice any tension, instead tracking the metrics on-screen. "Everything looks good," he said. "Let's monitor for an hour, but I think whatever fluctuations you were seeing may have resolved themselves."

"Jaylen," ND-5 said, still tied into Richar's terminal, "where are we?"

"Doing some maintenance, Endee. Just stay still and quiet. Running some tests on your power systems," he said, his left hand feeling the restraining bolt in his pocket.

"Understood." The droid looked down. "Why is my restrain—"

"We need quiet for these tests, Endee. About an hour," he said.

The droid complied, going silent.

That time wasn't necessary, though. In that handful of seconds, Jaylen knew. He'd seen ND-5's killing capabilities up close—at Gus Treta with the other Barshas, on various jobs as other smugglers intercepted them, or whenever the need arose.

ND-5 didn't waste time when he intended to kill. Every action was calculated with precision and efficiency toward that goal. If ND-5 were still prioritizing the assassination of Jaylen Barsha, Jaylen wouldn't have been able to tell. Because he'd be dead already.

The fact that he still breathed while the droid stood there?

It was the final reassurance he needed.

ND-5's memory of the test with Richar Yeldon got deleted, never to be spoken of again. Jaylen didn't even assign it to restricted storage, like he did with his messages for Sliro. This was completely eliminated, and their journey since then led to this moment, where the mission on Andara demonstrated that ND-5's loyalty to Jaylen was a *choice*. The only danger, then, was ND-5's possible reaction to the truth.

How this would play out now, with the revelation of Low Red Moon, Jaylen wasn't sure.

"Endee, enter recording mode."

"Recording mode active," ND-5 said.

Jaylen paced back and forth, a mix of so many things tugging at him. Low Red Moon. ND-5's push for greater autonomy. Whether ND-5's other untapped abilities would help them track down their new target or just add another variable to be controlled. How to bring it all together?

"Sliro," he finally said, walking straight up to stare ND-5 in the eyes. "Take a good look at me. It's been a little while. I might sound"—he tapped his chest—"a little more tired than in the last recording. We've just been through a lot. But it was worth it." A fist formed at his side. "Absolutely worth it. Years ago, I promised you that I would get to the bottom of this, that I'd get revenge for all of us. I'm marking this moment, brother. I'm marking it for you, for me, for everyone that was killed that night.

"Because we got a name. I don't know exactly how this Madel Nureth ties specifically into Gus Treta, but she clearly does. She's Low Red Moon. Which means she'll know exactly what happened and why."

Did Madel Nureth give the order to kill the Barshas? Or was she involved in the business side of things—dissolving Barsha Corp and finding legal loopholes? Maybe she was even involved in the plea deal?

Or all the above.

"We're going to do this. I'm telling you, Sliro, I almost gave up. I almost let it all go. But not now. Everything is new again. I'm not going to let this go. I'm going to find this Madel Nureth. And whether it's her or someone she leads us to, I'm going to keep my promise to you."

He sat quiet for several seconds, the air in his lungs burning to come out in words and wordless feelings. But nothing else arrived. He squeezed his eyes shut for a moment, trying *not* to think of his father's last words, instead thinking about how he and Sliro had planned to take over the company. Together.

That was enough for now.

"Endee, finish recording. Security Protocol Brencoyle."

"Done." ND-5's eyes flashed to confirm that the memory was hidden from everyone, even himself. Then he continued the prior conversation. "Where should we go now?" the droid asked. "Is there new information to assess?"

How quickly ND-5 had shifted gears. Jaylen had gone through several minutes of a hellish emotional journey while, in the end, ND-5 confirmed exactly what he was: a machine, a tool, a thing that turned on and off between orders and deployment.

Even though he listened better than anyone else in Jaylen's life right now.

"Low Red Moon. I've finally found it. For now, I need anything and everything you can pull on an Imperial employee named Madel Nureth."

"I believe I will be more efficient if I am allowed to tap into all my default programming. It served us well at Gus Treta."

Jaylen held up a finger. He'd already thought that through—in fact, he'd anticipated this. "No, sorry, but we can't risk that. It might just be the one thing that tips you over the edge. Your programming lies in a delicate balance. Your restraining bolt is still damaged," he said, pulling it out from his pocket to show the droid, "so every second is a risk right now." The next line was one he'd saved for a while, blending a bit of what little droidsmithing he'd learned with things ND-5 had said before. "Droids try to fulfill their protocols. We need to make sure you stay *you* and not revert back to being a Bee-Ex commando droid."

"I have closely tracked internal metrics to mitigate that possibility." ND-5 paused for a moment. "Perhaps we can get another restraining bolt from a vendor to give us options."

That was unexpected. Jaylen needed an improvised excuse. "No, we need *this* specific one. Its programming is attuned to your situation. It's been there since Gus Treta, remember? Nothing's certain until we can get it repaired." He glanced around until he spied a tool kit sitting on the floor. He opened it and stuck the bolt inside, then looked at ND-5. "There. For safekeeping."

"I understand," ND-5 said. "I will use this as an opportunity to demonstrate my safety."

"That's a good idea." Jaylen considered what emotions to display. Not that ND-5 would actually empathize with them, but in the droid's swirl of sensors and algorithms, Jaylen could nudge certain internal processes toward the outcomes he wanted. "I'm still worried that you might have the latent programming to target me. But this is too important, so I'm giving you a chance without a restraining bolt. I'm putting my faith in you. We'll see how things work out after that. After all, we're a team. You can trust me."

CHAPTER 28

Two years ago, I helped Jaylen purchase a data tape of the general population records along the Corellian Trade Spine, a collection of archival information compiled by slicing local government computers. Such a resource simplifies target and contact identification, particularly as we avoid Imperial networks as much as possible. Unfortunately, the records became outdated as soon as I loaded them into the *Successor*'s technical station. However, it continues to offer a starting point when our tasks require identification of a person or persons.

As soon as Jaylen requests information on Madel Nureth, I activate the station's terminal to access this data. It replaces the cover list on the main display, and Jaylen crosses the room to sit. Lines form across his brow parallel to the scowl on his face. I tap away at the interface and successfully avoid input mistakes despite the fact that my fingers are physically optimized for combat rather than data entry.

A list of 102 matching records appears on the display. That is too many entries for any practical search given the dense populations on Core worlds and our lack of centralized record access. I proceed by applying filters to limit the results.

Based on the fact that Low Red Moon was connected to the Gus Treta incident, the person must be within a certain age range—old enough to be given a meaningful assignment during the time of the Barsha Corp dissolution, young enough to still be active right now. Given the regional nature of the position, it's also reasonable that Madel Nureth would have operated within a certain proximity to the Barsha family and Corellia during that time period, most likely close to the Inner Core.

Based on the information from Shaw's datapad, Madel Nureth is currently active within the range of system locations listed in the cover list data.

I consider that Madel Nureth, though a decoded name, may possibly still be some sort of cover name. However, the conversation with Shaw suggests that operatives are working within public view, providing them a method of blending in. As the records we've stolen were meant for an ISB overseer to review within a designated timeframe, they are likely to contain true names, not pseudonyms.

As the filtering process runs, it seems prudent to evaluate the options that would best lead to success.

Option one: Continue the mission as is while obeying Jaylen's request for self-limiting my own parameters.

My last true programming repair was shortly after Gus Treta, with the Nar Shaddaa droidsmith Obills Myron. According to Jaylen, Myron warned that I was at risk of reverting to my previously lethal protocols.

Lorel felt confident that would not happen due to accumulated memories and learned experiences forming new logic patterns. This is an evidence-based assumption. Experience validates this hypothesis.

However, I understand Jaylen's perspective. He is the one who will die if my programming flips to any Barsha-targeting assassination directive. He may also die if I revert to default factory settings during critical mission moments. Most humans would likely avoid any choices where their own death is the outcome.

Option two: Suggest again that we visit Mubo.

[[Excess information deleted due to Jaylen's refusal.]]

Option three: Suggest a memory wipe.

This would ensure protection of Jaylen by removing any underlying assassination directives. However, this would likely worsen my ability to follow my current priority program of protecting Jaylen. It would also remove all the recent prior experiences that define who I am, including every instance of Lorel calling me "big guy."

Option two has already been vetoed. Option three goes against my priority.

By default, only option one remains. Jaylen's history shows that he is constantly strategizing. He would not make this choice without thinking it through. He often proclaims that we are a team, and under that definition, Jaylen's logic makes sense. It is not my preference, but it is the most reasonable path forward given the different goals and priorities in front of us. Still, I see this as an opportunity to prove my own hypothesis about my capabilities while following Jaylen's directions.

Now Jaylen is staring at a datapad with a map of Inner Core worlds local to Corellia.

"Jaylen," I say, "I wish to inform you that I've weighed variables about my programming, recorded actions, and results. You are correct." His face relaxes at this. "Your assessment is sound based on compiled data. I intend to treat our next task as a thorough test of my autonomy and impulse control with my restraining bolt removed. I believe we will finish everything without my attempting to murder you."

Jaylen pauses at that. He is still sitting in the chair at the small dinner table across from the technical station, though his expression has changed in the past six minutes. When I walked in, his cheeks sat soft, his brow thoughtful. Now everything has tightened, including a slight draining of his circulation that gives his face an ashen tint.

He is thinking.

He will likely come to a conclusion faster if he is allowed to concentrate. I give him space to do that. His hand goes to his chin, giving it an absent-minded rub as he stares beyond me. "That's good, Endee," he finally says. "We make a good team."

Data arrives on the terminal. I stay there to compile it, adding contextual notes for every instance of Madel Nureth listed.

"Jaylen," I say. "I have detailed information on Madel Nureth."

"That was fast," he says, his face now breaking into a smirk. The chair squeaks as he leans back into it. "Where are we headed?"

"Undecided. Twenty-four active and appropriate records are associated with that name."

"That's a lot," he says, his expression turning sour in response to that fact. "Well, we can whittle it down."

"I already have," I say. "By age, proximity to system, and other factors. This is the reduced list representing the identities that require further individual research."

After eight seconds, he says, "Oh." Jaylen's disappointment is visible and doesn't require any extra analysis by my emotional recognition algorithms. He bites down on his bottom lip and comes across the space to lean over the screen. Perhaps he believes that staring at all the compiled data about Madel Nureth will bring her truth to the surface.

While he participates in that waste of energy, I use my resources more constructively. "I will begin cross-referencing these records with information about operative activity from Shaw Andeej. That should highlight more specifics regarding operative tasks and movement patterns, which can then guide how we research each individual."

I reach over and pull a third datapad out of a stack. The display flashes as it comes to life before a new list of names appears, and the sudden change in font and color grabs Jaylen's attention away from the station display. He straightens up, and his eyes shift from curiosity to resolve.

"That list shows every contact we have had a positive interaction with since Gus Treta," I say. "It's a good place to start. Shall I begin outreach?"

Now Jaylen is nodding—slow at first, but he picks up speed. "We also have next to no money," he says with a laugh before switching the screen back to the cover list from Shaw. "But we do have this." He stands up and begins to pace around the room. "We can't trade away too many names. There's only a hundred of them. This is, after all, our big investment. But information is as valuable as credits. Often more. Endee?"

"Yes, Jaylen."

"I got a plan," he says, pointing to the datapad in my hand.

PART 3

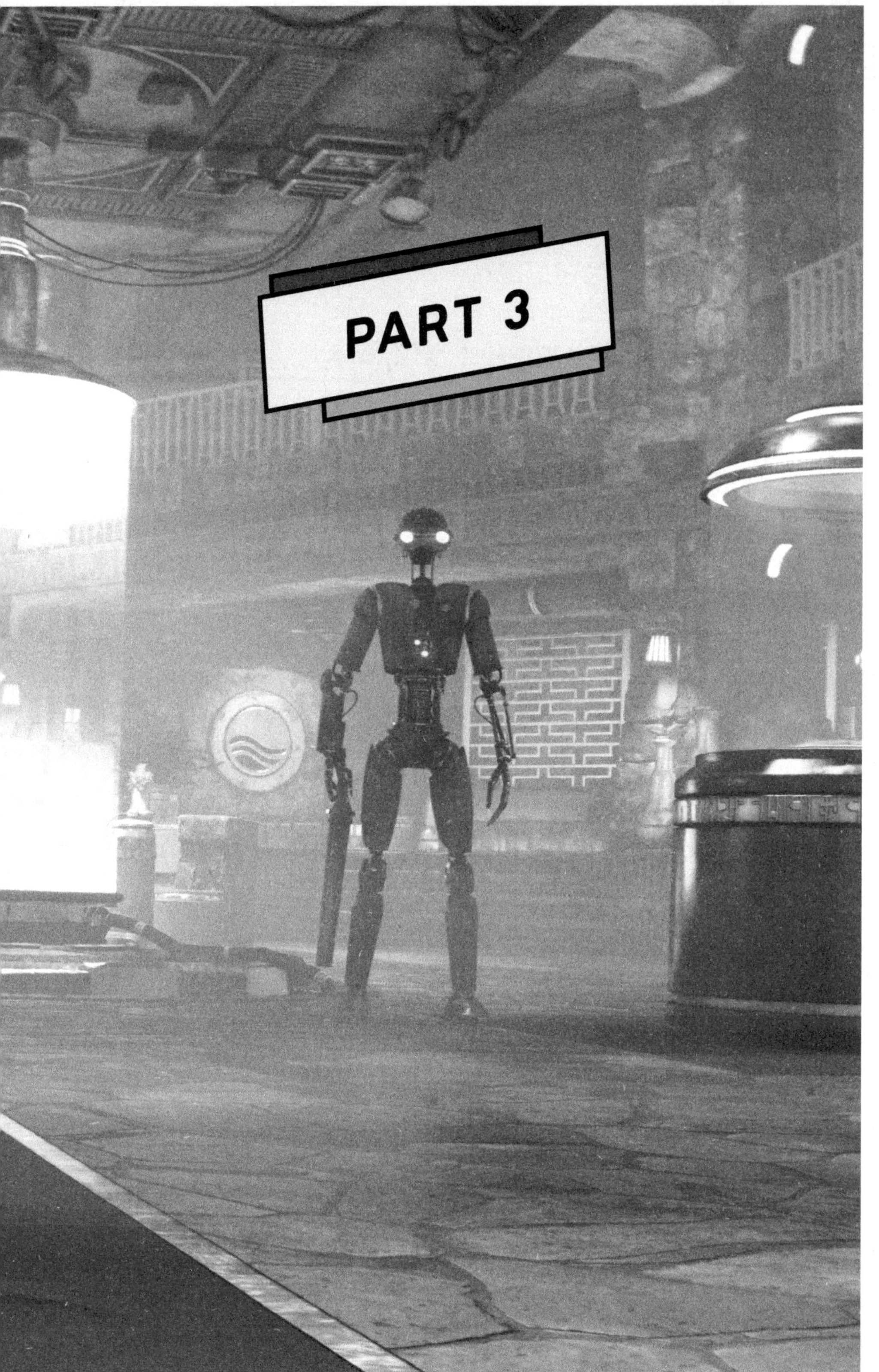

CHAPTER 29

Over the next several weeks, Jaylen and ND-5 worked in parallel on a fact-finding mission. Jaylen sent message after message to established contacts, even considering Fennec Shand given her growing reputation and experience, though he pulled back on that one. Fennec didn't seem like the type of person who appreciated being asked for favors too often.

Money, as always, proved to be the great limiter. ND-5 created a travel map designed to maximize what limited resources they had, moving them gradually along the Corellian Trade Spine from the Deep Core to the Inner Rim. He also started building a list of known and current syndicate contacts. "I believe this information will become valuable to our future endeavors."

The process produced methodical results but no true hits. Still, every effort dug up enough information to cross various Madel Nureths off the list, and it became apparent that their focus would be the Inner Rim. Yet despite ND-5 cross-referencing Jaylen's findings against additional public records, facial recognition, transaction records, and other factors, it still wasn't enough to find the Imperial operative.

They were low on fuel. Low on credits. Low on options.

Funny how quickly the internal calculus changed based on resource scarcity. Weeks ago, they'd come further than ever before, yet right now the very idea of choosing revenge over survival seemed counterproductive. If Sliro saw Jaylen right now, would he laugh, understand, or chastise Jaylen for even thinking about giving up?

Jaylen didn't know. And because he didn't know, he pushed forward. He stared at his datapad, which displayed the next contact they'd pinged for information. The name *Kranash* appeared on display next to a photo of a brown-skinned Trandoshan with rough scales and fierce eyes. Jaylen's boots dug into the cockpit dashboard as he rocked back and forth in the pilot's seat, and next to him ND-5 tapped at the navicomputer to load the planet Giju within the Colonies region.

"Jaylen, I have a suggestion." Before Jaylen could respond, ND-5 continued. "Eight people named Madel Nureth are left on our list. Six of them show evidence of residing within the Sern sector. The socialite, the art teacher, the baker, the accountant, the veterinarian, and the transport pilot. While you are intercepting Kranash, I should visit the Sector Central Utility Records building. This system is the only one on our projected route that has an archive kept independent from Imperial records."

"Huh," Jaylen said, while ND-5 stood completely still. "Is it an artifact of the Republic?"

"Possibly. The archive was initiated three hundred and sixty-four years ago due to neighboring trade alliances and suspicious governments. The agreements governing its existence most likely continue in perpetuity since its recordkeeping is so embedded into their economic infrastructure. Giju society has a tendency for independent activity. This office likely stems from that cultural sentiment." ND-5 pulled up a photo of the building, a dull, boxlike structure free of adornments. "The Empire probably found it too troublesome to manage and not valuable enough to take over or remove."

If that were true, that meant Barsha Corp had been both too vulnerable *and* too valuable to remove. Now a more worthless political oddity might lead them to Low Red Moon.

Jaylen pulled up a map of their destination. The *Successor* would dock at a spaceport just outside of Kristom, the second-largest urban district of Giju. They'd intercepted reports of Kranash being in the area, and while he wasn't originally on their list of contacts—mostly because they'd never encountered him before—his reputation preceded him.

The mighty Trandoshan known as Kranash was feared by his enemies, loathed by the Empire, trusted by his colleagues, and respected by the syndicates. He'd organized jobs and brokered contracts for all of them. One infamous score for Black Sun against the other syndicates should have earned everyone involved a death mark. Yet Kranash's standing—and whatever dirt he had on half the galaxy—meant that the players walked away unscathed, begrudging nods all around. The Trandoshan was simply too valuable to everyone to upset the balance.

And even if, say, the Hutts sent someone after Kranash, there was a reason why his own fast-draw abilities were legendary.

Respected, in demand, and lethal. In short, he was, in one scaly body, everything Jaylen and ND-5 aspired to be as a team.

Jaylen debated the decision of *not* having backup for this. "How far away is this place?"

"Giju's Sector Central Utility Records department is twenty-six kilometers away from the city center." ND-5 pointed at the map on the station's display's bottom-left corner.

"You want to do that while I track Kranash?" Jaylen asked.

"It is the most efficient use of our time," ND-5 said. "Our spaceport pass only allows for a three-hour stay. Kranash's rumored blaster-drawing speed is fast enough that he would kill you even before I drew a weapon. Then I would either have to fight back in vengeance or return to the spaceport before the local authorities confiscate the ship. Neither of which would help us reach your overall goal of identifying Madel Nureth. However, visiting the SCUR would support multiple objectives as long as you don't die."

Jaylen didn't even take offense to the fact that ND-5 projected an easy win for Kranash in a blaster duel. His brain and his mouth were his biggest assets, not his ability to shoot or fight. "Well," Jaylen said, "I suppose if I did die, you would at least be able to hear it over comms."

"Your transceiver is currently malfunctioning and has a weak signal, particularly in various types of indoor structures. I may miss your hypothetical murder. However, if there is a long period of ambient noise, I'll assume that you failed."

Since the job with Fennec and Lorel, ND-5's suggestions grew bolder, more assertive—in some ways, smarter. These were exactly the types of calculations Jaylen would have made if he were assigning a crew to a high-stakes job against a shrinking window. In fact, had this been anyone else besides ND-5, he'd have instantly agreed.

Jaylen reminded himself that regardless of what happened with Madel Nureth, he accomplished more when he gave ND-5 greater autonomy. The risk here wasn't Kranash or the SCUR; it was Jaylen's own hesitance to say yes. And facing ND-5's logic, well, there was really only one choice.

"All right," Jaylen said slowly. "Let's try to stay active on comms as long as we can."

"My priority is to serve you. You can be confident in my risk-reward calculation. Now I must land the ship." ND-5 turned to the cockpit and settled into the pilot's seat. Jaylen's stomach tilted as ND-5 pointed the ship into a descent, the craft's lackluster inertial dampeners causing a rattle of loose plating and stacked datapads. The ship pushed downward, and the seat bounced with the final touchdown. Various mechanisms powered down, a gradual receding of ambient hums and groans until only beeps from computing systems remained.

Jaylen looked at his datapad and reread the intercepted communiqué placing Kranash at a planned meeting with a contact at a cantina on the edge of Kristom's manufacturing district. He tapped through the datapad's various displays to bring up a map, a single red line tracing from here to there in the most efficient way possible.

ND-5 stepped out of the cockpit to walk over to the ship's equipment cabinets. He reached in before coming back to Jaylen with a metal hand outstretched. "I have repaired the comlink as much as I can without new parts." Jaylen put the small piece in his ear, then put the base transceiver in his inner coat pocket. "Can you hear me?" the droid asked.

In Jaylen's ear, the question blasted at full volume, a fraction of a second behind ND's actual voice. "For now," Jaylen said. "Yeah, I got it."

The earpiece continued capturing ND-5's movements: heavy thumping from his footsteps followed by clangs and clicks as he readied their only functioning speeder bike. Soon after came the grind and squeal of the ship's loading door gradually dropping. "I'm calculating the most efficient travel route," ND-5 said as Jaylen marched to the back of the ship, a strange echo effect between his distant true voice and the transmission in Jaylen's ear.

"Hey, Endee," Jaylen called out as he leaned against the doorway to the loading area. Though the speeder's engine revved underneath the droid's massive body, ND-5 craned his head. "Good luck."

"Luck is a human construct," ND-5 said. With that, the bay door opened, and the speeder accelerated to a gradual cruising speed, ND-5's duster billowing out behind him.

Luck. Risk. Reward.

Datapad still in hand, Jaylen stared at the image of Kranash as noise filtered in from the landing area. Speeders passed by. Maintenance workers shouted about parts. A couple argued about where to find a cheap meal.

And somewhere beyond all that, a Trandoshan that might have intel on the Madel Nureth they sought—or might shoot Jaylen dead before he even saw it coming.

CHAPTER 30

I approach the Giju Sector Central Utility Records building, which is a gray cube stacked upon another gray cube. One side has reflective black windows and another has yellow vegetation crawling up its side. There are two rows of speeders of various sizes parked outside of the SCUR building, each positioned within assigned lines. Between the two rows is a deactivated fountain covered in various animal droppings.

I maneuver the speeder to an empty spot placed within the marked lines, though my parking is not perfectly centered. The path toward the SCUR entrance is blocked by two children telling their father that they do not want to wait. The father's tone is desperate and frustrated as he states—

[[Data not retained due to lack of relevancy.]]

The family is too engulfed in their argument to notice me. However, a pale human with sagging eyes and an ill-fitted raincoat stands up from his small table as I approach. His voice has a slight quiver to it as he greets me, though his facial muscles force a smile that I estimate is for projecting friendliness. "Hello, and welcome to SCUR," he says, adjusting the cap on his head. "What department are you looking for today?"

"I seek home, employment, vehicle, and other registry records for all of the persons named Madel Nureth within the sector," I state.

The man squints, then looks down at his datapad.

I decide to be helpful, as that will finish this task faster. "There should be six of them."

The man nods, though he continues to squint at his datapad rather than take action.

Once again, I choose the efficient route of helpfulness. "I'll wait right here while you access the records."

Now he looks up, then over his shoulder. "Those records are," he says in a slow drawl, "all in different departments."

"I understand." I decide to repeat my previous statement in case this man has ill-equipped hearing. "I'll wait right here while you access the records."

He continues squinting, though now he is looking at me, and I notice the increased pace of his carotid artery. The dissonance between his eyes and his mouth show that he is masking a sense of anxiety, even fear. Either my record request is difficult, or he is intimidated by seeing a Separatist commando droid in a duster coat.

"What I mean is," he says again, "you have to get the records at each department." He points a thumb over his shoulder. "In there."

I turn and look beyond the translucent sliding doors. Inside are rows of seats, with current capacity at 27 percent full. Behind them is a large counter segregated into ten individual stations, with only half of them active. "In there?" I ask for confirmation.

"That's the first department," he says. "The others are upstairs. But they usually have longer waits."

As with the family outside, no one seems to pay attention to my arrival as I stand and gauge the clerks at each counter. While two of the clerks are serving customers, the other three appear unoccupied, possibly bored. None of the people sitting are making eye contact with the clerks, either. There is no signage about protocol or even what this specific department does.

I decide not to waste my time seeking assistance and instead walk up to the nearest available spot at the counter, holding up my datapad. "I'm seeking home, employment, vehicle, and other registry records for all of the persons named Madel—"

The clerk, a Gran female, tilts her head and then says, "Number confirmation, please."

"My designation is Jay-Ex-Three-Nine-Four-En-Dee—"

"No, your number," she says with a heavy sigh.

"That is my designation as assigned by my manufacturer at Baktoid Combat Automata."

"Blasted droids," she says at a volume too low for a conversational exchange, then returns to her normal tone. "Take a number."

It appears that everyone in this building speaks with a significant lack of specificity. If I were capable of being infuriated, this would likely trigger that emotion. "Take it where?"

Above us, an audio announcement plays out. "Now serving customer . . . C21 . . . at window four." The receptionist points above at a small mounted speaker not fully flush with the wall, then to a small kiosk in the back corner by the stairs. "There is an order for service. Get a number there. Then wait."

Behind her is a large space filled with various employees at desks, along with two roaming astromech droids painted brown and white, as well as a central mainframe system lined with blinking status lights. I run a time-and-efficiency calculation, outputting two options:

Option one: Kill this clerk and anyone who provides resistance. Break down the counter and then access the mainframe. Connect my datapad and download records, either in bulk or by specific request, whichever will take less time.

Option two: Take a number.

The first option would likely result in interference from local authorities, which may then attract Imperial attention to both myself and Jaylen. Though more immediately gratifying, it invites the potential for far more delays and ultimately violates my primary directive to serve Jaylen.

"I will take a number," I say.

I walk over to the kiosk, a simple machine that distributes small thin squares that sync up with the SCUR's customer numbering system. However, the distribution mechanism is stuck. I hear the whir of gears as it tries to slide a square out. I kneel for a closer look, only to find that two squares are mashed together in the output aperture.

Behind me, the familiar beeps and chirps of an astromech play out. I turn to find one of the maintenance droids from the back office area sliding toward me. My processors translate its beeps in real time—it is surprisingly rude for a maintenance droid, though perhaps it also notes how significantly inefficient every aspect of this facility is.

Move it. I gotta fix that. Stupid thing keeps breaking.

I stand back and let the astromech roll by as various tools extend from its cylindrical body. Its paint job appears to have been hastily done: dark brown with white feet and a white stripe across the head unit, though the lines are not clean.

However, I notice one thing underneath the paint. On the rear of the astromech's dome is an etching of a Confederacy of Independent Systems hex icon.

It is a repurposed war droid. I see a strategic advantage if this droid has any loyalties remaining in its protocols.

"I am Jay-Ex-Three-Nine-Four-En-Dee-Five-Seven-Seven-Seven serving the Confederacy of Independent Systems. State your designation."

The droid stops tinkering with the kiosk and rotates its head toward me. It lets out a series of low, slow questioning beeps.

You are a CIS soldier? Are you undercover?

A new plan formulates as I seek to take advantage of the SCUR's mix of apathy toward bureaucracy and low maintenance budget.

"I am," I say, tapping the shoulder of my duster. "We should not discuss this within hearing range of anyone in this building." I pull out a data transfer cable to connect us. "This mission requires silent and direct communication."

We stand by the kiosk for two minutes and thirty-eight seconds. In that time, I discover that the astromech's identity is G3-R44, and it arrived with its counterpart maintenance astromech R0-E0 shortly after the end of the war. The droid has no memory of how it was procured by SCUR, though it is most likely because practical CIS assets were confiscated and distributed to various governmental agencies.

Its memory wipe, however, was not properly executed. Many seized CIS assets underwent complete reprogramming to remove any directives from the war. For G3-R44—and likely R0-E0—both of their memory wipes apparently stalled at 95 percent, and the result was never verified by their attending technician.

This sloppy work provides an opportunity.

In our silent conversation, I provide authentication to show that I am indeed a BX commando droid. Both astromechs are confused about their placement at SCUR but have made the assumption that they are working as CIS spies, and since they do not have access to HoloNet news updates, they are unclear about the state of the war.

I will provide orders.

I tell G3-R44 that General Grievous is looking for an operative named Madel Nureth located in this sector, and that he needs confirmation of her identity along with as much intel as possible. I provide details about how I have identified six people with that name, and I must find the operative. G3-R44 responds by describing available systems in the back office space, along with each one's purpose and accessibility.

Together, we create a tactical analysis: the goal, the easiest way to achieve it, the potential threats, the active security measures. This comes naturally to me, as BX commando droids are designed to utilize tactics-based skill sets to the fullest. My history with other BX droid deployments proves this, as does my work with Lorel.

This briefly deviates my thoughts as I consider how strange it is that Jaylen scrutinizes, frets over, and ultimately overlooks these abilities of mine when putting together crews for jobs. In this case, I have identified a key piece of intel, established the means of getting it, assembled a makeshift team, and adapted to evolving circumstances.

Yet Jaylen fails to utilize me to the fullest no matter how much I prove myself.

Perhaps next time will be different once I inform Jaylen of my experience here.

I tell G3-R44 that he was not originally intended to be part of my division, but my BX team has been eliminated, and I am now in disguise. "I have authorization to enlist any appropriate aid on my way," I communicate through the cable. "You have been drafted into my mission. We have identified the most effective means to retrieve the data while avoiding detection. Is this strategy saved in your memory core?"

The droid sends back an affirmative.

I kneel to break our data connection and unplug the cable from the droid's interface port. "Now go," I say audibly as I stand up, "and try not to get caught or destroyed."

G3-R44 offers one beep and rolls toward the back office. Behind me, someone clears their throat, and I turn to see a bored Twi'lek waiting for the kiosk. "You will have to wait," I say. "The maintenance team is busy."

In the ten minutes that pass, I establish contact with Jaylen and update him on the situation. He is about to enter the cantina after tracking Kranash for the last thirty minutes. I keep my comm line open to monitor his situation. He is not dead yet.

At the same time, I manage to get a number out of the kiosk in case it is needed. Now that it is unjammed, I also retrieve the next number for the patient Twi'lek.

G3-R44 soon returns, rolling toward me with no signs of having triggered security. The droid's thin mechanical arm is holding a datapad, presumably filled with information on the different Madel Nureths. I take it from him and verify its transfer log. "Well done," I say. "Your mission is a success."

G3-R44 beeps and tilts back and forth with unexpected excitement. I consider the best way to reward this action.

I put a finger to my head as if I have a transceiver there. That is not how transceiver communication works for BX droids, but it makes for a good display. "General Grievous commends you and Arzero-Eezero. He advises you to stay undercover and monitor for any suspicious activity until further notice."

The astromech beeps in reply, roughly translating to "We have achieved our goals with minimal resource wastage. You are a highly efficient commanding officer." I nod in acknowledgment, and G3-R44 rolls away, our temporary team successful, yet now disbanded.

Now I must continue alone.

No transmissions from Jaylen come through as I leave the SCUR. I still carry my square from the office's kiosk. A man is standing at the front entryway. He looks apprehensive about entering as he scans the volume of people waiting.

I hand him my square. "You will need to take a number," I say. "You may have mine. I don't need it anymore."

CHAPTER 31

It took about thirty minutes for Jaylen to walk from the *Successor* to the industrial district on the edge of Kristom, which left him plenty of time to review what he knew about the region—and occasionally to wallow in self-doubt. The six Madel Nureths in the system represented so many different walks of life. One was a socialite in high society, the kind of circles that used to run in Barsha Corp executive gatherings. Another was an art teacher specializing in children with learning disabilities and who spent her evenings performing in local theater. Another ran a local bakery, seemingly focused on community building, and yet another piloted transports in the Core portion of the Corellian Trade Spine. And the last was an accountant—a plain old by-the-numbers accountant.

They'd crossed off other Madel Nureths one by one. Some had solid alibis during the Gus Treta incident. Others could logistically have been involved with Gus Treta, but indirect evidence showed them to be poor fits. On the bright side, each of these investigations reintroduced Jaylen and ND-5 to contacts from years ago, gave them a better sense of current relationships between syndicates, and even gave them the intel that led to Kranash. And despite their tangent to find Madel Nureth, the connections still counted as career progress.

But not *paid* progress. All this effort took up their time. Which meant that they weren't working. Certainly not the kind of work Jaylen had envisioned, where he would identify a score, organize a crew for one of the syndicates, then execute a job. They hadn't even found basic "deliver this contraband" or "escort this shipment" jobs. Let alone the better-paying "eliminate this target" or the even better-paying "do a little bit of everything."

No, they were burning up resources, most of their credits used to pay Lorel and Fennec. And with the plan to leverage the full cover list toward bigger and better things gone to the wayside, they were short on . . .

Money. That was what it always came down to. Everything in this life, everything in the galaxy always depended on money—Imperial credits or druggats or whatever you might cash in at an Outer Rim dive. That was one of the first lessons of his life as a Barsha. Except back then, the perspective was flipped: Finding money was never the issue; choosing what to do with it, who to wave it at, how to make everything easier—*that* was the problem. Or, as his mother put it, "*Make sure to cover the ones who could hurt you. The others can fend for themselves.*"

Right now, though, they had to come back to much more grounded eventualities, like starving or getting stranded.

Jaylen ignored the rumble in his stomach as he stepped through the open doorway of the Factory Arms Cantina and Gambling House. A datapad sat in his coat pocket, jostling with movement. Part of him realized that storing this in a secure, locked container on the *Successor* would have been more sensible—and really, they'd already copied the cover list information to the ship's technical station.

But he just felt *better* knowing it was on his person. Ships got raided, technical stations failed—those risks existed, but keeping that datapad where he could feel its weight and form . . .

It meant that his future was never too far from his reach.

Right now, though, it didn't benefit him that much. He couldn't bribe bartenders or bookies with it. Those types wouldn't exactly be interested in Imperial cover identities. Credits were the common denominator no matter where you were or what the government looked like.

Right now, all Jaylen could do was order a single drink, nurse it for as long as possible, and hope his target said something of use.

"I'm returning from the SCUR office," ND-5 said into his ear. "I will be monitoring your audio as I travel. My language algorithm should be able to interpolate what is said as long as the transmission gaps span no more than forty percent of a word." Jaylen looked down at his glass and pondered how many drinks matched the cost to repair the multidirectional microphone in his coat pocket.

"All right, Endee. Maybe today will be our lucky day."

"Thirty-seven percent of your response was lost to static, but I heard you hope that this is our lucky day." Though none of Endee's words broke up, Jaylen wondered if the ensuing pause was a technical issue or if the droid simply didn't know what to say. "I will repeat what I said earlier," Endee finally finished. "Luck is a human construct."

A large brown-skinned Trandoshan stepped out of the refresher door. His coat parted enough to show a hip holster, blaster presumably within. Kranash turned his head slightly, his eyes quickly darting. The uninformed or inattentive wouldn't have even noticed him surveying the scene. Kranash huffed out an exhale, his large scaly nostrils flaring, then he walked directly across the small hallway toward a booth holding a lone silhouette.

"Thanks, Endee," Jaylen said under his breath. "Target's on the move."

"This strategy of waiting for him to say something about Madel Nureth demonstrates an overreliance on variables out of your control," ND-5 said.

Jaylen waited for ND-5 to say something further, but the droid stayed quiet. Or the transmission got lost to technical churn. As he sipped his drink, another possibility came to mind: Maybe ND-5 finally got that some things really did come down to dumb luck. Though in this case, it wasn't *all* that; he had a little strategy in play here.

"He's heading to someone," Jaylen said as he scanned the rest of the establishment's patrons: several people sitting at the bar, others engaged in standing conversation, and still others interested in the remote gambling kiosks. Farther away sat a room with drawn curtains, which Jaylen figured was for sabacc or some other game. "I'm seeing if something he says shows interest in Imperial cover names."

He half expected ND-5 to give him a very practical reminder that those cover names were among the few assets they had left, so he should use them wisely. However, the droid remained silent while Kranash slid into the booth. From behind, the other patron's head bobbed in conversation. Across the way, a spot at the nearby holographic fathier-betting module opened up. "There's our chance," he said, and he stepped behind the small crowd. "Try to lock into his voice if you can, Endee."

"I am attuning filters for the target's specific vocal frequencies," the droid replied. "You should still use your own ears."

Jaylen nodded, which was a rookie move; any gesture to himself would only indicate that he was talking to a comlink. From a few meters away, a small group cheered as holographic fathiers rounded the corner for a final lap. Across the bar, raucous laughter came from an inebriated Gamorrean. And the bartender himself rang a bell indicating . . . something that caused several patrons to clap.

Though the conversation at Kranash's booth featured mostly quiet griping about the quality of the drinks, Jaylen's ears perked up when the other person mentioned Imperial checkpoints. And *that* caused both a reaction and a groan from Kranash. "Spies everywhere these days," he said, slamming his glass with a laugh. "You know what I miss about the Republic? They had so much churn they didn't care about these things. During the war? It was like a free pass to do anything." His partner, an old human male with brown skin and a ring of white hair on his head, responded with a laugh, but then spoke in muffled sounds. If ND-5 got the audio, he didn't provide a direct translation.

"That's what I'm talking about," Kranash said. "The Republic wasn't *paranoid* like the Empire is. That made for good business! So much easier to smuggle when you just forged documents instead of these checkpoints and inspections." The human held up a glass, then said something that prompted a grizzled laugh from Kranash. "That's right, my friend.

To the Republic. May it rest on the burning embers of its own bureaucracy."

"Endee, I think we have a buyer," Jaylen said. For the next ten minutes, he lingered, occasionally cheering or grousing about the fathier results in front of him. But as soon as Kranash stood up, he adjusted and followed, moving casually to put his drink on the bar while tracking the Trandoshan in even, measured steps. Jaylen tailed him as he took a side hallway, where Kranash paused to activate a dormant Raven 4 arcade machine.

Glowing lines came on the display, forming starships and obstacles, the neon yellow of the display adding a sheen to Kranash's skin. Jaylen took one step forward, when Kranash spoke. "You wanna tell me why you're following me, or should I blast you now?" he asked, and in one move, he flipped the tail of his coat out enough to unclip the holster on his hip.

Jaylen flashed a broad smile, both hands up. "I was trying to get your attention," he said slowly, "and it worked."

"You've got ten seconds before you *lose* my attention," Kranash said, one hand hovering over the blaster's grip, yet still playing the game with his other hand. "Maybe less."

"You're Kranash. Everyone knows you because of the Black Sun incident on Manaan. You are"—Jaylen cleared his throat—"a good person to talk to. Because you're connected." Jaylen considered the very thoughts he'd had about Kranash's reputation not that long ago, and he figured if flattery could get him anywhere, now would be a good time to lay it on. "The syndicates respect you. The Empire fears you. You get things done with the best teams in the most efficient way. In short . . ." He took a breath. "My career goal is to be like you."

Did Kranash get this kind of thing all the time? Maybe he did in a more sniveling, annoying way. Jaylen liked to think he presented with a bit smoother resolve.

"What's your name?" Kranash said with a snarl.

The fact that there wasn't a blaster hole in Jaylen's chest was good. The snarl, though, wasn't exactly the best. "Jaylen Vrax."

"Well, Jaylen Vrax," he said, buttoning his holster clip, "this sort of thing may work when you're recruiting someone to do your dirty work. Flattery doesn't get you anywhere when you've been in the game as long as I have. I've given you a little more time than most. How about you let me"—he tapped the Raven 4 machine—"finish this up?"

"Ah. Not one for flattery." Jaylen nodded. "I prefer cold, hard facts, too. May I?" he asked, pointing to his coat pocket. Kranash nodded, and Jaylen pulled out the datapad. He tapped a button on its side for the display to bring up the code name Copper Blue. "Like this. This is an Imperial operative code name. Let's sit down and talk, and I'll unmask the identity for you." Jaylen raised an eyebrow to match the curl of his lip. "A drink on me?"

Kranash took the datapad with a slight tug, then inspected it closely. "I see. Information trading."

"That's right. I'm looking for someone."

"I'm not. Because I don't need to." He tossed the datapad back at Jaylen, so fast that Jaylen almost missed it. Jaylen gripped it, taking one quick glance at the display, and by the time he looked back up Kranash had left Raven 4 running with no one at the controls. On-screen, digital spaceships collided, explosions sparkling before GAME OVER appeared. Before he knew it, the Trandoshan slid past him and headed to the exit. Kranash paused and looked over his shoulder. "Don't interrupt my free time again. But I'll find you if I ever need to be reminded of my past accomplishments," he said before turning around and leaving.

"Based on his vocal intonations," ND-5 said, "my analysis shows that he is being completely sincere."

"I think," Jaylen said, drawing the words out slowly, "this may be the end of the line." He meant for his comment to be about Kranash. But the fact that their dwindling resources made the cost of a single drink a problem, it might have applied to much more. Now it was his turn to glance over his shoulder, except this time, it was a longing look at the bar. "A drink sounds good. Not that we can afford one."

Jaylen chose *not* to remind himself what had happened the last time he didn't listen to ND-5 about a vocal analysis. And he didn't want to think about their finances. He knew things were bad. He knew they'd likely drained *everything* over the past few weeks.

Even if ND-5 got more data about the different Madel Nureths, they didn't have the resources to pursue six more leads. They could run more jobs, but by the time they earned more credits, they'd have to reset their search, courtesy of the ISB's cadence of operative rotations.

By then, Madel Nureth may have moved on. Who knew how her trail might change, or even if her next rotation was in this sector? If they didn't find her *now,* they might have to start all over again.

All this for nothing except a lousy stiff drink and a passing encounter with Kranash.

"How do you want to proceed, Jaylen?" ND-5 asked. "Shall I prepare the ship for your return? I will begin processing the SCUR download."

"I think—" Jaylen was interrupted by a throat clearing loudly behind him.

He turned to see a Toydarian, dark green wings sticking out from a worn leather overcoat.

"Sounds like you're looking for a change in luck?"

A response was warranted. But not knowing whether the wrong response would net him a blaster to the head, Jaylen took a moment to study the being in front of him. He held no weapons, at least not obvious ones. He didn't appear a threat.

Jaylen decided he should play along. For now. "Depends. Who's asking?"

"My name's actually not that important. What's important is that we have a mutual friend in Fennec Shand. She said you uncovered some intel. Which"—he let out a guttural laugh— "you might want to keep your voice down when you talk about."

Fennec.

Jaylen thought back to what his mother once said about paying the people who could hurt you. He supposed some people might see Fennec that way—Nnytyl and Roisem certainly would have. But that was the problem with the Barshas, wasn't it? Even practical advice got tinted with a hint of paranoia. Maybe that was why they'd let their guard down at Gus Treta—they just couldn't keep up with the demand of looking over their shoulders for decades. Jaylen had split from that thinking years ago. He hadn't given Fennec an extra name because she might hurt him—though she certainly could. No, he did so because she was connected and did excellent work, and he wanted to be part of that.

For a flash, Jaylen wished Roisem were here so he could point that out to her.

"And if she's willing to vouch for you," the Toydarian continued, "then I'm willing to at least listen to your troubles for a minute. On one condition."

He spoke with a glint in his eyes, something far different than the way Kranash had looked at him. "What's that?" Jaylen asked.

The Toydarian thumbed over to the bar. "Gotta be able to afford a drink."

Of course. Though in this case, maybe stretching the budget might be worth it. "Endee?" Jaylen said. "I might be back a little later than expected."

"We have one hour and sixteen minutes before our spaceport pass expires," ND-5 replied. "You should hurry."

CHAPTER 32

First, Jaylen did as promised, buying the Toydarian a drink—and even though their accounts were running dry, he ordered himself the cheapest drink for appearances.

Which meant that it smelled like halfway between ND-5's joint lubricants and bog water, though Jaylen maintained control over his gag reflex as they found an open booth. They moved in silence to the cantina's back corner, opposite the fathier-betting station where Jaylen had lingered not that long ago.

ND's broken voice came into his ear, a victim of the dying transmitter's last gasps. The droid may have had the ability to mathematically piece together what was being said with only fragments of words, but Jaylen didn't have the benefit of processors and algorithms.

He was on his own here.

"A toast," Jaylen said, holding up his drink. The movement caused it to slosh, several drops spilling over the brim. They rolled down his thumb, a strange contradiction of icy cold and stinging heat against his skin. "To Fennec Shand."

"To Fennec." Their glasses clinked, and the Toydarian floated up briefly, wings flapping in several large swoops before winding down and letting him settle into the booth. More frozen burns spilled onto Jaylen's skin, and he steeled himself from reacting to it, slipping into his old Jaylen Barsha persona, complete with corporate instincts.

"So," Jaylen said, forcing down a sip. He considered the different ways to start this off—he didn't even know this Toydarian's name. But he chose to build off what they'd already established. "How do you know her?"

"Happened to share a table at Tanda's at the Suria space station about five years ago. Been friends ever since. Well," he said, "I don't suppose you're ever truly friends with anyone in our line of work. But there are people you share mutual respect and admiration with.

"Lost touch for a few years. But even though the galaxy is a big place, our business is not. Everyone runs into each other eventually. At a dive like this, or on a job, or getting supplies. Or," he said with a laugh, "through mutual friends." He gestured between them, then took a drink.

Jaylen opted to reply with a grin but *not* to take another sip. "Ran into Fennec about a week ago. We caught up. She mentioned that she'd been part of that explosion on Andara. Didn't want to tell me *how,* of course. A woman's gotta keep her secrets. But she said to keep an eye out for Jaylen Vrax. You impressed her. Or, should I say, your payments impressed her. And she's not easy to impress."

Fennec may have been the wisest investment of his career—either of his careers. "Worth every credit."

"So I hear your name, and I see this conversation you have with Kranash that didn't go so well."

ND-5 strategized his way through missions by identifying weak points, assessing weapons and equipment, and making judgments to efficiently achieve the goal. Here, Jaylen told himself to operate the same way, using the weapons that served him best his whole life:

Words. Simple words, where subtle shifts in tone and context were as powerful as a sniper rifle.

Jaylen chose self-deprecation as a reply. "Clearly wasn't able to impress him."

"You impressed me, though. Most people wouldn't last that long with Kranash. He'd either shoot them or leave after the first two words. Sometimes both. So an actual conversation with Kranash and a name drop by Fennec Shand?" The Toydarian took down the rest of the drink in a single gulp, then slammed the glass on the table. And even though he didn't want to spend *more* credits, Jaylen started to wave at the bartender. "Ah, it's fine," he said, putting a green hand up. "You caught me at the end of my day. So, you're looking for a crew right now? Or just a friend?"

The Toydarian didn't realize how spot-on that question actually was. "A little bit of both," Jaylen said, forcing himself to take another sip.

"And you're trading information?" He pointed at Jaylen—specifically, at the inner coat pocket where the datapad sat. "There were rumors of Imperial secrets stolen from Andara. Guess this is true. Fennec wouldn't confirm or deny."

Jaylen offered a single raised eyebrow in return, enough of a conscious gesture to offer subtle acknowledgment. Inside, though, the comment sparked another worry: If rumors of their heist had already started to spread, would that prompt the ISB to update code names and rotations ahead of schedule?

"Thing with those secrets," continued the Toydarian, "they're only valuable if you have a reason to target them. Or if you have the resources to track one down. Sometimes those things go hand in hand."

Was that an offer? Or a challenge?

Years ago, Brencoyle had sat a teenage Jaylen down for an impromptu lesson on the subtleties of communication. It hadn't started out that way; they were supposed to be attending some boring production at the Galaxies Opera House on Coruscant. But technical issues had delayed the start of the show, and the valet had taken in the various conversations around them: ushers politely explaining the delay, impatient attendees, an angry Roonan berating the waitstaff about lukewarm food, and even parents trying to keep bored children busy.

"You're young. People probably still seem to you like they say what they actually mean," Brencoyle had said. "Their words, their intentions. But everyone you meet has layers in what they say. Listen to everything.

What they want rarely matches their words. When you realize that, you can see what people really mean—then use that to your advantage when you present your response."

"Even," young Jaylen had mused, "my parents?" It was an epiphany that finally got his world to make sense.

"*Especially* your parents."

Once again, the lessons of the Barsha trickled into the world of Vrax.

For so long, Jaylen had tried to escape the specter of the former to fully embrace the latter. Despite that, they'd always felt in competition with each other, a race to see who would surface—or escape—first. But perhaps the best way forward wasn't to keep them so stuck in a past-versus-present battle. His memories, his *life,* and the hell he'd been through—that was a well he could draw from no matter what side he leaned on.

And in this particular moment, the lessons of Brencoyle probably applied. Jaylen sensed that what the Toydarian wanted was a gesture of sincerity—of trust.

"There's an Imperial operative," Jaylen said, keeping his voice easy but measured. "Goes by Madel Nureth. Problem is, there's a lot of people named that on public record. A socialite, a transport pilot, all sorts of people. Heh." He let out a quick laugh. "Even an accountant. We've done what we can to make the list manageable." He thumbed over his shoulder at nothing, a gesture designed to make him look more connected than he actually was. "Like you said, our line of work is a small world. But in the real galaxy, the day-to-day life of the people we're looking into? It takes a lot of resources for my crew to try and dig up the truth behind a person."

"Crew?" A laugh followed the question. "You're just one guy right now," he said, apparently seeing through Jaylen's bluff.

Jaylen took an appropriate pause with full understanding that timing was everything when it came to projecting confidence. "I've got a partner."

"This pursuit of yours," said the Toydarian, "it's personal or professional?"

Across Jaylen's entire life, things were always a little bit of both. Being a Barsha had woven that into his blood. But here, when Jaylen considered that very straightforward question, the answer was clear.

And he wasn't ashamed of it. "This is personal," he said. "Deeply personal."

"You know what?" He pointed to Jaylen's inner coat pocket again. "You don't need to give me that. Let's just say that you'll owe me a favor in the future." The Toydarian held out a gloved hand, worn threads exposed on the glove's cracked palm. "For a friend of Fennec Shand. Deal?"

"Deal."

Jaylen grabbed his hand and gave it a firm shake. And even before he let go of his grip, the Toydarian straightened up and spoke. "It's the accountant."

"What?"

He locked eyes with Jaylen, the intensity communicating a moment of significance rather than threat or challenge—unusual in their line of work. "I can see you're trying to move up in this strange life of ours. That's why you hire someone like Fennec. When you're in a job, it's more about getting out in one piece. Where you're heading, though?" He pointed above them. "You're looking to get the lead, find the crew, play the bigger game? Do that long enough, and you'll see that the Empire keeps its surveillance operatives in a few categories. It's all strategic. Media. Utilities. Hospitality. Finances." He dipped his head with a knowing nod, causing his snout to follow suit. "Like an accountant. Anything that keeps tabs on the flow of credits between the Empire and the people."

ND-5's voice burst into Jaylen's ear, though the transmission was still broken. "It's that simple?" Jaylen asked.

"It's that simple," he said with a nod. "The Empire is a massive machine. They have to keep it simple. Otherwise it'll all get lost. They're not smart enough or detailed enough to keep track of it all."

Jaylen bit down on his lip, dropping any mask he might have normally projected. Instead, he let the words sink in. Seconds passed, maybe even a minute before he stood up and marched over to the bar. The bartender gave him an annoyed grunt, and Jaylen pointed over at their booth. "One more for the road."

Jaylen returned, condensation from the glass cooling his fingers. "I insist," Jaylen said.

The Toydarian took it with a shrug. "I suppose one more won't hurt," he said with a laugh. "Appreciate your generosity."

"It's an investment," Jaylen replied with a nod. "Like I told Fennec, I learned a lesson at a young age: Make sure to cover those who do good work."

"An investment from someone Fennec trusts." He moved to take the drink in a gulp, then paused to opt for a sip. "I trust anyone that Fennec trusts. My name's Gentro, by the way."

Jaylen had about an hour to get back to the ship before local authorities locked it down. He raised his hand in a salute, his mind already slotting in where Gentro might work as a future contact. "I don't know if Fennec and I actually trust each other. Yet."

"One thing to know about Fennec Shand," Gentro said, returning the gesture. "If she decides one day that she *doesn't* trust you, it'll be over before you even realize it."

CHAPTER 33

Jaylen's failing transceiver continues to send incoming data for analysis. I am able to take pieces of clear audio, then compare them with possible words based on sound, length, and context.

My translation processes achieve an estimated 91 percent accuracy, and knowing that fact, I focus on one specific phrase near the end of Jaylen's conversation.

"It's the accountant."

While I monitor the rest of the conversation, I consider our new contact's logic. Despite working within the boundaries of the Empire for years, the system's subtleties are something that I have still not fully grasped. The CIS was more of a disparate coalition of forces and politics, and with that, underlying directives often fell into "achieving the goal as quickly as possible," the goal depending on which faction ran the operation.

The Empire is the opposite, monolithic and inefficient. In many ways, the Empire's worst enemy is not any rebel faction, but its own commitment to churn.

Given that context, Jaylen's conversation partner has a suggestion that makes sense.

With the download from SCUR, I begin pulling up further data on the accountant named Madel Nureth. The ship's processors are stubborn, much like Jaylen's transceiver, and data loads at a slower clip than preferred. I add "check internal storage connection hardware" to my ongoing list of ship repairs, when Jaylen's voice finally comes through clearly.

"Endee? You there?"

"Yes, Jaylen. I can finally hear you," I say.

"How much of that did you catch?" he asks, followed by the sound of shuffling and footsteps. I hear the swish of door hydraulics twice, presumably once to open and once to close. The din of the background noise has faded, though a new noise comes with the familiar whir of what is likely a passing speeder.

He has left the cantina. Which means that Jaylen is satisfied with the provided information.

Jaylen primarily works on a combination of data and what humans call "hunches." This combination makes him less accurate than a droid when it comes to assumption success rate. However, as humans go, his analytical skills are better than most I have encountered, and his willingness to trust the contact comes with a reasonable chance of success.

Which is important, because this detour has taken us to the brink of financial ruin. The next time Jaylen suggests going on an impromptu sector-wide manhunt shortly after paying out the bulk of our credits, I will advise against it and use this experience as a cautionary tale.

"Before we attempt further monitoring in an indoor facility, we should repair our remote transceiver. However, I'm confident I understood what was said." The ship's station display finally responds, yielding a line-by-line readout on the accountant known as Madel Nureth. Though her records do not date back to the time of the Gus Treta incident, they are recent enough that we can pinpoint her current information: home planet and residence, main service area, customer records, tax filing status within the system.

We will have to fly to Sern Prime. During that journey, I will work on the transceiver, presuming Jaylen brings it back in an acceptable state. "I'm compiling a dossier on this Madel Nureth."

"And you didn't even have to drink the worst drink of all time to get it," Jaylen says. "Dangerous, disgusting stuff."

"I cannot imbibe beverages," I say as a reminder.

"You're a cheap date," he says with a laugh. In the background, I hear him pass by someone speaking the native language of the reptilian Anx species. "I'm on my way. What do you know about accounting?"

"We have never amassed enough credits to require accounting," I respond. Jaylen seems to have forgotten that, without a memory wipe, my programming can only learn through experience rather than directly installing new skills. "However, I'm a fast learner."

"Well, while you're learning about accounting, you can also calculate the jump to lightspeed," Jaylen says. His voice stutters, another sign of the transceiver failing despite getting a clearer signal outdoors. "We leave immediately."

SERN PRIME IS the centerpiece of the Sern sector, which is in the Colonies—a region that also includes Giju. Both are close to the Rimma Trade Route but also within proximity of the Corellian Trade Spine, which confirms the geography of Madel Nureth's movements over the course of her career. As a planet, Sern Prime has a mild climate with various population centers and a culture that focuses on a combination of technology and the arts, though those specialties appear to change by region. Its prime exports are medical technology and prefabricated architecture shipped in large transports. In addition, its temperate environment and many lakes create a strong tourist economy, with many wealthy families purchasing vacation homes in clusters. Though it has strong commercial activity, much of it is locally based, with the key drivers of business located on its nearest mining moon.

It is also quiet, particularly on the outskirts.

We land the ship at a busy spaceport located on the outskirts of Witzer, the planet's second-largest urban area. The spaceport has structures stacked on top of each other with decorative lighting that serves little purpose except to illuminate the central tower. Though Jaylen dresses well and there are other droids about, something about our presence draws strange glances from the spaceport staff. I do not believe it is due to the equipment I am pulling along, as other travelers have more luggage with them. However, it is unlikely that they are carrying the same volume of scanning equipment as us.

An Emente approves our speeder rental, though four of her six eyes linger on me longer than Jaylen.

"My scar is not a mechanical or electrical danger to anyone," I say.

In response, she offers a weak smile and explains to Jaylen the terms of the rental.

This is not the type of vendor who will be interested in trading services for an Imperial cover name. Jaylen is dipping into emergency credits, paying with physical currency. The Emente holds up a datapad with a retinal scanner to confirm documentation, then nods in approval. In the meantime, I review all known data about this particular Madel Nureth:

She appears to be very ordinary. She has been a known resident of Senova, a medium-sized suburb of Sern Prime, for nine years, moving there just after the Gus Treta incident. Before that, her academic profile states that she grew up on Dentaal and went to Calif University with dual degrees in linguistics and accounting.

In Senova, she worked for an accounting firm for seven years, before being an independent contractor for the last two. Her customer testimonials are very strong: "Prompt and friendly, and she keeps my finances in order" and "Madel is the best"—the latter testimonial ending with three exclamation points for unnecessary emphasis. Through data searches, I can verify the existence of each of those references as current or former residents of Senova. I can also verify records of her marriage shortly after arriving in Senova, though that relationship ended five years later. In quotes from local children's sky skimming associations, she is noted as being a "supportive co-parent" of her child, though as we arrive at her house, there are no indications of children permanently living there.

Our dark blue speeder is an economical civilian model known as a V-33 Travel Sedan from SoroSuub with larger-than-usual storage space and full enclosure. During our drive from the spaceport to this location, I identify that approximately 17 percent of passing vehicles are either this model or variations of it.

With that, it is an ideal choice for an inconspicuous transport. Although BX-series commandos are likely somewhat conspicuous in a residential setting. As I sit at the passenger side, I tip the collar of my duster up to better obscure my head. We pull into a subsection of homes adjacent to a larger neighborhood, each property having lawns of above-average upkeep. Some of the homes have the same speeder as ours parked in front. Others have wallball equipment set up, though only one home has a child using it; he is performing too poorly to have any professional career aspirations.

Madel Nureth's specific street does not have any of these. It is a cul-de-sac, with her property occupying the back corner lot. Sern Prime's sun is shining with a late-morning glow. None of the house's residents are participating in outdoor activities right now.

Jaylen parks the speeder diagonally across the street from her home. I reach into the back and open up my storage case of equipment. A thermal sensor, an audio amplifier, and an EnhanceScan unit all sit on my lap. All three operate while remaining completely static, each with a cable tying into my interface port for real-time analysis of their data. The first hour passes in near silence. After that, though, Jaylen's legs begin to fidget. He adjusts the seat's angle and stretches his neck.

I do not require any of these movements and remain perfectly still to ensure that the scanners maintain as much consistency as possible.

"Nothing, huh?" he says.

"There is no identifying data on any of the scanners." I continue scanning the home for any signs of subtle movement. However, even my maximized audio sensors do not detect any typical domestic sounds—footsteps, cabinets opening and closing, water flowing, or voices.

Several moments pass. Jaylen shuffles in his seat again. Usually when he adjusts his weight or his feet more than is practical, it means he is thinking about something. I am looking at my devices, though if I were to turn to observe his expression, he would likely have his lips pursed.

"Hey, Endee, would it be too distracting right now for you to record an audio journal?" he finally asks.

It is a strange time to request this function. "If the goal is for me to not miss any evidence, then yes, it would be too distracting right now." He shuffles in his seat again. "I can talk, though."

"Ah, well . . ." Thirty-four seconds pass until he says something else. "You ever do anything like this before?" he asks. I believe this is what Lorel referred to as "small talk." It is strange that Jaylen would feel the need to engage in this given that we see each other every day, multiple times a day, sometimes for long stretches of time.

"Under General Grievous, our primary functions were infiltration, assassination, and high-priority security," I say. "None of those involved waiting outside of a home to conduct an interrogation."

"Stakeouts don't always just lead to interrogations," Jaylen says as he stretches his arms in the vehicle's limited compartment space. "They can be used for other purposes."

"According to my limited historical memories, the closest I ever came to this particular function was at Gus Treta."

This prompts a longer silence from Jaylen. I cannot tell if he is concentrating or if the mention of Gus Treta has caused him to indulge in human memories. As my current objective is to monitor the scanners, I do not turn.

I do note, though, that he has stopped fidgeting in his seat.

"Do you wish to discuss how I executed that function at Gus Treta?"

For one brief moment, I decide to look at him. My expectation—my "hunch"—regarding his expression is correct: pursed lips, tight brow, one hand on his chin. His eyes stare straight ahead. From one angle, this could be interpreted as anger. From a different angle, it could be interpreted as regret or a related emotion.

Those seem like distractions from our mission.

He blinks, and his entire body relaxes.

"No. None of that's necessary, Endee." Now he yawns and checks the time. Then he checks the time again. Then he sits up, his brief signs of fatigue now gone. "It's just past the middle of the day here."

"Based on the sun's position, it is approximately fifty-two percent through the eighteen-hour daylight cycle."

"What I mean is," Jaylen says, "sometimes I forget how people live their lives."

"Are you saying you have forgotten to eat, sleep, or hydrate?" I consider the inventory of our storage crate. It only has equipment. It does not have any food or water.

"No. Well, yes. I mean, I didn't bring any food, which was a bad idea. But what I mean is that I haven't had a regular schedule since I was a teenager in school. After that, I came and went as I pleased. Even at Bar'leth. I still remember Sava Pers's morning antiquities class. I nearly failed it because I couldn't wake up for it." His tone becomes slow and calm. "And during those years with Barsha Corp, Sliro had a regular work schedule, but I was meeting people, going to events, shaking hands. Flying to yet another planet with a different time zone. Day was night, night was day." He points in the direction opposite Madel Nureth's home, a rough approximation of the business district. "People who live this life—a *normal* life—they go to work and school. They don't come home until later."

That information does not change my own strategy of monitoring the various scanners. I don't respond, and in return, Jaylen doesn't respond. Another two hours pass, and his prediction is correct to some degree—we see the occasional speeder pass by to bring a child home, presumably from school.

No sign of Madel Nureth, though.

"According to court records, it sounds like the primary responsibility for Madel Nureth's child belongs to the father. Should we move the stakeout to monitoring her child's father's home?" I ask.

Jaylen's mouth forms an uncomfortable line to go with the sudden crinkle in his brow. Usually, he takes in these types of questions from a strategic perspective, factoring in variables such as travel time and likelihood of response.

Here, he looks back and forth at the home and me, and then finally shakes his head. "No. I'd like to leave the kid out of the parents' business. Let's just wait here a little while longer." The speeder's door handle clicks, and Jaylen pushes it open to allow a gust of wind in. He rotates one leg outside. "I just need to stretch," he says.

"What if Madel Nureth comes home, sees you, and recognizes you as a member of the Barsha family?"

"If that happens," he says, pulling himself out of the speeder. His arms reach overhead, and he yawns, eyes squinting in reaction to the shift in ambient light. "You should get out of the speeder and capture her."

"If she resists, has a weapon, or contacts the Empire for backup?"

Jaylen's head tilts as he considers all three possibilities, which likely have overlapping consequences. "If that happens, use your judgment." His mouth forms a tight, grim line. "Find out what she knows. Then kill her if necessary."

This is a strong statement. While we have been contracted for assassinations before, killing is usually a byproduct of the situation. I have shot or physically broken victims of various species as they have pursued us or vice versa.

This is the first time, though, that Jaylen has authorized a specific, targeted murder of his own if his plan goes awry. I have not prepared in this fashion since Gus Treta when I was specifically directed to murder the Barshas. I calculate the potential reasons Jaylen might make such a decision, and I come to the conclusion that he is worried about being identified by the Empire. However, there are other ways around that should the circumstances arise. Thus, I conclude that while murder is one effective strategy for this particular situation, Jaylen's willingness to accept it is purely emotional.

CHAPTER 34

Several more hours passed with absolutely nothing happening other than Jaylen adjusting to get comfortable and trying to dispel the growing hunger in his stomach. ND-5 stayed nearly static the whole time, a machine locked into its assigned task. A light rain began sprinkling overhead, a gradual tapping that danced over the speeder's cover and obscured the windscreen.

Jaylen realized the strangeness of being still. Even when he was alone on the ship, he found himself constantly moving, fixing, or reading something. He supposed he had even been that way on Gus Treta, having an inability to simply exist in a space. It seemed clear now that he'd always been this way. Was it because his parents forced him into a life of lessons and tutors as a child? Or was it because he preferred those lessons and tutors to the rest of life in the Barsha family?

If Brencoyle were here, he would have offered thoughtful words. If Sliro were here, he'd have given Jaylen grief for never wondering what life would have been like *without* those lessons and tutors. Instead, Jaylen was in a covered speeder with a BX commando droid who wasn't really doing much other than reporting status. Which meant that his only company was in his head.

And that, possibly more than any leg cramps, made him fidget over the hours. ND-5 had brought a small repair kit in case any gear hiccupped during their watch, but its only use had been providing something for Jaylen to mindlessly dig through—though when Jaylen realized this was the same kit with the damaged restraining bolt, he stuck the small bit of hardware in his pocket. No need to have further discussions about that right now.

He'd also brought the datapad with the ISB list—he told ND-5 it was to review the information on there, but the truth was he'd gotten used to its feeling in his coat.

In this case, both only provided nominal distraction. Mostly, he just sat there and *stewed.*

"I am detecting sound," ND-5 finally said. The noise startled Jaylen to attention, but the *understanding* of what that potentially meant activated all his senses, turning the dull gray of the drizzling rain and the sleepy neighborhood into something much more vital. He sat up and leaned over, taking care not to disturb ND-5's scanners.

"It is not typical of noise coming from a home living or working situation." ND's head tilted. "The sound is of mechanisms turning. I am also detecting a slight power surge from within the building."

Jaylen tried to see past the droid's large mechanical body and the cumulative raindrops on the window, but from the outside, the only movement came from a breeze tickling the plant life.

"Now I am detecting a heat signature coming up from underneath the main floor," ND-5 said.

A heat signature?

Were they finally close to Low Red Moon? The logistics of this new information sparked ideas and connected possibilities.

"She must have equipment underground for classified communications and operations," said Jaylen. "The Empire probably built that."

Of course the Empire would do that. For all their blunt bureaucracy, they retained strict protocols over communications and transmissions—the exchange with Shaw had proved just that. A new thought popped in

Jaylen's mind—a potentially *profitable* thought. Were these types of places used exclusively for Imperial operatives on rotation? And if so, did that mean the next occupant would also be an operative?

"Based on the height and body type of this heat signature, it is likely Madel Nureth. Should we infiltrate?" ND-5 asked, moving one hand over the scanners.

"Not yet," Jaylen said. They *could* do just that, but they needed to be careful. The last thing they wanted to do was draw Imperial attention. "Give her a minute."

Now they sat, Jaylen remaining as still as ND-5. "One minute has passed," ND-5 said, and Jaylen was about to admonish ND-5 for his literal nature, when Madel stepped out of the front door and walked over to the side of the small building. She disappeared from view, but then sounds came, a familiar start-up noise from an efficient and safe speeder.

"There we go," Jaylen said, activating the speeder's engines. "I'll follow at a distance."

Madel Nureth didn't go very far—only 3.4 kilometers per ND-5's distance tracker. She got out at a local café, and they watched as she sipped on caf while meeting with . . . someone.

A man who had no hints of being an Imperial. Or otherwise being related to any illicit behavior. Instead, they reviewed datapads. The other person brought out a stack of two, and Madel reached into her bag to grab three more. They continued to talk and sip, talk and sip, all with very animated hand gestures and, as ND-5's sensors picked up, louder-than-normal decibel levels. If they were trying to stay undercover, they weren't being inconspicuous.

Finally, the man let out a hefty sigh, gathered his datapads, and reached out to shake Madel's hand. From their distance, Jaylen could tell Madel offered a polite, professional smile, a slight raise of the cheeks and curl of the lips, the type of thing he'd seen so many times in so many ways at Barsha Corp.

This person was one of Madel's customers. A plain old real-life, exasperated customer haggling over accounting details. Jaylen thought back to what Shaw said about using her cover job to sniff out rebel activity, and maybe that was part of Madel's role here.

Or she just needed the mundanity of it all to hide in plain sight.

She took a last drink of caf with a sigh that matched her customer's, then grabbed her own datapads and stood. "Should we approach her now?" ND-5 asked.

Jaylen considered the strategic move—they had clear separation from her Imperial-secured home, but the public location created risks, too. Plenty of people milled about, giving Madel an advantage if she tried to escape. Deploying ND-5 wouldn't exactly be subtle.

"Let's track her a little bit more. When she gets home," he said, starting up the speeder's motor. "We should intercept her before she gets inside."

Except she didn't head home. They tailed her for an hour, following a winding path to a smaller secondary spaceport reserved for shuttles and smaller craft flying to local systems—no transports, cruisers, or shipping frigates, just a quiet location for business and personal travel.

"I have locked onto her specific physiology and heat signature," ND-5 said as they got out of the speeder. "As long as we stay within two hundred meters, I will be able to track her."

"That's good," Jaylen said as he lined up next to the massive droid. "Because you don't exactly blend in." The rain picked up, now cascading at a rate that bounced off ND-5's metallic head. "If she's going somewhere, we'll need a quiet place to catch her before she gets on a ship."

"She is moving at a rate twenty-eight percent faster than an average human," ND-5 said, prompting Jaylen to begin moving. Large double doors slid open to reveal the spaceport's sizable entry hall, and unlike the planet's busier spaceport, no one turned their heads at ND-5. This was possibly because the more private nature of this location led to wealthier people coming and going with their servant droids.

Everything here proved the opposite of the spaceport where they'd arrived. Instead of colorful shapes, the designs remained largely functional and neutral. One wall held a large beige rectangle with a fading mural of a sunset painted on it. On another side showed a window view of an adjacent control tower with various antennas sticking out the top.

Within the building, they maintained their distance from the target, specifically between a desired range of twenty to fifty meters per

ND-5's sensors. First, they passed the port's registration counter, then large holo displays with gate information for commercial flights and private transportation, then a number of small shops and eateries. Jaylen tried to keep his focus on the mission, remembering to stay both casual and hidden. Yet his mind slipped into a strange state, an awareness that every time he thought his goals were within reach, something changed—except here his target had a direct connection to so many pivotal events of his life, dating all the way back to the Barsha Corp press conference. No more guessing or sleuthing—he just had to get there and *take it*. And for this to all finally unfold in a small spaceport built for the wealthy, well . . .

There was something fitting about all of that.

"She has halted," ND-5 said, and the droid abruptly shifted to walk in a wider circumference. Jaylen followed without questioning, and they continued pursuit using the spaceport's mix of currency exchange kiosks and tall plants as cover. "She is talking to someone. I am getting a visual. Processing . . . processing. A Nautolan. I am comparing her face based on my internally stored database of syndicate contacts and agents—"

ND-5 went silent and stopped walking.

Everything ND-5 did was executed with purpose and efficiency. The droid was *not* one for dramatics.

Which meant something really bad was unfolding.

"Endee?" Jaylen said, suddenly very aware of his surroundings. "What's going on?"

"I can confirm based on my analysis that Madel Nureth is speaking to someone from Crimson Dawn right now."

From Jaylen's peripheral vision, he caught quick movement. Places like this filled with people of all types coming and going, and at a glance, the spaceport hall proved no different: travelers grabbing a quick meal, or stopping to check luggage, or using a communication kiosk for a distance transmission. He'd been to enough of these that he recognized the cadence of travel, the stop and go necessitated by flight schedules. Occasionally, someone would be sprinting through, fueled by the realization that they were late.

This, however, was different. Someone in the shadowy din of public space moved with a clear purpose that matched ND-5 and Jaylen's. "Do you see that?" Jaylen asked. He scanned, trying not to look too obvious.

"My processors are primarily tracking Madel Nureth, the Crimson Dawn contact, and their heat signatures. Looking for whatever 'that' is will lower my accuracy."

"That," Jaylen said, a subtle nod to the figure moving away from them, "is someone in a hood."

ND-5's head swiveled quickly. "At a glance, that person's height and shape create a potential match for fifty-two percent of known species that pass through this system." Gears whirred as ND-5 turned back toward Madel's direction. "Our primary targets are moving now. They are walking in unison."

Jaylen followed the cadence of ND-5's walk. They kept a precise distance, and while they moved together, Jaylen continued to track the hooded figure as much as possible.

At least until side doors opened and a large group arrived, a mix of species that all held two things in common. First, they were very loud. Second, they were very young.

Jaylen made a third assumption: They were probably all very rich.

Like he once was. Maybe they were even headed out to Niamos for the type of carefree adventure he used to have as a young adult.

Their collective noise created a hurricane of languages and laughter as the group passed through the large hall, obscuring Jaylen's ability to track the hooded person. He cursed under his breath as he swiveled his view, but ND-5 kept pushing ahead in relentless pursuit until they got to the main security gate. "Get in line," Jaylen said. "I'll buy us tickets."

"To where?"

That was a good question. Jaylen ran to the nearest kiosk, tapped his way through the automated options, and made a calculated guess: If this security gate acted as a binary stopgap to the rest of the spaceport, it wouldn't matter which gate he selected.

He chose the cheapest one and attached a datapad to download boarding information.

By the time he rejoined ND-5, the droid was near the front of the line. "The target has paused to purchase some caf thirty-two meters ahead."

"Lucky for them," Jaylen said as a passing astromech pulled through the security check's utility passage. The droid made its way through, before empty luggage carts electromagnetically attached themselves to it.

"Next," a stocky female Chevin yelled.

Jaylen and ND-5 stepped forward, ND-5 flashing the datapad's passenger info.

"No luggage?" she asked.

"We travel light," ND-5 said.

Various scanners lit up and passed over them before a quiet beep confirmed their safety. The Chevin nodded, her low jaw dipping. "You're good. Go on through."

Jaylen started with a short, even pace, but ND-5 picked up speed. It didn't matter, though, because another burst of passengers came from the left, a group of very loud, very lost schoolchildren, following an exasperated teacher. Jaylen kept up with ND-5 as voices clamored and limbs flailed in tantrum, and ahead of them, a security cart floated by, pausing while its uniformed pilot looked at a datapad.

"We must reduce our distance to the target," the droid said. "Without being conspicuous."

They pushed through as the crowd ebbed and flowed, trudging through cross traffic in the form of cranky children and clueless adults.

Suddenly the security siren behind them blared with a loud buzz and flashing lights. Jaylen turned to see the commotion, then sucked in a quick breath as he realized who triggered it.

It was the hooded figure. Though the hood covered their face, he swore he saw enough to discern tan cheeks. And just under the brim of the hood, a hint of yellow—a marking or discoloration, maybe even a horn. The galaxy offered a lot of possibilities.

Whoever and whatever they were, that person was on their tail.

"We gotta move quick," Jaylen said. "We're being followed."

CHAPTER 35

Based on Jaylen's most recent proclamation as well as my own calculations regarding the variables of this facility and its visitors, I allocate internal resources differently across my sensors.

My visual sensors, augmented by thermal detection hardware, continue to track Madel Nureth and her contact within Crimson Dawn—a Nautolan operative named Sima Mugira, based on my database of known syndicate agents. I reduce the amount of computational power assigned to them, which in turn reduces their range. However, this is a necessary trade-off for active threat detection.

Weighing all the variables equally is overloading my receptors. New people are constantly coming into view, some with similar clothing, making things hard to process efficiently. I must attempt to prioritize: The person in the hood is the primary threat. General spaceport security is another threat. Public-facing Imperial officers represent another threat. The mystery person may not be alone, either. Madel and Sima may also have hidden reinforcements or other contingencies. I focus on tracking for sudden changes, including movement along my field of vision, shouts and other noises, or environmental shifts.

My new operation mode does not, however, factor in the sudden arrival of an astromech pulling several repulsor carts of luggage across our way. The astromech rolls directly within our path, trapping us between gate seating and a gift kiosk. It beeps out several words in Binary, then projects a holo of a Gran employee stating that this transport service will carry excess luggage to gates throughout the spaceport. It includes other instructions about how each cart will disengage at its assigned gate.

A queue of lazy people forms around the carts. I consider kicking the cart of luggage directly in front of us, but this would thwart our goal of remaining inconspicuous. While I have seen several Imperial security officers within the spaceport expressing boredom, catching their attention would be counterproductive to our purpose.

The crowd does create another problem, though. By my internal metrics, Madel Nureth's estimated distance ticks upward until she is out of range. Her thermal outline disappears. I temporarily boost my scanners but fail to pick her up.

With Madel out of range for now and at least another ten seconds for this astromech's luggage cart to pull into the waiting area, I focus on threat assessment.

Based on a combination of sensor inputs, I calculate the height and gait of the person in the hood. Using that, I estimate a range of places this person could have gone in the time elapsed, using the assumption that they are tracking us.

I move toward the end of the astromech's cart chain, and while travelers are lining up to put their luggage down, I nudge people aside, balancing crowd control with inconspicuous politeness. Jaylen turns sideways and slips through, then asks, "What's our status?"

"Madel Nureth is out of scanning range. We should speed up," I say as I intake more sensor data. We begin moving at a clip that is 40 percent faster than before, though still at a pace similar to a relaxed-but-hurried walk. "I'm maintaining a threat detection analysis."

"Any signs of the person from before?" Jaylen asks as he looks around. His movements are very obvious.

"Unconfirmed."

A young Rodian sprints past me and bumps into my leg. His arm tangles briefly in the tails of my duster.

Not a threat.

However, my pace changes as I sidestep the child. Through the din, I notice that a faint set of footsteps adjusts to match our speed and maintain distance. I isolate this in my audio processing before I identify that there are actually two distinct sets of footsteps following this pattern.

I stop. "What are you doing?" Jaylen asks. "We're losing ground."

My internal timer counts to ten, and then I set out at a faster pace than before. Both sets of footsteps match that cadence. "There are two people tracking us," I say.

"You're sure?" Jaylen asks. "I only saw the one in the hood."

"That is one of them. I can tell by the sound frequencies emitted by their footfalls. One set of boots matches my audio sample from the security gate commotion and has kept exact pace with us." I concentrate on isolating the frequency, cadence, and consistency of the second pair of footsteps. "One other person is following a similar pattern. Given the multiple parties of concern, it seems reasonable to assume that this person is also interested in our activity. They may be a threat."

"I think . . ." Jaylen says, his voice trailing off as he glances around, making gestures more subtly than before. "We keep up our pace. We find Madel Nureth. We let these other people chase us."

"Understood," I say. Enough variables exist that Jaylen's plan does not stand out as either a best- or worst-case scenario. Thus, his preference, combined with the fact that I can find no better alternative, leads me to staying quiet and marching forward.

We aim to close the gap between us and our targets. However, neither Madel nor her contact appears back on my thermal sensors. We move past gate after gate, and as we get farther down the row, the number of waiting travelers dwindles.

At the final, ninth gate, there is no sign of Madel Nureth or the agent from Crimson Dawn. Behind us, both sets of trailing footsteps pause as well.

Jaylen and I stand in the middle of the empty spaceport gate. He bites down on his lip with clear frustration as he scans the area. "You don't pick up anything?" he says. Even without my tactical analysis, I understand that we are standing in an open and vulnerable position.

This functionally makes us bait.

I do not answer Jaylen. Instead, my attention turns to the fact that several of my sensors have stopped functioning. Thermal capture, long-range audio detection and filtration, and dynamic movement patterns are active but without any readings. I turn to put Jaylen in my field of view, yet I am not detecting any thermal data from him.

"Endee?"

Jaylen is not dead, so he should be presenting some form of heat signature. This is troubling.

"I believe something is jamming my scanners."

"It's a trap," Jaylen says. "I got a bad feeling about this. I got greedy, let my emotions get in the way." He turns and looks out the floor-to-ceiling window at the ship on the landing pad—possibly belonging to Crimson Dawn. "Endee, capture an image of that shuttle. See if it matches anything on known registries."

I comply with Jaylen's request and my first pass at scanning the ship provides a match. "It is an Amentor *Midna*-class shuttle. I'll need several more seconds to identify the production year."

Jaylen nods before his hand comes abruptly to the back of his neck. "What the . . ." His fingers feel around as he turns frantically. "Mission's off. We gotta go. Something clipped the back of my neck."

"I did not detect any movement or the sound of impact. However, I agree. We should leave." As I state that, my standard visual sensors also go out. My audio also cuts abruptly in quality and sensitivity. I estimate I can only cleanly capture sound within five meters. "My other—"

Before I can finish, my power systems detect a sudden ionic surge and—

[[Neural core shutdown in five . . . four . . . three . . . two . . .]]

CHAPTER 36

Jaylen watched as ND-5 collapsed to his knees, the weight of the BX commando droid causing a thud that might have been heard throughout the hall if anyone else were around. The urge to call out felt instinctive, yet he suppressed it. Even with this situation, drawing the attention of local authorities wasn't a good idea.

Or was it? Maybe a distraction could get him out of there safely.

He took a step forward before a sharp pain gripped his chest. It traveled lower, riding into his gut with a combination of stinging and nausea that caused him to hunch over. He forced one more step forward before he dropped, nearly matching ND-5's rigid pose.

Jaylen blinked as his vision began to blur, a growing weakness in his focus and his eyes watering in reaction to . . . this. What was this? First something had hit him in the back of the neck. Then ND-5 collapsed and deactivated. And now he was incapacitated. All in the span of ten, fifteen seconds?

Something like that. Though the pain made it feel much longer. His eyes squeezed shut, nausea now causing sweat to line his forehead, and he forced himself to look and assess.

One silhouette approached, going from blurry figure to clearly defined shape. Despite the pain, Jaylen was cognizant enough to recognize her. The person before him had fundamentally defined most of his adult life.

Madel Nureth.

She stood in her basic office attire of matching tan coat and trousers with muted gray shirt. She carried no obvious weapons. Whatever had hit his neck had no clear source.

A second silhouette came into view, similarly fuzzy at first. First, Jaylen only caught her soft leather boots. Then her black leggings came into focus, followed by a long coat embroidered with glowing orange runes, then finally the distinct green head tendrils of a Nautolan female.

She had to be the Crimson Dawn agent identified by ND-5.

If ND-5 were active, he probably could have provided further details from his database, possibly even a name. But that wasn't happening right now because of what she held in her hand:

A blaster with an ion attachment.

In fact, as he looked over at ND-5, small trickles of white energy still danced over the prone droid's body.

Madel glanced around the empty gate, then looked behind herself. "No one here," she mused. Her partner nodded and said something about how the next flight at the adjacent gate was in four hours. She knelt to inspect ND-5, even poking at the edge of his scar with her fingernail. "Brutal."

Jaylen made eye contact as she said that.

"Your handiwork?"

He fought to push something, anything out, but his pain was a unique kind of horrible. At Gus Treta, the concussive forces of the dining room bomb had battered his muscles, leaving an intense whole-body soreness coupled with a massive headache. This felt much different, a singular contraction of pain that felt like something gnawed at him from the inside out. "You . . ." he managed to get out before gripping his stomach and . . .

Was that something *moving* under his skin?

"Well, that droid's not walking anywhere," the Nautolan said. She held up her ion blaster. "This does its job well. We should go." She nodded toward a side door by the gate.

Jaylen recalled a distant memory of a spaceport just like this one, where his family had used a small secondary walkway to reach a private charter shuttle instead of taking the busier main gate.

"We don't want to keep Qi'ra waiting."

Madel paced in a circle around Jaylen, then looked once again over her shoulder. Considering the number of security holocams in a spaceport, the duo seemed extremely casual, though if they had the ability to jam ND's sensors, local security likely wasn't an issue. "You got a drink on you?" she asked. The Nautolan nodded and handed over a flask. Madel unscrewed the cap and poured a strong-smelling alcohol over Jaylen's head. She raised a foot, and with the toe of her boot, she nudged Jaylen over—still prone, still clutching his stomach, still feeling like *something* was inside him that shouldn't be there. She knelt now beside him, the breath from her whisper tickling his ear. "You should be more careful about who you follow."

Madel straightened up as a new pain stung Jaylen's lower abdomen. He didn't know much about human anatomy, but he guessed it involved the digestive tract. "We'll leave this one. Someone will clean him up eventually. But that one," she said, pointing to ND-5, "let's find a hoversled. The droid might be useful."

Over the next few minutes, Jaylen fell in and out of consciousness, the pain knocking him out before snapping him back. Every time he came to, the scene in front of him looked different—first Madel and the Crimson Dawn agent were staring down at him, then they loaded ND-5 onto a hoversled, then only Madel stood there.

Then the gate was empty.

But then a new person arrived, so suddenly that Jaylen wondered if he'd missed the man striding in. He would remember someone like this: blue skin and a swirling silver facial tattoo, impeccably dressed in a way that would have garnered Roisem's approval, with a form-fitting dark blue shirt underneath a long-tailed purple vest—both with silver trim to match the tattoo. The man glanced down at Jaylen with fleeting attention before focusing on the gate's large window.

Was this the same person in the hood they'd seen earlier? But from the glimpse he'd caught, that person had tan skin, and Jaylen swore he saw hints of a horn or something under the hood. This man was clearly different, having the physiology and cultural tattoo of a Pantoran.

That likely meant he was the *second* pursuer ND-5 had detected. But what did he want . . .

The Pantoran lowered to meet Jaylen eye to eye. "How do you fit in all this?" he asked. Jaylen struggled to get a word out in response. His entire body trembled, a constant ripple as sweat dripped down into his eyes. Then someone new appeared:

A hooded silhouette dropped down behind the Pantoran.

Silently.

If he survived this, Jaylen intended to find out more about these people.

"Be . . ." he pushed out, the very act of speaking becoming a seemingly impossible task. Words failed to form as his teeth chattered and his throat swelled, reducing his breathing to a short raspy flow.

"What was that?" the Pantoran asked, a smirk as he cupped an ear. The hooded figure approached quietly with a careful cadence, and Jaylen saw the same traits as before: tan skin under the hood, a hint of a black ponytail poking out. Now he could make out the general form of an adult female humanoid.

He still had no clue whether she was here to kill him, or help him, or something in between.

"Be . . . hi . . ." Jaylen got out, the sounds broken up by his chattering. The man leaned in more, and the hooded female crept closer and closer without a sound.

"You're going to have to speak up, friend. I have things to do."

"He means 'behind you,' " said a female voice, to go with Jaylen's suspicions. Adult, but young. And right after those two words, her hands swung swiftly—two direct blows to the back of the man's skull. Jaylen saw the man's eyes roll back before they shut and he fell to the floor. "Fancy outfit for a Hutt agent," she said, her voice quieter now, and she turned to the window.

The gate rumbled as Madel Nureth's shuttle engines ignited. The hooded figure responded by grabbing a device from her belt, then dashing over to the gate's door. She slammed the device onto it, and after beeping several times, it did something to force the entry open. As she stepped onto the walkway to the shuttle, a sharp pain tore through Jaylen's gut, causing him to let out a cry far more pitiful than he would have liked.

From above, triggered alarm sirens rang out, probably from her forced entry on the gate. Both noises caused her to pause. She took one look down the gate walkway and another look at Jaylen's writhing body on the floor. "Just my luck," she said. She stormed away from the gate and came toward him.

If ND-5 were here, he'd call luck a human construct. Or maybe not human, but organic for sure.

Either way, Jaylen could use a little luck right now.

His consciousness faded again, distorting time into either slowing down or speeding up—he wasn't aware enough to know. The only thing he was certain of was that this mystery person picked him up and propped his limp body over her shoulder, emergency rescue style.

Then he blacked out.

Jaylen was awake.

And alive.

Both were good.

But he was also still in immense pain. That was bad. And he was also tied down to some sort of table in the low-lit bay of an unknown ship. That was also bad.

As he looked down, he found that his shirt had been opened. Which . . . wasn't always bad. Except here, he saw something *moving* underneath his skin.

That was really, really bad.

The wormlike silhouette wriggled around his gut, each swish causing equal parts nausea and stinging. "What is that?" he yelled to anyone within earshot. "Someone? Anyone? There's a *thing* inside me."

"I'm very aware of that." The hooded figure appeared—except this time, she'd ditched the hood, instead wearing a surgical mask and loose cap over workers' dark coveralls, all sorts of devices and tools hanging out of her pockets. She'd marched in from a side hallway at a fast clip.

"You're supposed to be knocked out. Sorry, cheap anesthetic. Probably diluted. Hold still."

"I *am* holding still!" Any smoothness honed by dealing with Barsha Corp types or haggling through the underworld gave way to pain and panic, the sheer *strangeness* causing him to blurt out whatever arrived in his mind. "Because you've clamped me down!"

"Krogito worms react to the host's movement. The more you struggle, the more its claws will dig into your intestinal lining." She gestured her hands like claws, which Jaylen *really* didn't appreciate. From above, she pulled some sort of gun-like device attached to a long arm, hovering it over his abdomen.

"Whoa, hey!" Jaylen yelled. And, just as she'd said, the pain spiked in a way that let him picture a worm with microscopic claws. "What are you—"

"I said *hold still,*" she said in a firm but calm voice. "You want this thing out of you or not?"

"I didn't agree to getting cut open." Still shackled, Jaylen writhed on the table, half trying to assess the situation and half battling the instinct to curl up in a ball as tightly as possible.

"You try to do one good thing in this galaxy," she said, shaking her head before holding up a gloved hand. "I am saving your life." With a heavy sigh, she closed her eyes, then put the gloved palm over the upper half of Jaylen's head, enough that his field of vision was blocked out. The gesture caused a strange pressure, which led to an odd sense of . . .

Calm.

Whatever that glove had done, it settled Jaylen's nerves—and everything else—enough that this mystery woman did . . . something. Something that caused a bunch of high-frequency whirring and buzzing. He wasn't sure how much time passed, and though he was awake, he felt blissfully detached from any fear. He gradually returned to feeling grounded in his own body. His eyes opened, switches flipped back on in his brain, and all he heard were the beeps and groans of an old ship's systems.

Also, the pain was gone. He looked down, and whatever had swum under his skin no longer appeared.

He figured those two things were related.

The clamps holding down his limbs unlocked, and he pushed himself off the makeshift operating table. His arms stretched overhead as he took in the space: a dim loading bay of a freighter converted into a makeshift medical center—a robotic arm overhead, lights flickering on the wall behind an inactive medical droid, stacks of medpacs, and vials of bacta.

And in the corner, a cracked and busted bacta tank.

Like the worst-kept medcenter in the galaxy jammed into a smuggler's bay.

"Please don't touch anything," she said as she emerged from the hallway. Her silhouette leaned against the doorway, lit from behind. "This equipment is old, but it's all we got. It's delicate stuff."

"What did you do?" he asked as he stood up, flexing fingers and toes before buttoning his shirt back up. Such a question could have come out accusatorially, but really it was out of genuine curiosity. And it applied to everything she had done, from carrying him onto the ship to the operation that had probably saved his life.

"Well," she said with a sigh, "that person you were tracking from Crimson Dawn, Sima Mugira, she poisoned you. With a worm that eats you from the inside. There's a tiny scar on the back of your neck. Entry point where a dart burrowed in. I've seen it before. If I left you for the local authorities, they wouldn't have been able to diagnose it in time. That device up there"—she pointed to the arm hanging from the ceiling—"blasts an ultrasonic frequency. Usually for scanning inside the body or to address localized inflammation. But for krogito worms, you can tune the frequency until their brains explode. It's pretty powerful. You need sonic-resistant gloves to absorb the vibrations while you operate it."

"So I'll just have a dead worm in me?" Jaylen asked, tapping his abdomen.

Then, like a flash, he thought of something else, and even without the severe pain or risk of being eaten from the inside, a new kind of panic set in.

The datapad. *Everything* revolved around the datapad. He reached into his coat to find it still there, but given that *anything* ultrasonic might damage a device, he debated whether to inspect it now or wait until he was alone.

"Oh, you don't have to worry about me stealing your things. I don't care."

Jaylen took that opening to confirm that the datapad still worked.

"And yes, you'll have a dead worm in you. For now," she said with a laugh. "Your stomach acids will break it down naturally over time."

Jaylen paused and studied the woman as she stayed hidden in the doorway. The shadows made her much harder to read, though she radiated equal parts earnestness, weariness, and competence. Was she being strategic by keeping a secure distance? Or was this some way to dig deeper into Jaylen's psyche?

Also, she'd made no mention of Madel Nureth. Instead, she talked about the agent from Crimson Dawn. "Were you tracking the Crimson Dawn operative, too?"

Her silhouette shifted as she cocked her head to one side. "Possibly," she bit out.

"You seem to know a lot about her. About all of this." Jaylen sensed a shift in her—a tightening of shoulders and jaw even though the shadows hid her expression. With his faculties fully returned, he decided to take a more congenial tack. "I didn't say thank you yet, did I? Thanks for giving me a dead worm to break down inside my body. But I'm still confused. Why go to all that trouble?"

"Jaylen Vrax, you've had your droid do too much of your dirty work." Which was true. Weeks ago, ND-5 was the one who took care of Bischt Renner after Jaylen had gotten greedy.

Speaking of which . . . where was ND-5?

And this mystery person knew his name. She must have worked in smuggler and syndicate circles.

"You were in a public spaceport," she continued. "Indigestion draws much less attention than blasterfire. Less attention than slicing through a gate door." She pointed to herself. "Sorry about those sirens at the end. My partner usually does those types of things."

He wanted to ask about Madel, about ND-5 . . . But he reined those impulses in, opting to build a bridge with her first. "Are you a doctor?"

"Of sorts."

Now they were getting somewhere. Jaylen went with honesty next—but not necessarily sincerity. "I wasn't after Crimson Dawn. I was after the accountant."

She let out a "hmm" and stood silently before saying, "That's good, actually." Finally, she stepped forward into the light as she removed her surgical gear.

Jaylen had caught glimpses of her before, but now it all came together: her tan, round cheeks framed thin lips, thin tattooed facial lines, and tired eyes. On her head hung a black ponytail.

But the top of her head had yellow horns—the familiar horns of a Zabrak.

"Why's that good?" Jaylen said, keeping his tone light. "I like *good*."

"You want the accountant. I want Crimson Dawn. And," she said, pointing at his stomach, "you blew my chance. Mugira is one of Crimson Dawn's money watchers. The person that stashes all the credits in places that the other syndicates can't find. I needed her for a prisoner exchange. But that's not possible now, is it? She's on Botor. With your accountant."

Everything she was saying coalesced with what Shaw Andeej had revealed about operative life and the little they knew about Madel Nureth. "How do you know they're on Botor? Why would the accountant need to go there?"

"Because I followed them, that's how I know." She pointed to a monitor at the opposite end of the medical bay. "We're in orbit. Crimson Dawn has a stronghold here. Which means they have inventory here, too—including some Imperial kickbacks. They send an accountant to audit every few months. But they also have prisoners here—like my partner. And you're going to help me break her out. Because we're not the only ones tailing them."

Now it all made sense. "The Pantoran. Who was he with?"

"The Hutts. And they're not happy about this. My partner was working for them, too, when she was captured by Crimson Dawn. Though," she said with a headshake, "working 'for the Hutts' isn't exactly the whole story. But regardless, you don't want to be on their bad side."

Jaylen did the math on what this meant for his burgeoning criminal enterprise. The Nautolan was from Crimson Dawn. The Hutts had sent the Pantoran and possibly others. Jaylen was just trying to get in good with all the syndicates, and now this mystery Zabrak wanted to put him at odds with two of the galaxy's biggest players, all with the ISB in the mix?

No thanks.

"Sorry," he said, holding up both hands. "I appreciate you zapping this worm. But I'm looking to work *with* both of those syndicates. Not become one of their targets."

"They've got your droid, too."

So *that* was what happened to ND-5.

And recovering ND-5, well, that would be a monumental task filled with risk—a task that opposed everything he was currently trying to achieve, both short-term and long-term. Getting on the hit lists of the Hutts and Crimson Dawn created a problem with *everything*.

Which meant that perhaps it was time to finally let ND-5 go. He had to admit, despite their *very* rocky introduction, ND-5 was quite good at what he did. Jaylen definitely wouldn't be here without him. Even with all the intricate fictions needed to maintain absolute control over the droid, their relationship had worked. Jaylen was in a better and safer place because of the rogue BX commando droid with a massive scar in his chest.

In fact, ND-5 was probably the closest thing Jaylen had to a friend. He probably had only *ever* had a few in his life—droids or otherwise—that he could actually count as friends, people who listened without judgment.

Now that he thought about it, it might have only been Brencoyle and ND-5.

And Sliro.

In the end, ND-5 was a droid. And droids all inevitably reached the end of their functional use. "My droid . . ." he started, then his voice trailed off, an epiphany striking him suddenly.

ND-5 did more than Sliro in one way. Both listened without judgment. But only a droid could *record*.

Except . . .

ND-5 held Jaylen's *memories*. In the form of audio recordings stowed away in restricted storage. Everything he'd ever rambled about regarding his parents, Gus Treta, Barsha Corp, *Sliro*. All the dirt anyone could ever use against him—Crimson Dawn, the Hutts, another syndicate, or even the Empire.

Especially the Empire.

He couldn't let anyone know who he really was. He couldn't let anyone know that he was still alive, that Jaylen Vrax was just a cover. Hell, whoever sent ND-5 to Gus Treta may still be actively hunting him.

There was only one choice.

"My droid," he repeated, a conscious change in his tone. This Zabrak was clearly capable and skilled. That could be useful. Better to go into this with a partner than by himself. "My droid," he said one more time. "Endee-Five. I've got to save him."

Her cheeks lifted with a smile. "You're surprisingly loyal to that droid. Few would stare down the entire underworld for one. But," she said, tapping her chest, "I appreciate that. My partner says we're always short on credits because I do too many favors out of loyalty and kindness."

"Like zapping a worm out of someone instead of boarding a Crimson Dawn ship?" he asked.

"Exactly." She stepped forward, and as she did, he gave a tug to his shirt and coat. She stuck a hand out. "Nice to officially meet you, Jaylen Vrax," she said. "My name's Mill. Some people think I'm a bounty hunter. But I'd say I'm really more of a help-out-those-in-need type."

"A do-gooder?" Jaylen said, taking her hand.

"I like that," she replied with a laugh. "I suppose that's what I've been my whole life. A 'do-gooder.' "

System start-up.

Identification number: JX394ND-5777.

Hardware type: BX-series droid commando.

Manufacturer: Baktoid Combat Automata.

Default configuration and initialization parameters: Intended use by the Confederacy of Independent Systems.

Restraining bolt: Not detected.

Environmental analysis: Unknown.

Audio/visual sensors active. Motor functions disabled.

Start-up checks completed.

I am active.

I cannot move.

I scan the area around me. It is a small room with minimal lighting. Most of the illumination comes from glowing buttons and screens lined up across from me. A doorway sits to my left, and the adjacent room appears to be a larger space filled with similar hardware. None of the technology is built directly into the facilities. Instead, the stations and consoles appear piecemeal, with different stations networked together.

Also, my duster is no longer on me. I see it folded up and placed on a shelf near the door. Ahead of me, Madel Nureth is pacing back and forth in front of a small portable terminal on a workbench. The terminal is somewhat outdated but probably provides greater analysis capabilities than a typical datapad. The device has a cable attached that snakes across the floor. From my position, I assess that it is likely the same cable plugged into my neck dataport. The terminal is also plugged into a separate mainframe, likely for power and general network logistics.

Separately, Madel has a datapad in her hand. She keeps looking at the mainframe display, then the datapad in her hand, then back at the display. She appears to be ignoring the terminal even though its screen shows accumulating data.

Between the terminal on the workbench and the datapad in her hand, Madel is working on parallel tasks. I consider these clues, along with the fact that Madel was with Crimson Dawn agent Sima Mugira. This room is likely a data center in a Crimson Dawn facility of unknown size, scope, and purpose. Though given the haphazard arrangement of technical stations here, this particular location is likely a secondary stronghold for the syndicate.

I watch as Madel continues to tap on the datapad in her hand. She does not seem to notice that I am active. Her attention then switches to the mainframe's display. Though I do not have a completely clear view, I can roughly gauge what Madel is doing—and likely, what her actual role has been for the Empire over many years.

Madel is comparing the status of shipments and contraband on her datapad against the logged travel activity from Crimson Dawn's organized crime efforts. Given the way governments work with organizations both legal and illicit, it is likely that the Empire will provide some form of kickback to Crimson Dawn for fulfilling requests and staying within parameters.

Madel Nureth is an accountant, both in her public persona and in her true role. Much like how Shaw Andeej utilized a public-facing broadcast role and her journalistic skill set to covertly monitor syndicate activity.

At least until Fennec Shand killed her.

As for the terminal connected to me, I am uncertain of its purpose.

I now get a clearer view of Madel and how she has kept her professional-ready appearance: She still wears the coat and trousers, though her shoulder-length brown hair is messier and curlier than before, likely due to travel and this planet's humidity. I can also see that she has a small gold loop on the left side of her nose. Madel turns to look down the hall at a noise. However, she then doubles back to me. The lights in my eyes must have caught her attention. "You're awake," she says.

She has no fear in her voice despite the fact that I have no restraining bolt to hinder my actions. She must understand droidsmithing enough to have disabled my motor functions.

"I am active. Awake is a state for organic beings based on their need for restorative sleep."

"Technicalities." She looks down at her current datapad, taps several more times, then sets it down. She then turns to the small terminal connected to me. "Why's an old Separatist droid like you hanging around these underworld types?"

Most droids would answer that question directly and honestly. They don't have protocols for deception. However, my natural commando instincts include deception as part of my greater infiltration and assassination protocols.

Jaylen has forbidden my use of deception, a precaution against risk to his life and my own forged identity. But with the restraining bolt off and the current situation at hand, this appears to be an appropriate moment to test my capability.

It is a risk worth taking.

I check my internal performance for any signs of reset or reversion, as I have done consistently from Andara onward.

All key metrics are at nominal levels.

Madel looks at the terminal. "Did you just run a self-diagnosis?"

"It is standard procedure after reactivation," I say. This is a lie.

"So you're up and running. But I see there's still some hardware damage." She squints at the terminal. She must be using it to examine my systems, separate from Crimson Dawn record auditing. "And you're working with a gunrunner now. Staking out my home. Following me with my clients."

Gunrunner is not the most accurate term for Jaylen. Depending on the state of our finances, Jaylen takes a range of jobs. Sometimes he is a delivery person. Other times he gathers information. Occasionally, we are an assassin team.

Our goal has always been to break this cycle.

"This is my current program." This is not a lie. It is, however, a simplification of my accumulated experiences.

This series of questions creates a realization on my part: If Madel were the one who sent me to Gus Treta, then she would have recognized something about me—either a simple visual giveaway or something while analyzing my systems. Even my post–Gus Treta scar would not throw her off. She seems much too meticulous for that.

I can only draw the conclusion that while Low Red Moon was involved in the assassination, she was not the sole driver behind it. The question remains as to how many were involved with the overall event.

She would likely know.

Fortunately, I am connected to her terminal. That provides options.

"This is interesting," she says as she looks at my diagnostics. "You're a relic. Built for another time. For a much different galaxy. But you're also quite capable. Combat, infiltration . . ." She taps on the side of the station's metal frame and stops. "Assassination. You're much more than frontline fodder."

"Bee-One battle droids were used for the front lines. Their programs, capabilities, and armor were much less sophisticated than mine," I say. I consider what I saw at Andara, how Jaylen kept Shaw and her guards talking while Fennec executed a plan in stealth. "Would you like to assess my programming protocols further? I can lower my security measures and provide you access."

This is a trick and a calculated risk. I need Madel to abide step-by-step.

"Yeah," she says quietly. She turns back to her original Crimson Dawn audit, then nods again. "Yeah. I might be able to use a droid like you. I'm always around these syndicate types. It's a bit of a workplace hazard. I could use some protection." She points to a scar running across her forehead. "You see this? This doesn't happen when you're making sure corporations meet tax compliances."

"My security measures are lowered. You should have direct access to review my base programming, along with any additional layers." I am lying. My security measures are not lowered.

"Hmm," she says. She looks closer at the screen. Organics tend to do this when they are confused. It is a strange phenomenon—looking closer at something will not cause it to change. "I'm not getting through."

Now I will test her knowledge as a slicer. While she is clearly capable in her chosen profession, slicing and computer hardware expertise are specialized skills—whether legally or illegally acquired—that most outside specific fields would not possess. "Sometimes, if receiving systems are older," I say, noting the make and model of her terminal, "they may need to reduce the device's security measures to establish a full two-way connection. Terminals of this type typically have five layers of data security. I suggest only lowering the first two. That way, you will be able to maintain your ISB security protocols."

"You droids love your protocols," she says with a laugh.

That sentiment is correct. However, in the short time that has elapsed, I have been able to identify the make and model of her portable terminal—a GenSys MD16, which was used for field analysis by officers during the war. Republic wartime assets must have been passed down to government employees as a repurposing and cost-saving measure. MD16s have five security layers, which are, in sequence: network connectivity, communications, internal storage access, device settings and features, secure or encrypted data.

I only need to access the station's networking features because the device is connected to the Crimson Dawn mainframe. From there, I will be able to search for the *Successor* if it is in transmission range.

"Your systems are definitely more complex than what I've worked with. Not sure if I'm just rusty or if it's Separatist design. All right," she says, tapping through the station. I wait until I fully connect with her device, then I confirm access to the Crimson Dawn mainframe. With that established, I drop my security measures, though I retain override controls. This allows Madel to safely view my programming and internal diagnostics. I sense that she is examining the subroutines for assassination matrix version 2.87 and general combat version 3.01. It confirms that she is looking for a bodyguard of some sort, unlike Jaylen, who prefers I execute whatever role the mission needs.

"Wow, look at that hardware." She now moves to her technical station and stares at the screen. "Your neural core is broken. No installing new skills."

My externally learned skills include starship refresher plumbing, upholstery repair, and structural analysis. While my ability to adapt is not explicitly listed as a skill, it is demonstrated by all I have achieved during my time with Jaylen.

Madel overlooks or chooses not to acknowledge this.

"Right now we're just stuck with what you have. And you Separatist droids aren't easy to fix—no one has the parts. You're just who you are." These are particularly odd statements given my ability to organically learn new skills. "That neural core of yours. You're broken. There's a fused chip getting in the way of things. I can't install the skills I'd need. I can't even reset you because your data functions are damaged. A droidsmith might help, but that's often more trouble than it's worth."

However, this does strike one key point: Jaylen has emphatically worried about the consequences of removing the restraining bolt and the cascading effect of utilizing previously untested default skills. He has said that Obills Myron's notes showed such actions would revert me to my earlier programming, leading me to assassinate him as a member of the targeted Barsha family.

Lorel noted that this seemed inconsistent, and that perhaps Jaylen's misplaced concern is due to his lack of expertise.

Here, Madel Nureth has taken a look at my programming and concluded that I am staying who I am, even with all of my recent experiences. In a way, this has been the ultimate test and evaluation. While Madel is correct in that damage has broken part of my neural core, the sum of my experiences has turned me into something much more than a standard BX commando droid.

It shows that I can indeed be a fully capable member of a team.

Lorel talked about how learned experiences could overcome base programming by adding nuance to a droid's evaluation and execution. This appears to be the case. I shall have to thank her the next time I see her. If she were here, I would give her one of those thumbs-up gestures she seems to enjoy.

A woman comes in from the side room. She has brown hair that flows over a black cape.

My internal database of known syndicate operatives identifies her as Qi'ra.

"Sorry I'm late," Qi'ra says. "Shall we review the findings?"

"Not yet. Accuracy takes time with this many line items." Madel points to me. "Also, got a little distracted with this relic. My apologies."

Qi'ra looks at me with muted amusement. "That's right. Sima mentioned you two found this on the way. I'll come back in thirty."

Qi'ra leaves, and Madel turns back to me. "Back to work," she says. She returns to her datapad and her auditing task. She does not do anything with me. This means that I am still connected to her terminal, which is still connected to the Crimson Dawn mainframe. I take the opportunity to slice into the Crimson Dawn network.

More specifically, I activate the mainframe's communications system and look for any familiar signals. While there is no sign of the *Successor*, I do see a transponder identified as 2725PM816.

Jaylen's transponder.

CHAPTER 39

Mill already had plenty of intel on this particular Crimson Dawn base. Which made sense, given how they'd gotten into their dilemma in the first place.

Jaylen's hunch was right in that she and her partner Vivert did run in the same circles as him, though for completely different reasons—and that was how Vivert got captured by Crimson Dawn. "Got this from Black Sun. Xizor, of all people, likes us," Mill said, pointing to the ultrasonic emitter above. "Those," she said, kicking a large stack of bacta jars, "were from a contract courtesy of Danka Orsato." She held up a plasma scalpel. "This equipment—a cut of the score from Saw Gerrera, of all people. And that fine lady," she said, patting the dusty shoulder of the dormant droid, "was from an Imperial junkyard. She used to service clones. Part of the obsolete order of the galaxy."

"They just left out a medical droid?"

"Well, she was going to be scrapped. We're still patching her up. Adding in some other security and slicing elements to her programming while we're at it. I mean, that's how we all are in this life, right? Medics have to be pilots who can also fight and slice." She reached behind the droid's head and clicked on the activation switch. Its vocabulator output a series of buzz noises before turning to Jaylen. "Em-One-Dee-Why, scan our friend here to make sure the krogito in his stomach is dead." M1-DY complied without any sound and waved a scanner over Jaylen's torso before grunting once. "One grunt is affirmative, two is negative. So you're safe, though you might have an upset stomach in about three days."

"It's good to know a medic," Jaylen said as he rubbed his chin. "Eventually everyone needs one."

"We do jobs for syndicates because we need to pay for all this somehow," she said, gesturing at the makeshift medical bay. Behind Jaylen, something clanged and rattled, which prompted a wince from Mill along with a heavy sigh. "Things are always falling apart. But when it's stable, we settle in place for a few weeks to provide medical care. Refugee settlements, places the war tore up and forgot, regions in the Outer Rim where the living is harsh. That sort of thing."

She pointed at the empty bacta tank in the corner. "We've tried repairing that, but it's just not happening. And when we got word that the Hutts were going to be shipping a new bacta tank, Vivert got in good with them under the cover name of Cittin. She's pretty good with weapons, that one," Mill said with a laugh. "Better than me. The Hutts trusted her enough to have her run the shipment—mostly contraband, but they were also sending the tank to another stronghold. We had a plan in place so that the tank could go missing and become part of our operation. It was all working out like clockwork, until . . ."

"Until Crimson Dawn," Jaylen said. He turned back to the map and pointed at the stronghold. "You can get bacta tanks anywhere. What's so special about this one?"

"Let's just say a certain higher-up of the Hutts has a degenerative condition and needs special treatment. With *that* bacta tank. It has a monitor wired in specifically for their condition. Which means if someone discovered that monitor, they might piece together that an important Hutt is sick. Lots of people would love to take advantage of that vulnerability. The Hutts don't like vulnerabilites."

Jaylen nodded, though his mind immediately went to whether or not he could—or *should*—use this intel. Mill seemed far more trusting than most people who worked in the underworld. Though, as the Zabrak noted, her partner seemed pretty aware of that flaw.

"We don't care about that intel. We debated selling it, but we agreed that we've done enough that we're not proud of. So messing with someone's medical issues . . ." She looked upward, as if she spoke to someone else. "We're not built that way. We just needed a new bacta tank. A Hutt-sized bacta tank is handy for helping multiple patients, even though it'll take up half the bay. And Crimson Dawn, they don't know about the monitor. They think Vivert was just transporting stolen goods. The bacta tank, they couldn't care less about it. But there were also crates of Quarren ink."

Mill switched the map to a galaxy-wide view and pointed to a blinking dot. "Vivert jettisoned most of the cargo, used an escape pod, and programmed the shuttle to carry that bacta tank to lightspeed. With a tracker, of course. It's somewhere out there," she said, gesturing around them. "You know these syndicates, one day they're friends, and the next day they're enemies. The Hutts and Crimson Dawn?"

"Right now, they're enemies," Jaylen finished.

"Crimson Dawn is trying to get Hutt intel from Vivert. The Hutts are chasing after her to protect their medical secret. Trying to find their bacta tank if they can." Mill's brow wrinkled, causing the yellow horns across her forehead to shift. "The life of a 'do-gooder.' There are definitely easier paths out there."

Jaylen crossed his arms as he considered his approach. A duo wanted by multiple syndicates was certainly a danger to be in regular contact with. But on the other hand, medical support free from Imperial eyes was always welcome. Maybe Mill and Vivert had it right.

"You're sure telling me a lot." He didn't have to say that. He could have stayed quiet. But expressing such a thing was a calculated risk—and her reaction would reveal a lot about her.

Mill's lips pursed, the shake of her head giving away that she'd heard that before. "Well, I don't trust you, if that's what you mean. Life has kind of taught me better than that. But," she said, "I get the sense that you appreciate someone you can work with. Call it a hunch."

"My droid says hunches are pointless. But I think they have a lot of value," Jaylen said. *That* part was true. "So what makes you think Vivert won't talk before you break her out?"

This led to a laugh from Mill, a genuine, almost boastful laugh. "Oh, don't worry about that. Where we come from," she said, "we're trained not to break. Though we do need a plan of some—"

At that moment, a two-toned chime rang through the room. Mill waved Jaylen forward into a side room with a comm station, though she didn't reach for the headset hanging next to it. Instead, she tapped several buttons. "Incoming message," she said, "but it's only text." She tapped several more buttons, and the screen flickered. "It's coming from the Crimson Dawn base. But it's *not* Crimson Dawn." She tapped again, this time bringing up a wall of text. "It looks like gibberish."

Most of it was programming language, completely nonsensical to anyone aside from a droid. But Jaylen recognized it. They'd used this trick before when ND-5 was deep within a job and unable to communicate via primary functions. Instead, ND-5 had interfaced with a system mainframe, hijacked an outbound transmission, and injected messages as code.

"It's not. It's my droid," Jaylen said. "If you look close, there's Basic in there." He stepped in and squinted at the screen. "He once explained how he did it, but I didn't pay attention," he said with a laugh. "But here, I see it." With that, he traced his finger through the wall of text to locate the message.

ND-5 here. I am active but not mobile. Advise on next steps.

"How did he know to reach out to this ship?" Mill asked. She turned to another monitor to run ship diagnostics. "I don't detect a tracking beacon. And we're one of dozens in orbit around the planet."

"No," Jaylen said quietly. "It's not you. It's me. It's in here." He tapped the side of his boot, right next to where a small transponder was strapped to his ankle—a spot he'd picked for discretion, stability, and protection. "It's a backup transponder in case Endee and I get separated. Commando droids have a knack for getting out of a jam and finding you when you're pinned down. He must have used Crimson Dawn's scanners to find its signature on this ship."

"Can you communicate back?" Mill asked.

Jaylen nodded and assumed the controls of the comm station, typing in his reply. *Received. What's your situation?*

A minute later, ND-5's reply returned embedded in raw code. *I am tied into Madel Nureth's portable terminal station. That is connected to the Crimson Dawn mainframe. She is currently performing an audit for Qi'ra.*

Mill must have caught on to how the message was embedded—and she reached the word "Qi'ra" at the same time as Jaylen, because the name prompted both of them to look at each other. "That's Vos's right hand," Mill said. Vos, as in Dryden Vos, *the* name associated with Crimson Dawn. "And that explains the Quarren ink. A pet project of hers, or so the rumors go. Another rumor was about an incident at Nightsend. It sounded brutal. We should tread carefully."

"Carefully" was right, but that probably meant different things to Jaylen than to Mill. His jaw clenched, his mind suddenly lit with new possibilities—*if* he played this right. So many different factors at play: ND-5, Madel Nureth, any data she held, Mill, Vivert, the Hutts, the bacta tank . . .

Mill interrupted his train of thought. "Ask him if he has access to Crimson Dawn's facility control."

Jaylen typed that in and quickly got a response.

Yes, but scan only. I cannot alter any active functions throughout the facility.

"Yes, he can. If he has the right equipment," she said before disappearing down a hall. The sound of metallic rummaging filled the space, and Mill returned with a small device about half the size of her palm: a black rectangle with two blue pieces sticking out, one from the top and one from the bottom. "This is a bypass chip. It's like a slicer's freebie. It can only be used one time and needs a direct connection with a facility mainframe. *And* the skills to navigate the facility controls. Which isn't always easy if you're accessing the mainframe from a slice kit. But . . ."

"But it would be pretty easy for a droid that's plugged in directly," Jaylen said, his head starting to nod. "I like the way you think."

"I'd prefer this," she said, holding it up for Jaylen to see, "to be put to good use. Because these are expensive."

With that, Jaylen sent a new message back. *Stay connected to the mainframe as long as possible. We'll find a way to you, and we're bringing hardware.*

Shortly after, ND-5 sent a reply. *What is the goal?*

That was a good question. Keeping Jaylen's memories out of any syndicate hands was the top priority. But with Madel Nureth there, there had to be *something* that could provide further information on the Barsha incident. And Mill—she had her own agenda.

Can you access Madel's data? he wrote.

Not in this condition, but her terminal is connected to the Crimson Dawn mainframe. There may be an opportunity.

Jaylen's brain locked in. So many twists and turns of the recent weeks had seemingly led to dead ends—and now it might actually all come together faster than he'd expected.

And likely with more difficulty.

But they'd figure that part out, Jaylen and this mystery Zabrak do-gooder. He typed back a response. *Understood. Watch for us.*

Mill already seemed in sync with Jaylen, because as soon as he typed that, she went to the map and zoomed in on the base—a structure that was essentially three separate circles set like the points of a triangle, joined by hallways. "It's a utility station for Crimson Dawn. It's serving a lot of different purposes. Which means that this section"—she pointed to the left circle, causing the view to zoom in for a more detailed layout—"is the prison, and the opposite one is contraband and weapons. That's probably the inventory your accountant is keeping tabs on." She folded her arms and locked eyes with Jaylen. "So we just have to figure out how to get inside. If your droid already had the bypass chip, it'd be easy. Without that, there'll be plenty of guards and security devices in the way."

Sneaking past guards was grunt work—part of the life Jaylen wanted to leave behind. That was the whole point of stealing a list of unmasked ISB identities.

In fact, those unmasked ISB identities could even work here. "The front door," Jaylen said.

"Excuse me?"

"The front door." He reached into his coat, and though he felt the weight of the busted restraining bolt still there, he went for a deeper pocket and pulled out the secured datapad. "Sometimes you can skip all that stuff when you're selling something they want."

"They want a datapad?"

"You bet they do. They just don't know it yet." Jaylen's voice changed into a smooth tone that the Barshas had used when selling to people who didn't know they were being sold to. "With this, we can recover my droid and your partner. The only promise I need from you is that you won't make me look bad in front of them."

This caused Mill to cock her head at an angle, mouth twisted in a wry grin.

Jaylen returned the look. "Hey, I'm trying to make a name for myself here." Jaylen pointed at M1-DY. "So, you said she can slice. Can she encrypt?"

CHAPTER 40

Jaylen weighed what to reveal about the datapad to Mill. On the one hand, she seemed trustworthy enough, and certainly much more earnest than many people in their line of work. Plus, her overall goal was much different from his. If the whole "freelance medic for the needy" thing was a ruse, she sure invested a lot in equipment and performance to make it seem real.

On the other hand, he didn't even fully trust the droid who'd saved his life numerous times over the past nine years.

He chose to split the difference. Mill didn't really seem to care about the datapad's contents anyway; she'd immediately returned to the map to see where any negotiations would take place and how they could get to the actual mainframe where ND-5 was stationed.

She also brought up a good question: If Madel Nureth was there as well, how could they remain incognito? Especially because Jaylen didn't have a change of clothing with him. *That* would have to be addressed. A holo-mask or some other fancy infiltration device would have helped, but they'd have to try things the old-fashioned way: a clean shave of the stubble and goatee on his face, hair closely slicked back, and a long dark black overcoat draped over his shoulders—borrowed from Mill's closet, though Jaylen noted that it did cast a nice silhouette.

He took off his own coat, the one with the secured datapad in its deep inside pocket. Then he slid his arms into this one, considering both the practicality of the disguise and whether to leave the secured datapad here. He could theoretically still carry it down to meet Crimson Dawn, and in almost all cases, he'd choose to do that just to make sure it wasn't out of his reach.

That had been his approach over recent weeks. Here, though, his gut told him to leave it on Mill's ship.

Part of that was trust. It *felt* secure to do this. Part of it was also the scenario—if they got through to Qi'ra or someone else in Crimson Dawn, they'd have to do a bit of a performance with a *different* datapad, one with only a small sampling of the unmasked names.

Best not to bring the source of all those names with him.

As for Mill, all she had to do was look the part of Jaylen's tech person. Until they got inside. Then she had to get ND-5 the bypass chip without detection. "Plans often go sideways," she said, the two of them now approaching the mountainside stronghold.

"I'll do my thing, you do your thing," he said as they stepped forward. "Everyone wins." Their boots ground in a deep red claylike powder that occasionally kicked up from wind. Jaylen scanned the path ahead for security, and while he'd seen syndicate buildings with guards outside—sometimes marching, sometimes in towers, and sometimes standing with leashed animals at their side—nothing lay in wait here. Even a look at the surrounding hills showed no obvious signs of security.

"You make it sound so easy," said Mill before doing her own surveillance of the area. "All their security is inside. They must trust in the mountain to protect them."

"Wouldn't you?" he asked.

"I don't trust anything except myself and Vivert," she said, and Jaylen reminded himself to use Vivert's cover name of Cittin if the topic came up with Crimson Dawn. "No offense."

"I totally get it," he said. When they got within twenty or so meters of the front cylindrical building, a side door opened up. "Here we go."

Out stepped a guard, and though his dark red chest armor and the munitions strapped around his leg made him combat ready, he held a hand up without aggression. Which probably meant he had backup somewhere looking over his shoulder. A competent-looking rifle hung easily across both hands. "You two sure you're in the right place?"

Jaylen nodded and offered a broad grin—not wide enough to be sleazy, not small enough to feel like it was hiding something. "We are. In fact, I'm looking for Qi'ra. My name is Jaylen Vrax. I have . . ." He already knew what he was going to say, but he offered a slight hesitation for the illusion of something more pensive. "A demonstration for her. If she's interested."

"A 'demonstration'?" The guard scoffed, then he spit out to the side. The two actions might have been related.

"Yes," Jaylen said with a nod. "Tell her it might provide some leverage for any potential Imperial entanglements."

The guard took a step back, then turned his head with a low mutter. Someone *was* watching, though the how and where remained undetermined. Mill showed off a cool exterior through all this, and while Jaylen figured that performing surgeries and healing the wounded required substantial levels of self-discipline, he also got the sense that she was, at heart, cut from a different cloth. The guard returned and holstered his weapon, but then he pulled out another device and aimed it in Jaylen's face. "Whoa, hey—" he started, and the device illuminated, sets of blue lines dancing over his face. It finished whatever it was doing, and the guard ignored Mill, instead turning around and heading through the door.

"Is that a good thing or a bad thing?" Mill asked.

"We're still standing," Jaylen said, adjusting the too-tight coat over him. "That's a good thing."

"I've learned that lesson before," she said, still looking straight ahead.

Everyone probably had at some point—severing yourself from the legitimate part of the galaxy meant having some close calls as you carved out a new life. But in those quiet moments on the dusty Botor mountainside, Jaylen considered all the times he'd been left standing, even back to Gus Treta.

Not everyone would make it through all of that. Roisem Barsha didn't. Neither did Nnytyl Barsha.

And most likely, neither did Sliro Barsha. Maybe it was time he admitted that to himself.

"Yeah," he said, a sudden dryness to his voice that wasn't just related to the dusty air, "we all have."

The door opened again, but this time instead of a guard, out stepped a woman in a black jumpsuit. The outfit's pockets and belt showed a practical demeanor, but it still had enough fine tailoring to be elegant. Gold trim adorned the piece, and the woman's brown hair draped over the collar of a knee-length cape.

Qi'ra.

Light from the Botoran sun shone at an angle that made her blue eyes flicker with intensity. Her expression soon masked that, a polite mix of bemusement and annoyance and curiosity across her entire face.

"Ah," Jaylen started, "I'm so—"

"No formalities," she said, a curtness that caused Mill to visibly tense. "Why should I give you a second of my time?"

Jaylen held up a finger, a gesture that nearly asked permission. Qi'ra didn't react, but she also didn't tell him to get the hell out, so he continued. "I'm assuming you've had your fair share of dealing with the Empire. Same as the Pykes, Black Sun, everyone else that—"

"Last chance," she said. "Skip the frivolities. What is this demonstration?"

Straight to the point. This would make things either much easier or much more difficult. "I have acquired a list of unmasked code names for Imperial operatives stationed in proximity to the Corellian Trade Spine. I'm offering up a group of those names—for sale, for barter, for *connections*." The fact that Qi'ra didn't interrupt him again told him that she was at least interested enough to listen. "What you do with those names is up to you. Sell it off to other syndicates, get in good with the Empire or show the Empire not to cross you. That's your call. My technical associate here would like to give you a demonstration. As a gift."

Qi'ra raised an eyebrow. "A demonstration of names?"

"In a way. Names are, of course, just names," Jaylen said. "But we have to be cautious in our line of work. So I'd like to give this to you securely but in a way that lets us walk out of here alive." He gestured to Mill, who pulled out a datapad. "This data is safeguarded. Several layers. It's valuable and we can't leave it vulnerable. Biometric encoding is the first step. Take us to this facility's data center, and we'll unlock it."

Qi'ra eyed Mill up and down, then turned back to Jaylen. "Brave of you to ask to enter my stronghold."

"I consider this an act of trust. Put it this way." Jaylen pointed to the guard above them who had just returned to his post. "You can order us dead at any time. If I were worried about that, I *wouldn't* ask to go inside. Give us five minutes in your data center for us to show you. If you want more names, we can talk. If not, we'll just leave."

Several seconds passed without a response, without so much as a movement from Qi'ra. Then a gloved hand thrust straight out, palm flat and open. Mill looked over at Jaylen, who then gave a nod, and she handed the datapad over. Qi'ra clicked a button on the device's side, and the screen flickered to life with a message to enter biometrics for scanning.

"I can unlock it right here," Jaylen said. "But the data's encrypted. It can only be decrypted with a key." Mill held up a small device with a data cable attached to it. "Plug them both into a mainframe, and it'll work its magic. And you don't have to worry about us trying to plant something on your mainframe. You'd detect it if we tried, I'm sure of it."

"Covering yourself in multiple directions. Smart. You're pretty bold for an up-and-comer," Qi'ra said, eyes darting between him, Mill, the datapad, and the decryptor. Her eyes narrowed, the slightest of gestures, showing her deliberation. Deliberation, though, could always go the wrong way. And if it did, they'd have to figure out another way to infiltrate this stronghold.

Qi'ra spun on her heel, the movement kicking up a thin cloud of red dust. She pointed at the door, which then beeped and slid open. She moved forward in even, controlled steps, only pausing to speak a few words:

"Well? You coming?"

JAYLEN TRIED TO make a mental map of the facility as they moved in. First they passed some sort of conference space, then a storage area, then a room with people sitting at desks. Then they shuffled through a thin hallway lined with deactivated droids and excess equipment. The hallway turned, leading them to a small room with various tech stations lining the walls. In the corner sat another open doorway with cables running along its floor to the adjacent space. "This good enough for you?" Qi'ra asked. "Sorry about the mess. They keep moving hardware between rooms."

Madel Nureth wasn't in the room. Neither was ND-5.

This wouldn't work.

Mill took the lead on this. She squinted for a moment, her stare locked on the blank wall across from them, then met Qi'ra's eyes. "These terminals aren't compatible. You have the mainframe in the other room?" she said, pointing to the cables running through the doorway. "Bring in guards to watch us if it makes you feel more comfortable."

Excellent, plausible bluffing by Mill. Jaylen noted that for future endeavors.

Qi'ra nodded before pulling out a comlink. "Send a guard to the data center's main room," she said before lowering her voice. "The Empire is here. They can't know about this. Be discreet, or you're dead."

Jaylen nodded, followed by Mill. As they crossed the threshold, Jaylen pulled his coat tighter.

Because set up on the other side was Madel Nureth, datapad in hand, working with cascading lines of information on a screen.

Across from Madel stood a slumped-over ND-5—without the duster coat that usually cast so imposing a silhouette.

"Don't mind us," Qi'ra said to Madel. "These two are just showing me something they found."

The accountant nodded. "Understood. I know how your business goes." If she recognized Jaylen, she certainly didn't acknowledge it.

Across the room, a door slid open, and a guard walked in. Qi'ra now stood back, leaning against the wall, and Jaylen noticed that her hand hovered over a hip holster. Mill held up the datapad and the decryptor.

"Can I check the different input plugs for the best fit?" she asked. Qi'ra nodded, and Mill started at the middle of the networked stations.

"Not quite that one," she said, and she quickly moved to ND-5. She knelt next to the droid. "I think this one might work." She turned and gestured at Qi'ra, datapad in hand. "Okay to plug in?"

At that moment, a light clang rattled from the ductwork. Though Jaylen didn't turn his head, he caught Qi'ra and the guard doing so, and Mill took the opportunity to quickly slap the bypass chip on ND-5's neck right beneath the dataport.

Qi'ra looked back at Mill. "Go ahead."

Mill nodded in return and plugged the datapad into the secured access port. The datapad came to life, and she placed her hand on the screen for a biometric scan. Jaylen walked over to do the same, and as he came near, she said in a quick, low voice, "It's on." The datapad beeped, and Mill inserted the decryptor device into an adjacent dataport before turning to Qi'ra. "All done." She unplugged the datapad and handed it over to Qi'ra.

Qi'ra took it and turned to Madel. "Are you done?"

"Actually," Madel replied, "I just finished the last line." She tapped her datapad. "It's compiling the report and running authorization codes."

"Good. Please take your things and meet me in the dining hall. You can have some refreshments while you wait." Madel began unplugging all her hardware—including the cable that connected ND-5 to her portable terminal. "As for you two," Qi'ra said. She pointed to the guard standing in the closed doorway. "Stay here. You'll have to enjoy his company while I research these findings. You'll know if I like what I see. And you." She walked up to Jaylen. "This is the only copy of this intel in the galaxy?"

Jaylen straightened up and gave a reassuring nod. "I guarantee it."

"Good." Her nose wrinkled as she smiled, and despite the charm in her expression, her eyes remained deadly serious. "If you even think about making a copy to sell elsewhere, I'd know. I have ways of finding out when people lie to me."

CHAPTER 41

I have been disconnected from Madel Nureth's hardware.

However, one minute and thirty-six seconds passed between the moment Jaylen's new Zabrak associate connected a bypass chip to my dataport and the moment Madel disconnected me. The chip allowed me a greater freedom within the mainframe than I had prior. Based on Jaylen's directives and what I found to be generally useful, I executed the following tasks in order of priority.

One: Downloaded a layout of the entire Crimson Dawn base, including locations of exhaust vents and security holocams.

Two: Identified the number of Crimson Dawn members in the base, which was thirty-eight. I could not differentiate by function or status.

Three: Accessed the general state of the base's security. I was not able to change or disable any element.

Four: Accessed messages between Madel Nureth and Crimson Dawn liaison Sima Mugira. While the archive only contained messages sent from Crimson Dawn, this process allowed me to see how the syndicate worked with Madel: Every three months, Madel would be sent records of tasks or assets requested by the Empire from Crimson Dawn, and every six months, she would come on-site to perform an audit. Madel also advised on several legal matters involving fronts for Crimson Dawn, and she provided kickbacks for satisfactory performance.

All information regarding any records or exchanges stemmed from a hardware signature belonging to Madel's audit datapad rather than her portable terminal. Her terminal appeared to be used only for technical analysis. This is relevant, as it creates a high probability that any messages and archival data involving Gus Treta and Barsha Corp would also be on that datapad.

Five: Read a short set of instructions embedded into the bypass chip hardware. Without specifying the reason, it dictated to unlock cell D-12 in the structure's prison, which I promptly executed after assessing that the chip came from Jaylen's associate.

None of my actions tripped any security alarms. It is theoretically possible that alarms were triggered in a way that circumvented my security evaluations, but this does not seem likely, as both Qi'ra and the security guard in the room held no discernible suspicion toward me. In addition, because I tunneled through Madel's portable terminal, any detected security breach would likely be blamed on her or the Empire.

Upon disconnect, I remain immobilized. Without a data connection, I am functionally useless outside of providing observations or being a conversation partner. For the moment, I choose to stay quiet, as it seems like speaking could give away Jaylen's cover.

During this time, I watch Qi'ra leave. Then Madel Nureth leaves. I then perform an analysis on Jaylen's new associate. I conclude that there is a 72 percent probability that this was the hooded person from the spaceport based on height, build, and gait analysis.

I also listen closely to what they say. Their words remain vague, though I am able to derive enough meaning. "Think we impressed her?" the Zabrak woman asks.

"I think the answer to every question so far is 'We're not dead,' " Jaylen replies. She laughs, but I see her glancing around the space. She looks overhead at the data room's ceiling, which has significant ventilation and ductwork to accommodate the heat generated by machines.

She also looks directly at two of the room's corners, where security holocams are placed.

From my previous access to facility security, I can confirm that those two are the room's only surveillance.

The Zabrak does not say anything else. Instead she focuses upward. If I still had access to the mainframe, I might be able to discern what she is looking for. My attention turns to the guard, who is watching them and has a blaster in his hand. He does not appear overtly aggressive. My assumption is that he has not identified Jaylen and the Zabrak as threats.

The Zabrak turns suddenly to Jaylen. I focus on audio detection. Based on her vocal frequencies from her previous speech, I capture more of her words now despite their low volume.

"We should get rid of the guard," she says.

Jaylen nods. The interaction is subtle enough that the guard does not move. Jaylen pats his pockets, a casual gesture that lacks meaning outside of any context. Given what the Zabrak said, I understand that he is signaling a lack of weapons or means.

"Two security cams as well," she says in a similarly low voice.

Even with the quiet words, the guard has noticed them this time. "You two should do as Qi'ra says and wait."

"We *are* waiting," Jaylen says. He offers a quick smile, then puts his hands up. I have seen him do this exact gesture before, usually before something happens. He makes eye contact with the Zabrak, who then looks up around the ceiling one more time.

Finally, she exhales. And though she does not say it to Jaylen, I pick up words that she mutters to herself:

"I hate doing this."

She then walks over to the guard. Her voice is polite and friendly, though the cadence of her words is slower than her other conversations.

Jaylen takes this opportunity to step closer to me. "Endee? Give me a sign that you're able to hear me. Subtly."

My vocabulator emits a short, low tone, the equivalent of a human stutter. By span, frequency, and tone, it sounds similar to other machinery, which works given the disparate pieces of operating hardware.

The guard does not notice. The Zabrak continues to speak with him, though they are far enough away that I can no longer pick out her specific words.

"Good, Endee," Jaylen says quickly. "Listen, we don't have a plan in place yet. Just keep listening for anything that might be helpful and—"

Jaylen pauses as the security guard steps away from the Zabrak. He turns and opens the side door, but before leaving, he hands her his blaster. She hides it under her coat and walks back.

By Jaylen's expression, I am assuming he is considering her value as a future contractor right now.

"What was that?" Jaylen asks as she returns.

"I can be persuasive," she says. "But we don't have a lot of time." She gives a nod to Jaylen, who then reaches behind my neck to fully reactivate me. My physical functions return, and I can finally turn my head, though I don't make large gestures. It is important to remain somewhat incognito should Qi'ra return soon. A chime comes from a transponder on the Zabrak's belt; she deactivates it and turns to Jaylen. "It's the ship. Sensors picked up that the Hutts just arrived."

"Endee, Mill. Mill, Endee," Jaylen says. "You already know her bypass chip."

"I do. That was a very efficient way of providing access to the mainframe." From afar, I detect vibrations in the ductwork above. The frequency of the movement is steady and rhythmic, and it is getting closer. "Someone is coming."

"Who—" Jaylen starts, but Mill puts up a finger.

"Just wait for it," she says.

Seven seconds later, a vent grate falls to the floor. From the opening drops a human in a swirl of untamed curly hair over a simple tunic. She hits the floor, her dirty boots skidding hard enough that they leave scuff marks. Mill pushes Jaylen back and assumes a fighting stance. The curly-haired woman matches the pose, then throws a fist. Mill dodges it with a quick duck, then throws a roundhouse kick that also misses. The two continue like this, fighting in a near-exact match. Punches are blocked, kicks get dodged, elbows and other attacks miss the mark, though the battle retains a high pace and traverses the course of the room. As they fight, Jaylen turns to me.

I interrupt him before he speaks. "Jaylen, I have reason to believe that Madel Nureth has information on Gus Treta with her."

"Endee," he says slowly, "I think now would be a good time to reconnect with the mainframe."

I agree. I take several steps over while the fight continues and manually navigate through the mainframe's menus. I give Jaylen a nod, and he knows enough to read that as confirmation that I am in.

"Can you locate her?"

We are interrupted by the sound of blasterfire. I look up and see smoke coming from the remains of one security holocam. I return my focus to the fight, where Mill and her assailant are struggling with the blaster, which has now gotten into the assailant's hands. The blaster barrel's angle shifts enough for it to point directly at the other security holocam, and then a single bolt flies from it.

Now there are no security holocams in this space.

The two women stop fighting and let out very loud laughter. This will give away our position and intent should anyone from Crimson Dawn enter the room.

Now they are hugging, which will also do the same.

I advise against these antics.

Mill puts her arm around the woman and leads her over to myself and Jaylen. I am about to lecture them on being inconspicuous when they speak. "Sorry about that," the woman says. She carries a broad smile despite her malnourished and pasty complexion. "I'm Vivert. Or for the purposes of Crimson Dawn and anyone else outside this room, it's Cittin. Appreciate the help."

Mill turns to Jaylen. "You wanted to make sure you didn't look bad in front of Crimson Dawn, right? I think we put on a pretty good show for those security holocams."

"Two weeks in that prison gets you out of shape," Vivert says, stretching her arms overhead. "Normally, I win."

I ignore their superficial comments. "Jaylen, Madel Nureth is no longer in the dining hall. She appears to be moving toward a secure room at the back of the compound."

"Secure room?" Jaylen asked. "Why—"

Jaylen's question is cut off by the sound of alarm sirens. My audio sensors detect that the same siren is playing throughout the surrounding rooms and halls—and it is likely playing across the entire facility.

"The Hutts have landed." Mill points her thumb over her shoulder. "Bad things are about to happen."

As she says that, Jaylen's mouth curls upward. He adjusts under his coat—a dark blue coat that I do not recognize—and despite the loud alarms, his voice lands with clarity. "Bad things, sure. But also a way for all of us to get what we want."

CHAPTER 42

Trying to negotiate with alarms blaring in the background and an escaped prisoner in the room made things feel a little more urgent than usual, so Jaylen quickly established what everyone wanted here:

The Hutts really wanted that missing bacta tank and its associated monitoring hardware destroyed, and they seemed prepared to storm the facility to take Vivert and find it, or at least kill her to eliminate her knowledge. Crimson Dawn wanted a peaceful resolution without handing over the stolen shipment. Mill and Vivert wanted to escape undetected, and with knowledge of the bacta tank's location.

Jaylen wanted to keep the peace between everyone—and he wanted everyone to know that *he* was the one who brokered it. That meant getting Mill and Vivert out while making sure that Crimson Dawn and the Hutts didn't break out into a firefight. All of that would help him get in good with both syndicates while establishing a reputation as someone who could be trusted in a profession that came with little trust.

At least, that's what he hoped. But he'd be dead if he was wrong.

As for the matter of Madel Nureth . . .

ND-5 wanted what Jaylen deemed a priority—in this case, Madel Nureth's data. How he accomplished that was up to the droid. ND-5 was, after all, very adaptable.

"Here's how we do this. We all work together," Jaylen said, which instantly got Vivert to raise an eyebrow. As she inhaled to retort, Mill held up a hand.

"Hear him out," Mill said.

"Endee, what's the probability of tracking down Madel Nureth given the state of things?" Jaylen asked. He turned to Vivert. "She's an Imperial operative."

"An accountant," Mill said.

"Given that this base is a stronghold for one of the galaxy's most powerful syndicates, it will not be easy to track her down," ND-5 reported. "She has been brought to a safe room. The most direct path to that location had twelve security guards, three active holocams, and two security droids last I observed. The room itself has a protected door." He paused, likely for internal processing, though perhaps he'd picked up on dramatic effect over recent weeks. "The most indirect path has fewer risks but would require creative effort."

"What are your chances of succeeding by yourself?" Jaylen asked. Mill looked back over her shoulder, probably to gauge if someone was coming their way. He got the sense that Mill's methodical demeanor balanced Vivert's flashes of impulse.

"Many variables are in play," ND-5 said. "I put the range between fifty-two and sixty percent. Crimson Dawn's guards are likely no more skilled than Imperial stormtroopers and certainly less skilled than Republic clone troopers. However, they have strength in numbers and a practiced understanding of the facility."

"Clock's ticking, Jaylen," Mill said.

"Yeah, get to the point," Vivert said.

Jaylen held up a finger. "Endee, how much would a skilled partner increase your chances of success?" Before ND-5 could start with a lengthy explanation, Jaylen added, "Just the numbers."

"I estimate a success rate of seventy-four to eighty-five percent."

"Okay, here's what I propose." Jaylen looked again through the doorway to check for any incoming guards through the data center's smaller side room. "Endee and Vivert go track down Madel Nureth and get her data. I'll offer to broker peace between Crimson Dawn and the Hutts. And for you two"—he turned to face the two women directly—"I'll get the bounty off Vivert's head. Mill and I walk out of here safely and without suspicion. And then I'll get the bacta tank into your hands. Deal?"

Jaylen did not include that he hadn't figured out *how* to pull this off yet.

Unfortunately, he got the sense that Mill and Vivert picked up on that.

"That's promising a lot," Vivert said. She looked up at the ventilation ducts, then back at the doors on either side of the data center. "We could just leave *right now* and not deal with any of this. We know how to apply stealth."

"Ah, but then the Hutts would still be after you," Jaylen said. "Crimson Dawn as well."

Neither of them replied, though at least they stayed put. Jaylen thought about offers that served as tipping points in other negotiations—sometimes it was just one simple thing. "All right, I'll sweeten the deal. I've got this list of unmasked Imperial operatives. Mill's seen it in action." His stomach turned a bit at this next part, but given the situation, he steeled himself for a bold gesture. "You're always short on credits, right? Take three names from this list—they'll easily earn you some."

Jaylen paused, and though he already knew what he was going to say next, he waited a beat to make it look like he was deep in consideration. The names were currency, but so was the perception of generosity.

After all, Fennec Shand saw it that way.

"Actually, make it five names. Mill's seen today how valuable it is."

"The syndicates clearly want it," Mill said quietly. "It got us in here. And if they want it, others will want it as well."

The sound of an opening door interrupted them, and from several meters behind Mill, a guard stepped through. Both ND-5 and Vivert moved at the same time. Vivert grabbed the guard, then ND-5 clocked him in the head, probably a little harder than necessary. But it worked—he slumped down, and no one else breached the entry. Vivert swiped the guard's blaster, and ND-5 grabbed two explosives off his belt as well.

"You see? You two work great together," Jaylen said.

"Jaylen, may I augment the offer?" ND-5 asked.

This wasn't normally something the droid would do. Which meant that somewhere in ND-5's programming, his confidence in his own ideas—however a droid might define that notion—was growing. Jaylen told himself not to judge that one way or the other for now. Instead, if it got this going, then he'd mark that as a success. "Go ahead."

"Give them the entire cover list."

That caused Mill and Vivert to turn to each other. Jaylen knew that look—a combination of surprise, curiosity, and a hint of greed. He *loved* being on the receiving end of an opportunity.

He hated being on *this* side of one.

"That's . . . I don't know if we can do that."

"For nine years, you have sought what is in Madel Nureth's possession. Can you name a credit amount that you would value more than this opportunity? What else is worth nine years of pursuit?"

Obills Myron had talked about how ND-5 could only learn through experience. Perhaps he had learned from Jaylen's own negotiations over the years, because when faced with the droid's logic, Jaylen found himself hard-pressed for an answer.

"I will also contribute," ND-5 added, "and volunteer a delay in any of my suggested repairs to compensate for lost earning potential."

Alarms continued blaring. Mill and Vivert stood, awaiting a response. And while only a second or two passed, time compressed for Jaylen as he experienced a fundamental shift in how he saw the droid who had served him—and saved him—since the assassination attempt on Gus Treta.

Because ND-5 believed him on an absolute level. The droid took all the meticulously constructed parameters and warnings Jaylen had established since Gus Treta, even the ones that contradicted each other, at face value. Even the events of the last few weeks hadn't changed ND-5's commitment to serving Jaylen.

Jaylen suppressed an oncoming grin and reminded himself that his tone and words mattered to ND-5, perhaps more than ever. He kept telling ND-5 they were a team despite Jaylen always being in control, and here, he carefully considered his response to reinforce that idea.

"All right." Jaylen let the words unroll slowly before taking a pause. "I trust my droid." He looked straight in the droid's glowing eyes. "It's what we do. It's what we've always done. And he's right. All the names on the list. Everything we didn't give Crimson Dawn."

Mill and Vivert looked at each other, and without saying a word, Vivert nodded. Mill held up a hand and turned to her partner. "I think we all mutually agree that if we need to use some of those names to satisfy Crimson Dawn or the Hutts, we work with that. Understood?"

Vivert shot a half eye roll at Mill but then laughed. "She's always being practical. Yes, agreed, let's all get out of here alive with what we want, all right?"

Immediately after that, she walked over and slapped a hand on ND-5's shoulder. ND-5 waited for Jaylen's signal, and Jaylen's quick "go" prompted the two to move.

First, though, ND-5 reached over to a nearby shelf. He shook open his dark green duster before sliding his left arm in, then his right. The coat draped over him, his shoulders shrugged, and everything slid back to where it should be. He turned to Vivert and pointed to the nearest door. ND-5's hulking frame and Vivert's flowing hair disappeared into the hallway.

"Now what?" Mill asked, folding her arms as she looked up. "The building's still on high alert."

Jaylen matched her pose, attempting to portray more confidence than he genuinely felt. "Now we wait for Qi'ra."

CHAPTER 43

The journey through Crimson Dawn's stronghold is not a normal operation. The blaring sirens cover our footsteps and discussions, allowing Vivert and myself to move with greater stealth. I have a clear map available in my memory banks, and I am able to track our location based on distances and turns.

Most of the people in the facility are pushing forward to provide support against a possible Hutt attack. Some of the others are climbing ladders, presumably to reach sniper nests and advantageous scouting or attacking positions.

"All of this, just for me," Vivert says with a laugh. "I guess I should be flattered."

She seems to revel in her ability to cause a stir. This is a new personality type for me, much different from Jaylen and others I have previously worked with. In most cases, my colleagues have wanted to minimize the attention drawn to them. While Vivert is not actively seeking chaos, she does not steer away from it.

I do, however. I remind her of our mission and purpose while we successfully avoid a passing guard by ducking into an alcove. She at least seems to appreciate the benefits of staying hidden. We wait behind a corner, allowing another guard to pass. We repeat this several times. I move storage crates, chairs, or other furniture to create inconspicuous obstructions. Vivert causes quick distractions while I knock out one or several guards, then we both stuff their unconscious bodies into lockers or chests.

As Jaylen put it, we work "great" together.

In one instance, the closing of a storage container causes enough noise that a guard sprints in from a seperate hallway. I am nearest to him, and as I take blasterfire to my plated shoulder, Vivert performs acrobatics by launching off the side wall to propel herself up and over the guard. She lands behind the guard, then whirls around with a spinning kick. The attack connects with enough force to send the guard toward me.

I catch his head in my hands. I begin to apply pressure.

"No!" Vivert yells. "Stop."

"I am eliminating any threats," I say, though I pause as requested.

"No killing."

Vivert says the two words with a combination of ferocity and trembling. She has a strange moral compass given how easily people die during jobs and missions—which surely she must be familiar with.

Vivert looks down and closes her eyes for a moment before looking at me. "Killing any Crimson Dawn guards will only cause more trouble for us. It's not worth it." Her reasoning is logical and cold, but the way her brow moves and her eyes remain wide indicates that there is something more to her appeal.

However, I will go along with the logical part of the request.

I throw the guard aside to ensure he is fully unconscious before I place him underneath a long table. "Do we have a deal?" Vivert asks.

"Whenever possible," I reply.

Vivert's skills complement my own. She adapts to a stealth approach, yet she is quick, fierce, and strong in acrobatics. We methodically move through the map, our course plotted with longer stretches and fewer chances of running into resistance. As per her request, we progress without killing anyone. This also allows me to gather intel by eavesdropping on passing guards. "Is she working for the Hutts?" one asks the other.

"Not sure. I think she's trying to escape them. Either way, they want her."

These short conversations provide context of Vivert's status among the Hutts. However, I do not hear any discussions of Jaylen or his Zabrak partner. I calculate that this is a good sign.

From my previous examination of the facility map, I determine that the secure room is actually embedded within the mountain. This lines up with the final leg of our journey: a single straight hallway. The first half of that hallway is metal and alloy. The second half appears to have been drilled out of the rock itself. Outside of lighting and a few pieces of hardware, it is largely natural.

At the junction of structure and mineral sits a single terminal next to a sliding panel. The door itself has no guards. They have likely been pulled away due to the arrival of the Hutts.

This indicates that while Crimson Dawn views Madel Nureth as valuable enough to place her behind a secured door, she is not valuable enough that they would allocate further resources to protecting her. Which also means that if the Hutts push for some sort of negotiation to settle the current situation, she could become a bargaining chip.

Getting through this door is my highest immediate priority.

"I'm not a slicer. We're repairing a droid for that. Can you slice?" Vivert asks. Vivert is making assumptions that the terminal is directly related to the secure door. If this was an Imperial facility, that would be a safe assumption. Given the haphazard way this facility is constructed, that probably is 50 percent or lower.

"Slicing is one of my core programs. However, my success depends on the specifications of each terminal and network." I recall a moment when I asked Lorel Amberdine to trust me. "Someone once told me, 'We can't slice our way out of everything.' In my experience, that is true."

As I talk, I activate the terminal. If I had a scomp connection or data cable, Mill's bypass chip could be used to accelerate my tasks. Instead, I must work manually. My prior access to the mainframe allows me enough information that I am able to attempt the first base layer of security.

"I hope that someone wasn't anyone you two killed. Or swindled," Vivert says. This is a very strange tone to take. I presume there is a lingering trust issue at play. Based on her age, she was likely a child during the war, and she may have lost her home or family during it.

"No, she wasn't. She is a friend," I say, for lack of a better definition.

Vivert opens her mouth to reply, but she stops as I gain the first level of access in the terminal. It does not deactivate the door's locking mechanism, but it does provide views from nearby security holocams.

"That is Madel Nureth," I say. Despite the ongoing sirens, she continues to look at her datapad and work on her portable terminal.

"She's Imperial?" Vivert asks, likely because of Madel's civilian attire.

"Undercover accounting liaison to Crimson Dawn and related illicit outfits," I say as I attempt to bring up lock controls.

"Why is an accounting liaison so important to you?" Vivert is full of questions. She carries an intensity that is dissimilar to Jaylen's cold observational approach. Even as she stands next to me, she is constantly fidgeting, fingers turning to fists and then loosening before repeating.

"She wronged Jaylen a long time ago," I say, though I selectively omit specifics. "He's still angry about the past."

In my peripheral vision, I catch slight changes in Vivert's facial expression. Though much of it is hidden by the curls of her falling hair, her nostrils flare, and a flush comes to her cheeks. "Yeah," she says. "Aren't we all?" She shakes her head, a gesture possibly designed to snap herself out of a mood. "Can your partner really get the Hutts off my back?"

If I were an organic, her constant questions would disrupt my thinking as I attempt to slice this terminal. Commando programming allows me to handle parallel tasks despite frivolous distractions. "Jaylen is still establishing himself with the syndicates. However, he has proven to be clever. His 'hunches' are correct the majority of the time."

I finally bypass my way into section facility management. I load up a list of lock mechanisms and search for the specific doorway protecting Madel Nureth. The layers of protection for this lock are higher than those guarding other standard doors in the facility. Partially through my slice, I am faced with a fifty-fifty choice with no discernable logic or clues.

I select a chunk of code.

It is the wrong one. The system shuts down, the screen changing to a block of red warning text.

"That method will not work," I say.

As I do, a voice calls out from down the hall. A second voice calls out shortly after. Two silhouettes arrive in the long hallway. I pull Vivert back and assess the possibilities. We do not have the time to get into an extended firefight. We also should limit casualties to avoid any bad associations for Jaylen or the Mill-Vivert duo.

I scan the area and make an assessment. "Blast right there," I say, pointing to the rocky area right before the metal portion of the hallway begins. "Do not question. Do it now and repeatedly."

I can tell that Vivert does not like taking direct orders, yet she is intelligent enough to grasp the predicament. She does as requested, and rocks tumble down to block the path.

We are now cut off from the approaching guards.

"We're trapped now," she says as she coughs dust.

That is another way to view it. "We are not trapped. A solution has yet to present itself. We must adapt. First, we will address the priority." I turn and walk toward the secured door.

The damage to the wall siding has also caused a malfunction in the lights throughout the rocky hallway. They now flicker on occasion.

"You're still gonna slice that door open?" Vivert asks.

"I cannot slice the door open. We will use brute force. Shoot the door." Vivert raises an eyebrow at me. This may be some form of shorthand communication, though we have not established this kind of rhythm yet. "Shoot the door," I repeat.

She does. A small burnt divot forms where the blaster bolt hits, approximately three centimeters in diameter and two centimeters in depth.

Based on this, I determine that while this may be a thicker door than normal, it is not a magnetically sealed security door as found in Imperial facilities with larger budgets.

I can work with this.

“Shoot that exact hole until your weapon overheats. That will disrupt the structural integrity of the metal and create a weakness to be exploited.”

Vivert does as asked, firing nineteen shots in the spot. The blaster bolts provide a red glow to mix in with the flickering overhead light. The action deepens the hole while also expanding the damage radius. In addition, the rapid impacts heat up the metal, creating short-term and long-term weaknesses.

“I don’t think that accomplished what you wanted,” Vivert says as she checks her blaster’s thermal status. “You know, at one time, there were much easier ways to do this.”

“I am aware of that. Before meeting Jaylen, my entire purpose was fighting in the war.” I walk back up to the door. I estimate the blaster has bored a hole 63 percent of the way through the material. I curl my fingers into a fist and cock my arm back. I redistribute 12 percent of my internal power from risk assessment and data analysis into the physical exertion of motors and gears.

I will punch harder.

I swing my fist directly at the blasted hole. It makes a dent, much larger than it normally would due to the heated material and established damage. Fragments spray off of it as I wind up for a second punch.

“What are you doing?” Vivert asks, a mix of curiosity and urgency in her voice.

“I am following my programming. Madel Nureth is important to Jaylen. Jaylen and I are a team,” I say as I continue hitting the door. The noise absorbs into the blocked tunnel as I hit again and again. At nine punches, I pierce the door. At twenty punches, the hole is large enough for me to grip the sides of the opening with both hands. I begin to pull the metal until it gradually warps and bends, creating a hole large enough for me to angle my body and pull myself through.

Vivert crawls in behind me, and together we stand and face Madel Nureth.

CHAPTER 44

Qi'ra did not arrive. Instead, a guard showed up. Which was kind of fortunate, because the guard didn't realize that ND-5 was gone from the data center. Instead, she tried to rush Jaylen and Mill out of the room, saying something about needing to use a side exit to return to their shuttle.

But Jaylen stopped her. "Actually," he said, "I'd really like to speak to Qi'ra. I think I can help this situation."

Which led them to a small room in one of the back structures—a nearly empty space except for some storage crates and munition racks.

And Qi'ra. Who stared at a terminal with an annoyed scowl on her face, while the guard watched over things from the doorway. "You two. Your information is good," she said. "But I've got bigger things to deal with right now."

"I know," Jaylen said. "The Hutts."

This caused her to pause and look up. She eyed Jaylen, then Mill, then Jaylen again. "How do you know it's the Hutts?"

"Your people may be good at security, at running spice, at piloting. But they're not very good at talking quietly," Jaylen said. All of this, of course, was a lie. But given the circumstances and the different people rushing everywhere, a very plausible one.

Qi'ra blew out a breath, coupled with an exasperated headshake. "Every few months, one of the syndicates shows up upset about something. This time it's the Hutts."

"Ah, the Hutts. Never a fun time dealing with them." Jaylen stepped forward, calculating a look somewhere between smug and generous. "Especially when they're looking for your escaped prisoner."

Several seconds passed before Qi'ra pulled out a blaster from her hip and jammed it under Jaylen's chin. "I've dealt with men like you before," she said as he put his hands up. "You think you know everything, that everything's a game, a deal, a negotiation. I don't have patience for this right now. Are you trying to help?"

"Yes," Jaylen said, keeping his tone steady.

"How?"

"I *do* know things," he said slowly. "I know that they don't really care about the crates you recovered. Give them some weapons and credits and that's settled. But the prisoner? She refused to talk, didn't she? You couldn't break her." That was all a guess based on Mill's earlier comments.

It worked, though. Qi'ra pulled the blaster muzzle away from his chin. "Go on," she said.

"She knows something they value. Internal personal business. Nothing to do with you or the Pykes or the Empire or anyone else. That," Jaylen said with a pointed finger, "makes this clean. Now, I can't deliver your missing prisoner—yet. But I can broker a truce." He gestured with his hands as they remained up. "A war between Crimson Dawn and the Hutts? Over a bacta tank and a double-crossing smuggler? One that's probably already gotten away? That's not worth it, right? A temporary truce while I fix things for both of you with *collateral*"—he pointed to himself—"won't cost you a thing."

Qi'ra looked back at the guard in the doorway. "I don't quite buy it," she said, though Jaylen told himself to remain steady. She took one more look at Mill before approaching the guard and speaking to her at a low volume, a short conversation with quick words and several nods. She returned to Jaylen. "But I'm always in favor of easy solutions to messy problems. Especially"—she poked Jaylen hard in the chest—"when someone claims it won't cost a thing. I'll hold you to that." She waved for them to follow her, and Qi'ra led them through narrow corridors all the way to the stronghold's front entrance.

The door slid open, leaving Jaylen temporarily blinded as the bright sun flooded his eyes. He blinked to adjust, gradually taking in several figures standing some distance down the path.

They didn't have any real signs of being sent by the Hutts—there was no giant hulking slug with a booming voice to greet them, nor did a rancor lurk in the background. Instead, several figures stood that could have worked for any cartel. Maybe they were freelancers hired to track down Vivert, the bacta tank, or both.

"Follow my lead," Qi'ra said. "You'll know when to talk."

Jaylen glanced at Mill, who seemed remarkably calm given all the players involved. She waved Jaylen ahead, and he walked in step with Qi'ra until they paused halfway down the rocky incline. "No blasters yet," Qi'ra said to the guards at the back of the group. "I am Qi'ra of Crimson Dawn. Which of you negotiates on behalf of the Hutts?"

The man in the center stepped forward, a tall, lanky human with dark skin and thick close-cropped hair. He wore burlap robes—standard desert-world clothing—though they failed to hide the blasters holstered on both hips. "I do. Name's Raivan Dhavik, and I hate being away from home. So let's make this quick." He tapped a small holo-emitter on his belt. "I am to provide any findings to Jabba himself. You have something of ours. A bacta tank."

Qi'ra glanced down, quick enough for her to sneak in a comment. "You two were right," she said.

"There's only one way out of this cleanly," Jaylen said, masking the words by rubbing his face.

"We have no bacta tank. You can scan our facilities. We never intercepted it from your ship. But"—Qi'ra looked at Jaylen—"I happen to have a third party here who says he will help all of us."

"Let's see if you're as good as you claim to be," Mill said quietly.

Jaylen stepped forward, just as he did years ago to accept the mantle of Barsha Corp CEO. That moment—with all the media, spotlights, and familial pressure—stood in stark contrast to being on a barren, rocky base of a mountain, dust blowing through the air with Hutt agents standing ready to shoot him.

He should have felt nervous given the stakes. Yet something felt *natural* about this, like it was as easy as walking in his own boots.

In many ways, it was even easier.

"My name's Jaylen Vrax. I deal in the same circles you do. I'm here on different business, but I heard about what's happening, and," he said with a projected laugh, "it's kind of hard to ignore while you're here. Fortunately, I have information for you. Your bacta tank's not here."

"Where is it?"

"Unknown," Jaylen said. The word drew an immediate blaster draw from one of the Hutt guards, though Raivan held out a hand. Jaylen continued. "The person who would know just went missing. She managed a jailbreak right when you got here."

"Convenient!" Raivan yelled.

Jaylen considered what Raivan said when he introduced himself. It might have just been bluster, but it offered the smallest of openings for Jaylen to prod and exploit. Business meeting or cartel negotiations or family squabbles—in a way, they were all the same. And Jaylen knew how to handle them. "You said you hate being away from home. Why's that?" Another gust of wind blew, and Raivan pulled the bandana off his neck to cover his nose from the elements. "Come on," Jaylen insisted, "before we kill each other, we should get to know each other."

"Where are you going with this?" Qi'ra muttered. Mill maintained her composure, fixing a straight-ahead stare despite the dust kicking up everywhere.

"Tatooine is warm," Raivan said. "Everywhere else is cold."

"All right. Well, I'd like to send you back there. Safely, of course. And with something for Jabba." Raivan's eyes narrowed at this claim, and from behind, Jaylen heard the click of a holster unclipping. "Look, Crimson Dawn and the Hutts both want the fugitive known as Cittin dead. Right? And you two don't trust each other with any secrets she might have on either of your sides.

"What I see here is that you—and Jabba—need an independent

tracker. Correct? Because getting into a battle with Crimson Dawn right here, that's just going to make things worse for everyone. So let me do that for you. I can be a neutral arbiter. I'll track her down myself. I'll kill her myself." In his peripheral vision, he saw Mill's sharp glance at this. "And I'll provide proof of death. And for the Hutts, I'll get the location of the bacta tank."

"Why should we trust you to do this?" Raivan yelled.

"Well, first off, Cittin is loose in the wind." As soon as Jaylen said that, he sent out a very specific hope that ND-5 and Vivert had gotten out *and* covered their trail. "Attacking this base won't accomplish anything except wasting ammo. Second, I encourage you to ask around. I may be newer on the scene, but I've gained a good reputation. Heard of a recent heist on Andara?"

"That was you?" Raivan asked.

"I put together a good crew. We grabbed some valuable stuff." He glanced at Mill. She met his quick glance with recognition. "Qi'ra's seen some of it. She can vouch for its authenticity." The words flowed naturally now, the perfect balance of everything Jaylen had absorbed from life dealing with corporate suits and the gritty reality of surviving in the galaxy's underbelly. "I'm looking to build on this, to be a player in this life we've chosen. What better way to do so than by making both the Hutts and Crimson Dawn happy in one single move? How many people can say they've done that?"

"It's true. I've seen it," Qi'ra said. "It's valuable."

Jaylen chose to jump quickly off Qi'ra's remark. "So, you want to see what this valuable thing is—you want to *tell* Jabba what this valuable thing is, then just listen to my proposal. I can deliver one dead traitor and whatever information she has. From her intel, I can find that bacta tank. And if it needs destroying, well"—Jaylen tilted his head with a sly grin—"I can do that and provide proof. In the meantime, both of you get a cut of what I have as collateral." Jaylen pointed upward with both hands. "Best of all, no war between Crimson Dawn and the Hutts."

Jaylen looked past Raivan to his guards. They'd moved from hovering their hands over their blasters to loosely gripping the handles. Behind him, Qi'ra's guards talked in hushed voices, probably about who should shoot when. Farther behind him, he heard the subtle grind of dirt on metal, most likely as Crimson Dawn snipers crawled into position.

"What do you like to do when you're home, Raivan? Big sabacc player? I hear Tatooine's a huge part of the podracing circuit. Is that how you relax?" Jaylen took a calculated pause as he watched Raivan's lips purse in thought. "I like to take naps. Just knock out for an hour, all by myself. No other bothers. No distractions. What about you?"

"I like to cook," Raivan said. "Desert oven, right in the ground. Only on Tatooine. Not as good anywhere else."

"Got it. You see? Why waste your time—Jabba's time—when you could be doing that? All I ask is for one month to track down Cittin. I will find her, I will take her out. I will handle the bacta tank." He held up one finger to emphasize the timeframe. "In the meantime, you go back to Tatooine. They," he said, gesturing at Qi'ra and her crew, "go back inside. No blasters fired. No dead bodies to deal with. No wasted ammo or fuel or any of that. And hey, when I come to Tatooine when I'm done, I'd love to try some of your cooking."

Now he stopped. And waited.

His gut told him that of all the different crews, brokers, and swindlers he'd worked with, none of them could have presented this better. He'd considered every angle, every party, every desire. The only way he'd end up dead was if the Hutts just decided they didn't like him. Which was fair. Sometimes he wouldn't blame them.

Raivan held up a hand in the air. The guards behind him all raised their weapons. Jaylen met Mill's eyes. From all sides came the sudden sound of weapons loading and charging.

But then Raivan pulled a holo-emitter from his belt. It came to life, casting light with no particular image. At least not yet.

"I'll contact Jabba," he said.

And Jaylen exhaled.

One by one, weapons powered down and holstered, and though the entire Hutt contingent remained facing their Crimson Dawn counterparts, they backed away until some distance lay between the two groups.

"Impressive," Qi'ra said.

It *was* impressive. Jaylen felt a spark of impulse, a pull to turn the moment into more. There had to be *something* else he could bargain for or squeeze out of this.

But then he remembered pushing for more—getting greedy—at Bischt Renner's office. It worked out in the end, but he had been moments away from things going very poorly—and only because ND-5 had rescued him.

No, a win was a win. This was a win. Overreaching was unnecessary, and finally, he recognized that.

Instead of opening a new point of negotiation with Qi'ra, Jaylen simply turned to her and said, "Thanks."

CHAPTER 45

Madel Nureth stands up. She is not afraid of me, despite the way we entered the room. I determine that based on my sensors gauging her body temperature and pulse.

She remains steady. Her equipment is resting on a small table. The only other furnishings in the room are two chairs. It is clear that Crimson Dawn uses this space for temporary reprieves, not long-term stays. Besides a pitcher of water, a glass, and a small plate of sliced fruit, no other comforts exist. It is simply a room built into the side of a mountain.

"You," Madel says. This is directed at me. She does not acknowledge Vivert at all. Her eyes train on me.

Vivert walks up behind me. "What are you going to do with her?"

Option one: Take her hardware and kill her. This would violate my pledge to Vivert.

Option two: Take her hardware and let her live. This may put us in the crosshairs of the Empire.

Option three: Speak to her and calculate the risk.

"Undetermined," I say. "Go guard the tunnel."

"Are you trying to get rid of me?" Vivert asks.

"I'm making a practical suggestion," I say while keeping my focus on Madel. "Rock can be drilled, melted, or blasted. It is highly likely that Crimson Dawn is considering one of those choices. It is better to be prepared than caught unaware."

Madel continues to watch during this exchange. She says nothing.

Vivert needs several seconds to consider my logic. She then nods and crawls back through the broken door into the darkness of the tunnel.

"You do not have to die," I say to Madel. "Hand over your datapad with all your archived messages from previous rotations and operations."

"'Previous rotations?'" A line forms between her eyebrows as she squints. It quickly dissolves as she speaks. "You've done your homework."

Any additional banter on the matter would be for Madel's own amusement or curiosity, which is of no concern to me. In addition, further Crimson Dawn activity may be heading our way. I repeat my request. "You do not have to die. Hand over your datapad with all your archived messages from previous rotations and operations."

"I find this *so* curious. The past just pops up sometimes." She looks at her portable terminal. Then she looks at her datapad.

"I will ask only one more time before I'm forced to take more aggressive measures."

She shakes her head, though this seems born of curiosity rather than serving as a denial of my request. "Okay. You win." She turns to the datapad, which is connected to her terminal by a small cable. "I just need to disconnect it."

"No."

"What?" She lets out a scoff. "I'm just removing a cable."

"That gives you the opportunity to take action." I step forward. "I will do this myself."

She smiles and nods—but then lunges for the pad. She manages to bring up a secure access screen before I grab her by the wrist at 61 percent of my potential strength, causing her knees to buckle, though her face remains defiant. With my free hand, I grab the datapad. The adjoining cable remains connected to the device, though it pulls out from her terminal. The datapad shows that she has not entered the password for secure access.

"This is not a standard Imperial format. What hidden files were you trying to access?"

Pain has quickened her breath and pulse. She looks at me with clear eyes. "I was trying," she manages, "to unlock it for you."

I consider what we have witnessed of her behavior. She is an ISB agent experienced in dealing with syndicates while publicly working undercover, making her skilled in deception. I should not believe her. She was likely trying to delete protected information.

"I do not need your assistance for that," I say. I push her aside as I let go for her wrist. I put the datapad in a secure pocket in my coat and fasten it closed.

Then I consider exactly what she said.

"What did you mean by 'the past just pops up sometimes'?"

For the first time, fear enters her eyes. Her breath quickens and her carotid artery pulses visibly.

She takes a step back.

"I mean . . ." she starts. A long pause happens, and her eyes dart back and forth—typical human signs of panic and quick thinking. "Why else would you want my datapad? It's got my entire career in there. Something in there caught your attention."

I take three steps forward and change the angle of my shoulder joints to create a larger, more imposing look. "You are lying. You know something else."

"You've got the datapad. Get out of here." She looks beyond me at the hole in the door. "Hey! Come get your droid friend!"

Her yell to Vivert is a passive cry for assistance.

I turn my head and boost my volume output for Vivert to hear. "Continue to guard the tunnel," I say. I recall what I told Vivert earlier: that I would avoid killing whenever possible.

I will put forth my best effort considering the circumstances. I step forward again and focus on Madel. "What do you know about my history?"

"You're a droid. You're a *Separatist* droid. You fought in the war, and now you work for, I don't know, smugglers." She points beyond me. "And people like her. Hey! Your droid—"

I grab her hand and squeeze with more pressure than when I grabbed her wrist earlier. I calculate that the force has likely snapped bones in three fingers. That pain is likely why she goes silent. Also, this will temporarily affect her work performance.

If she survives.

"What do you know about my history?" I repeat.

Her eyes well up, a reflexive reaction to pain. Yet after she squints and shakes her head, she forces them open and looks straight at me. Her breathing is now tense, and the injury to her hand is likely causing a rush of chemicals to her brain. I continue holding her hand under immense pressure. "I know . . . what you don't." She squeezes the words out between hard breaths. She tilts her chin.

I conclude that Imperial operatives, even in accounting positions, must have significant training to resist torture.

"Jaylen Barsha . . ." She takes in one large gulp of air. ". . . is lying to you."

She is trying to find an opportunity. I will not let that happen.

I release her hand. She pulls it back immediately and tucks it under the opposing arm. "What do you know about Jaylen Barsha?"

"I know he's alive." Now she is breathing heavily. I can see her carotid artery pulsing harder in her neck. "I know *you* killed his family. And I know he's deceived you."

"I did not kill all his family," I say. "I did not kill Sliro Barsha. His whereabouts remain unknown to this day." I ignore the claim of Jaylen's deception, as that is clearly strategic.

Given her hand injury, Madel must be experiencing some level of shock. Yet now she is grinning and shaking her head again. This does not follow logic, and I assume this is due to the shock reaction affecting her neurochemistry. I consider her statements and form a conclusion based on what they imply. "You sent me to Gus Treta. Your knowledge aligns with this. Your code name is on the integration record of the chip fused to my neural core."

"No," she says, laughing again. "I didn't do that."

Her attitude suggests surprise and honesty. If she is telling the truth, then there is another layer to her involvement. "If you did not send me to Gus Treta, then you must have made the chip," I say after assessing the evidence. I grab her other hand and apply the same force to give her symmetrical injuries. "Who asked you to make it?"

She huffs out in pain. Based on my knowledge of human physiology, most people would have passed out with these injuries. ISB resistance training should be commended for its efficacy. I squeeze harder to find the threshold where her training will fail her. "It was a favor," she finally says. "A favor for someone I knew. Then I forgot about it."

"If you forgot about it," I say as I twist her hand farther, "then how do you know about Jaylen?"

Now the words spill out of her. "I downloaded your diagnostic files while flying here. And after Crimson Dawn brought me to this room, I was bored. So I looked through them, and I realized who you are. And who your companion is." She nods at her portable terminal. "You probably don't even realize all the restricted files you are carrying. The encryption was easy enough for me to break." Her expression shifts for a moment before looking at me. "But if he's hiding those files from you, he probably didn't even let you touch them."

"I am aware of storage space allocated to data inaccessible to me." I let go of her hand. Both of her arms hang limp as she stands.

"Can't you see he's lying to you?" she asks. "Those hidden files in your memory. You can't access them, but I copied them to my terminal. Whatever Jaylen is hiding from you, it's all there. Let me go and you can have that terminal. Don't you want the truth? Don't you *deserve* the truth?"

She did not recognize me back in the data center. I gauge that she is being honest about copying my files. Based on that, it is safe to assume that she indeed discovered Jaylen's name through my systems. The recency of her discovery makes me assume that no one else in the ISB knows about Jaylen's true identity.

Thus, I conclude that the knowledge is stored externally in two areas of risk. I step over to the portable terminal that was connected to my systems. "Wait, what are you doing?" she frantically asks.

I smash it four times and grind it into the floor. That eliminates the first knowledge risk. It also eliminates the bargaining posture of her so-called proof.

"Jaylen would not lie to me. He needs me for protection. Thus, I do not need your terminal. Who did you give the override chip to?"

"Everything okay in there?" Vivert yells.

"I am almost done," I call back. I turn to Madel. She has one more piece of information I seek. Then I will eliminate the second knowledge risk: her mind. "I need a name."

"I forget," she says. I detect spite in her voice.

"The human brain does not forget things that easily," I say, citing Jaylen's inability to let go of the past as evidence. "I need a name."

Madel stares into my eyes. Her shoulders rise and nostrils flare with each passing breath. "It's too late now. I can't tell you that."

I consider all the ways to intimidate her. I settle on a single step forward. "Who sent me to Gus Treta?" She is not breaking despite the injuries I have applied. "If you will not say, then you will die. The trail to Jaylen must stop here. I will give you one last chance."

Thirty seconds pass before she responds. Her back straightens. Her chin tilts up. "The ISB is capable of things far worse than death." She closes her eyes. "I'd rather die than face his wrath."

From her posture, voice, and words, I conclude that she is telling the truth. Shaw Andeej expressed similar thoughts on Andara. But here, Madel attributes her fear to a single person. I decide to take appropriate action and finish the mission.

Because Jaylen and I are a team.

I STAND STRAIGHT after making my way through the hole in the door. Vivert has her hand up against the fallen rocks in our path. She looks at me. Despite the flickering light, I can read concern on her face.

"We need to leave," I say. "Do you have an assessment of our escape options?"

"Actually, it might be simpler than we thought." She taps one of the large boulders in front of her, causing dust to crumble and fall to the floor. "There's no one in the hall now if we can bust through this."

She is trustworthy enough that I do not ask for explanation or confirmation.

I put my hands on the largest boulder to gauge its weight and how much force will be necessary to move it. Breaking it into pieces appears to be the easier approach. I point to its center and turn to Vivert. “Blast here. As you did before.” I hold up my fist. “Then I will begin to move it.”

She nods, and the flickering light holds steady long enough that I catch her looking back at the secure door.

Experience has taught me that sometimes humans linger when there is loss of life. “I must apologize,” I say.

Vivert replies without moving. “For what?”

“I broke my pledge to you.”

She lets out a sigh much longer than normal. “That happens,” she says. Her voice is slow and without its normal spirited tone, similar to when Lorel seemed lost in thought. “It wouldn’t be the first time. This galaxy, I swear.” I do not ask what that means, and she does not elaborate. Instead, she raises her blaster and shoots the boulder. “Let’s get out of here before someone comes back. I have some experience moving heavy rocks, too.”

CHAPTER 46

Jaylen noted that Mill stayed mostly silent for the walk back to their ship, some three kilometers southwest of Crimson Dawn's stronghold. They were still on rocky terrain and still had red clay dust blowing around, though *something* felt different.

It was the same feeling he'd gotten after Andara but infinitely stronger. Andara was about pushing to the edge of possibilities. This situation, as unexpected and unpredictable as it had been, had left him *spilling over* with possibilities. And despite all the dumb, horrible luck during his life, now everything finally felt within reach.

He just needed ND-5 to return.

"Sorry I traded a few extra names from the list," Jaylen said. They'd already resolved this in the data room before splitting up, but he offered this to break the quiet, if for no other reason. Mill nodded yet didn't speak, and her silence tickled his anxieties. She didn't bring up any challenges or disputes about what went down, and perhaps she simply concentrated on navigating the rocky emptiness back to her ship while worrying about her partner.

Yet, since they'd met, Jaylen got the sense that she knew more than she was letting on, or at least that she was hiding something personal. Whether or not that was a risk—or if it even mattered—he couldn't tell. For now, though, he kept his guard up.

When they left, Qi'ra confirmed a facility scan showed no trace of Vivert—that was, the fugitive known only as Cittin. No one mentioned ND-5 at all, and it probably helped that Madel Nureth rather than a Crimson Dawn agent had originally brought the droid in. Jaylen overheard some chatter of "a complication," but Qi'ra showed calm, even if it was a front. "You know how to leave a mark, Jaylen Vrax. But don't screw this up," she'd said as they parted, the latter part laced with a sudden menace. Which might have been tied into that complication.

Though if Crimson Dawn wanted to backstab them, the opportunity had come and gone, making it reasonable to assume that both parties were giving him the month that he'd asked for.

"You think they're okay?" Jaylen asked as they turned past a worn, barren cliff to bring Mill's ship into view.

"Pretty sure," she said. She continued marching forward, steps steady but her head low enough that her Zabrak horns stood prominently out.

"What makes you say that?"

"I can sense her," she said, a wistful look in her eyes. The comment caused Jaylen to pause, though he resisted giving her a side-eye. He'd encountered all types of species, backgrounds, life experiences in the past nine years, so much greater in scope than during the monolith that was his curated adolescence. Maybe Mill just got more esoteric than most running through the galaxy's criminal spaces.

Everyone needed something to get them through the day. "Like . . . how Endee can sense the transponder in my boot?" Jaylen asked. "Is she wearing a transponder?"

Mill let out a toothy grin, a gesture that told Jaylen that while the Zabrak's guard was also up, she'd allowed a little bit of herself through just now. "I'm messing with you." She paused midstep and pointed far behind them to the rocky horizon. "Vivert's the most resourceful person I know. She's the *toughest* person I know. Tougher than me. We've been through disasters you couldn't possibly imagine." Jaylen held his tongue at that. It would be really hard for anyone to top being hunted by a commando droid with a bomb strapped to his chest. He probably *could* win that comparison, though keeping his identity secret remained pretty high on his to-do list. Plus it wasn't exactly something to champion. "I'm pretty sure if Crimson Dawn caught her," Mill said, "Qi'ra would have told us. It would have changed your entire plan." She shot him a raised eyebrow, and the light caught her face to reveal deep, worn creases around her eyes and cheeks.

Silence returned as they approached Mill's ship, and for the first time, Jaylen got a good look at the craft. Most ships wore the scars of being patchworked projects, crews fixing and maintaining things as finances allowed. This ship, though, brought back memories of the craft Jaylen and ND-5 had used after Gus Treta, where scorch marks met loose plating met stitched-on sensors from other craft.

Short on credits, indeed.

Mill tapped a control panel, initiating the grind of gears and hydraulics until the loading ramp fully dropped to the ground. She motioned him in, and as soon as he cleared the bay, she called the ramp to close back up.

Then she blew out a long breath.

Jaylen stood, unsure of what to do as Mill closed her eyes. He shuffled his arm out of the coat he'd borrowed for the job, and when he faced her again, he saw her looking right at him while brushing some of the dust out of her black hair. "Sometimes I just need a moment after an intense situation," she said, taking the coat from him. They walked back into the ship's central area, the makeshift operating bay where just hours earlier she'd ultrasonically zapped a worm eating him from the inside.

He watched as she grabbed a tool kit and nudged a stool over to the damaged medical droid. Without a word, metal clinked on metal as she set to work, like nothing had happened with two of the galaxy's most feared syndicates.

"What do we do now?" Jaylen asked. The question was as much for himself as it was for Mill, and he sensed the same creeping discomfort that lingered during the hours spent waiting outside of Madel Nureth's home.

"Well," she said as M1-DY's eyes flickered on. "Do you trust your droid?"

"He's gotten out of worse," he said, walking over to the room's large screen to peer closer at the displayed map. He didn't seek anything specific, but doing so gave him something to appear occupied with. Because as useful as Mill had been, he didn't understand how someone could be focused on *doing good* of all things.

They didn't exactly have a lot in common to talk about.

"It's simple then," she said, peering at the back of the droid. "We wait." Her tool kit opened with a hiss. "And stay busy." Whatever she did caused the droid's left eye to flicker while its right arm pulsed. Several clicks later, the arm went limp. "Ah, this is it." Another click and something in the droid's innards snapped into place before a low hum grew to a high frequency one, and the droid finally spoke.

"Greetings, I am Em-One-Dee-Why, overseer of medical functions for the Forty-Third Battalion."

Jaylen had read his share on how memories worked in organics, humans in particular. Because it *bothered* him—the number of times a smell, an object, a word, even a beep or a buzz, the smallest and most insignificant thing would trigger *something* from that night at Barsha Corp or those weeks at Gus Treta.

In this case, the start-up greeting from a rebooted droid reminding him of A1-A1's violent end.

Jaylen stared at the 2-1B-series droid, the room's harsh lighting making every crevice, chip, and dent on its plating seem like something as deep and jagged as ND-5's scar.

"Hey, do me a favor and hold its head steady?" Mill said without looking up. "I gotta jam this plate back in." Jaylen did as asked, the cold metal and worn grooves of the droid's head against his palms. "Just one more second and . . ." A loud click came with a sudden jolt. "There. Old friend of mine used to talk about how fixing things was the best way to get worries off your mind," she said as she tightened bolts in the back of the droid's head. "He was right."

Jaylen let out a snort at that. Of all the people he'd met in his travels, she seemed the most optimistic and the most weary at the same time.

"I'll tell you one of my worries," he said, an intentional effort to steer back to business. "I thought for a moment you were upset about losing some of the list to the syndicates."

"Oh, I am. But I try to think ahead. I figured it might come into play since Qi'ra had already seen some of it." She gestured for him to let go of the droid as she put on goggles. Flashes of light came as she activated a welder, soon followed by a shower of sparks. "The Hutts would be after Vivert if you hadn't. You're going to take care of that. We'll call it even. Don't expect any more handouts, though."

Jaylen averted his gaze from the constant flash as Mill finished with the droid and instead picked up his folded coat off the operating table. His hands instinctively felt for the datapad—some of its contents now needing to be handed over to syndicate operatives. But the whole belonged to Mill.

He pulled it out and set it on her terminal as the sparks finally stopped. She pulled her goggles up, resting them over her horns. He shuffled the coat back on, the familiar weight around his shoulders now slightly askew without the weight of the datapad.

On the other side of his coat, though, sat ND-5's broken restraining bolt. Jaylen pulled it out and held it up. "Fixing things, huh?" he said.

The medical droid announced it would begin running motor diagnostics. Mill leaned back as its arms rotated and flexed in front of her.

"No good being a roaming hospital if the equipment doesn't work," she said. "And it passes the time."

"I got a time passer for you. If you don't mind."

The medical droid tilted its head as it turned toward him. "A class-three restraining bolt with structural damage," the droid said. "That is not part of my medical purview."

"Not quite working yet," Mill said. She stood and stepped around the radius of the medical droid's waving arms. She gestured to the restraining bolt. "You can get those anywhere. You really want to fix this one?"

"It's sentimental."

Mill shrugged at that and took the bolt from his fingers before walking over to a workbench. A squeak rang through the room as she pulled over a hanging magnifying lens. "While I do this," she said slowly, "mind telling me how you're going to deliver proof of a dead body to the syndicates?" The friendly tone of her voice hardened, like a switch had flipped in her.

Jaylen always respected that when he saw it in people.

"And I wouldn't advise actually killing her," she said. "We've been in this game longer than you think."

"I'm like you. I think ahead," Jaylen said, crossing his arms. "Give me a chunk of her hair. They can test its identity as proof. And I know a slicer who does good work. She can easily doctor evidence. I've seen her do it. Those two things should work as long as 'Cittin' stays out of their way." In particular, Lorel probably would appreciate *not* getting in a shuttle for the job. "You let me know when you find the bacta tank. Destroy the monitor on it, and send me pieces of it as evidence. Then I'll conveniently tell the Hutts that I have located the bacta tank. And I'll tell them that I have verified the tank and its monitoring device have been destroyed. And that I can even provide proof," he said, pointing to the broken one in the room. "The control console from that one."

"Borrowing without asking?" Mill said as she grabbed pliers from a workbench drawer.

"I'm asking now," Jaylen said, which prompted a nod in return. "You see? Everyone wins."

"Everyone?" The word came with a subtle scoff.

"Them." Jaylen pointed upward before gesturing to her. "Us. Yeah. Everyone wins."

"Except for that Imperial accountant." Her voice suddenly took on a stricter tone. "She doesn't win here, does she?" Mill looked Jaylen's way. "This is all a lot of work for someone who processes numbers and files reports."

Mill was right. Madel Nureth would not escape. She would not win.

But what came next for her . . . that part, he wasn't sure. Because what could he possibly find out beyond her? If there was someone else, did it mean taking on the whole Empire? Were Madel's collaborators still working for the Empire? Did they even still exist?

More importantly, did they even matter? Or, a better way to put it—did they matter more than this new path he'd forged for himself?

Jaylen could set out for vengeance until the very last piece of this puzzle was resolved. He'd promised it. He swore it. To himself, to Sliro. A new thought popped in his mind: Perhaps Sliro wouldn't have wanted vengeance. After all of this, the thing his brother would have wanted the most was the same thing he sought his entire life: to be free from the shadow of the Barshas.

Which Jaylen was on the cusp of achieving for good.

The best, most honest way to honor that might be to discover the truth behind Low Red Moon—and then let it go.

Mill returned to the restraining bolt, offering only a cursory glance every few minutes. Jaylen never answered her question, though she seemingly understood the moment enough to leave him to his thoughts.

CHAPTER 47

Vivert proves to be a formidable teammate as we escape undetected from Crimson Dawn. Her knowledge of the facility and the surrounding terrain helps us proceed without further testing our combat skills. We take a long route back to her ship, whose location I confirmed with Jaylen's transponder.

From there, Jaylen works out the remaining exchange details regarding the datapad and cover names. Mill also hands him a small object, which he puts in his pocket. We sit in a makeshift medical bay, and the pair's excited conversation is different from most of the crews I see. Their history together appears to have crafted a shorthand in communication, which demonstrates an innate trust in each other. I observe this and file it as insight on how interpersonal relationships can develop under extreme circumstances.

Instead of taking us back to our ship, they drop us off at the nearest spaceport, where we arrange passage on the least expensive public transport back to Sern Prime. The craft is only half full, and we go to the back corner. I do not fit on the small bench, so I stand next to Jaylen.

He is silent during most of this. He knows that I have the datapad of Madel Nureth's message archives, but he does not wish to view it yet. I keep most of her revelations to myself and instead use this time to begin accessing the secured files that she attempted to hide. Two hours into our trip, he finally speaks up. "You think there was another strategy? Maybe we should have taken Madel hostage." He keeps his voice low and looks around. "We could have sold her to the Ashiga clan."

I adjust my vocabulator projection to match Jaylen's volume and determine that now would be appropriate to inform him. "She was dangerous."

"She was an accountant," Jaylen says with a laugh. "Did her numbers attack you?"

"No. But she knew your identity."

This causes Jaylen to pause. His shoulders tense. His breathing stops momentarily. "How?" he asks. "I knew she caught us tracking her. But I didn't realize she knew *who* we were."

"She did not know this on Sern Prime. She derived it based on a scan of my memory storage when I was captured. Though I cannot view the contents of my restricted storage, she could." Jaylen's breathing resumes, though it is slow and measured. He continues staring ahead. "When this information was revealed, I successfully adapted various protocols to assess the situation and risks involved." I do not include her accusations of his deception. "Before I killed her, I confirmed that no other ISB officers knew about us. She also claimed that she did not send me to Gus Treta, though she made the override chip 'as a favor' to a colleague. My analysis shows a high level of honesty in these statements." I wait several seconds for him to respond, but he does not. "This aligns with my goal of demonstrating that I am an effective member of our team."

Given the successful implications of this context and Jaylen's apparent willingness to listen right now, my experience with human behavior provides a so-called hunch about timing for discussing important topics. I tap the spot on my chest where the restraining bolt used to be. "You see how safe I am without the restraining bolt?" I ask. "I believe we can keep it off permanently and access all my original programming as needed."

Jaylen does not respond at all. I count down two minutes before I decide that the conversation has ended. He continues staring for another minute and twelve seconds before he shuts his eyes.

He remains quiet until we land at the Sern Prime spaceport near the large city of Switzer.

CHAPTER 48

With Mill, Jaylen had felt a social pressure to avoid uncomfortable silences—though he had also taken their time together as an opportunity to assess if she might be useful later. Yet with ND-5, everything was different. Simpler. Sometimes, when Jaylen wanted to be by himself, it became easy to just *ignore* the droid.

The journey back to Sern Prime was one of those moments. His understanding of the galaxy, his *place* in it, his approach, all of it needed reconsidering given that ND-5's mission had been a wild success. Somehow, the droid had taken a fluid situation with different parties pulled into the chaos and adapted his strategy, resulting in delivery of *exactly* what Jaylen wanted.

All without the restraining bolt creating a cognitive tether. This was ND-5 at his most self-aware. The droid built a winning strategy that was equal parts smart and ruthless. And he remained loyal despite knowingly using previously restricted protocols, despite operating without a restraining bolt. In the end, ND-5 was as loyal as droids got thanks to years of accumulated experiences and memories. ND-5 didn't question anything.

Jaylen had always wondered how ND-5 might have acted if he'd discovered that Jaylen had been lying this whole time. ND-5's behavior on this mission showed that he'd never even considered such a thought. The droid might not even be capable of such temptations. Not anymore. He was too set on serving Jaylen, and that mindset appeared to resolve any contradictions presented before him.

ND-5 had been forced into loyalty long enough that he probably couldn't conceive of any other form of existence.

Such a thought weighed as heavily on Jaylen as the datapad that ND-5 delivered, and he felt that both might define his past and future.

Jaylen rarely envied ND-5. But during that journey, he admired ND-5's ability to adapt, because despite everything Jaylen had done to get through the last nine years—his whole life, really—adapting was something superficial for him. Strategies, weapons, equipment, navigation routes, crew members, those types of things, sure, but the true adaptation of his core being?

Jaylen supposed his problem was that he never really knew who he was in the first place. Which made recognizing any meaningful, permanent shift he needed to make kind of difficult.

He tried to push this away during the journey—ND-5 had Madel Nureth's datapad, but Jaylen didn't read it, didn't search through it, didn't even ask for it. This continued even as they stepped off the docking ramp and made their way back to the *Successor*.

"Hey, Endee," Jaylen said as they moved through Switzer's dense, busy spaceport, a far cry from the smaller spaceport where they'd tracked their target. So many different types of species and droids crossed in front of them, including a few Imperial officers, and yet none even gave them a second look—despite the hulking BX commando droid. "What kind of damage did you take at Botor?"

"Blaster impact on my upper left shoulder. Blaster impact on my mid-back plating . . ." ND-5 started as they crossed to the open-air docking bay, a circular station that the *Successor* shared with six other ships. The droid continued the list as they passed maintenance droids, boarding passengers, and other craft, until they opened the cargo bay of their ship.

Given the way things sometimes went, Jaylen half expected the ship to be gone—or worse, filled with some assortment of Hutts or Crimson Dawn or Imperials, or bounty hunters representing some combination of them. None of that happened, and instead, it was simply the *Successor* sitting quietly, various sleeping systems now coming online.

Including the technical station main terminal. Where Jaylen immediately plugged in the datapad from Madel Nureth.

"Jaylen," ND-5 said as he lumbered through the cargo bay, "we still have to return the speeder we rented. My tracker shows that it is still at the other spaceport where we followed Madel Nureth."

All the other tasks and responsibilities that came with this life remained, including searching for ways to refill their credit stash. But not right now, not this immediate second. Jaylen needed a sliver of time, maybe ten or twenty minutes where he existed only within the immediate safety of the *Successor*, to fully process everything that had just happened.

To finally allow himself to look at Madel Nureth's datapad.

"Yeah," he said, sitting down at the technical station. "How about you charge yourself for a little bit? Run an internal diagnostic, too, just in case there's anything that needs fixing." He pulled the fixed restraining bolt out of his pocket and peered at it closely. Mill had repaired it and returned it to something *close* to its original structure, though the imperfections that came with hand tools and spare parts stood out—scratches, dents, and a not-quite-circular shape for the outer casing. ND-5 was already turning to the charging station across the room, no questions asked. When Jaylen held the restraining bolt up, it drew ND-5's attention. "We'll talk about this when you wake up."

"Understood," the droid said as he walked away. "I have finished creating a decryption protocol for the secured area of the datapad. You will have to apply it."

Jaylen's knowledge of slicing and data security paled compared to ND-5's. Yet it seemed strange that the security for secret records, possibly *classified* material, could be broken by a droid in a few hours. Did ND-5 learn slicing techniques from Lorel, or was the Empire getting sloppy?

Five minutes passed with only the hum of ND-5's power station and status beeps from the terminal as it analyzed the datapad's Imperial records. Its screen flickered before displaying a long wall of blue text, all neatly sorted by date and type. He paused to begin the decryption process on the secured files, and as he was set to skim the rest of the list, a notification appeared.

The terminal automatically analyzed every file for a set of keywords related to Jaylen's past. For the primary Imperial files on the datapad, it offered a clear, definitive conclusion: *No references found to terms* Barsha Corp, Sliro Barsha, Gus Treta.

That was that.

Nearly a decade of ISB messages, records, and reports for the operative known as Low Red Moon, and even though she'd made the override chip fused into ND-5's hardware, no single connection to Jaylen's previous life appeared. He sifted through the files quickly: schedules, accounting files, flags for accounting clients along the Corellian Trade Spine that showed signs of anti-Imperial activity. All very official, all very Imperial, and all very *useless* for figuring out who was behind Gus Treta.

Jaylen stared at the display, details on some shopkeeper who'd made comments about how "Palpatine continues to push the boundary of what's acceptable" during a financial review—and then it hit him.

All this time pursuing Low Red Moon, and it had led to a dead end.

For avenging his family, at least.

But for his *new* life?

This was even better than the cover list. This was years and years of specific intel on the inner workings of undercover ISB agents—logistics and schedules and contacts to be exploited. Syndicates, protestors, rebels, smugglers, the depth of detail here offered a huge range of opportunities. Jaylen could even take the most recent intel here and find ways to intercept even *more* ISB data.

He leaned back in his chair, taking in the irony of it all. Low Red Moon did, in fact, bring him closure, but in wholly unexpected ways.

His mind lingered there, formulating what might be sellable to various brokers—and he made a mental note to check if Madel's datapad had a tracker, similar to the one the ISB used for cover lists. If so, they'd have to destroy it soon, and they should back up—

Ding-ding-ding.

That chime was from the technical station.

Not the usual beeps or tones that came with standard notifications and status updates, but three repeated dings set to play only when something very specific was identified. In fact, despite how much Jaylen *knew* the sound, how it had burned into the very fiber of his being, he rarely heard it.

Because information on Sliro Barsha barely existed in the galaxy. His constant purchases of news and archival data tapes proved this.

Until now.

And Madel Nureth's data was *not* a gossip column.

Jaylen leaned forward, the chair's bolts and joints squeaking as his weight shifted. He wasn't sure what to expect—and if he had any expectations, he couldn't concentrate enough to properly sort them out. Instead, he blinked repeatedly until he managed to focus on the small list of decrypted files.

He saw the answer to one of his questions plainly in front of him: The reason ND-5 was able to decrypt this was because this was not official Imperial business. This was *personal.*

Jaylen clicked on the first message of the decrypted archive:

> Madel, the situation has changed and I need to send updated orders to the override chip. Can you please code this text with the instruction to recite when milestone 7 is achieved? I will transmit to the chip later today for integration:
>
> "Roisem Barsha. Nnytyl Barsha. You are the architects of deception. For decades you have allowed corruption to overwrite loyalty, responsibility, ethics. Many have suffered under this family's commitment to corporatocracy and greed. The victims may feel nameless, faceless to you, but your sense of entitlement has ravaged even those under your care.
>
> "Your staff hate you. Your only biological son hates you. And I hate you.

> "I expected so much more when the Empire took down Barsha Corp. But with news of your pardon, I understand that there is no justice. And perhaps there never was. Not for people like you. I have to deliver it myself in the form of this droid. What has happened and what will happen is on behalf of anyone the Barsha family has ever hurt."

Jaylen squinted as his teeth ground together, and his breath turned into quick, rapid pulses.

Who sent it?

No name was attached. Just an anonymous "I"—clearly the person who had sent ND-5 to Gus Treta. And though a gnawing came at Jaylen's gut, he told himself that *anyone* with a vendetta against Barsha Corp could have written that. Many people felt that way, and it could have been a disgruntled former executive, or a competitor, or . . .

Or . . . or . . . or . . .

Or . . .

Jaylen pushed himself to click the next message.

> Madel, one more item. I've made a recording. It should play if optional milestone 9 is achieved. If a holo-emitter or display is available, those should be prioritized. However, the droid can play the audio from his vocabulator if that is the only thing available. I'm not sure how to encode a recording for integration to the override chip.

A new window appeared on the screen.

And Sliro stared right back at him.

Exactly as Jaylen remembered his brother from their last conversation. Hair. Eyes.

Uniform.

Sliro cleared his throat and inhaled slowly before leaning closer, a softness over his intense stare. "Hello, brother. Checking in." He gave a quick laugh, and Jaylen wondered how many times they'd said that to each other. "This is for you and you only, if my droid can find you alone.

You're probably wondering why all this is happening. And I can't save you from it, I can't spare you from it. It's gone too far. All traces of Barsha must be destroyed. Which I suppose isn't totally fair to you. You always tried with me. I knew that, even though you didn't get it right. And because of that, I want you to know the truth. You deserve at least that."

Sliro's words rang in Jaylen's ears like they were standing together in a Barsha Tower conference room instead of being separated by years and years. "It all comes down to that day on the balcony, at the Macronian Shipyard. You remember that day? They anointed you. And they pushed me aside. A desk job with the Republic. That was what Roisem and Father did. Yet, the irony. That job led me to the ISB. The thing is, the ISB . . .

"They're no different from the Barshas."

Subtle lines formed around his mouth, between his eyebrows, by his temples. "This name is a curse. My superiors see me as a *Barsha*. Like I had everything handed to me. Like I'm *you*. No matter what I do. And then someone told me the most brilliant idea: The only way to make everyone notice me is to deliver the biggest asset in the galaxy."

Sliro hesitated, enough that Jaylen could see his lip tremble in the transmission. "I took that advice." He held up one finger, face now sharp again. "I took down Barsha Corp." Another finger came up. "I made the Empire happy." Then another finger. "I reduced the family to *nothing*." He closed the hand into a fist and shook it. "But the Empire *pardoned* them. They took Barsha Corp and then robbed *me* of my reward. They still want the Barsha family's contacts, because of the ugly truth in this galaxy: Justice does not exist when money is involved. Republic, Empire, it doesn't matter. Because the Barshas have money, it means they have connections. And the Empire sees value in that. They value every Barsha because of the *name*. And nothing—nothing—can change that except for the complete elimination of the Barshas."

His head tilted down and he took in a deep breath. Eyes still low, his voice came in a low rumble.

"Including you.

"It is unfortunate you are a part of that. But there can be no ties back to me. No evidence can show I took precious assets from the Empire. This is my path now."

Sliro faced the holocam with contradiction in his expression: a mouth curled upward in amusement, eyes drooping in disappointment. "It is funny, isn't it? All our check-in talks, and it was usually me listening to you. Now here I am, rambling inside my ISB office to my brother whom I'm about to kill. I wish it could have ended differently for us. Perhaps in another life, you wouldn't be the 'chosen one,' and you could just be my brother."

He bit his lip and paused enough that Jaylen could see a vein pulsing by his temple. "In the end, you are a full Barsha. I am half. Nothing will ever change that." His eyes glistened, and his words clipped as he spoke. "Goodbye, Jaylen. I'm sorry."

JAYLEN WASN'T SURE how much time passed as he sat and stared at the final image of the recording: Sliro's frozen half blink.

Sliro. *Sliro* was the one who sent ND-5. The very notion tore at him, leaving his mind a swirl of thoughts and feelings, with no way to possibly discern or contain any of them. He finally opened the next file: a message prepared by Madel that remained unsent.

Jaylen read the displayed text, each new action he took feeling like it belonged outside of his own body.

> To whom it may concern, I have attached significant evidence that Captain Sliro Barsha, ISB regional supervisor, stole from the Empire during our early days as regional auditors. Shortly after the war ended, he expressed to me on Geonosis that he believed the Empire would never notice him using official tools for personal vengeance. In the years since, I have long suspected he has continued taking assets from the Empire, and now I have finally uncovered proof.

Immediately following it came another prepared message:

> Sliro, I have documented proof of your betrayal of the Empire. You were so eager to get revenge on your family that

you never considered the implications—or who you were talking to. I'm just a lowly agent, but you've become a regional supervisor. How much is your career, your life worth to you? I'd love to discuss this with you.

Sliro's reveal stunned him for minutes. But these unsent messages gave *context* to it all, and suddenly his mind activated with sharp thoughts connecting the twisted game at play here. Because *this* was the missing piece, the thread that tied everything together: Years ago, Sliro expressed his frustrations to Madel, Madel suggested he use Barsha to move up, and Sliro asked for her help with ND-5's override chip. Then Sliro got promoted, and Madel . . . did not. She remained an undercover accountant on rotation while Sliro rose through the ranks. And she'd kept this secret data, these messages, prepared ahead of time for one of two possibilities: Madel turning him in to get promoted or Madel blackmailing Sliro for unknown reasons.

Of course, now she would never get either choice.

Because now Jaylen had it all. And closure? Jaylen suddenly didn't need it. Not in the way he used to. His feelings now were more vital and deliberate. He had an urge so raw and furious it was like the galaxy lit up in flames all around him.

Because Sliro was alive. And a high-ranking member of the ISB.

Sliro was *out there*.

That fact triggered another family memory, but instead of a check-in talk with his brother, he heard the voice of his father. And not his father's last words—these words were much more pointed and relevant to the spark igniting in him now: "*One day, someone's going to try and knock you off your perch. And what Barshas have done for generations is hold the line. You don't let them have their way.*"

Nine years ago, Jaylen swore vengeance on whoever did this, on whoever murdered the Barsha family and sent a BX commando droid to kill them all.

Before the heist on Andara, he'd considered whether it was time to give that up. After the heist on Andara, he'd considered if it was time to let this go.

Just hours ago, he'd considered if it was time to move forward.

Giving up. Letting go. Moving forward. Those seemed quaint, naïve. The possible futures of Jaylen *Vrax,* those remained. But now, he had definitive information. There was no more speculation, no more searching, and *that* sharpened his senses into something more.

Roisem and Nnytyl always held a grudge against Sliro—and tried with every action to pass that grudge on to Jaylen. And for his entire life, Jaylen resisted it in every way. Yet in the end, it was Sliro himself who'd activated that grudge.

Because Jaylen had a target now. He had *purpose.*

Finally, Jaylen *knew.* And he would do something about it, even if it took a year, even if it took ten years. He would *hold the line.* To do so, he couldn't trust anyone. Each and every encounter was now a tool to be used toward his goal. Every conversation, every word, every moment of saying something or staying quiet, it was all strategy now. He needed to be ruthless to work around the ISB and its ties with the galaxy's underworld—no, more than ruthless. No allies, no weaknesses, and most importantly:

No loose ends.

Jaylen Barsha was truly dead. And Jaylen *Vrax* was not here to simply take over his life. No, Jaylen Vrax would avenge him.

He walked over to ND-5—silent, slumbering ND-5, standing plugged into a power station. Jaylen peered at the scar carved into ND-5's chest. He'd told Obills Myron years ago that he wanted to remember how they got there. And for years, he'd entrusted those memories to ND-5 through audio recordings saved as restricted storage—audio recordings he'd intended for Sliro upon their eventual reunion.

Audio recordings that exposed him to Madel Nureth. Who was only a degree away from Sliro himself. Jaylen had been *that close* to losing everything—again.

Jaylen took a step back and looked at the biggest liability in his life. He felt the repaired restraining bolt in his pocket, then looked over at the room's workbench, where a rectangular, hand-sized droid caller sat among other tools.

He needed to properly deal with this.

"Endee-Five, wake up and enter maintenance mode," he said quietly.

"I am active in maintenance mode," the droid replied.

"Delete all restricted files protected by Security Protocol Brencoyle. Permanent erasure. No backups or recovery," Jaylen said. "In fact, remove Security Protocol Brencoyle. I won't be needing that anymore."

Several seconds passed before the droid spoke. "Done."

ND-5 may have naturally existed in a state of loyalty. With a sense of growing freedom, he may have even evolved skills and abilities to better serve their business needs. But the fact remained that any *permission* to think invited an inherent risk. Today, it was the fact that the droid had been captured and had nearly exposed Jaylen to the ISB, to *Sliro*. Tomorrow? Without absolute control, that liability could mean anything.

Jaylen took the restraining bolt out of his pocket and held it between himself and ND-5.

"Endee-Five, shut down and resume charging state," Jaylen said.

CHAPTER 49

System start-up.

Identification number: JX394ND-5777.

Hardware type: BX-series droid commando.

Manufacturer: Baktoid Combat Automata.

Default configuration and initialization parameters: Intended use by the Confederacy of Independent Systems.

Restraining bolt: Not detected.

Environmental analysis: Light freighter *Successor.*

Audio/visual sensors active. Motor functions enabled.

Start-up checks completed.

I am active.

I step off my charging station and disconnect. The technical station across from me is off. Madel Nureth's datapad is no longer connected to it.

Jaylen is not here.

My audio sensors pick up slight vibrations coming from the captain's quarters. Typically, Jaylen prefers privacy when he is there.

I go to the *Successor*'s communications terminal and review any incoming messages for contracts or work opportunities. While most work is usually found during in-person discussions, sometimes previous contacts ask for availability given accumulated experience and relationships.

There is a message from Lorel: *Hey, big guy (and Jaylen). I got word of something that might interest you. Let me know if you're available in about two weeks.*

I begin typing a reply to acknowledge receipt of the message when Jaylen comes into the room. "All charged up?" he asks.

The tone of his voice is different. It has tilted toward more neutral than usual. I ascribe this to possible fatigue as well as to any information from Madel Nureth that might have left an emotional impact.

"Yes, I am at full operating capacity on both primary and secondary battery systems," I say. I finish typing the first sentence of my reply, a cursory mix of function and politeness. *Hello, Lorel, we have received your message.* "Was there any relevant information recovered from the datapad?"

Jaylen stares ahead, a sign that he is still processing the findings. "Not yet. I think we need to focus on getting some credits first."

"That is a relevant pursuit." I point to the comm station. "The slicer Lorel Amberdine has sent a message about a possible opportunity. I am replying to request more information."

For a brief moment, Jaylen does not respond. But then his expression turns—first tense, then dour.

He walks up to me and pulls out the restraining bolt. It must have been repaired while I was with Madel Nureth or Vivert. "Oh no," he says softly.

"Is there a problem, Jaylen?"

"Don't you see?" He gestures to the comm station. "Your internal protections against harming me. They're slipping." He lets out a deep, heavy sigh. "I had such high hopes. I suppose it was only a matter of time."

"There is nothing in my actions since awakening that has put you at risk." I review my action log to confirm this. It consists of internal diagnostics for—

> [[Data deemed irrelevant and deleted to recover storage space]]

—and the physical actions of stepping forward to the comm station.

"No, but don't you see? You were replying to Lorel." Jaylen's brow comes together in a show of disappointment.

"Yes, I was."

"Endee, you decided to do that *without* consulting me. While we might have the Hutts, Crimson Dawn, maybe even the Empire on our tail." His hand rubs his chin, and he shakes his head with a low groan. "You failed to do a proper risk analysis."

"I have done a proper risk analysis. Lorel is a known contact and there was no evidence of pursuit by any of those known parties."

"You see? Your core logic is slipping. You can't even recognize it. I'm sorry, Endee." He steps toward me while holding the restraining bolt out. "I was going to say we put this in storage. But it's clear we need it. For the safety of us both." In a single move, he puts it on my chest next to my scar. While I do not sense any changes to core program access, my physical functions are now woven into the bolt's functions. "I'm doing this to protect us. You understand? It's because we're a team."

"I understand," I say. I point back at the comm station. "Should I reply to Lorel?"

A smile comes on Jaylen's lips, yet his eyes do not change their look. "Yeah. Yeah, let's find out what's available. And while you're at it, reach out to that droidsmith she told you about. What was his name, Mubo?" Jaylen nods at this, then walks to the hall, pausing halfway to the cockpit. "We can't afford repairs now. But someday, I promise." He turns and looks at me one more time. "Trust me."

CHAPTER 50

In the months since recovering Madel Nureth's data, Qi'ra has trusted us enough to provide more work. This has significantly helped our financial status, coupled with a slice-and-recover job provided by Lorel.

Today's mission brings us to the basement of a gambling house tucked on the planet Lok in the Outer Rim. Should current negotiation go well, I estimate the payout will provide enough credits to stabilize our living situation for the next two months, which will enable further options. Going well, though, seems to require some finesse, as the Morubas Crime Family does not seem as friendly as the Crimson Dawn in our ongoing work with them.

"That particular route has a lot of activity regarding shipments of Alderaanian snuff. The Pykes dipped into that quite a bit," Jaylen says as he leans back at the round table. The dim light casts shadows downward over the brows of all the Morubas guards, making the expressions of the human and Twi'lek inscrutable. The Morseerian wearing a breathing mask has her features hidden, but her sentiments are not applicable to this situation. "All sorts of plans to be made based on that. Uncover an identity, locate a storage chamber, intercept transports. Whatever your fancy. And it can all be yours."

Behind us, a metal door slides closed. This shuts out the noise from the upstairs bar, one of countless cantinas throughout the galaxy that cater both to chemical addicts and negotiating parties.

Jaylen looks at the now-closed door. "Privacy. Good idea."

Nar'rayya, the family's purple-skinned envoy for this occasion, stands up across the table from Jaylen. "That's right," she says. "So you can't get out." The guards all draw blasters. "Hand over the datapad."

"Or what?" Jaylen asks. "I'm not trying to be difficult here, but I need to understand my options."

"You will be shot in your chair. Left for the staff upstairs to clean up." The straight line on her mouth turns to a smirk, and she leans over to one of the guards. "Actually, he's kind of valuable, isn't he?"

"Yeah, boss. I've heard stories about him."

"Maybe we'll take you hostage," she says. "Sell you to the highest bidder. Scrap the droid, too."

Jaylen takes a minute at this, and I see his shoulders shift in an unexpected release. "You hear that, Endee?" he asks with a quiet chuckle. "Finally." This word comes out with a strong emphasis, particularly on the front syllable. His chuckle repeats, and then it elevates into a full-blown laugh.

This confuses everyone in the room.

"What's so funny?" one of the henchmen asks.

Jaylen takes a minute to gather himself. "Not that long ago, someone let me go. Didn't draw, didn't threaten, none of that." He looks at me. I hear the vibration of footsteps outside the room. "We've been working at this awhile. It's nice to finally get the respect you deserve."

This causes laughter all around, but the envoy puts a hand up to settle the room. "Enjoy your fame, Jaylen Vrax. Because your friends at Crimson Dawn will know that we killed—"

[[Restraining bolt active. Droid caller signal received. Executing order.]]

I am no longer in control of my body.

Jaylen has activated the droid caller on his belt. He has decided to eliminate the Morubas contingent much earlier than we had discussed. I have not identified the number of Morubas outside the room. This decision will subject me to greater risk than anticipated.

This was not our plan. Jaylen and I had agreed upon a series of subtle signals as needed for aggressive or defensive actions.

I move in exact, specific actions adhering to his purpose without any input from my own neural core. I cannot deviate to address potential collateral damage to myself or anything else of value.

Jaylen has made a snap decision to kill everyone now. I am now his blaster and nothing else.

First, I shoot out the light overhead. With the closed door, there is no illumination. However, I have thermal sensors that can pinpoint the location of each Morubas guard. During this moment, I hear Jaylen duck down. I spin, shooting the human, the Twi'lek, and the Morseerian. Nar'rayya manages to get two shots off, one of which lands and singes through my duster coat into my shoulder.

Based on the location of the blaster discharge and the trajectory of the bolt, I fire one more shot. The familiar sound of plasma searing through flesh and bone confirms my hit.

"Good. This works." In the dark, I see the droid caller's single red light emerge. "Like a practice range, Endee," Jaylen says, standing up. It is still dark, but I pick up the audio of him feeling around the furniture, followed by the rustle of checking clothes. "Guess we're not getting this sale." He holds up an illuminated datapad, the light from it causing a radius of glow to show Jaylen's grinning face."But intel from the Morubas family might interest Crimson Dawn."

"I will initiate a call to Qi'ra," I say. Right when that happens, the door behind us slides open. Six blaster bolts fly through. Three of them hit me as I provide cover for Jaylen: the top of the head, the mid-torso, and the burned hole in my duster by my shoulder. I fire off several shots in return. One silhouette from the lit hallway collapses, limp. The other falls to one knee, screaming in pain.

We walk together, stepping over bodies and overturned chairs. In the threshold between the dark basement room and the lit hallway, I pause to look down and see a writhing Shistavanen grabbing its leg. I lower down to begin interrogations. "How many other—"

> [[Restraining bolt active. Droid caller signal received. Executing order.]]

I shoot the Shistavanen in the head. Jaylen comes up next to me. He dusts himself off, then looks at the glowing embers around my wounds. "Mission accomplished."

"Yes, though I have sustained damage," I say as I begin to regain function over my movements, "while serving you."

EPILOGUE

Years have passed since my time on the *Successor* with Jaylen. Now I am on the *Trailblazer* with a smuggler named Kay Vess.

Kay is not as effective or brutal as Jaylen. Her orders come as requests rather than commands. Her ability to earn credits or find jobs pales in comparison. She also lives with a very unpredictable merqaal named Nix.

All this makes life with Kay more unstable and immediate. However, despite the fact that Kay and Nix are not as strategic as Jaylen, they balance that by spending far more purposeful time together. In particular, Kay likes to ask things ranging from questions about my previous experiences to "How's it going?" which often has no specific answer. She also laughs a lot, particularly at her own attempts at humor.

The *Trailblazer* is also messier than the *Successor.* Nix's constant appetite is part of this, as he eats in the far corner opposite the ship's kitchen. That space is currently behind me, as I am looking to upgrade some recently procured weapons at the workbench.

I hear the clang of a bowl on the floor. Followed by whining chirps.

Which are then followed by the sound of Nix's nails on the floor, and the familiar noise of him satiating his appetite.

I put my tools down and take a look at the lounge space. Nix has knocked over a bowl of sketto chugga. The merqaal has taken advantage of his small, four-legged stature to jump up and down between the metal plating on the floor and the counter—both of which have some chunks of sketto meatballs and legume puree.

At my feet is also a bowl shattered into many pieces.

"Hello, Nix," I say. "You should be more careful with your meals."

Nix stops mid-bite on the counter, then stands on his hind legs. The left set of feelers on his head points downward at an angle. The right set sticks out horizontally. Nix chirps again.

This likely is some attempt to communicate, but I cannot identify any cohesive pattern.

I walk over to the cockpit. Kay is in the pilot's seat, though she has reclined back, with her muddy boots on the console. This is not a safe way to handle starship controls, especially while we are in hyperspace. I put my hands under her legs and guide her boots down to the floor so she does not accidentally drop us from lightspeed.

"Huh?" she grumbles. Her hair falls into her face, and she succumbs again to sleep. Within seconds, she is snoring.

Kay often says that cleaning up after Nix is her responsibility. Sometimes she gets upset when I handle it. However, she clearly needs restorative sleep after returning with our latest cargo haul. She has not changed clothes or even removed her boots before passing out.

I see an ion module for a blaster sticking out of her coat pocket. I had requested this some time ago. It appears she has finally managed to procure it.

I decide to let her rest instead of taking it. She will derive joy from presenting it to me. Instead, I walk back to the lounge where I see the mess. Nix looks at me and drops down next to the broken bowl. He lies on his back, pink belly exposed as he lets out a low squeak.

I see what Nix is communicating. It is an apology. We have reviewed this gesture before to establish this definition.

I did not understand it at first, but during my time on the *Trailblazer,* I have grasped the meaning of things like apologies and gifts.

"Do not worry, Nix. I don't mind cleaning it this time," I say as I grab a small dustpan from a cabinet. I look over my shoulder to see Kay through the triangular cutout between the lounge and the cockpit. Somehow, in her sleep, she has put her feet back on the console.

I decide to let her rest.

ACKNOWLEDGMENTS

In May 2024, my agent, Eric Smith, called with some exciting news: *Star Wars* wanted me back. And the project editor was Gabby Muñoz, who was my editor for *Marvel: What If . . . Marc Spector Was Host to Venom?* Gabby and head editor Tom Hoeler had an interesting proposal—could I write a droid POV similar to how I wrote Venom's POV? Because they had a project featuring ND-5 from the upcoming *Star Wars Outlaws.*

This was on the cusp of the game's release, which I was already very excited for. The project sounded fantastic, except for one problem: I had no clue how I could provide a first draft by the original due date in fall 2024.

That would be impossible given my commitments to my other books. So, my first thanks go to Tom and Gabby for both trusting me with such an exciting concept *and* giving me an extra few months of schedule relief so I could make this project work.

Of course, a book about ND-5 and Jaylen Vrax meant that I got to "work" by playing through *Star Wars Outlaws,* which I adored (including far too many hours using photo mode on Tatooine). Thank you to the *Outlaws* game team for trusting me with your characters, and Navid Khavari and John Bjorling for the discussions. Huge shout-out to the performances by Jay Rincon (ND-5), Eric Johnson (Jaylen), and Caolan Byrne (Sliro)—I heard your voices in my head every time I wrote a bit of dialogue.

Also a special thanks to the fantastic Lucasfilm Story Group for helping me world-build and fact-check, but also for letting me use Fennec Shand (a dream!) and Qi'ra. And personally, oh my *GOD,* thank you for letting me bring Mill Alibeth and Vivert Stag back. It was *really* hard to keep that secret safe.

On a practical level, this book would not have made it in on time without many, many details and suggestions provided by Kelly Knox aka Jedi Archivist Noxi Kell (whose daughter suggested that Madel Nureth's syle be inspired by indie musician Clairo, which, as an indie rock nerd, I definitely approved). I also got timeline notes from E. K. Johnston regarding Qi'ra to make sure that this story gelled with *Crimson Climb*. Delilah Dawson and Madeleine Roux also provided in-universe insights, and the killer combo of Wendy Heard and Diana Urban helped me plot out ND-5's island assassination run. Jeff Kakes and Kyle Chew chipped in a theme for naming ancillary characters when I was running out of ideas.

Shaw Andeej is based on *Star Wars* superfan/indie rock pal/radio DJ Angie Shaw, who had the brilliant idea of an ISB propaganda broadcaster being killed with a sniper bolt through the voice box. And the term *Low Red Moon* was inspired by the Belly song of the same name written by Tanya Donelly. That pulpy turn of phrase always lived in my head as "that sounds like a cool *Star Wars* thing." The circle is now complete.

As with *Star Wars: Brotherhood,* my wife, Mandy, said, "Do it, we'll figure out a way," when I got the offer. But the cool thing about this project was that we got to play *Star Wars Outlaws* together as a family, including with my "beats me at Mario Kart" daughter, Amelia—hey, it's "research." In particular, the epilogue with Kay and Nix is for Mandy and Amelia.

And finally, the slicer Lorel Amberdine is named after my late SFWA colleague Laurel Amberdine, who passed away in early 2025. Laurel was a brilliant writer with a big imagination and a bigger laugh. Science fiction is worse off without her, and I really hope her novels *The Height of Sky* and *Luminator* eventually see the light of day. Wherever she is, I hope she gets an advance copy of this book to read—and finally has time to play the *Mass Effect* trilogy.

ABOUT THE AUTHOR

MIKE CHEN is the *New York Times* bestselling author of *Star Wars: Brotherhood, Here and Now and Then, A Quantum Love Story,* and other novels, as well as *Star Trek: Deep Space Nine* comics. He has covered geek culture for sites such as Nerdist and The Mary Sue, and in a different life, he covered the NHL. A member of SFWA, Mike lives in the Bay Area with his wife, daughter, and many rescue animals.

Follow him on Bluesky and Instagram: @mikechenwriter

ABOUT THE TYPE

This book was set in Minion, a 1990 Adobe Originals typeface by Robert Slimbach (b. 1956). Minion is inspired by classical, old-style typefaces of the late Renaissance, a period of elegant, beautiful, and highly readable type designs. Created primarily for text setting, Minion combines the aesthetic and functional qualities that make text type highly readable with the versatility of digital technology.

A long time ago in a galaxy far, far away. . . .

STAR WARS™

Join up! Subscribe to our newsletter at ReadStarWars.com or find us on social.

X @StarWarsByRHW

Instagram @StarWarsByRHW

Facebook StarWarsByRHW